LUCREZIA BORGIA

A NOVEL

JOHN FAUNCE

Crown Publishers
New York

Published by Crown Publishers, New York, New York.
Member of the Crown Publishing Group, a division of Random House, Inc.
www.randomhouse.com

CROWN is a trademark and the Crown colophon is a registered trademark of Random House, Inc.

Printed in the United States of America

DESIGNED BY ELINA D. NUDELMAN

Library of Congress Cataloging-in-Publication Data
Faunce, John, 1949–
Lucrezia Borgia : a novel / John Faunce.—1st ed.
1. Borgia, Lucrezia, 1480–1519—Fiction.   2. Italy—History—1492–1559—
Fiction.   3. Women—Italy—Fiction.   4. Nobility—Fiction.   I. Title.
PS3606.A87 L83 2003
813' .6—dc21
2002009751

ISBN 0-609-60974-2

10   9   8   7   6   5   4   3   2   1

First Edition

For my mother and father
and for Elizabeth Karl

The Borgias have served their Church well, for they are the cherished scapegoats that have been used to embody and obscure the sins of every dark pontificate before them and after.

NICK TOSCHES
In the Hand of Dante

My life is a myth. My first adultish memory, I always tell myself, is of my desire for my mother, father and brother Cesare. All three are conjoined with Cesare's horsey aroma and mixed with a tang of maternal scent, of her Arabian perfume, of her opaline, moonish breasts, which I'm told I abandoned late. A Virgin's portrait in oils hung on the wall, a burning lamp always before it on a ledge. I've childish memories of earlier events and people, but they've no hunger in them, even of an immature sort, and they're without the lovely fear that only an adult can sense, a shadow opening out over decades. True children don't feel such apprehensions.

I was named for the valiant Lucrezia of Etruscan Rome—who Livy says stabbed herself to death rather than endure the public shame of rape at the hands of the Roman King. Stories about me have been written by many on graffiti-walls, pissing booths and in shelves of well-bound books. I've entire scriptoria of my own foul-mouthed Salimbenes that scribble lies on vellum and cheap Florentine paper. One has me, à la Frederick Augustus, murdering a certain Cardinal at dinner to settle a bet with my father whether or not a soul at the moment of death could be seen escaping the body. In most of those, as that one, I confess a degree of proprietary pride, especially in the more outlandish. I wish, as I peruse them, that I'd had the imagination to live such an impiously purposeful and unfettered life. But are any of these books true, the ones that declare Lucrezia Borgia, though beautiful, the vilest, most sinful woman since Eve? Some, more or less; some, less or more. I've accepted the bones of what they've said of me as simple fact, since none would credit my true, less exotic tale; and, like all souls, I wish to be believed. A small epic I've written here in the still-pliant lambskin of my soul. My father didn't fashion it, nor did my brother. This is all mine.

I remember that day, August 15, 1486, I think. Our *tinctus taxus*—our "venomous" or "tinctured" yew—dining table, bathed in morning sun and a family happiness that I then thought merely a ceaseless condition of life. It was massive, seamlessly carved of a single great tree trunk, with ivory inlay wrought down three of its legs with scenes from Our Lord's Life and the Lives of Saints Peter and Paul. On one dark leg He was transforming the wedding water into black chianti. Behind Him stood the bride and groom. I remember being beneath the table and making a small prayer that when my wedding moment came, I'd be happy as this yew maiden.

On another of the table's legs Peter and Paul bent stiffly together over the Host and Chalice of His Blood. On a third leg Peter and Paul again, this time in their agonies of martyrdom. The rough-hewn fisherman hung on his upside-down crucifix, and Paul's bald, intellectual's head waited on the headsman's block, which bore the initials *SPQR*.

"Nero martyred Peter and Paul on Vatican Hill," Papa'd told me. "That's why it became the Capitol of the World. Peter was buried, where Saint Peter's Basilica now stands, right under the altar. Paul's there, too."

The fourth leg, I don't remember, something maybe of the Magdalen. The table's top was heavy with a real-life feast. Golden goblets of Tuscan red wine and Venetian glass goblets of golden, sweet sauterne from France, golden apples of the Hesperides, the yellow noodles of China mixed with tomatoes of Sicily on Chinese crockery, bursting-sweet Moroccan figs, a German-style goose, a Friulian piglet as stuffed with truffle as any piglet might wish in her piggy vision of Heaven—and pies, savory and honeyed. Our new flatware bore the Borgia crest, even on the forks that backward priests condemn as tiny imitations of Satan's torturing trident, all in gold. I remember my father, fifty-three years old at that time, thick, but with a younger man's presence and not yet fat. His chest, head and legs were bare. All he wore was a short pantaloon, a common outfit when at home, and an incongruous pair of silken red socks, held up by red leather garters. He was seated at the table. To me he loomed a continent of lovely skin, forests of dark, curly hair, a chest like the Rus steppe, his hands—one bearing a ruby ring that would've fit me as a bracelet—as fine as mistletoe sprigs.

Vanozza Cattanei, my mother, whom Papa always called "Vanita," because she well knew how lovely she was, was in her breathtakingly well-maintained early thirties then and she sat on his lap, wearing a thin, ivory gown as gossamer as Arachne's web. She wore it because it pleased my father. He'd smuggled the gown past the Sultan's Janissaries from the Orient, where he'd been momentarily a secret emissary to the Sultan to discuss the timing of a new Crusade from Pope Callixtus III, Papa's uncle. Papa's arm was now around her and his ringed hand splayed over the web-covered, faultless surface of one of her breasts, obscuring it so gently amidst their laughter that her necklace's diamonds wobbled and sun-danced with their pleasure of one another. Their dress—or lack of much—and their physical happiness in each other felt to me not at all shameful, unforeseen nor unusual. My parents were often so in Vanita's country villa of Subiaco, Sixtus IV's election-gift to Papa in a village northeast of Rome and in 1464 the site of Italy's first printing press, as he incessantly remarked. Saint Benedict, the great bibliophile monk of Nur-sia, was said to have first fled to and inhabited Subiaco in Anno Domini 505 to escape the *"Lucifer Vaticani"*—before his Rule and before his first scriptorium. Roderigo and Vanita, on the other hand, took what Benedict would've deemed vain pleasure in one another's beauty and touch as often, openly and tenderly as April rain.

I watched and listened to them both from my lair beneath the dining table, where my brother Cesare and I were waging surrogate war over a game of chess. That was also the spot where Cesare often read to me from my first book, *The Golden Legend*—he loved the title—a popular children's book of the Lives of the Saints. But he'd only ever read me the story of Saint George and the Dragon, which even then he'd told me was the Christianized version of Εραкλσσ, or Roman Hercules. He'd read the Saint George part, then read me slowly the Dragon's, which he'd have me repeat, as if I were reading it.

He'd say, "Have no fear, child! Throw your girdle around the Dragon's neck! Don't hesitate! I'll save you!"

I'd throw my long braid at the Dragon's neck, impersonated for us by my bay Venetian rocking horse. Cesare'd read me the next line.

And I'd repeat, "When she'd done this, the Dragon followed him like a dog on a leash, crying, 'Woe is me! I shall become dog meat.'"

"Eaten well done!" Cesare'd laugh, rolling on the rug.

I'd roll as well. I'd fallen in love with my Saint George; he was so hand-some, brilliant and brave on his palomino charger, his golden armor, helm and vermeil sword flashing in the sun through Mama's window. The chess set was a Muslim one with ivory Islamic Janissaries and ebony Crusaders, board and pieces also lifted from the Grand Turk's Sublime Porte. Cesare'd begun to teach me chess on this set when I was three. Even then I found it easy as tick-tack-toe, easy as pretending to read. Cesare was a master of the Knights' Opening, which, like real reading, he never taught me. He'd usually attempt to win his game using only the two horse pieces, which wasn't possible, but he'd try anyway, forking my king with intricate and daring intelligence. I was attempting my usual, childish Siciliary defense. His knights now stood to the right and left of what I'd thought my impenetrable double wall of castles and bishops, my king in check and only his queen's bishop's full-board diagonal from checkmate. Damn. I knocked my king over—Cesare hadn't even taken my queen yet—and let the rhythm and intonations of our parents' voices wash over me.

"Roderigo, you're the most attractive Child of God on earth," Vanita whispered.

"Vanita of *veritas*, you're wrong," Papa said. "On this earth there's hardly room for another speck of charism; it's so filled with your own."

But Cesare whispered, "Check. Mate in one."

"Shut up, Cesare." I sighed. "I resigned already."

I continued to ignore him. I opened my mouth, silently repeating my parents' expressions with lips and tongue, so I might taste them like wine, roll their shapes and savor around my tongue so I'd remember how to form the words, when my time to say them came. I tried to strike this moment into my mind like an image struck into a coin. This moment happy together—Cesare and I eavesdropping below—in each other's arms and everything embraced by the feast's and other scents would remain my model of Paradise for the rest of my life, remains so till this day, as years after I form with a white Irish feather the black letters of its description. I've often wondered whether it would've been better for them to have treated me and one another cruelly, to have furnished me with a vision of Hades, instead of the Elysian Fields, so that the ensuing agonies I'd pass through as an adult might've felt familiar, instead of alien and bitter.

Papa raised his gold goblet again to Vanita. "To the second most beautiful goddess in the world," he said, his voice sounding like a benediction.

My mother frowned, but they drank the toast, heads together and pouring wine into both their mouths at once from the same goblet.

"Roderigo Lenzuoli Borgia, you're my true love, but an ungracious pig," she said. "Why am I second? You just said none on earth compare to me."

He turned his head toward me, his short beard scraping over the skin below her neck. "You were once the first, Vanita, but you've given birth to one even more perfect."

As she smiled dubiously down at me, I felt blood rising into my face; the pink pleasure of victory filling my entire body, which felt now grand as Aphrodite's. I shook my hair, single-braided to my waist like a comet's tail. I'd become the sudden Empress of the World, basking in the sun of God's Election. My blond hair was my mother's obsession. Countess Nani had invented a process for blond hair that Vanita insisted on twice a week. The recipe called for two pounds of alum, six ounces of black sulphur and four ounces of honey, all the mixture then slathered on my head; then sit in the sun for three hours. I've kept it up all my life and my hair's become legendary as the Golden Fleece.

Then Cesare in his yellow-golden doublet grabbed that sun-shining tail in his fist and wrestled me gently to the floor beneath the table with a faux-wolfish growl, scattering the chess pieces and cracking my queen in two. My brother was twelve years old then, I was six. I thought him a lovable giant cockroach, a description with which I'm sure many who've known him since would agree. The cockroach part, anyway. A bundle of spikey, badly humored, torturing malevolence, he seemed in those days. As golden-haired as I, his eyes, like mine, blue, but of a somewhat colder cerulean. A smirk that, as a child, could strip the self-assurance from the gayest little girl as readily as one day it would undress her from across a room. Malice was a part of his attraction, as the Dark Prince's has eternally been. Cesare was always so beautiful that for him to launch an attack, on me or anyone else, pleased the assault's subject, as if he or she ought be flattered that anyone as luminous as Cesare Borgia took sufficient interest to bother. Around our table's legs he now continued his mild assault and we wrestled like Greeks. I gave as well as I got and my reacting glee was as delighted and raucous as his. Above us I heard the laughter of our parents, laughter that turned me in a flash from lovely empress to patronized tot. I finally pulled free of Cesare, leaving my golden hair-ribbon clutched in his great, conquering mitt.

"Look, gold!" he exulted. "It's mine."

Cesare loved gold since birth, since he'd reached from his crib to the Catalan golden rattle that dangled on a gold chain above him. I can remember my mother laughing that only the gold rattle or her breast could quiet him in his babyhood. My parents in those days thought his gilt fascination amusing and perhaps their delight in his delight informed his lust for gold. He now chased me across the room, me screeching and he childishly cursing. My beautiful parents, as was their habit, meanwhile paid our war no notice.

"If you think us so lovely, Roderigo," my mother said, "you should marry her mother and rescue the child from bastardy and me from a slut's reputation."

"I wish I could, my love," Papa said. "But I'm previously wed to an even more jealous slut than yourself."

My parents laughed at that, his hand still over her breast. Cesare had chased me within my father's reach. He leaned down from my mother, scooping me up in his arm, rescuing me, and plopped me onto his opposite thigh, so that I was across from her, both of us in his lap. I looked across the landmass of him and smiled. I smiled with love, but admit it was a smile of triumph, as well. I'd become her equal, if only for a moment. He stroked my hair and kissed me. Not even Vanita had hair like mine.

"And do you want to marry your father, as well?" he asked.

"Yes, Papa. Will you marry me?" I said.

"We'll see," he said. "But remember, the man chooses, Lucrezia, not the girl. Even if it seems unfair. It will be your brothers' and my choice."

"Of course, Papa. Mama told me that."

He then laughed with such a pleasure in the sight and feel of me that I knew I could bend his choice any way I someday would, no matter what he said now. I knew, even if only with my child's understanding, a man's power to be at best only a big seeming. Even Jesus, though He ruled the Universe, could be bent to the will of His Mother. Else why should we pray to her?

"But I think, from the look of you," he went on, "any man you wish will beg your hand. The most powerful man in Italy, if you'll have him."

I knew I'd been right again.

"I'll be the most powerful man in Italy," Cesare whined. "The most powerful man with the most gold in the world. And nobody is pretty enough to marry me."

"But Cesare," Papa said, "no one is good enough for you? You'll need a woman, you know, young man. You cannot birth my grandchildren all by yourself."

"Thank God for small favors." My mother giggled.

"Don't be so sure," Cesare said.

Papa looked at him sternly. "Try not to act a swine, my boy."

"That's unnatural, Cesare," Mama said. "But you'll find your desire for a woman is just around the next corner."

Cesare scowled. "A wife, Plautus says, is the very antidote to desire. Well, maybe. But I'm not taking just any girl."

"No?" Papa asked.

"I'm going to wait until I find a girl of gold."

My parents laughed again, thinking that another amusing example of Cesare's obsession. Cesare looked unaffected. But I saw in their faces the worry that Cesare, at twelve, was still acting childishly. I didn't think so.

"You mean like Lucrezia?" Papa asked him, stroking my sun-gleaming hair again. "You'll never find a more golden girl anywhere in the world than your sister. Maybe you should marry her."

Cesare looked horrified. "It's against the law."

And I repeated, "It's against the law."

"No law that I know of has ever interfered with a Borgia's inclination." Vanita smiled. "Shame on you, Roderigo, for putting shameful ideas in little heads. Do you want God's curse on your House?"

"Shall I dance for you, Papa?" I asked, to get his attention back.

My father was again delighted, the way the prospect of my little dancing always made him. To dance was my most potent, attention-grabbing weapon with him, no matter which of my siblings by various mothers I wished to eclipse. This included poor poxed Pedro Luis and Jeronima, who had both recently died, leaving my fellow bastards, Juan, Isabella, Rodrigo, little Jofre. But Vanozza's gorgeous Cesare was the only one, while growing up, I knew well and saw regularly. Papa put me down. I attempted to perform a tarantella I'd seen peasant women do to drain poison from the tarantula's bite. The more sensually they dance, it's said in the villages, the more likely the bitten will live. As I went on, my parents applauded, especially my father. I tried my best, but I'm sure I was terrible. All a child can fathom of the voluptuous is a sort of drunken-sailor roll of her hips, combined with a show-off and toothy smile. Sexiness is only revealed in the dancer's intention, which a child hasn't the body awareness to form in herself. In my rear I felt the bobbins of Cesare's annoyance, his face as black as any spider's.

"Not that dance," Cesare whined. "Do the one I showed you."

"I'm dancing for Papa, not for you, Cesare. Papa likes this one."

"Go ahead, but you look like a peasant."

And he was off on a tantrum. Yell. Yell. Yell. All about my silly dance. Accompanied by stamping his feet. His tantrums occurred ever since I could remember, even before I could remember, since long before I was born, Mama said, whenever he'd get frustrated or cross. They drove Papa crazy, but nothing she or Papa did or said ever stopped them.

We then heard the bells from Benedict's monastery—and sister convent—of San Sisto. I could see the hot air vibrating with the chimes. In fact, bells were ringing all the way from Rome. They rang in the Vatican, which would alert the nearest northerly church and they'd ring their own bells, which would rouse the next church's or monastery's North Starward, and so on, until they came to our San Sisto's. The bells were a thing I hated. They took my father away and left my mother crying. Papa stood up, Vanita slipping from his lap, her perfect breast from beneath his protecting hand. It was happening. Nothing would stop it now. No tantrum of Cesare's, nor dance of mine, nor even my mother's beauty. We three froze as stony still as a carved frieze on some Ptolemaic sarcophagus.

"I have to go," my father said. "The whore is ringing her bells."

He glanced at his ring and strode from the room into their bedroom, the tears already welling into Vanita's eyes.

"If you leave us, Roderigo, I'll kill you," she called after him.

He didn't answer.

For several minutes all was quiet, but for my mother's soft weeping and Cesare's loud scowl. It was always this way, because we'd never know how long till Papa's return.

I remember on another sizzling morning, in 1492, we four found ourselves again in the same dining room. I was twelve; Cesare was just eighteen. We'd just finished a similar meal, the remains again strewn across the table. Cesare and I were no longer at chess beneath the table, but sat politely at our places, watching sunlight sparkle on our crystal, which I loved, and gold-plate, which he did. He was dressed in a gold breastplate the exact muscled shape as himself, with a cloth-of-gold cape. The drapes fluffed in the hot breeze at the windows. Vanita was again, or perhaps I should say *still*, in Papa's lap. I glanced down at the beheading and crucifixion of Saints Paul and Peter on the table's leg and abruptly

San Sisto's bells again began to toll, as they'd done six years past. It was July 25, 1492. The sultry air before me once more shivered with the sound. But today was different from six years ago. Our dining room was draped in black silks Papa'd smuggled from the Sublime Porte. Innocent VIII was writhing on his deathbed in the Vatican and Papa'd pre-ordered mourning at Subiaco. As I sit here, years later, writing in my frugal little room, I know finally what it was. It was a trembling of the Holy Spirit. Innocent VIII had just died that day, moments ago, at that very hour. Every bell in Christendom rang. But I didn't know that. The Holy Spirit made the air vibrate the way it did with flame on the first Pentecost. We heard Papa's voice.

"The great pimp is dead. I must go and be seen to have been at his bedside at the time of God's call."

"The Pope, Papa?" Cesare said, his voice cracking. "Is the old bastard dead?"

Papa turned abruptly on Cesare. "That 'old bastard' gave me the means to buy you all your ridiculous gilt costumes," he said bitterly. "Don't be disrespectful."

"You just called him a pimp."

"I'm his friend. . . . I was, anyway. I'm allowed."

My mother's eyes flashed. "You can't know what those deadly pricks may do to you, Roderigo," she said. "It will be like your death for me if it happens."

"Don't worry, my little family; I've always been lucky when it comes to God's Will."

" 'God's Will'? God's Will is the selfsame damnation I'm afraid of!" Vanita cried.

Something definitely was in the air; the bells rang more hollow and there was something far different from his previous leavings and also fear in Vanita's voice like I'd never heard before.

"Papa, I'm afraid," I pleaded. "Please, don't go there."

"Don't worry, sweet Lucrezia. God shall not let it happen to such a sinner as me."

"Yes, he will," Cesare snapped. "And it will be God's best Will if it does happen. Better for all of us."

Vanita raised her hand to slap him, but with visible effort relented. "Cesare, how dare you say that?"

"He won't let *what* happen?" I said.

"I must get dressed," Papa remarked, and went into Vanozza's and his sleeping chamber just off the triclinium, in which we sat.

What was this terrible possibility no one even dared speak of? Was Papa going to Hell? Was the Holy Office to make an Inquiry of him? Was there a plot against him? Wasn't Papa too smart to be successfully plotted against, too powerful to be Inquired into, except maybe by the Pope? But Uncle Innocent was dead. What possible Hell-deserving sin could smudge the soul of such a manifestly good man as Papa?

I heard his returning footsteps. He stood in the archway that led from their private dining chamber into the bedroom, the chamber in which they'd enact the mysteries of Aphrodite out of my jealous sight. He'd dressed in his robes. Brilliant, shiny red like a drape of satin blood. About his neck hung the pectoral cross with a great ruby at each of Christ's Wounds, his skullcap an exclamatory halo. He wore his red gloves with the massive ruby ring over the glove on the right ring finger. He looked, and he was, a great man, even greater-seeming than in his pantalooned nakedness. To think so is my sin of pride, because Nakedness is God's Image, as the artists and Turin's Shroud show us, but it was true. Archbishop Roderigo Cardinal Borgia, Prince of the Universal Church, Senator and Consul of the *Respublica Christiana*, earthly Vice Chancellor for the Lord of Eternity, Vigilant Right Eye of the Body of Christ, Hammer of Satan and all his Devils, thereby entitled to sit at the right hand of the Servant of the servants of God. Cesare's and my father, and lover of Vanita.

"Roderigo Borgia, if you leave me, I'll murder you."

"I'm Paris to Vanita's Helen," he said. "Our fate is permanently enwrapped."

"No, no. You're Aeneas to Vanozza's Dido," she retorted. "You'll go away to found an empire and I'll just burn on the deserted beach."

Vanozza Cattanei, my precious mother, was a whore. Not exactly a whore, but a courtesan. She'd been brought up in the convent of San Sisto just below Subiaco by the Dominican Sisters there, where unwanted bastard girls of otherwise blue blood were often deposited by their mortified parents. My mother was a Cattanei by her mother's blood, a spurious issue of one of the lesser noble Houses of Italy through the female line, since her sire was unknown to her. After deposit, these well-but-poorly born demi-orphan daughters were guided into life by the good offices of Church and Sisters. One rainy spring afternoon, Vanozza, by that point older than a girl, had been alone in the convent's chapel, feather-dusting, as was her duty, her favorite devotional statue of Saint Sebastian, who by custom had been portrayed by the artist in a mystical undressed ecstasy of Diocletian's arrows and his own blood, sensually flowing over his body. Why Sebastian had been so under-dressed for his martyrdom is never explained in the hagiographies, no more than is the definitely sexual quality of the particular saintly writhe he's forever engaged in. But he's always naked and always writhes. The supple beauty of Sebastian's male nudity, Vanita'd giggle as she'd tell me, was why he was her favorite. She'd been tenderly swabbing grime and dust from Sebastian's muscled bum, when a young, blue-eyed priest with wide shoulders appeared at the rail below another devotional statue, this one of the Virgin. Papa had wandered down from Subiaco to offer a prayer of thanksgiving to the martyr, since he'd received the mes-sage that day that he was to get a cardinal's hat.

"Mary's arms in her blue vestments were stretched out toward me, as she stood behind this priest," Vanita told me the day of my First Com-munion, as in my little white dress I watched her, standing in morning sunlight by the carved-leg table at our villa's window. She was gazing at the convent and its chapel below. "As if the Virgin were offering him to me as a gift. He was the most beautiful thing I'd ever seen. With his soft, young beard above that long black of his cassock. I'd yet seen few men at all, but Venus's choice is never based on knowledge or discrimi-nation; it's a gift of Grace, outside time and locale. Never forget that, Lucrezia, and never deny the Virgin's Grace when it sings to you. This priest was of flesh and blood and more beautiful than a convent-grown bastard girl was likely ever to get, especially one of my soon-to-be old-maid years. I fell in love with the flesh and blood of him in the time it takes lightning to run from Heaven to earth."

She first made love to young Father Roderigo Borgia, she told me, "in fluttering candlelight and shadow below a statue of Saint Christopher, carrying Baby Jesus across the Jordan," in the sacristy behind the chapel's altar at sunset that day.

She'd never left him. Then a young cleric of a noble family, he could afford to keep her comfortably and did so at his villa in Subiaco, given to him by Callixtus III and at his town house in Rome, which Pius II com-pared to Nero's *Domus Aurea*, his stupendous Golden House. His family was Spanish, but Roderigo's mother, Isabella, had followed her uncle Cal-lixtus to Italy. Once there, family legend went, she'd accidentally dropped the white-swaddled baby Roderigo from the seawall at Savona, and he'd only been saved when he cried to the Holy Mother from beneath the water and she interceded by rendering him abruptly buoyant. Roderigo'd bobbed up into the Church, as second noble sons do, as the one place that offered an insignificant-yet-ambitious young man the opportunity to build a greater House on a lesser foundation. On ordination he dedicated his life to the Virgin in thanks for saving him and vowed to be a "protector and defender of the Virgin and All Women" for his priesthood's duration. Ambition and God's Call—and the help of a few women—led him to become monsignor, bishop, and archbishop in a year—all at an age scandalously young, and shortly to Cardinal Archbishop, Lord Prince of God's Kingdom, at twenty-five. All these wonders' wheels, of course, were greased somewhat along by the Pope of his young manhood, Callixtus III, Papa's uncle, and by Pius II, the following Petrine Apostle, for whose election Papa'd been instrumental by securing a strategic bribe.

But when they met, all that was unknown to Vanita. That day he wore only a simple black cassock.

Lord Prince had become Papa's title, but such women as Vanita are titled only "whores," whether their loves are blessed gifts of the Virgin or pimps' commodities. I recall how everyone these days always raves about what a perfect model of a modern man a "courtier" is. Someone ought write a book, so we may finally shut up about courtiers. But "courtesan" is only a female courtier. Why is stigma attached to the feminine syllables, while honor and fashion accrue to the masculine? And why did Pope Gregory VII, shortly after the turn of the last millennium, banish families from the official, sacramentally blessed lives of our priests in the first place? The vast majority of priests all the way back to Peter—a few say even Christ—were married. But Gregory had become sick of priests dying and leaving their estates to their wives and children. He naturally thought it would be better for *all* these monies to descend into the Church's coffers—his own, in other words. To find the peas he was looking for in this shell game, he commanded theologians to come up with a series of more pious-sounding cover stories for doing away with priestly marriage. In the old days all the Apostles had wives. Saints Peter and Bartholomew's wives performed a sort of nightly resurrection on them after their Pentecostal, rugged days' works. So what was the result of trying to keep ordained men and their women apart? No one paid a speck of attention. Mistresses, boys and courtesans immediately replaced wives in priestly beds, and for the five hundred years since have multiplied as fast and eagerly as black bunnies through every seminary, parish house, Episcopal residence and Cardinal's palace in Christendom—everywhere but in the Papal apartments, and even there on a few disastrous occasions. The marriage ban has turned nearly every priest into a sinner and reprobate and their ladies into "whores." How many priests, after a life of otherwise selfless service to God and His Children, suffer eternal torment in Hell from this lunacy, gifting Satan the joy of seeing souls melt in his flames with the shining marks of priesthood on them? Or does Christ at the moment of Judgment, as I prefer to think, listen to the Virgin's prompting, remember the Magdalen and the loving wives of His Disciples that knew Him, and simply decide to unknow those things He deems it unworthy for His Omniscient Mind to think of? Most of those bile scribbling theologians, the sort who pulled priestly families apart, abide in monasteries, where they satisfy their God-granted Urges on one another. But I don't think it's theology makes them abominate females. It's that they fear us, fear our power to affect their own flesh, mind and soul, as if whatever powers we may have to rouse them weren't as much from God's creating Hand as any capacity of their own. Our bodily powers are God's Gifts. No one may refuse God. Vanita was a woman of strength, wit and elegance, more than fit to hold company with kings, popes or emperors, more than their equal, anyway, in my First Communicant's opinion.

But on this July 25, the year of my Confirmation, in Vanita's Subiaco, Roderigo Cardinal Borgia walked slowly toward us in his glory. Red satins, silks and white linen lace whispered with his steps like angels' wings over a deathbed. He took my mother in his arms, cupped once again her breast in his ringed hand and kissed her, their tongues wrapping about one another's. When their kiss ended, he kissed Cesare and me tenderly on each cheek. I saw tears in his eyes. His face looked like the face of one of those men I'd see at the foot of the scaffold, bidding his family farewell before the Hell of the Holy Inquisition. Papa turned on his heel and swept from the room and down the great stairs, leaving my mother and me in tears, Cesare with an odd, knowing pout on his dazzling face.

Papa's sudden absence left me angry and chilled. I knew my mother could feel me shaking and she gripped me all the harder, trying to comfort and warm me. If I'd known then the times-to-come, maybe I would've tried to comfort her. I was aware of her crying, but with a child's selfishness I assumed my own hurt worse than anyone else's in the world. I've many times debated with myself, as I've grown, which of the two of us, Vanita or Lucrezia, in the intervening years has suffered more? Vanita from Papa's absence? Or me from his presence? There's no way to know. Absence is only emptiness, from which the lucky recover. But presence, though filled with transgression and horrendous hurt, is also rife with moments of love and soul- and body-satisfying peace. I still don't know the answer. Will the Virgin tell me in Heaven? Or more likely will Eve in Hell? But I do know what *my* answer will be, in whichever place. I'd choose presence. Better alone with the Inquisitor than alone with oneself.

In the broad, graveled driveway in front of Subiaco a grand enclosed carriage waited for Roderigo Cardinal Borgia, all red and gold and with the Spanish Borgia coat-of-arms, a charging red bull on a sable field defending its doors. Pigeons and doves zoomed back and forth from window to window of the villa, as they have always in the Roman countryside. Papa's footmen rushed after the pigeons with bird rakes to make sure the fowl left no unattractive deposits on Papa's silks, or even worse, on his head. Papa walked like the prince he was, toward the carriage, servants bowing and dropping its steps for him. He entered and flopped into its Libyan ostrich-leather seat, plopping his feet on the silver footrest. The coachmen leapt onto their bench and whipped the six snow-white geldings with the red-leather traces. The postillion mounted the saddle on the team's left lead horse, making certain his wheel-lock pistol was drawn in plain sight. Armed cavalrymen spurred their palominos, and coach and company clattered away down the dirty road in a massive, dusty rush, leaving in its wake panicked roosters and sight-hounds.

On the scorching morning of Saturday, August 11, 1492, Jehovah's Eye was focused, as It has been and will be for all time and beyond all mornings, on Vatican Hill, one of the seven low lumps that comprise the Eternal City. The appellation for the "Vatican" lump descends from the ancient Etruscan site of seeking prophecies, or *Vaticinii*, from the Seers, or *Vates*. Divinity has lived forever on this hill. Above the peaked crown of the Pope's private Chapel, the Sistine, soared a crow. It's called "Sistine" some say because Sixtus built it; but the truth is, because it "holds firm," *sistere*, the tottering world. The crow circled a witchy and decrepit chimney, which thrust from the finished, curving tile of Sixtus' roof. With a circular wobble and messy flutter of wings, God's black Messenger alit on the chimney's peaked top, calling and cawing. God loves birds, else why give angels wings?

But snow-white smoke billowed massively from the skinny smokestack and in a panic God's crow flapped from his resting place and away, a fell fluttering dot, into a cloudless summer sky. Below that roof, the Sacred College of Cardinals, all the twenty or so created by that time, including my father, sat in sweat-soaked red robes in a vast horseshoe below the Sistine's main altar. Each Cardinal sat on his own smallish throne. Above each throne hung a spotless white canopy. The wraithlike Portuguese Cardinal Costa, eighty years old, served as *Camerlengo*, or Chamberlain, for this Sacred Consistory. He was, for no apparent reason, informally referred to by that temporary title for the rest of his long life. "Camerlengo" is a title an Electoral Consistory gives by custom to the most ancient and therefore most venerable member of the College. He runs the Apostolic Household and Papal Administration for the period of election, while Peter's Throne is vacant. Ninety-five-year-old Cardinal Gherardi was actually the eldest, but age had by then dispensed with his mind, if not yet his soul; evidently the two are not coexistant. He'd become entirely non compos mentis. Now Costa put aside the gold and bejeweled chalice on the table before him, having counted the little slips of paper in it, one of which, of course, was senile Gherardi's. He whispered to an aide-monsignor, stood shakily and tottered like a crimson ostrich into the center of the horseshoe. He raised his rheumy, cataracted eyes heavenward and then closed them. Offstage a monk pulled a string. All the white canopies thereby collapsed, one after the other in a rapid-fire, semicircular clatter into their respective chair backs. All the canopies but one. The one over Roderigo Cardinal Borgia. Over Papa, so to say. The one over the new wearer of the white cassock.

The Camerlengo faced my father. *"Annuncio vobis, Roderigo Borgia, gaudium Papem habemus,"* he said as loudly as he was capable of, his aged voice as squawky as any Latin-cawing crow's. "I announce to you in great joy, Roderigo Borgia, we have a Pope."

Peter's Throne had been as usual viciously fought over. Massive chests of gold, jewels and silver had crisscrossed Rome from embassy to embassy, as always, attempting to leverage Peter's chair to accept the buttocks of some cardinal-citizen of this or that embassy's homeland. Any number of murders had occurred, as usual, to sway God's Will toward this or that aspirant. Rumors flew like Eumenides, the gods of vengeance, through Rome, describing new plots or contingencies at the rate of six or more an hour. But "He who enters the conclave a Pope," the proverb says, "leaves it a cardinal." At the balloting's start, after nine steamy, enervating days of mourning for Innocent, Papa hadn't been the first choice, the second nor even on the list. Everyone had been jealous for years over his youthful advancements, and besides, most felt he still ought to toil in the vineyard more years before quaffing the wine. Going into the Papal Election, or "Scrutiny," the new Camerlengo himself was assumed to be the next wearer of the Fisherman's Ring and white slippers. The most *"Papabile."* That was because the red princes were so divided and antagonistic to one another, split into factions of this or that part of the world or this or that interpretation of this or that Sacred Doctrine—never mind cash and personal hatreds—that no favorite emerged. When such a thing happens, the eldest sane cardinal is generally elected, since the others reckon he won't live long anyway and so there'll be another Scrutiny in a year or two, by which time, God willing, maybe one's own faction will have accumulated enough gold and influence and killed enough enemies to prevail and elect someone, preferably oneself, who will grant his brother supporters yet more power and gold.

Second choice in the Divine Sweepstakes, depending on whom one asked, was said to be Cardinal Giuliano della Rovere, head of the Ligurian, Rovere/Riario faction. He descended from a vulgar sardine fisherman— "like Peter," he was fond of saying—and was a nephew of the unlamented Sixtus IV. Della Rovere had also always appeared to childish me somewhat elderly, though nowhere near so old as the semiembalmed Camerlengo Costa. The favorite rumor that week, naturally enough, involved Costa and della Rovere. Giuliano Rovere was an ambitious cutthroat and former military man and arch-humanist, who'd left campaigning to come to Rome for the Papal election, leaving his nephew, also of dubious lineage, in command of his army. Italy one day would pay through its bloody nose and heart for della Rovere's military vocation. He surely had none for the priesthood. The nephew was as famous for his crimson suit of red-gold armor—a gift of his uncle—as he was for his cruelty. "The Red Devil," his own troops had nicknamed him, though anyone heard speaking that nickname was executed forthwith. His favorite military discipline was to ram a white-hot sword blade up this or that misspoken soldier's fundament. The unfortunate then baked to death from the inside.

"Roast this man's sausage!" was the Red Devil's customary death sentence.

All his soldiers by now hated him. Nephew Field Marshal with his uncle's troops were parked below the walls of Ronciglione, laying siege to the ancient castle. The fortress's capture was critically important to della Rovere, because Ronciglione was a twin to his favorite castle that he already owned at Ostia, the formidable, militarily advanced Rocca, built there in 1482–86. The Rocca was designed to resist cannon, the new scourge of man. Both castles fronted on the Mediterranean. Also Ronciglione's treasury, he thought, might provide him with just the extra gold he needed to buy the Scrutinies of several Austrian and German Cardinals, whose votes would be enough to tip the election in his favor. The Sacred College's first five votes in the ancient Sistine had seen the Camerlengo fade and come closer and closer to declaring della Rovere the next sitter in the Fisherman's chair.

But, so the Furies' rumors said, Camerlengo Costa still burned with the Satan-lit fire of ambition, biblically elderly though he was. Immense power and wealth dangled within his mummified grasp. In furtherance of his election, he sent a current girlfriend to make a surprise visit to della Rovere's nephew below Ronciglione. This fine slut was a legitimately born scion of an Imperial Elector, but nonetheless a legendary, exquisitely talented and epically expensive whore. She arrived with a train of ladies-in-waiting, her so-called "whorelettes," at the camp. The general was surprised but delighted to see this magnificently cleavaged, relatively clean prostitute—prepaid!—as well as her spiffy retinue, since he'd become bored of satisfying his exuberant lusts on skinny, cow-poxed camp followers. That night, after hours of sexually ecstatic *tenor robusto* screechings had wafted from his crimson tent through the camp, Costa's odalisque transformed the Red Devil into a boy soprano with a curved German *Trockenbeeren* harvester, while hundreds of his troops listened outside and Ronciglione's defenders eavesdropped athwart their ramparts.

"What's that new screaming from the general's tent?" a young soldier asked. "It doesn't sound like pleasure anymore. It sounds like a man in Hell."

"Pleasure, pain, it's all the same to him. He enjoys hurt so much? Let him wallow in it" was the captain of his bodyguards' growling reply.

John Faunce

It was reported the Cardinal's nephew bled to death. It was also said the courtesan and her maids had brought him to their "Egyptian little death," a sexual rite for which she and her girls were infamous in palaces all over Europe, before they'd sliced him to his big one. But the general's littler and bigger deaths had somewhat altered the Papal Scrutiny's possibilities. When Giuliano della Rovere heard the reports, he offered several masses for the benefit of the youngster's doubtlessly roasting soul, but since he no longer had hope of Ronciglione's gold, his hope of the white cassock vanished. At least for this election. But he'd be damned if he'd let Costa win. Della Rovere hated him, because two decades ago the Camerlengo'd strangled a particularly prenubile Magdalen of della Rovere's in a fit of jealousy. So he now informed the Camerlengo's supporters in the Sacred College that if the old man were to be elected, della Rovere would order his troops to nail Costa's girlfriend with spikes through her privates to Ronciglione's cherry-wood drawbridge—since she and her suite were still in the hands of della Rovere's delighted army.

This return threat, everyone imagined, put a damper on the Camerlengo's enthusiasm for Peter's Throne, since it was known he loved this skillful paramour like a daughter. But in the Sistine seven more indecisive votes were cast, making twelve Scrutinizes in all. After each, black smoke floated up the Sistine's chimney to be seen and cursed by the anxious human ocean in Saint Peter's Square. The night after the twelfth vote, the Camerlengo Costa and Giuliano della Rovere came to Papa's cell. The cell contained, besides Papa, those amenities considered vital to all the Cardinals: a seat for the discharges of the stomach, two urinals, four boxes of chocolates, one box of sugared pine seeds, Austrian marzipans, a pound of cane sugar, biscuits, jugs of water and of wines, red and white, and a silver salt cellar. But all this had been recently removed to motivate the Cardinals to a decision. By now, all the Red Hats had was bread and water.

Papa instructed his guard to leave. "They won't assassinate me," he told the guard. "I don't have enough votes to kill."

The guard having left, the Camerlengo said, "Brother Borgia, I've prayed to God. He's answered, praise Him. I give the votes in my control to you."

Papa whirled on his discharge-seat in shock at that utterance. He later told me he was stunned to his depths, but also said this news was such a thunderbolt, it felt as if only God Himself could've sent it.

"And what do you want from me in return, brother?" Papa finally asked. "Assuming you're right about His Will?"

"My gentle maiden at Ronciglione. I want you to send Papal troops to escort her from della Rovere's militia of horny swine. I want her alive and unharmed. I've no longer the strength to play Abel to Brother della Rovere's Cain."

Della Rovere sighed. "I've sought the Lord, as well. I give you my votes, too, Borgia. You were the most skillful of us all, merely to watch and wait till the rest of us ran out of cash."

Papa was flabbergasted. Della Rovere's or the Camerlengo Costa's votes by themselves were impotent. But both together were more than enough to decide the election. Papa later told me he felt like a sudden Saint Paul, lightning-struck on the road to Damascus.

"And you, Brother della Rovere? What do you require?"

"I require Ronciglione. Once your white and golden-yellow troops have rescued and retrieved the whore-of-plenty, swear to me they'll stay and help me take the fortress."

"What for?" Papa asked. "The purpose of its gold to you will by then have vanished."

Della Rovere smiled. "For the aesthetic of the thing. Ronciglione is half of a matched, seaside set. Gemini isn't Gemini with only one twin. And gold is always useful. Perhaps I can buy salvation."

"Your own?" the Camerlengo cackled. "Even Midas lacks the gold for that."

Papa looked at the two men. He bowed his head, closed his eyes and looked within his soul for the Will of God. He saw nothing. That is how decisions that move the world are made. The Pontius Pilate method. I've seen Papa and Cesare do it in council and have done it myself a hundred times. After all the advisers and learned advices are done and fruitless, one looks inside oneself for Heaven's answer; but regrettably there rarely is one. So all there is to follow is the soft voice of one's own desire, which only God knows may be Himself, whispering destiny in one's ear, or the Demon, murmuring perdition.

Papa took the Cardinals' hands, one in each of his own. "I know it's God's Will," he said with not a beat of further hesitation.

But why did they give their votes to Roderigo Borgia, when there were a dozen others, in addition to della Rovere and Costa, who would've leapt at the white cassock? There waited in the wings, for instance, Ascanio Cardinal Sforza of Milan (two votes), who'd campaigned viciously and might've even won, but at thirty-seven was judged insufficiently elderly;

also the Neapolitan Cardinal Carafa (one); Cardinal Michiel, Archbishop of Venice, who certainly had Saint Mark's cash and imagined himself already a Pope in Venice (two); and Bernardino Cardinal Carvajal, the choice of Spain's Catholic Majesties, Ferdinand and Isabella (one).

Papa never knew, though legend says bribery had much to account for—something of donkeys carrying silver. But legend, in my experience, is itself a donkey, unsafe even for Christ to ride.

"That's the mystery of my life," he said on more than one occasion. "Maybe it was the bread and water in my cell."

"But you all had bread and water."

Papa'd shrug. I've never heard a satisfactory explanation; though alone at night I've imagined a thousand. They've all failed in the end, except the only incontestably true one, which comes as I fall asleep. It was the Will of God. The College's next Scrutiny, their thirteenth, had elected my father. He sat now beneath his erect canopy, weeping in heaving sobs, as white smoke chased away all the crows from the roof. Though many later accused Papa of hypocrisy and cravenness at that moment, his tears were genuine. Genuine, because it was Vanita, and his impending loss of her, that filled him. It was one thing for a priest, bishop or even cardinal to have a mistress—they all had at least one, richer ones several or a dozen—but entirely something else for the Pope, the holiness of whose position has always been vastly more sensitive to blackmail and to accusation. Children—Cesare and I and even our several brothers and sister—would be acceptable. We were only previous accidents of nature and God's manifest Will. But it's one thing for a latterday Sebastian or Paul to bless the occasional willing acolyte with a swift fornication, something entirely else for the Christ Himself.

"God's sacred Finger," the Camerlengo now cackled to the horseshoe of red men and white thrones, "has been thrust at you," and he pointed at Papa, "Roderigo Borgia."

This somewhat ambiguous pronouncement gave Roderigo an instantaneous vision of the Almighty's doubtlessly Holy Digit, he later told me, thrust aggressively and eternally into his face in a simalacrum of the well-known, indecent gesture. My father raised his head. Tears streamed down his face. "I beg you, brothers, I'm unready. Let this cup pass from me to another."

A bit disingenuous and grossly presumptuous, that particular diction, but my father was a great man and at the moment it was honest, since he knew he'd never again feel Vanita's breast beneath his hand. He was trying to remember exactly the way her nipple would "charmingly rise beneath the silk," as he'd put it, at a chill of momentary breeze, the way he'd seen and felt it do a thousand times. He rubbed softly the acorn-shaped end of his throne's arm to re-create for himself the sensation. But even with that gold mnemonic, he told me, he couldn't at that moment bring the image to mind.

"I've never been able to again," he later said to me. "Though I've let my hands play over the breast to that end of many a statue of Aphrodite. It's part of my soul that's lost to me."

"The Chalice of God's Blood cannot pass," the Camerlengo chirped. "You must drink it, as Our Savior drank, to its dregs or to its glory."

Roderigo looked up at the Crucifix behind the altar, at the Virgin's statue below and to its left. His eyes moved over the horseshoe around him. His doubts vanished. He'd struggled against these death's heads for thirty-five years. A hundred times in council he'd been right and they'd been wrong, but they'd prevailed, even though he'd been Vice Chancellor to His former Holiness. Was it truly God's Will that fools make false or devilish choices for His Church? He'd plotted, struggled and become one of them and now they'd offered him mastery over them all. He'd hold the spiritual reins of the world, and the tools to reign over more than its spirit. Not a man among them was unworthy of his contempt. Now he'd crush any of them at will. Now he'd be their liege lord and their true Lord. He'd fulfill his oath and deliver Costa's whore, as promised, that being of little cost or lasting consequence. Ronciglione's gold? Well, that was a choice to consider—maybe, maybe not—once he sat in Peter's chair. He bowed his head to Heaven's Will.

The red semicircle applauded, and called, "Bravo!" as if he were some peasant singer, who'd just finished a vaguely pleasing aria.

"What name shall you take, Roderigo Borgia?" the Camerlengo asked.

What name? What name, indeed? The time ticked on, as they all sat and dripped sweat in puddles. Five minutes. Ten. A dozen Saints passed through his decision. He knew he should take the name of one he wished to become. But who? He wished only to become himself, but more so. Fifteen.

"It's time," the Camerlengo said. "Decide. A Pope mustn't dither."

Papa looked threateningly up at him. Costa bowed his head to Papa in contrition.

"Alexander," my father said. He couldn't remember a saint of that name, he always said.

"Alexander," the circle responded, attempting to sound approving, but unable to hide entirely a vibrato of fear at that particular pagan name.

"The Conqueror," Camerlengo Costa said in as upbeat a manner as any octogenarian is capable of. "May you conquer the East, as your namesake did, and free Jerusalem from Allah's curse."

"And prevail against the very gates of Hell," della Rovere added, which Papa mused meant della Rovere was telling him he ought to go there.

All the Sacred College rushed from their thrones, still applauding, to congratulate Alexander VI. Cardinal della Rovere, all of them. They knelt before him. They kissed his hands, feet and the bottoms of his robes. The Camerlengo read to Papa Christ's Words from Matthew 16: " *'Et ego dico tibi quia tu es Petrus, et supra hanc petram aedificabo ecclesiam meam, et portae inferi non praevalebunt adversus eam.'* 'And I say unto thee thou art Peter and upon this rock I shall build My Church and the gates of Hell shall not prevail against it. And I will give unto you the Keys to the Kingdom of Heaven; whatsoever thou shalt bind on earth shall be bound in Heaven; whatsoever thou shalt loose on earth shall be loosed in Heaven.' "

Sotto voce, like the fearful flock of red birds they were, they muttered, "Holy Father . . . May your reign be great . . . Papa."

Now all mankind would call him Papa. I learned of his election from one of the Palatine Guards that came to fetch Cesare and me from Vanita's Subiaco later that evening. I remember the sound of a dozen big horses, their heavy shoes crunching and clattering to a stop in the driveway outside our villa, like Macedonian cavalry. I recall heavier footfalls than any I'd ever heard, accompanied by thick clinks of armor, rushing louder as they came up our marble stairways. I've the image forever in my mind of my brother and me watching Vanita, who tried desperately to hold the triclinium's door closed. I remember beyond the door Germanic voices like wet rasps. Finally they forced Vanita to give way. The door swung open and the guards in their striped, clownish uniforms and gleaming armor poured in. Vanita rushed toward Cesare and me, screaming at the guards not to touch her children, but before she could reach us, two massive Palatines grasped her.

"Don't worry, Mama, it'll be all right; they're here to take us all to His Holiness!" I heard Cesare cry.

She whirled in the guard's arms at Cesare, as another grasped him by the arms. "They're here to take *you* to him, not me!" Vanita screamed.

She whirled back at the Palatine and left a bleeding nail-scratch across his face. "Let me go! Don't touch my children!"

I saw the captain coming toward me. I remember him gigantic and inescapable as a moving Alp, face craggy as a col. He dipped down and scooped me up in his striped arms. I didn't know why, but I was unafraid to be in those arms; nor did Cesare look the least bit upset. They carried me and rudely escorted Cesare from Subiaco. The last thing I recall of my first home is my mother, held by two Papal Guards, screaming for their blood and them prying a knife from her hand. I was unafraid for her. I saw the way they were handling her was meant to calm her, not to subdue her by force nor to hurt her, either of which they could've easily done; broken her neck with a swat of a mailed hand.

"It's God's Will, Mama," Cesare called back.

"I will kill God!" she screamed, as I lost sight of her.

The Palatines blessed themselves in horror.

"Don't worry, Mama," I called back to her. "We'll be all right."

The prophetic implications of her fear finally gushed over me. The guards rushed down our stairs with Cesare and me. Outside was a carriage. It was Papa's, but on its door I now recognized the yellow-gold and white Papal Arms and crossed Keys of Peter.

Vanita called to us in the driveway from her bedroom balcony. "Don't forget me! Remember me, no matter what they tell you or how much they give you! Remember there will never be another who'll love you like me!"

"Where are you taking us?" I asked my guard.

He deposited me gently in the carriage. "You're going to the Vatican."

"Why? Papa hasn't become *the* Papa, has he?"

"You're to live there. He's been blessed beyond all men on earth. He's become the Christ." He made again the Sign of the Cross.

The captain shoved my brother in and the door slammed shut. A whip cracked, its report echoing against the hill. Our carriage began to move. Subiaco's bells began to ring. Three hours later on our way up another hill, Vatican Hill, I wondered what the captain had meant. I knew who Christ was, but what would it signify, that Papa'd become Him? Was the Pope actually Christ? Uncle Callixtus hadn't looked like Christ; neither did Papa. It'd be spectacular news for Papa, I imagined. I remembered Jesus had been a bachelor. Was that why Mama couldn't come, too? But hadn't the courtesan Magdalen gone everywhere with Him?

Cesare and I were soon to be ensconced in the newly built palace of

Cardinal G. B. Zeno, the Santa Maria in Portico Palace, to the left of the entrance of the Papal Residence. There was even access to Saint Peter's from the Palace's chapel, through a secret door that led into the Sistine.

In this life Vanita was never to be alone with her beloved again. She left the Subiaco the next morning, to go I never knew where. I kept hearing rumors of her over the years: She'd bought an inn, at which she was sup-porting herself. She'd become a high-priced madam to the senior clergy. She'd become rich from real-estate speculation. She owned hair salons, at which the girls would slather Countess Nani's sulfurous gook on their dark heads. She'd given a party here or there. But I never knew if any of the rumors were true. My own, preferred belief is that she shut herself up in a convent, if possible the one in Subiaco, where she waited impatiently for Papa or death. It would be years before I spoke to her again and I'd miss her every hour of those years. But in fact Papa installed a fresh courtesan in the Santa Maria in Portico—two of them, actually, Adriana Mila Orsini and Giulia Farnese—but he never loved them, nor they him, as well, long or faithfully as Vanozza Cattanei.

Giulia was a beauty. She befitted a Pope. Her brother-in-law, Lorenzo Pucci, infamously wrote, "I called at Santa Maria in Portico to see Madonna Giulia, who, when I found her, had just been having her bath, and she was with Madonna Lucrezia, the daughter of Our Lord, and Madonna Adriana beside the fire. Madonna Giulia has become most lovely to behold. In my presence she undid her hair, which fell to her feet, her body's only covering, and then had it put up again to reveal Paradise to all of us. Thereafter she covered it with a sort of net as light as air and interwoven with gold threads that seemed like the sun. Madonna Lucrezia did the same in all detail, but the threads were barely visible, her tresses golden already. She wore a Neapolitan wrap, but after a while Madonna Lucrezia went to take it off and picked up a gown, scandalously lined almost entirely with purple satin. She re-covered herself and, as she did, I inwardly cursed this second banishment from Eden."

What was "infamous" about this description at the time was not our nudity, but the ease with which I dared advertise myself in imperial purple.

The coronation of Alexander VI took place about ten days later, the third week of August, 1492. Rome still stifled and sweated. There'd been so much activity and heat in the Vatican those ten days. The Curia had installed Cesare and me in the Santa Maria Apostolic Palace, where Papa was to live, on a separate floor, of course. As for Papa, Cesare and I rarely ever saw him, except at a distance, when he'd stride across some great hall we were in, trailing a dozen variegated, whispering apostles, either cardinal- or bishop-members of the gigantic Curia, *plumbatores*, the sealers of Papal Bulls or any number of his twenty-six secretaries.

"Every one of these functionaries has purchased his Holy Office," Papa said.

"Why?" Cesare asked.

"Our churches, priests, altars, sacred rites, Our prayers, Our Heaven, Our very God are for sale," Papa whispered.

I'd run to him. He'd stop, wave off his attendants, kiss and hug Cesare and then lean down to me, kiss me and pick me up in his arms, as if we were the two most important souls on earth. But he'd soon be off again. We'd become orphans in those days.

And everything was so big. Big rooms, big food, big furniture. Big hair and busts on the women and big hats and codpieces on the men. My new bedroom in the Apostolic Palace—all my own!—was bigger than big. I kept expecting to see clouds just below the soaring ceiling. The cadre of nuns, into whose charge I was placed, were many and friendly, as were all the Papal Guards and the hundreds of guests and prelates we constantly met. Every moment we were presented to someone or other with a clump of titles longer than the Sermon on the Mount. These people all bowed, to *us*. When we were presented to the representative of the Holy Roman Emperor, Maximilian, and even *he* bowed, I thought Cesare would flop over dead. Everyone was friendly—beyond friendly, positively toadying—to my brother and me in a manner and to an extent I couldn't remember anyone being before. Everybody greeted us with monstrous grins and would sweep the floor with their gigantic hats, while bowing, to pay us homage. I ate anything I wanted, even gelato for breakfast. An old monsignor gave me setter puppies. The male I named Sweetlips, the bitch, Pretty Poison, because she had a beautiful coat and overpowering gas at night.

"Great bird hunters from England," Cesare said.

"They're puppies from Tivoli, silly," I answered. The puppies peed in the Belvedere's three big fountains: the Tiber, the Nile and the Cleopatra. I did too, yet no one yelled at me. I tried to get Cesare to join us.

"Papa's going to make me Cardinal Archbishop of Valencia," he said. "Don't you think plashing with pissing girls and puppies in a big birdbath is maybe beneath my dignity?"

"If it were a gold birdbath, you'd do it."

"It's not. Only, the pee is golden."

Tailors came to measure us both. Cesare was delighted at the tailor, because he told my brother he was going to make him a suit all of cloth-of-gold for the coronation. I knew all these extraordinary solicitations of us had only to do with the fact that our papa was about to become Christ, something I understood was miraculously good. But it was impossible for the girl I was to make the slippery assumption that I was not myself, somehow deserving of all this. Cesare, on the other hand, never bothered to consider that maybe he was being treated this way on Papa's account. Cesare was as accepting as a Seraph next to the Throne of God, nodding and smiling at the praise of the Universe, as if meant for him.

"I'm about to be a prince, after all," he kept saying. "A *princeps* like Cesare Augustus."

The evening before Papa's Coronation we saw the "The Sprint of the Race Whores" in the Campo dei Fiori. Thousands of Roman whores too poor to be courtesans stood in various stages of undress at the crest of a steep hill. At a signal they screamed bloody murder and, breasts flying, barreled down into the arms of hundreds of teenage boys, mostly gangsters, each of whom shifted and dodged to put himself in the path of the more attractive sluts. Those whores who knocked a boy on his ass were declared "Race Fillies" and got a gold ducat from the Papal Treasury.

On Coronation morning Papa performed the *Possesso*, the Procession, with which he took formal "possession" of the City of Rome. Papa was at the procession's end, under a golden baldachin. In front of him went Captains of all the districts of Rome, Knights of Saint John, the Roman Barons, Papal secretaries, the Papal singers, non-Roman clergy, Abbots from the city's monasteries, the Cardinals, the Curia and finally Cesare and me, him on a palomino, me on a white horse. The Pope-elect processed from the Piazza San Pietro to the Castel Sant'Angelo, then crossed Ponte Sant'Angelo to Monte Giordano—where he met Rome's Jews.

"Ecce vicit leo de tribu Juda, radix David," they davened. "Behold the lion from the tribe of Judah, scion of David." I saw one roll his eyes.

Papa reminded them he was Alexander, not another Leo, and that Christ was their Jewish Brother and yet Jews murdered Him. They wailed in sorrow a sound like a grieving of owls. The procession continued and passed close to the southern end of Piazza Navona, where there was a bull-shaped fountain* that spurted water and red wine, then proceeded to the Church of San Marco, traversed the Capitoline Hill, through the Forum, past the Quattro Coronati to the twin *colossi* of Alexander the Great, a quick obeisance to the equestrian pagan, Marcus Aurelius, in front of the Lateran and then circled back to Saint Peter's—the last three stops symbolizing the passage of World Imperium from Hellenic Empire to Roman Empire to the Empire of Christ. All this grand circuit I was just behind Papa, feeling like Athena behind Zeus in my golden chiton—in honor of the new Alexander, I was told and platinum, diamonded corona. The coronation finally was held—Papa became God—with huge pomp on the main altar of Saint Peter's old Basilica. But just before the coronation was a painful, queer little ceremony in Saint Peter's sacristy, its dressing room, which was old, dark and as big as an entire normal-size church. Abbots escorted Papa in, the entire College of Cardinals awaiting him. Everyone paused; Papa turned and looked toward the door. Three giant Jesuits, whose Order is charged with enforcement of the thornier conundrums of orthodoxy, carried a wide, short throne of marble and porphyry into the

---

*The Bull, as is known to all, is the heraldic device of our family.

sacristy. They grunted and gasped from the effort. This throne was the *Sedia Stercoraria*, Cesare told me, the "Chair of Shit." There was something odd about its shape. The seat was very high and cut into a keyhole shape, the stem open to the front. It looked like a commode for Goliath. The back was at a curious, reclining angle, far too laid-back, it seemed, for any bodily movement. The legs were unusual, as well—two slabs of marble down either side, ending in flourishes in the shape of lions' claws, but leaving the center, under the keyhole, open and unobstructed. Papa then lifted his robes and sat on this weird throne.

"Would the youngest member of the College step forward to perform his duty?" the Camerlengo squeaked.

Two decades ago that had been Papa and two weeks hence it'd be Cesare, but as of now it was Ascanio Cardinal Sforza, Papa's too-young former competitor. He stepped out from the College and knelt before Papa. He reached under the chair where the keyhole was and moved his hand upward. Papa's eyes snapped open in surprise. Ascanio then felt around for a moment, as Papa winced and glared.

"I hope you're enjoying yourself, Sforza," Papa said, and the whole College chuckled, except Ascanio, who then stood up.

"*Penis est. Testicula habet,*" Sforza said. "*Hominus est.*"

"There's a penis. He's got balls. He's a man."

Hardly Ciceronian, but the College demurely applauded.

"Not surprising," della Rovere piped. "His Holiness is well known to attract ladies as a magnet attracts steel filings."

This chair and ceremony are to prevent a repeat of Pope John VIII, who became Pope in the tenth century and reigned for seven years, until Christmas Eve, 956. It turned out John VIII had defrauded God and was in actuality Joan I. This embarrassing interlude was only discovered at the end of a particularly exhausting Midnight Mass, celebrated by Joan on that 957th Christmas Eve.

"*Ite, Missa est,*" John had said, and immediately gave birth to a baby boy, while dragging herself toward the manger set up for Christmas on the steps of the High Altar. The irony of this wasn't lost on the midnight Mass worshipers, who ripped mother and stillborn child to shreds on Saint Peter's outer steps and scattered sanguinary bits of them all over the city.

Following the "balls" ceremony, all the prelates performed προσκυν-

hand. He looked at Peter's Ring on that fourth finger, over the kid. He looked at Cesare. He peered out at the multitude, the Kings' and Emperor's representatives, the nobles and Saints all doing him homage, then up into the sky of church above him, as if at the angels, likewise exalting him. I could see him adjust to the forty-pound weight of crown. He glanced again at the Fisherman's Ring on his finger, his tear still glistening brighter than the ring's central stone. He once again loomed in his robes a whole continent, the greatest man in the world. Greater than all Asia and Europe combined. Not just to me, but to everybody in this church. To every particle of the Body of Christ. To everyone in the world and beyond the world. He was Omnipresence in a gold chair. His tears of a moment ago had shrunk him, I reasoned. He'd wiped them away and been reborn. He'd become Alexander, Suzerain of the Cosmos. Papa impatiently gestured the Cardinal of Warning away. He pulled Cesare down and kissed him on the lips. He kissed my golden hair and turned my face to himself.

"Lucrezia, Our child." He gently laughed. "Will you dance like you used to for the Kings of the world?"

I began my tarantella at the foot of Papa's throne. Cesare looked at me, boredom and potential tantrum filling his eyes, and then back at our father.

"Not that ludicrous, peasant's dance!" he sudd groaned. "I don't see any spiders. Think of where we are!"

Everybody in the place could doubtless hear him, which I'm sure made him no difference. But Alexander only laughed. From a gentle beginning to a great, powerful laugh, his crowned head lolling back with it. His body began to shake with mirth. His laugh didn't feel like it was mocking me. It felt so fine, I began to laugh, too, in the middle of my dance, laughing with Papa. We went on and on. Soon the Cardinal of Warning, full-throated, then the Camerlengo's cackle, joined in with us and laughed. Finally della Rovere and the entire Sacred College. Then the lesser ranks of prelates with their red and purple chucklings, then priests and monks, the inferiors gaining permission from the laughter of their betters. From the altar our mirth then blew across the rail into the congregation, which at first hesitated, fearing a laugh might be sacrilege at such a time and place. But when they saw the three Kings' plenipotentiaries and finally the Imperial envoy bending over with it, unable to restrain themselves and at one with us, the whole basilica raged fire with a noise of joy. Papa grabbed me and raised me up into his throne. He grabbed Cesare around his waist. He hugged us both. His Holiness showered us with kisses on the mouth, on our hands and cheeks and even noses, his laughter still mounting, the whole church by now a cacophony.

Just behind us a Cardinal amidst his own laughter whispered to della Rovere, "Such joy, Cardinal. An auspicious beginning to a Papacy, is it not?"

"Is it truly auspicious, Eminence, do you think," della Rovere answered, "for Christ's Vicar on his Throne before the world to take such joy in his bastards?"

The first nodded back gravely in response, trying unsuccessfully to stop his Jupiter of a belly from shaking. I glared at them. Papa was right. These men were worthy of contempt to question joy like this. Joy is only a moment, passing quickly as a flash-paper. To distrust joy is a sin. Remember Lucifer, the onetime "Joy of the Morning Light"? Then we heard it—a sound like a thunder. Like the tidal waves that are said to come ashore from the Atlantic in the New World, bursting into Saint Peter's through Filarete's "good and beautiful" bronze doors. The laughter of fifty thousand faithful from Saint Peter's Square outside the Basilica. I was certain, as Cesare and I laughed with our father, that God had never, since Noah crawled onto dry land, heard such a grand laughter. I thought so then. But years later, as I write, I think God's Ear, bent by the Virgin to her will, actually paid our grand laugh that day not a speck of heed. He was too busy watching Vanozza Cattanei, who was a hundred or more rows back in the congregation, out of sight of Ambassadors, Cardinals, Dukes or Popes. She looked to God a tiny figure. A worldly nothing, as the Virgin might've looked to Him that Friday from His Cross, lost and alone amidst the throng of happy, Roman Centurions and celebrating Pharisees.

No one in history ever had less calling for a life in the Church than Cesare Borgia. Nonetheless, two weeks later Papa created him Cardinal Archbishop of Valencia. Cesare was well aware of the gulf between his aspirations and any Cardinalate.

"You mean I have to go to *Spain*?" he whined miserably.

"You'll be a great churchman with the ear of their Catholic Majesties, Fernando and Isabella," Papa reminded him. "You'll have power and gold. We had to give 150,000 ducats to a Cardinal that voted for Us; We'll give you 100,000."

"I appreciate the gold, but I don't want to be a glorified monk and I don't give a damn to be friends with a pair of Inquiring butchers. Let my brother Juan be a prelate. He'd vastly prefer that to the soldier he's become at your command."

"When did We command that?"

"When you made him marry the King of Spain's cousin."

"I—? Never mind. We know you want something. What?"

"I want to be my name. Wasn't that what you meant by choosing 'Alexander'?"

Papa considered that question for a moment. " 'Cesare Borgia'?"

"In Latin."

"Ah. You want to be Caesar. We can't say you lack ambition. These things are not mutually exclusive, as you well know."

"Papa, this 'We' business makes me keep looking for someone else next to you."

"That's God, you know."

"Naturally. You and He. 'We.' "

"We both apologize for any confusion."

Juan was overjoyed to be a soldier, loved everything about it, as Cesare was well aware, though Juan did truly loathe Spain's cousin and everybody said he hardly ever slept with her. Perhaps in the playing of this part Cesare learned the art of dissimulation, of which he became a grand master and which later became one of the more demoniacally tiresome pages of his particular myth.

Cesare was just eighteen and looked ludicrous during his "Creation" in his huge, red hat and old man's robes, but bore himself well, considering. But his resulting concealed rancor, I'm sure, played a signal part in alienating him from the rest of the world. He spent the remainder of his convoluted young manhood from that day forward in frigid isolation—the first and last refuge of the disappointed—from all but me and Papa. His former sensitivities, of which there were many, as my mornings with him under the yew table demonstrated, were thereby torsioned into cruelty. His solipsism was his castle, and he employed his inhuman bravery and arrogance to serve other gods than the One in whose Name he'd been created Prince: power and its concrete manifestation, gold.

For a year or more the new Holy Father and I lived more or less happily. I bought a copy of the *Mirabilis Urbis Romae*. I couldn't read it, but it had maps and pictures for the hundreds of thousands of yearly pilgrims, most of whom couldn't read, either. I visited Saint Peter's marble Tomb, where I also saw the Sudarium. That's the cloth with which Veronica washed Christ's bloody Face on the way to Calvary. I went to Saint Paul's Basilica and its fountain, which sprung up from the spilling of Paul's blood. But I couldn't find there, though I looked all afternoon, the SPQR block. I saw the Basilica of Saint John Lateran that had the heads of Peter and Paul. Within Porta Latina I saw the place where John the Evangelist, my favorite Saint next to the Holy Mother, was boiled in oil while writing, "I see the Holy City, the new Jerusalem, descending from Heaven." I saw the Christ Child's Manger. I saw a hundred more relics, tombs, miracles and holy doors. Rome seemed a grim place, at least it used to be. But Rome, grim or not, doesn't exist the way other cities do, as a human community. It's rather a vast, mysterious and potent sanctuary, the Gateway of Heaven, to which Peter holds the Keys. The proper way to see this *Caput Mundi* is not with eyes of the mind: to perceive, to analyze, to comprehend; but with eyes of the soul: to behold, to contemplate, to venerate and praise. Rome's not just an idea, as the Classical cliché went; Rome's an Idea in the Mind of God.

We lived at the Pontifical Palace in the grandest suite of apartments I've to this day ever seen or can imagine. Papa'd begun the "Borgia Apartments" under Master Pinturrichio's direction, but they weren't ready yet. I'd watch him and his men—one a woman!—apply *The Descent of the Holy Spirit* or *The Assumption of the Virgin* to the walls and cry that we could make a Universe of colored plaster, as God once had of dust. Had men—formed in His Image, after all—become God with these paintings? At the end of the year we moved into the Borgia Apartments, which, I'm told, will retain their name for eternity. In 1494 there came a time when the Vatican and all Rome buzzed in terror at the invading approach of the King of the Franks, Charles VIII. People compared him to Alaric, the Visigoth, and prayed Papa'd put up a better defense than Innocent I, under whom the Visigoths sacked Rome in triplicate in A.D. 408–10. Dread spirits and black magic began ravishing the country. In Puglia one night three suns appeared in the sky, surrounded by clouds and thunder. In Arezzo an infinite number of horsemen were seen for many days, passing through the sky with terrible clamors of drums and trumpets. In many places throughout Italy Sacred Images openly sweated and bled. Even in the Sistine I saw an image of Saint Anne bleed wine-dark tears from her eyes. Monsters of men and other animals were born. The whole peninsula filled with terrible fear at the renown of French power and ferocity of the Gauls, who'd once before plundered all Italy, sacked Rome and laid all waste with fire and death, never mind the Visigoths. With the whole Boot in a panic, Charles invaded Italy in search of the Kingdom of Naples, which he insisted was his rightful inheritance and liege property by way of his Angevin and Anjou ancestors, those same Angevins who claim just about *everywhere*, from Ireland to Jerusalem, as their property. The vicious and violent King of Naples, Ferrante of Aragon, had just died *sine luce, sine Cruce* and *sine Deo*, without light, without the Cross and without God. Charles thought this was his opportunity, now that such a terrifying beast as Ferrante no longer sat on Naples' throne. Alphonso II now sat where Ferrante had, thanks partly to Papa's Bull of Investiture. Meanwhile, Cesare, now Cardinal Archbishop of Valencia, had begun to negotiate on his own with their Catholic Majesties to get the throne away from Alphonso and give it to the Frankish King for two tons of French gold, much to Alphonso's and Papa's chagrin.

"That midget traitorous brat; and after I gave hi he red hat," Papa complained.

"Papa, if Cesare is such a friend of Charles, maybe you can use that friendship to a holier purpose," I whispered in his ear.

"Lucrezia, you pleasantly surprise Us. We should've given *you* that hat."

I lit inside with girlish vanity, twirling my braid. "I do look surpassing well in red."

To get to Naples from Alphonso, of course, required Charles to traverse first the Alps and then almost the entire Italian peninsula from the Sforzas' Milan, allied with Alphonso, through Papa's Rome, to the Bay of Naples and Alphonso's stronghold at Torre del Greco. Like all successful conquerors Charles had a tendency to lay waste to everything on the way to his target. He didn't bother wasting Milan, but only because the Duke of Milan, Ludovico Sforza—that traitor—signed a Treaty of Permission to let Charles pass through his lands. But everywhere else he razed to the level of truffles. Charles was said one day to be only a few dozen miles outside the Eternal City. Everyone was anticipating rape and plunder with fatalist dread, but this type of dread, as usual, had at many addresses the opposite effect than what might be expected.

Many people were in a dissolute mood, saying to themselves, If not orgy now, will we ever get another chance?

I was playing that afternoon my favorite playacting, which I called "Imperial Courtesan," parading up and down the hall, as if I were dressed in a gem-encrusted gown, and kissing a bust of Marcus Aurelius, a grim dalliance. The hallway adjoined a big throne room, the Hall of Sibyls. I could hear Papa's voice, raised angrily in response to the Bishop of Allatri, who was Charles' ambassador to Papa. The bishop had come to arrange the timely surrender of the Vatican and to get a new Bull of Investiture from Papa for Charles VIII, replacing Alphonso in God's Eyes. He sounded as soothing and velvety, I could tell, as he could make himself. I surreptitiously peered into the sun-drenched throne room.

Papa sat below the still-wet *Prophet Hosea and the Delphic Sibyl.* "We order it!" He was almost shouting at Allatri. "We command it. Do you defy Us?"

"But Holiness—"

"Your master will remove his troops from before the city."

"It is not my master for whom it is obligated to remove troops."

The two were alone together with a smattering of Palatines. The Palatines had been in Vatican service about a dozen years at the time, having been imported by Sixtus IV as part of a deal with the Swiss Cantons. It's sometimes said today they were Julius II's idea, but that's only one of the more mythical paragraphs in the ever-expanding della Rovere myth, like the one that it was *his* idea to hire Buonarroti to ruin old Saint Peter's and shove up that unfinishable, nouveau riche monstrosity. At any rate, the Palatines were solid as mountain ice and faithful as Saint Bernards. They were known to be somewhat less devout than, let's say, Iberian or Irish Guards might've been. They were also exceedingly punctual, tidy demons against the anomalous, as well as almost pathologically neutral in political matters, a trait common amongst inhabitants of insignificant and vulnerable lands. And politics were far more dangerous than religion to a Pontiff in those days. I especially loved the Palatine's striped uniforms and silly helmets, which always reminded me of the Bohemian clowns I'd see at festivals.

"But Beatitude, your oath to my master," Allatri was saying, "was not to oppose him in his rightful reacquisition of his own property. Now you say he must remove his army entirely?"

"Alphonso's Kingdom of Naples may or may not be his property, according to God's Will. But since when was Rome his property?"

"But you swore to allow whatever my Liege deemed necessary."

"That was then, Excellency, with his army drunk in Marseille. This is now, with his army sober at Rome's gate."

"But Holiness, an oath is eternal. There is no 'now' nor 'then,' no drunk nor sober in regard to an oath."

"Don't be a fool, Excellency. Each thought that occurs to Us, as We think it, is the new Eternity, replacing the old. Compare 1 Kings 20:31–42 or Psalms 68:20–23 to Luke 6:27–38."

"Your Holiness knows the Bible! Who would've thought?"

"Ah! Irony. I recognize it. Perhaps We'll clap *you* in ironies."

"Mea culpa, Sanctissimus."

"The Most High, Eternal Yahweh, ethical Foundation-Stone of the Universe and Righteous Murderer of at least 30,250 of His Own Chosen People in the desert, in thirty-three years transubstantiated Himself into the One, who feeds the hungry and turns the other Cheek to Tiberius' tax-collector and crucifying centurions. *He changed His Sempiternal Mind.* What We will is God's Will now; something else was His Will then. Today He wills your master live. Tomorrow ▮▮ . We will what He will."

"Whatever you command, Holiness," Allatri oozed, "must be done, as the Crab must scurry in the wake of the Twins." He began slowly to walk a circle about Papa's throne. I saw guards' eyes move toward him and hands tighten on halberds. "But if you were to command the King of the Franks to remove his troops, which he's brought transalpine at severe cost, I'd imagine I hadn't heard you aright and, come dawn, I fear we would find the troops had not moved."

"In defiance of Our Will?"

"Mirable dictu. Not a defiance of your Will, Holiness. Rather in spite of it, as the Devil may tempt us in spite of Our Lord's admonitions to the contrary. Even Your Beatitude is not more powerful than Our Savior in these matters."

"You argue as your mentor Satan argued with Our Lord in the desert," Papa shouted. "We command this. These troops will be removed from before Rome by morning, Excellency."

"The troops will not move for your sake, Holiness, as the Alps refused to avalanche for you. And do not forget, my master has Cardinal Borgia, your son, as collateral from their Catholic Majesties of Spain to assure us you will fulfill your promise. I have but to send word and Baby Cardinal Borgia will ascend to Heaven—to which I'm sure he's bound, in any case."

"You will kill Cesare regardless. Is that your master's meaning?"

"My master could never do such a thing, to let a guest come to harm. But I, being but a churchman like yourself, hanker for the *summum bonum*, the best result, not chivalry. That particular meaning is my own."

"Take care on your exit from Vatican City. Don't forget that Our Will is God's Own and none but He, not even emperors and Saints, knows the hour of a man's death."

Allatri cocked his head, as if listening to something. "That chiming, Holiness? Do you hear it?"

I listened and heard no bells, no chiming at all.

"I saw your hallowed lips move," the Bishop went on. "But couldn't make out what they said. Do tell, was it a threat?"

"What chimes?" Papa said. "What nonsense are you talking about, Excellency?"

Allatri made a gesture around his grotesquely hairy ears, as if abruptly something else were horribly wrong with them. "Ah, please God, *Sanctissimus*, I'd be a lip-reader. But alas . . . it must be Satan's evil anvil, hammer and tong," he said, "ringing in my belfry."

That was too much for me. This twit was defying Papa and was going to kill Cesare.

"It's not Satan's evil anvil in your belfry!" I screeched. "It's Satan's horrible hairpiece in your ears!"

I dissolved into gales of giggling and choking laughter, as adolescent girls are prone to. I emerged from my hiding place, now that I'd blown my cover. The power of unexpected laughter drifts through the rest of our lives. I still remember Papa's chuckle on seeing me and hearing my childish insult, replacing his foul aspect of a moment ago.

"You think as men think, not as We think, Most Reverend Sir." Papa sighed. "Out of Our sight, Satan."

"You may expect His Majesty to enter Rome in a trinity of days," Allatri called back, as he turned to go.

Allatri's eyes were glued to me as I passed through the huge room. I'd seen him before and his eyes always were affixed somehow to my fanny. I was young yet, and could only insufficiently imagine why, though I knew it was allied somehow to concupiscence. But what was that? Soon my understanding would be vastly enlightened.

"As you command, Holiness," Allatri said, the Satanic blacksmith evidently having taken a sudden vacation. The Bishop, eyes still fixated, now aimed also his oily, wrinkled smile at me. "And please convey my blessings to your blasphemously celestial daughter," he went on, making a Sign of the Cross in the direction, I was sure, of my nether regions. "Though simply to be daughter—or is it 'niece'—of Christ's Vicar should be blessing enough for any girl. This one has a budding divinity all her own. She seems not the daughter of a mortal man, Holiness, but of a god. Lucrezia *Formosa**, you could tempt Christ."

Allatri saying that made me feel fearful, proud and powerful, all at the same time. Papa scowled. I couldn't figure why. Why should Papa care whom Allatri's eyes played over and coveted? How was that a Pope's affair? I could take care of myself vis-à-vis such a withered branch. He bowed deeply to Papa, kissing his ring, and began to withdraw. Papa held out his beautiful arms to me. I ran and in a moment was happily ensconced on his white lap. He was all in white, the way I'd seen him every day for the past year and more. White cassock with a white simar, white cloth-covered buttons down the cassock, white fascia. He wore Peter's ruby Ring and a big, pectoral cross, all encrusted with diamonds, as well as white slippers, hose and skullcap. Even in his formerly dark beard there arose newly emerging strands of white, as if in sympathy with the rest of him. His whiteness seemed to roll through the Apostolic Palace and now the Borgia Apartments. I'd grown a lot since I'd been six, and Papa had lost somewhat that continental feel he'd had for me earlier. Now he was always in white, and also now he was without Vanita and her love to hold his feet to earth; he'd risen from landmass into a cloud. A somewhat fatter one. Not a thunderhead, though I knew him capable of a sudden, lightning flash, but one of those summer cumulus giants that arcs colorlessly over the Mediterranean.

He kissed me on my head and hands. "And what vile sins have you been about, you bantam, blond Beelzebub?"

---

*Most beautiful.

I'd just come from my lesson. It'd been a sewing bee with a bunch of giggly, sewing nuns, who spent the bee guffawing at salacious double entendres they'd make to each other. Then they'd look at me and their eyebrows would dance up and down like Commedia clowns. Lots of cracks about "pussy cats" licking "cream" and about themselves or me twirling around "maypoles." Is it Heaven's Mandate that nuns have bad senses of humor? But giggle all the time? They thought I couldn't understand their unfunny jokes. But what I couldn't understand was why I was made to sit like a dumb lump and sew and not be allowed to study history, like Cesare always had.

"I've been learning to sew," I now said. "It's as fun as watching milk sour."

"It's a thing young ladies must learn," Papa said.

"Why? Cesare studied history and war in Latin and Greek books. I want to read books. Why may I not study history and war?"

"Cesare studied these things because one day he'll make them. A girl studies sewing because one day she'll sew."

"Girls never make history, unless it's as some great man's slut," I said. "Aunt Adriana said so in my lesson. But I think that's bullshit. Look at Cleopatra."

" 'Bullshit'! Lucrezia, don't be a foul-mouth."

"Cesare used ● ay it and you never minded; he's where I learned it. Why can't I say it? It's the Borgia device, isn't it?"

Papa groaned. "A *bull* is our device, not his . . . excrement. As if we were matadors, not stable boys."

The Madonnas Mila and Farnese were my tutors and both were—so everybody said—Papa's present paramours. I doubted Papa was overly happy about that, since Aunt Giulia was a habitual flirt and kept sleeping with this or that handsome guy all the years she shared her bed with Papa. He'd always have to send soldiers or some cardinal to drag her from one villa or another, where she'd be shacked up, usually with her estranged second husband, Orsino Orsini. Papa hated the Orsinis, too. We studied drawing, dancing, embroidering with gold and silver threads, playing the lute, general politesse and protocol every weekday in a chamber at the end of the Borgia Apartments. The room was just next to the grand library, which Papa said was the best in the world. I kept trying to get Giulia or Adriana to take me there instead, but they insisted on my learning to curtsy and to eat pasta without slurping.

And how to be dainty and of comfort to my future husband with his battle wounds, whoever he might be.

"Oh, he'll be a great nobleman and he won't stand for a wife who doesn't know how to tidy his castle and dust his antiques," they'd said, to my intense annoyance.

"Bleccha," I'd responded. "What're servants for, after all? When was the last time either of you did any dusting around here? I'm not going to live in a cold, drafty castle; I like palaces."

"Lucrezia, the nuns and your father—the Most Holy Father, by the bye—have forbidden you the library or to read any books. They're bad for you."

But I'd finally thought enough was enough and followed Papa to the library's entrance on the ground floor by the Papagallo, keeping warily out of sight. But Papa didn't go in. He just passed on by. I'd never yet passed through that entrance.

When he'd been gone a few minutes, I gathered up my courage. I grasped the round iron-rope handles of the enormous, hanging doors. I swung them open, looking back over my shoulder to make sure their creaking hadn't alerted anyone.

"Oh, my God," I bubbled from the hallway at the sight of the library's interior. It looked like God's Own Vault of Mysteries, suddenly flung open.

"Little Lucrezia," I heard behind me. "What are you doing here?"

"Papa!" I then made a shamefaced shuffle toward him—not exactly toward him, so much as sidling toward the shelves of beckoning books. "I wanted . . ."

"Yes? You wanted what?"

"I want to read the books."

"You're a rare Lucrezia indeed. Neither Giulia, Adriana nor even your mother ever opened a book's cover. The fairer sex has no interest in literature."

"They haven't? They don't?"

"No. Writing or speaking in general are forms of unchastity, you know."

I gathered up my courage again. "How do you know, Papa? Have you ever asked one? Did you ever ask Vanita if she'd like to read?"

"I didn't have to. The greatest author, Aristotle, tells us it's not in the nature of women to seek the more abstract knowledges. 'The male principle in nature,' he argued, 'is associated with active, formative and perfected characteristics, while the female is passive, material and deprived, desiring the male in order to be complete,' he says in his Την Φισιν, *The Physics,* or *Nature.*"

"Like Vanita desired you?"

"Roughly." He chuckled. "But in Greek."

"Was Aristotle a Greek woman?"

"Of course not. He tells us Sappho was the only woman, a sluttish Greek of deviant nature, who ever thought to write a book."

I bit my lip. Should I say what I was thinking? Oh, why not, I thought; he's Papa. He's the nearest thing to God. He'll understand. He's omniscient. "Then Aristotle's a big ass."

I was sure he'd break into a fury, but no. He only laughed, rather happily, I thought. I was shocked to find I could turn Papa with words. I was scandalized to learn such power resided in them. Could that be why he loved it here? And protected it from me? Many in later times have rumored Papa to be inelegantly lettered, ignorant of the Classics and far from a humanist. That's untrue, but it's become part of his myth, regardless, I think because his Latin, extempore, was on rare occasion halting, as were his Greek, Hebrew and even Tuscan.

"Well, the great master's been often wrong in other instances," he said amidst his chuckles. "He's wrong about government and war and the role of princes. Maybe he's wrong about women. An occasional woman, anyway. Contemporary thinkers prefer Plato; he's so much smarter and up-to-date. By Plato's reckoning, the Ideal Soul, the *imago speculi,* the burnished image, upon which the souls of all women should be based, would be the Virgin. Perfect, except, of course, that no one accused the Virgin of being as bright as Sappho. Many say she couldn't even read 'The King of the Jews' on the Cross."

I gazed about into the library at the thousands of books weighing the shelves into subtle, downward curves. What a grand mind I imagined one must have to write a book. Could I write one? Standing there with mouth open, smelling dusty parchment, sour sweat and the moldering-liver scent of gallotannin on leather, I prayed I'd someday write one, having then no idea of the task I'd set myself. I hope its frontispiece will be after my favorite portrait by Bartolomeo de Venezia, for the look of that painting is the look my Alphonso of Bisceglie knew. I'm half naked in it; that should sell. But that day in the library I was consumed with jealousy in the face of all that scribbled brilliance. "How does one go about writing a book, Papa?" I asked him. "It's awfully hard, isn't it? How does one go about even thinking about it?"

"Well, let's see." Papa at long last led me into the library.

A hundred-foot-long, forty-foot-wide cavernous tunnel of thousands of books confronted me on shelves that began at the floor and climbed to a thirty-foot, rounded and decorated ceiling. Three great rooms in succession made up the library. The Latin and Greek Rooms, open to the public, the *Bibliotheca Secreta*, for the most elaborate and costly books, and the *Bibliotheca Pontificum*, filled with Papal documents, some a millennium and more old.

"Behold the Image of Aristotle's Lyceum," Papa said, as he went into the Greek Room, "as We are the Image of God."

Did he mean *We*? I wondered. There were sliding, golden-yellow ladders, like Jacob's, ascending to the upper shelves on both stories. Papa smiled and began to walk along the spines, softly describing individual books to me as we went. I heard in his voice how he loved them. I was so jealous of that love. I wanted it. I wanted to know these pages well enough to love them, the way he did. Or to add that love to what he already had for me, me filled with all their knowledge. Were these wooden shelves made of Eve's apple tree? Was the Knowledge of Good and Evil hanging on them? Where could such Knowledge be, if not here?

"In the heart," Papa said, chuckling, when I asked him.

Sets, clusters and single volumes. Many books were brand-new. The new ones were characterized by the newest fonts, formed in imitation of the letter style in ancient books, as described in Feliciano of Verona's treatise on the Roman alphabet, which was also here. There was a copy of Cassandra Fedele's *Ordo Scientiarum*—a Κασσανδρα*, indeed, as I'd find out, when I'd read her. Also there was Bartolomeo Goggio's 1487 publishing scandal, *In Praise of Women*, plus Cusanus. Ficino—today's philosopher of immortality—Averroes in Latin translation and Plethon, among hundreds of other moderns.

"Goggio's prose is tedious and oleaginous," Papa said. "But it asks and discusses for the first time the four questions our age must answer about the feminine body and soul."

---

*Cassandra, the prophetess, warned the Trojans about the Horse, suggesting to them they "never trust a Greek bearing gifts." They didn't listen.

John Faunce

"Which are?"

"The question of Chastity. The question of Power. The question of Discourse. And the question of Knowledge."

"Will I know the answers if I read all these?"

"Probably not. We still don't."

Many other books looked hundreds of years old. Pindar, Jerome, Chrétien de Troyes, Cicero, dozens of Homers in Greek and Latin, Xenophon, Pliny—father and son—Caesar, Herodotus, Euclid, Saint Augustine, Chrysostom's *Homilies on Matthew*, Athanasius, along with scads of Greek Fathers, dozens of Virgils. A *Complete Works* of Josephus, Philo's *De Vita Moysis*, Gregory of Nyssa's book of the same name and cheek to cheek a thousand other Hebraic and *Contra Judeos* titles. A leather, book-shaped box, Papa showed me, with *The Chaldaic Oracles* stamped in gold on what would be the spine of a regular book.

"Who's this by?"

"Zoroaster. He says God is light."

"Isn't He?"

"Perhaps. But it's 'translated' by Plethon and some say it's a fake; that Plethon just made it up."

"It's fake, so it's darkness?"

Opening the box, he leafed over the loose, handwritten pages of weird scratches, as if t were rusted gold, tea-colored with hundreds of years. He showed me Books of Hours, the most glamorous things I'd ever seen, their pages dancing with every color and passion. There were dozens of those Books of Hours, each filled with God-inspired pictures and black-, red- and gold-ornamented text. Dozens of Testaments, Old and New, in Latin, Greek and Hebrew. Many of the volumes were bound in calf in the newest style, Bernard of Clairvaux, Maimonides the Jew, John Foxe, Seneca, Petronius Arbiter, Aristotle, Saint Ignatius, Anaxagoras, Saint Thomas Aquinas and Plato—

"Plato brought philosophy down from Heaven to earth," Papa said.

"How?"

"He says we're all prisoners, sitting around a campfire in a cave. That we can see only the shadows thrown by the fire on the cave's wall."

"Like the shadow puppets I make with my hands?"

"Exactly. And we imagine those shadows are reality instead of only images. He tells us that the truth—your hands making the puppet—is deeper and greater than the shadows, even if not so enchanting; that with persistent toil we can know the truth—the highest and best calling of artists and poets; that there are morals based on truth for us to mind, of duty and decency, and that there is a supreme unity in the cosmos, the God we've chosen, such that nothing, however apparently insignificant, is ever lost."

"We chose God?"

"*I* did."

"I'll never be lost if I read these books?"

"You'll never be lost if you trust your Papa."

"Does Aristotle say anything?"

"He tells us what a good life is."

"What is it?"

"A life of 'excellent activity in accordance with reason,' which always seemed to me the very subtitle of our current times."

An age of 'reason'? Ours? Not unless reason's lit by bloody gloom.

"What is 'excellent'?"

"Courage, temperance, generosity, magnificence, greatness of soul, ambition, good temper, friendliness, wit, justice and two more I can never remember.*"

"That's you, Papa." But what were the two he couldn't remember? I wondered.

And we looked at less weighty authors, entertainers such as Aeschylus, Sophocles, Euripides, Terence and Seneca the Stoic, who tells us to cultivate misery for its own, exquisite sake. He showed me atlases of the world which revealed all secrets of place and distance. Papa was devoted to the New World, as revealed in Vespucci's *Atlas*. He saw it as the greatest opportunity in history for the propagation of the Faith, rather than a fresh occasion for rape and plunder, as he published in his Bull of 1501. It was he that in May 1493 had divided it between Spain and Portugal, casting Christ's dominion over the earth's new half, about which whole new libraries will undoubtedly be written. A few have even suggested the New World be called "Alexandria," in his memory. And sheep's vellum–bound volumes, too, thousands of them in their white covers. Ovids, Catulluses, Horaces, Lucians, Juvenals, Plautuses, Epicuruses, Livys, Apulius, Vitruvius' *De Architectura*, Quintilians, Sallusts and dozens of Latin, Greek and Arabic poets, some original, some copied. Those in their white covers were especially

---

*Truthfulness and shame are the ones he couldn't remember.

beautiful, I thought, poised on their shelves like the slow-moving ice mountains the Swiss say move an inch toward the sea each year. Anything that
old and still white ought carry a reader to only aboriginal and pure truths, I
was certain. A hundred sets. A thousand snowy volumes, at the least.

"What's that one?" I said, pointing to one whose vellum was roseate.

"That's the *History of Salvation Symbolized by a Building* by Hildegarde of Bingen," Papa said.

" 'Hildegarde'? Isn't that a woman's name? I thought only balmy
Sappho wrote books."

"Hildegarde was crazy mad as Satan's anus," he replied. "She was
driven so slowly, as was Sappho, by her scribblings, which start rationally,
but soon become even loonier than herself. The Camerlengo's told me
my taste is . . . well, it's 'catholic,' is what he said—small *c*. You've seen
me send monks to Ostia, to meet arriving ships? It's books they're after
in their holds, you know. Since I ascended the Papacy, I've become a
secret bibliophile. I've expanded this collection, begun by Nicholas V
and tripled by Sixtus IV. I've decorated the chamber, as you see, in the
manner of Pliny the Younger's description of the garden suite of his villa.
It's my ambition to one day replace the lost libraries of the Athenian
Academy and Alexandria."

"Have you read all these?"

"At one time or another."

My God, I thought, Papa must really be omniscient. All right, a touch
of blasphemy. But I knew I should never question a man as great as
would collect and read all this. I didn't know anything except sewing.
"Has Cesare read them?"

"I believe so." Papa laughed.

"Can I?" I asked.

He chuckled again. "Do you know Latin and Greek?"

"No."

He reached up and took two slender volumes from a shelf. "These are
Greek and Latin grammars. Do you know how to read at all?"

"Yes," I retorted with a crabby glance. It was half true, at least, since I'd
always make the old nun follow the words with a finger when she'd read
me a saint's life or a tale from Aesop. "I know my letters. The old nun
taught me; it's amazing what you can learn sewing sayings on pillows." I
blamed the old nun, not wanting to get the aunts or younger nuns in
trouble.

"Memorize everything in these two books. Then maybe we'll talk again."

I took them and ran. Over the next months I front-to-back memorized them. These two grammars, written by priests with Celtic names and printed, respectively, by Johann Frobens in Basle and Aldus Manutius in Venice, were frustrating as ill-fitting, whalebone corselets. And all the instruction in these two books was *in* Greek or Latin. It was easier to learn those languages from any pair of priests, I soon discovered, who happened to be conversing in those tongues. Latin was all over the Vatican, because it was God's Official Language. Greek was all over the Vatican, because there were hundreds of clerics there, exiled from the Grand Turk's lately Muslim Byzantium. I'd sit next to them and listen, pretending to play with a doll. They were generally engaged in the fierce debate between follow-ers of Plato and those of Aristotle—between the primacy of mind and spirit or of things and bodies—which had been raging in Rome since the fall of Constantinople in 1453, when the Eastern scholars had fled to Rome, Venice and Florence. From these Byzantines derives our interest in Greek literature, thought and art that now vies for attention with the world of Virgil. Their arguments flew over my head, but I memorized the grammars and the priests' vocabularies, nonetheless. I'd then go to the library at night and begin to read. It took me a few books before I really could relate what'd been in the grammars to an actual page of words, but not long. I'd also loiter at the *Studium Urbis*, Papa's rebuilt University of Rome near the Pantheon, where I'd listen to students argue in Greek and Latin, whether Christ's Blood, shed in His Passion and reassumed in His Resurrection, remained united to His Divinity during the three days His Body lay in the tomb and thereby rated the *cultus* accorded divinity proper. All the rage that year, but I couldn't follow it in any language, except to think us saved not by His Blood but by His Death.

"People think Borgias are all mad," he said. "What's the harm?"

"Do you want her, Holiness, to turn into another Sappho?"

"Men will never allow a girl with a form like hers to become Sapphic. It would contradict Plato *and* Aristotle."

"What if she becomes a nun?"

"You mean Sapphic?"

"Holy Father!"

"Resign yourselves, sisters. It's Our Will."

And that was that.

One by one in the moonlight I'd slip the precious books from their shelves, open them as if I were opening the Covenant's Ark and read them. Some were as big and heavy as myself and were trials to unload from the creaking shelves, but I found I liked those the best. As I drank in the words, they assumed a strange sort of life inside me. I felt my mind, my soul—is there a difference?—begin to alter in its very character. Is there anything more potent in the world, I wondered, than the rebirth of a soul? Odd, I thought, how these paper and leather objects do so easily and pleasurably what the Inquisition's fires, frequently fed with similar books, have never done. Ink puts out even hellfire. I pray, as daily I pick up my quill, this book before me might have such reforming powers for some other blond. Moonlight made my book reading slow and there were thousands of books. I couldn't go the nights of the New Moon, since my reading lamp those nights had fled the sky. But I learned gradually to love the flipping pages of books, their smell, dust and everything about them.

But that earlier day I was still on Papa's lap. Allatri had just withdrawn.

"And what have *you* been up to, Papa?" I asked.

Alexander glanced toward the archway, through which the Bishop had just fled.

"Making history." He paused. "Making *bad* history. It's very difficult to be Pope. Much harder than We thought, before We were Ourselves. To be is harder than to desire. That's an apt lesson for either man or woman."

"Cesare will never learn it," I said. "Because—"

But Papa wasn't listening. He was absorbed in thought, puzzling over the Brunelleschi Crucifix that hung, according to Pinturicchio's design, on the far wall. "We'd simply have Allatri killed," he said softly, "but he knows it, and is careful to go nowhere alone."

"Can I help with Allatri?"

"You can't help. You're only a little woman. Women only kill flies and the odd lobster."

"Let me kill Allatri for you," I whined. "I'll stick a knife in his breadbasket, like Aunt Giulia says Cleopatra should've done right off to Mark Anthony."

"Giulia says that?"

"All the time."

"Why?"

"Because he slept with other women."

"I hate to disagree with Aunt Giulia, but I don't think that's such a good reason."

"You're saying 'I,' Papa."

"Absolutely not. A terrible reason. A mortal sin of a reason. We'll have to talk to her."

"Let me kill him, Papa. I can do it. He's only a donkey bishop."

"We were once a Bishop," Papa said. "Were We a donkey? And so then did We sire a little lady, who's an ass?"

"Allatri's always calling me 'divine,' " I said. "And trying to get me to sit on his lap."

"Really?" Papa said. "But you don't?"

"There's something funny in his eyes when he says it."

" 'Something funny,' indeed. Lucrezia, I want you to come to my chambers just before suppertime. Will you do that?"

"Oh, yes, Papa."

I had a feeling I was about to make some history of my own. Maybe someday there'd be a book in the library about me! I thought of Cesare, for whom whatever I was to do was being done. He'd probably be having a tantrum at the thought that I was about to do it, instead of himself. Go ahead, I thought, have one. Screech, scream, stomp, spit, and bang your head on the floor. Be my guest. But I'm going to save your life, and you can't.

At dusk Sister Angelique, Papa's "Maiden of the Bedchamber"—no pun intended, really; she made the bed, cleaned the room and chamber pots and was quite a devout girl—escorted me to the Pope's gigantic bedroom and left us by ourselves. Gigantic and magnificent. Or rather an embryo of its future magnificence. The artists hadn't yet decorated it with their oily miracles, as soon they would, with some of the most beautiful murals in the world. "The way walls look in Heaven," Master Botticelli would exclaim, when first he saw them. But I knew this was already the dream room of the Cloud King. The Cloud King sat on his creamy white, satin-covered bed. Just to its side rested a table made entirely of ivory. On the table was a golden goblet of red wine. Later that night there was supposed to be a Papal banquet, Papa told me. He turned to me and asked if I'd like to go. I was stunned. I was to be invited? Me? To a State banquet?

"Papa, isn't it forbidden for girls or women to attend State banquets at the Vatican?"

"Innocent VIII of sacred memory violated that rule daily. That's how it's said he got sixteen little apostles."

"An adult dinner? At night? May I have a new gown? A blue one to go with my eyes?"

"What a vain little girl, daughter of Vanity. But yes."

"Yes? And earrings?"

"Yes."

Was he joking? Of course I'd go. I felt like the queen of the world. This is a room where dreams come true, I thought. Nothing like this had ever happened before, though I'd begged a hundred times. Papa then started giving me instructions on what I was to do and say and how I was to act at the banquet.

"Papa," I said. "You don't have to. Aunt Giulia already spent about a hundred years teaching me this stuff."

"Well, I'm sure that's true, but you'll have some special duties at this particular dinner."

" 'Special duties'?"

I'd do anything he might ask if it meant I could go to tonight's affair. I stood before him. His lesson went on and on. Lots of stuff I knew about—which spoon for this and that, to whom to curtsy, whom to ignore. Then he began to tell me the "special duties" I was supposed to do for Allatri. In his white Papal cassock he demonstrated for me a new way I was to walk. He looked ridiculous. He was prancing like a prostitute in his big, thoroughly male body and tight white skirt. He looked like a hirsute, brawny Vanita, in fact. Finally some odd things I was supposed to do and say only for the French envoy.

"And after dinner, when everyone's talking, when they've had a lot of wine and are making a lot of noise, you just get up from your chair and walk up to the Bishop the way I showed you," he said.

"Like this?"

I performed for him my best approximation of the mincing walk he'd shown me.

"Not so much," he admonished. "Just swing it a little. But don't be vulgar."

To oversashay, he said, was "trashy" and would attract stinging wasps, instead of the honey drone a girl wants. I didn't quite know what that meant, but I'd be damned if I'd be vulgar. I walked to him. My Vanita imitation felt both bizarre and in some perverse manner evocative, as if its hippy little switch contained an ocean's incipient tide. I figured it must be working, because Papa certainly looked approving, and he was as much a connoisseur of a woman's walk as any man on earth. I felt exhilarated. Even my waist-long braid felt as if abruptly more blond. I felt irresistible. I couldn't have said how a new walk had accomplished all that, but it had.

"Exactly." Papa grinned, pleased surprise on his face. "And when you get to him, what did I tell you to do?"

"I don't step on his purple robe. I say, 'Oh, Eminence, may I sit on your lap, please?' Except I draw out the word *please* real long, like I want to sit there more than anything in the world."

My father imitated Allatri's answer. "Of course, divine girl."

It turned out he wasn't so bad an Allatri. I sat on his cloud lap.

"Now wiggle your bottom. Just a little," he said.

"Do I have to?"

"Never mind. Just do it."

So I did. I wiggled just a bit, trying my best to be unvulgar.

"That'll make his bells ring, I'll wager," Papa said. "The Frog Ambassador will love that."

"Are you sure?"

"Then what do you say?"

"I ask . . . if I can kiss him."

"Don't make a face like that, even if he looks especially amphibian this evening. He'll lean forward. When he does, I want you to take this ring—"

He took a ring off his pinky finger. Not the Fisherman's Ring, of course; that would've been too big; another that I hadn't seen before. It had a ten-carat central stone.

"Sapphire as your eyes," Papa said. He took the ring and slipped it onto my thumb. "Then put your hand with this ring over his wineglass." He held my ringed hand over the goblet of red wine on his ivory side table. "And while he waits for his kiss, open this stone." He showed me how, flipping open the hollow blue eyelid from the ring by its tiny gold hinge. "Then turn your hand over and let the blue powder inside fall into his wine. Make sure you do it into dark red, strong-flavored wine, an Amarone or a port." He manipulated my hand, so I'd know just how. "Then kiss him and offer him—politely, be sure—his wine to drink. Understand?"

"Do I have to kiss him? He's *always* froggy."

"It will please Us and We're your Holy Father."

"Why am I doing all this?"

"It's your own idea. Don't you still want to help Cesare? And because We wish it. God and I."

So, *We* wished it. I knew that meant him and God. Wouldn't it be blasphemy to deny Them a wish? "Why do you Both wish it? Why do *you* need to wish it, too? Whatever He wishes just happens, doesn't it?"

"What I wish today on earth is what God wishes eternally in Heaven. Has always wished. That's the way I understand being Pope works."

"Oh. And so I'm to kill Bishop Allatri with the powder? Isn't that a mortal sin?"

"If what he says is true, Cesare's life is forfeit if you don't do it. How could saving your brother's life be a mortal or any kind of sin? In fact, the Two of Us decree it isn't a sin. Will you save him?"

"Of course. Do you want me to?"

He took a long pause. "It's up to you. You're almost a woman; your choices aren't mine to make."

I could sense that was at least partly true, or seemed so at the time.

"Really?" I asked.

"All I can say to you is, be a Borgia. Take the world and bend it to *your* will. Don't let the world do the bending. Do you want to surrender your brother to our family's enemies?"

"Will you still love me, Papa, if I become a murderess?"

"A 'murderess'?" he said. "It will please me, Lucrezia. You will have saved Our son, after all. And I'll love you with all my heart, were you to become Lucifer. You wouldn't want to lose Papa's love, would you?"

"That would be the worst thing in the world."

He smiled. His hand grasped my thigh. A tingling warmth that in those days was unwonted, but since I've become a woman I'm well accustomed to, spread through me. For the second time during that conversation, that particular warmth.

He put his lips to my ear, so they brushed it and my cheek, as he spoke. "You must swear the most sacred oath, you'll tell no one else, ever, about our design to save Cesare. Enemies could kill us all with that knowledge."

"Don't worry, Papa, I never will."

"Say it. Swear on the Blood from Christ's Wounds, washed from His naked Body by the Holy Virgin's hand."

That was the most terrifying image I'd ever heard. The Savior's Blood, rushing from those horrible gashes, over Mary's hands, as if the still-living Gore were His Life's final Cry to her. Even more terrifying than the imprecation and condemnation, which I'd heard many times the Inquisition pronounce on sending a man or woman to the burning death, a curse that had always made my skin bump with icy cold.

"I swear, Papa. On the Virgin's bloody hand," I said, quivering as the words came out of my mouth.

He softly laughed, evidently at my malapropism.

Several hours later I found myself in a brand-new, baby-blue gown the giggling nuns had made me, seated on a damask-cushioned chair at the biggest gleaming oval table I could remember, at a Papal banquet in the State Dining Room, the grandest meal I could imagine. When people ate in Heaven, I knew, this was how, stuffing their souls with Divine Grace just the way we all now stuffed our faces with divine rarities. At the grand oval sat two dozen or more members of the Sacred College, with their marvelously dressed courtesans—so much for no women— as well as several knights, their ladies and sundry noblemen and noble-women and a scattering of Borgia relatives. Conversations bubbled all around me, laughing, shrieking toward the cloud- and cherubim-printed ceiling. Wines were so copious, I imagined Papa must've turned the foun-tain water outside into wine, though I drank only one tiny white and one red glass, as he'd instructed me. There were crockeries and goldwares that could've ransomed kingdoms. The most heavenly music wafted and piped from an orchestra that played as they strolled through the room, dressed like cherubs with wings and Beelzebubs with tails. Foods from every land encircling *Mare nostrum* were brought from the Vatican kitchens on silver trays the length and breadth of altars.

Papa sat at the head of the table. All evening I watched him. All the guests acted all night as if they adored him, which surprised me not at all. He looked handsome and confident as some Mephistopheles, without a care in the world. Allatri sat in the seat of greatest honor for a guest, at the exact opposite end from Papa's. If all night I watched the Pope, then all night Bishop Allatri's eyes were, no surprise, fixed on me. It was a relief to be seated at a table, so he couldn't focus, at least, on my fanny. Near the end of the banquet, when all the noble guests had become nobly drunk; when the revelry was at its height, as Papa had said it would be; when the old French Bishop, drunk as any and more than most, was nearly drooling at me, I climbed from my damask, legend-embroidered pillow. "Antequam

Satanam fieret, EGO SUM," it said in red letters. I looked straight at Alla-tri. My hard glance stiffened his usually bent back. As I did my mincing lit-tle walk toward him, he wet his lips as if a fox approached by a gosling.

"Oh, your Excellency," I said, when finally I reached his side. "May I sit on your lap, puhleeeze?"

"Of course, divine girl," he said, exactly as Papa had imitated.

I knew at that moment that Papa's intention and God's must really be the same. I sat on his lap. I did it as I imagined Vanita would've, no longer having to think how to do so. I realized that only thinking so had previ-ously rendered it foolish to me. He was overjoyed. He fed me a sweet of Austrian marzipan, trying to worm into my good graces. I looked at him. He was mine. I knew it. I was a girl; he was a King's envoy, Lord Bishop of the Church and commander of thousands of murderers. In spite of that, I was his mistress. As I chewed the marzipan, I rolled it in my mouth, as I'd seen Vanita do once with a butterscotch. I knew this would ensnare him further. It did. I wiggled my fanny over his lap.

He rolled his eyes in Parisian ecstasy. *"Ooh la la."*

"Oh, Excellency," I said. "May I kiss your wrinkly cheek, puhleeze?"

"Child, you may kiss me on whatever wrinkly part you like."

He leaned in for his kiss, just the way Papa'd said he would. As he did, out of his sight line I moved my ringed hand over his Burgundy. All around us was such merrymaking chaos, music and laughter that no one paid the slightest mind to a girl and an old man. I opened the ring. I tipped my hand over his goblet. I couldn't see the powder fall, but I knew it had. It was God's Will. I kissed him on his nose, the only unwrin-kled, unrobed part I could see. As he sat back from my kiss, a wide slash of lascivious, red grin had conquered his face.

"A cooling sip of wine, Most Reverend Lord?"

I politely offered him the goblet of the purple French Burgundy. He grinned at it. After a toasting motion in the definite direction of my fanny, Allatri gulped it down in a single swallow. Papa watched us, a hun-gry smile over his face. I offered a prayer for the Bishop's soul to the Holy Spirit, but behind my back, just to be sure, I crossed my fingers.

Three days later, on New Year's Eve 1494, Charles VIII and his army occupied Rome. Though they'd murdered and plundered all the Jews, compared with Goths or Vandals they were really behaving rather well. Nevertheless, all the prelates, and most everyone else, were hiding in their palaces' basements, stables and outhouses. That morning Charles came to the Vatican. Papa waited for him, enthroned alone in the Borgia Apartments, a shivering clump of Curial Cardinals hiding in his bedroom. I stood next to him. Charles entered the throne room. I was shocked. I was expecting some latter-day Charlemagne, a great, imperious commander. But Charles VIII was a crippled, crooked dwarf with blubbery lips, dull eyes, a vulture's nose and twitching hands. He was four and a half feet tall, but looked even shorter, owing to his back's massive hump, which crunched him over toward the ground. He had to bend back at the waist to see anything higher than his shoes. His execrable image is preserved forever on the first sheet of Attavante's otherwise wondrous Bible, a sacrilege. Following Charles, Cesare strode into the room in his red robes and cobalt eyes, tall, straight, handsome. Now *this*, I thought, is Charlemagne. Charles hobbled and wobbled up to Papa. He sunk to his knees on the steps to the throne and kissed Papa's foot, already inches from Charles' nose. Papa then stood and lifted Charles to his flapping feet.

"Majesty," the Pope said. "Your politesse shames Us. We should be kissing your foot. You are the Alexander here. Rise. Rise."

"Most H-holy P-p-papa," he stuttered, words bursting from fat lips like articulating flatulence. "We've come to offer Our felicitations and to report We've acceded to your c-c-command and have moved Our army from before Rome's walls—"

"Yes, *into* Rome."

"—as well as to return to You Cardinal B-b-borgia, your gracious child."

"*Deo gratias.*"

"We've taken great joy in him Ourselves. We've often taken him hunting and campaigning with Us. We've found him a b-brave, aggressive and noble knight. He once saved Our life from a r-raging r-r-razor-b-back, much in the manner that Meleager saved Theseus from the Calydonian B-boar."

"Cesare, my son, you do Us honor."

"We've also found him, considering especially his hab-b-bits *d'amour,* not so n-noble a ch-churchman, however."

"Horrors," Papa said. *"Quelle surprise,* as you people say."

"Be that as it may, We've awarded him the Order of Saint Louis and have knighted him for his services to Us. We are heart-b-broken to now b-b-bid him adieu."

Cesare beamed.

Charles reached up, pulled Papa down to himself and kissed him on both cheeks.

Papa stood up. "We must now have lunch," he announced. "It won't be as fine as a lunch in Paris—"

"C'est la g-g-*guerre."*

"—but it'll be adequate, We're sure."

We all went in to lunch. I walked next to the Pope.

Charles asked him, "We seem to have misplaced Our envoy. Have you seen him, the Most Reverend Allatri?"

"Oh, yes. We had many excellent exchanges with him. We had dinner together only three evenings ago."

"We're aware of that, b-but soon thereafter he seems to have vanished. We've heard a rumor, unfounded, We're sure, that you are holding him in a guest suite at the Castel Sant'Angelo."

"That's absurd. We swear to God he isn't living in Sant'Angelo. Lucrezia, you were next to the Bishop and got on splendidly. Did he say where he was off to at dinner's end?"

"He went home with a guard of French knights," I replied, which was true.

That afternoon, after a Sicilian lunch of sole amandine with a sauce of olives and sun-dried tomatoes, Cesare came to see me. I was in the library.

"Cesare, you've not come to read, have you? Papa said you've read all these already."

He knelt down next to my chair. He kissed my slipper. Then he took my hand and kissed my palm, then his lips moving up my arm, he said, "I've heard you've become a murderess on my behalf. I've come to thank you and to tell you that your brother loves you."

"Where did you hear that?"

"That I love you?"

"The murderess thing."

"Last night I took to my bed a redheaded Dutchwoman with a hideous name that could only have been propagated athwart a dike. Hroswitha was

Allatri's conventual whore, until three nights ago. She told me she thought you'd poisoned her Lord Bishop. 'I tasted almonds on his lips,' she told me."

"Sole almandine."

"Or poison, made from extract of almond?"

"What color is extract of almond?"

"I've no personal knowledge, of course. It's said to be bluish."

I took an intake of breath. "She won't tell anyone else, will she?"

"I doubt it. For your sake I throttled her with a woven silver garrote that I had as a gift from *Le Roi*."

I sighed with relief.

"What happened to the bodies of the Bishop and the Dutchwoman?" I asked.

"Do you know D'jem?"

"Of course."

D'jem was the twenty-fourth son of the Grand Turk, Baz al D'jet Ottoman. D'jem was tall, hook-nosed, painstakingly cruel in a way distinctly Turkish and held in resplendent hostage to some or other Turko-Vatican treaty. He was Cesare's favorite whoring buddy.

"D'jem agreed to send some fez-headed soldiers. He told them to take the carcasses to Castel Sant'Angelo, put them in a cell in the new section Papa's building for secret escape and then brick up the cell's entrance. They're now lost to history."

"And the Turkish masons?"

"Dead, as well."

"Papa told the truth. Allatri's not 'living' in Sant'Angelo."

I thought long and hard, as we sat together after his story, and he sipped sweet wine. I realized I knew so little of the way of the world and knew even less of the ways of Papa and Cesare, though my love for them remained undiminished, especially since my murder had been sanctioned by the Father in Heaven. Would I know more after my readings of all those books? Whatever I might learn therein, then I was sure of only one thing: I must not forget this lesson.

It's commonly said on the Italian street and repeated in scads of learned volumes and broadsides that my ring poisoned an Apostles' dozen more prelates for my father's benefit during my life. That is my myth, but it's a lie. My ring took but one more life.

Charles' passage through Italy, on the other hand, wrecked the entire peninsula for decades. He brought the seeds of unnumbered destructions, terrible events and changes in all our states of affairs: alterations of dominion, subversions of kingdoms, desolations of cities and countries and the cruelest of massacres. But also new fashions, new customs, new and vastly bloodier ways of battle, to replace our chivalric and chesslike form of formal war, and new, unknown diseases—like syphilis, the French pox—that have killed million of Italians during my life. If Allatri had lived, might our penances have been still worse?

three

I didn't fall in love with Dante until just days before Charles' invasion. Not with Alighieri himself, but with his divine trio of books in our library. Every foot and line of his Ptolemaic architecture bristled hairs at the back of my neck like infantry in the moonlight, either from fear and terror or from my recognition of the poet's the power to expose humanity's mysterious core.

Dante's book, and Virgil, its ghost-guide, for the last few nights had been lighting me up from within such that I imagined I saw my soul's skeleton, projected against my skin. And the thing most stunning about it, even more than the story or characters, each as vivid as a moment of birth, was that it was in Italian. Italian! I knew my mind might've turned to Latin and Greek, but my soul always breathed Italian. I'd never before come across a book in our tongue, having only seen brief phrases of it attempted previously on signs or in vulgar graffiti on walls. I'd not even yet heard of Petrarch. People have forgotten that before Dante's *Divine Comedy* there'd been no such thing as Italian. Venetian, Tuscan, Bolognese and a hundred other Latin- and/or Greek-derived dialects were spoken throughout our boot, though none of those were written in any way more literary than, let's say, "Marco Barbo is an ape," or "Vittoria Colonna has big tits." Dante was the one who in his three-line stanzas first invented a common language such that anyone from the Swiss border to the farthest outposts of Sicily could understand and write it. I vowed to someday write a book in Italian. I wondered how many whittled goose quills a whole book would take? I wanted to become another Dante; not that I imagined I'd ever imitate his quality, but just to fill sufficient pages with ink to create a book someone might read felt to me a miracle. I wanted to write an Italian book of the blackest ink, scribbled on the kind of opalescent vellum, so-called "abortive," that's made of the skin of unborn lambs of God, but with my name on its cover; so that no future little girl could ever again be told in her papa's library that reading was sinful. I resolved someday to write my journey into life, as Alighieri had written his luminous journey into death. *Quod est demonstrandum.*

One night, I'd reached *The Inferno*'s Canto XXXIV, Hell's climax scene, in which Virgil and Dante at last confront Satan in his Ninth Circle pit of ice, but dawn had interrupted my reading and I had to run the book back to its shelf unfinished. As I write this now, the memory of Canto XXXIV crackles still so coldly in me after all these years that it makes me shiver in despair, as the great Florentine poet every day makes hundreds of us scribblers quiver. We shake, because we know we can never be the poet Alighieri was, no matter how sharp our feathers. He had the courage to write to the Ninth Circle, the pit where Satan's interior justifications for his transcending evils lie with his reasoning for the endless pain he's caused the world and the God who loved him and probably loves him still. I know I lack the courage to write to Cesare's and Alexander's final pit. What strips my nerve is love. I love Cesare and always will. I love Roderigo and Alexander, my father and Holy Father, even now. I love them on my own account and because I know Vanita loved and loves them. At the entrance to my understanding's ninth circle of them stands the Guardian Devil, who we lesser poets expect to be Hate, but I find instead calls himself Love. But I promise to write until the feather turns to flame in my hand. I pray to the Virgin to reach, at least, the eighth circle.

I'd been cursing myself all the next sleepy day for not reading the end first, by far the least scary way to read a scary book. In bed again I had to know how *The Inferno* turned out, and not tomorrow, but right now. So I got up and wended my barefoot way through the cold, stone-floored apartment, to our library doors. They were already open when I got there. This had never happened before. I made my way inside, terrified I'd find some insomniac nun to scream at me. But as I began to make my way past the stacks, I could see, sitting at the big oaken table far at the moonlit end of the massive room, a distinctively golden figure with a red full-stop at his crown, hunched over a pair of vellum volumes nearly as big as himself. The documents were opened flat across the table.

"Cesare?"

The night-clothed figure looked up. "Lucrezia?" he replied, whispering, as well. "What are you doing here?"

I walked to the table and sat across from him. "You won't tell the
nuns, will you?"

"There are no bitches allowed in here," he snapped. It was as if he
were speaking to a rat.

I saw in him the first signs of tantrum. He hadn't grown out of them,
never would. I panicked his thunderclaps would wake every wen-waggling
sister in the place. But as I watched him, coronaed in the taciturnity of the
moonlit sky, saying nothing myself, his eyes began to soften. Then he
smiled that smile of his that was always so gorgeous, a tiny sweet laugh
underneath it. "I love you, Lucrezia. If you read, you'll wind up in Hell—"

"Maybe in the ninth circle."

"But you're my sister. I won't tell the sisters."

I couldn't breathe. It'd been so plain, direct, so unanticipated—he'd
never been the type just to say a tender thing or one filled with such innocent feeling, so I thought it could only be the simple truth. I couldn't
remember him ever saying anything that way to me before, or to anyone,
though through the years he'd been forced at birthday celebrations and
the like to say he loved me for public applause. He'd recently said that to
me in thanks for saving his life, but never so spontaneously, so without
self-centered intent. I couldn't think of so impulsive a previous instance. I
filled with happiness and a safe, protecting warmth. I looked around us at
the thousands of moonlit spines, most of them vellum white.

"You've read all these?" I said.

"I don't know. I never kept track."

I stood up and moved quickly along the shelves. "This one?" I pointed.
"Yes."

"This one?"

"Yes."

"And how about this?"

"Uh-huh."

I pointed to a complete Aristotle in Greek.

"Yes."

To an *Anabasis* and a *Septuagint*.

"Of course."

On I went, Cesare answering, "Yes," for a dozen or more shelves.

"Okay, I get the point. From the *A* of Achaeus to—"

"The *Z* of Zosimus."

"You've read them all. Just like Papa."

I hadn't come close to reading a hundredth of all the books in here with my year of moonlight readings, nor had it ever occurred to me consciously to try. I'd rather just pulled down whatever randomly looked interesting or called out to me on this or that night—I read *Paradise* before *Purgatory*—which remains to this day the way I pick a book. What a Spartan discipline of mind his reading must've taken, I thought, and what an Athenian breadth of spirit must be its result. I'd known my brother was smart and dimly I remembered we'd read *The Golden Legend* together, but like me and Papa he'd somehow done most of his reading in secret. At least secret from me.

"What are you reading now?" I forced myself to ask.

"Look," he said.

He pushed the two folio vellums toward me across the table, opened them upside-up. "What do you see?"

"I see a map of ancient Greece and another of modern Italy."

"One by one. But what do you see, when you consider the two of them together?"

"What do you mean?"

"Lucrezia, there is no 'Italy,' just like there was once no 'Greece,' before Philip of Macedon and his son, Alexander the Great, first created such a place. Like Classical Greece, Italy now stands divided into many political units of insignificant dimension; or in Herodotus' construction, 'islands on dry land.' 'Italy' today is nothing but a dreamt vocabulary from Petrarch's and Dante's heads."

Dante? I was surprised he'd read Dante, too. But then, he'd read everything in here. In fact, I could see the map of Italy was divided into a plethora of independent, variegated regions on a sliding scale of sizes, each ruled by a different city-state or Ducal seat at the center of each color. Sea blue Venice, pink Florence, darker blue d'Este, green Bologna, a dozen others. The largest, of course, was the Papal State, the "Donation of Constantine," all in bright yellow and ringed in gold with its Vatican City capital at Rome. The Papal State, roughly matching the borders of antediluvian Latium, included a dozen ancient and modern towns and lesser cities and covered most of the peninsula's center. The map of Greece, the primordial land of the Argives, was similar, divided into the dominion colors of long-ago Corinth, Athens, Sparta, Thebes and so forth.

Cesare moved his hand down the Greek peninsula from Macedon to the Peloponnesus. "But Philip the βαρβαρικοσ, the 'Barbarian,' Alexander's father, turned this chaos into Greece and from there into an empire, so finally Greek became the semantic of all the ancient world, before Latin ever was. His sword's iron turned into his imperium's language. Language can be a curse, or a blessing; language can be soft as a kitten. But language first is power, and Empire, the ultimate power, an epic poem in the greatest language. Why else read all this? Alexander's linguistic realm was the forerunning model and Sibylline Book of the Latin Empire. Read Valla's *Oratio in Principio Sui Studii* of 1456, where he calls Latin *'Sacramentum Auctoritatis,'* 'the Sacrament of Power,' if you don't believe me." He pointed. "It's over there."

"I will."

"You see this library you and Papa love so much? I know you love it. I know how often you sneak in here. But do you know what created it? Do you know by what power it exists?"

"Papa's Papacy—following Boniface, Nicholas and a dozen Popes since—created it, the power of Christ and His Universal Church."

Cesare gently laughed. "No. The Roman Empire did. The Papacy is only a ghost of Roman power. *Fasces Romanum.** You're not one of those naïves who thinks that a peasant from Galilee would or could make such a monstrous secular power as His Apostolic Church, are you?"

"Yes."

Cesare lowered his voice even further and leaned across the table, till I could see the top of his red skullcap. "Christ has power to create and maintain a Heaven, an Empire of the Spirit, a speck upon which a billion angels may dance; but on earth God hasn't taken any visible interest or intervened in history these last fifteen hundred years. Since His Son's death He's become far too transcendent a Fellow to concern Himself with our nasty substances here below. God knows, He used to. Or at least, over time that's the God He's become. In Old Testament days

---

*In ancient times the *Fasces* were a bunch of rods, surrounding an axe. They represented the authority of Rome. The rods stood for the power of punishment, the axe for the power of death.

perhaps He'd share a smoldering shrub or a urinal in Ur with a favorite worshiper, but no longer."

" 'The Kingdom of the Father is spread upon the earth, but men do not see it.' "

"From the Gospel of Thomas. But Holy Mother Church has declared that book anathema. Damnatum est, non legitar."

"But the Virgin, Christ's Mother, wasn't too proud to dredge her hands in anything human. When He died, she washed the Blood from His Body."

"Lucrezia, you've become a secret theologian. Before I know it, you'll be mad as Hildegarde of Bingen. You're partly right, of course, but Saint Anne's immaculate daughter wasn't God, was she? Only His servant. And His Inquisitor would swab your mouth with molten iron for even breathing such a heresy aloud."

"I suppose he would."

Could Papa's Church, I wondered, torture people? I always knew it did, but the connection between my family and screaming death had never coalesced in my mind before. And where was Cesare going with all this? I felt goose bumps on my forearms.

"What the age we live in knows, lost for twelve hundred years, is that on earth *men* create and rule. One day in the *Anno Domini* fourth century the Roman Emperor and man, Constantine, woke up. During his breakfast he looked out his casement over his world. He glanced at the dozens of temples of Roman and Greek gods in the Forum. It occurred to him how much happier any one of these gods would be if he or she alone were declared the One Single Living Suzerain of the Universe in exactly the same way as he, Constantine, was happy to be and should be regarded by the people as the one single Emperor Absolute. The God Caesar, who also happened to be Jupiter's *Pontifex Maximus** of Rome. He searched his vast library—probably much like this one—for any Divinity who might be of the then blasphemous opinion that he or she were the only Sacred Being, a Heavenly Reflection of the Augustus Caesar *Imperator*, Constantine himself. He lit on the Hebrew God, whose desert bad temper and unremitting insistence

---

*Chief Priest, the oldest, most revered office in the ancient Roman hierarchy and also the formal title of the Popes. The Romans thought Brutus a criminal, not because he killed a Dictator—that was honorable—but because he killed Julius Caeser, the *Pontifex Maximus.*

on single-minded fealty to Himself seemed at first to make Him an ideal candidate."

"Cesare, cardinal or not, they'd cut your gut open and yank out your intestines for that comment."

"Every opinion I ever have would be a disemboweling offense in a lesser man, but a man as great as I will be the gut-cutter, not the cut. God became man, after all, so that man might become God."

I pointed to the shelf of Sophocles. "Ὕβρισ, brother."

Hubris is only in Greece. . . . However, reading the Torah, Constantine found some damned fine stories, but the entire Judaic enterprise seemed to the Emperor too difficult, too complicated. And then there was that upsetting circumcision thing."

What was that? I wondered. I could feel oscillations of doubt and simultaneous admiration for the startling brilliance my brother must possess to formulate such an ingenious hypothesis as he was describing, no matter what the final truth or untruth of any or all of it turned out to be.

"But study of the Jews led him to the historian Josephus, which led him to written rumors of Blessed James of Jerusalem, the brother of Christ, which led him to the Gospels. ' Ὕρικα!' he must've cried."

" 'Eureka'?"

"Exactly. He thought back; he smacked his forehead with an open palm. 'So *that* was the thing in the sky at the Milvian Bridge!'

"He called his Imperial Council and the Senate into session and informed them that from that day the Roman Empire would be the Roman and Christian Empire, which I've no doubt knocked their tibiale off at the time, Christianity still being primarily the religion of slaves and mealy-hearted lovers of slaves."

"Cesare . . . that's amazing. Let me read the book you found all this in."

"It's in no book; it's my own."

Cesare turned his head toward the map of Italy. "And the ancient Romans conquered Italy in the same way as Phillip the Barbarian conquered Greece, city by city. And from Rome they created their golden empire, replacing Greek with Latin. Constantine's Roman Empire was built on the conquest of Italy."

"Yes? So?"

"Past is future, Lucrezia. Papa and I will do the same. From our 'Donation of Constantine,' those parts of central Italy deeded by Constantine

to Christ's Vicar, Sylvester I, on account of his curing an Emperor's lep-
rosy—a miraculously sweet deal—and now known as the Papal State,
we'll paint all Italy Papal yellow. I'll polish its boot to a golden sheen.
And then one day all the world will learn Dante's Italian in order to
understand its new Caesar. Caesar is Roman, not Frankish nor Teutonic.
Max*imus*, not Max*imilian*. Neither should 'The Holy Roman Emperor'
live in a wild mountain valley, as he now does, in the land of schnitzel.
The world says ours will be a new Augustan Age. How can it without
the new Augustus?"

"You? Cesare, you're out of your mind. Does Papa even want to do any
of this? Besides, the 'Donation of Constantine' is an eighth-century for-
gery, as Valla proved in his *Treatise.*"

He smiled, this time with absolute confidence. "We'll see," he said.
"Possession, as they say . . ."

He'd never before spoken to me like this, either. For me this had been
an entirely new and surprising Cesare, one that measured himself
against a Julius Caesar or a Barbarossa. I looked at him. He was barely of
age. What other man this age could've marshaled me such a brilliant and
persuasive history lesson, tossing aside every sanctimonious truth we'd
grown up with—ones burnt onto our hearts from birth—as if they were
so much ash in a windstorm? But neither was he exactly a man, though
he wore the skullcap of a Prince of the Church. What would he become
by twenty-five, or forty, with such a beginning? At his age Great Alexander had begun to subjugate cities. If only a boy had just made such a
boasting, whispered tirade, it might've been simply—though undeniably
brilliant—a thing to be laughed off. But what if a truly self-aware and
completed man had said it? Would such a speaker be a brash boy, or the
incipient Imperator? I'd a vision of a colossal Cesare—an entire gold-
leafed page in an illuminated manuscript—astride a lapis horizon, driving the hard, ink-black iron of his intellect into the palms of a prostrate
and thorn-crowned world. I remember involuntarily shivering, as I had
on my first reading of Canto XXXIV.

❦

About the same time as Charles' invasion—anyway, it was 1494—I was fourteen. I'd begun to fill out to womanhood with all its timely lusts, fears and

foreshadows. I'd forgotten, as all young women do, every self-protective lesson I might've learned from childhood. I'd forgotten Allatri and his Hroswitha of the Dike and Cesare's and my parts in their deaths and burials. It would take me years to remember, and by then too late. I'd molted, thank the Virgin, into a beauty. This isn't vanity, I don't think. All the men, the woman-loving ones, in any case, who visited the Vatican—priests or monks or laymen, from furry Angles to naked Ethiopes to overly cultured, ex-patriot Muslims and Byzantines—every one said as much. Every one had his eyes affixed now where Allatri had always glued his. Or more often they were fastened to my expanding breasts which I thought just right and wore high, as Vanita had worn hers. And they weren't my sole inheritance from her. My teeth were Papal white and not rotten or falling out, unlike most women's. My sun-gilt hair hung always in its loose, single braid to below my waist. My eyes had kept their childlike lapis blue. My cheek-bones were high, as well. My body stood slimly as the manikins that I've seen our more fashionable tailors use, both to show their wares to best advantage and to give a flattering impression to the rich-but-overfed of how those wares will wear.

I stood in front of enthroned Papa, who wore his ring, miter and pallium and carried his crozier. "But he's old, and ugly, and *fat!*" I screeched at Christ's Vicar, my eyes closed, mouth open, stamping my feet and my hands in little fists like Cesare.

Papa batted not an eye. He was well accustomed to my methods of getting my way and had grown as impervious to this one as to most. He looked much the same in his white cloud of robes, though the whiskers of his beard had grizzled a bit cumulus whiter than before. There had also arisen in the years since he'd ascended Peter's Throne a not uninviting and ever-expanding bulge of pot-stomach. But he was still a most attractive man, an attractiveness only amplified by the ease acquired over the course of a thousand interviews, struggles and sacred public occasions with which he'd come to wear his power. When he'd first become Pope and even in his tussle with Allatri, he'd employed his authority like a painter of delicate still lifes, a smidge here, a feathering touch there. But as he sat longer in Peter's chair—especially after Charles VIII—he was becoming more and more a megalithic sculptor, hewing great strokes of stone away when necessary to achieve his desired effect. He'd seemed to make this power transition naturally, in the way any artist's style might grow in a baffling trice from apparently insignificant to creative genius. By now his power struck me as being worn by him as easily as a heron might've learned to wear its gracefulness. He was ready finally for Cesare to tutor.

"'Fat of body, fat of soul,'" Papa calmly quoted me in reply one of his little aphorisms, the kind he loved to pick up at his annual audience with a few hundred homeless beggars, scoured from the Roman streets by the Palatine Guard, during which Papa would wash their feet *in imitatio Christi*. I'd always giggled at the notion of Papa's foot-washing, until I noticed that as each homeless person would leave the private audience, in which the cleansing had taken place, he or she had a smile of ease and happiness, which I can only describe as beatific, utterly unlike their characteristic grimaces of loneliness and pain. What was Papa doing? I snuck in one day out of his sight to see how he was working these Christ-like miracles.

Papa sat the derelict on a bench. He washed her feet in warm water as tenderly as Vanita once cared for his own. He dried them with fresh linen and gently kissed them, all the while discussing with her the desperate minutia of the poor woman's life as if they were the most interesting subjects this Pontiff had ever heard. He blessed her, granted her remission of all her sins and a Plenary Indulgence, and finally, as the unfortunate stood to go, Papa surreptitiously slipped a gold florin—enough to buy a fine horse or a year of suppers—into the dirty palm. The vagabond stared at its glint in wonder, its gilt reflection lighting her eyes, as the Holy Spirit's Grace, I'm sure, was lighting her soul. The beatific smile then spread over the lined and sun-burnt face. These poor, Jesus said, have been always with us. Quoting their pithy sayings now, as I stood before his throne, no doubt made Papa feel quite Franciscan, but only served to throw fuel on my anger.

"Lucrezia, Our unreasonable child, you must do this for Us."

"I hate him!"

Papa sighed. "Lucrezia, Count Giovanni Sforza of Pesaro is a most delightful and powerful man. Cesare has visited his lands on the wild Adriatic for Us. Has even viewed his treasury. And he is a Sforza, as is the Duke of Milan, whom We presently require as an ally."

"Who is yet older, uglier and richer and with a bigger army than Giovanni," Cesare cheerily quipped. "Lucrezia, be fair. Lord Giovanni isn't that old or fat."

"Compared to whom?" I snapped. "He's a decade older than you and you're old—I'm only fourteen—and he's fat as Papa."

"We are not fat," said the Pope, sucking in his puff of pot. "At least *I'm* not. I leave God's corpus to judge for Himself. You're nothing but an *audacula*."

"And an *homuncula*," added Cesare.

"I am not a 'pushy little bitch,' nor a hermaphrodite; I'm a *virguncula*."

They stared at me, eyes and mouths agape.

I was outraged. "I'm certainly small. I'm still intact and unbedded, God damn it. Though attractively so. What?"

They gaped on.

"You don't think I'm a virgin?" I squealed in indignation.

"What on earth's a *virguncula*?" Papa asked. "And how do you know what it is? Is it Greek, Latin, Hebrew, barbarian?"

"Latin. If you were listening, I told you what it is. It's a 'small, chaste virgin.' "

"Ah!" Papa said with a proud smile.

"Ah!" said Cesare. "I knew that."

"Ah. That's a relief," from Pesaro, with a sigh.

My brother stood next to Alexander. Cesare had fulfilled the promises of his young manhood in every physical measure I might've been said to fulfill my own. He was tall and straight. His striking eyes caromed through a room as if blue gryphons in search of prey. His hair curled like a gold crown. He was dressed that day, as he often was, in a doublet of Oriental cloth-of-gold, fitted tightly as another skin to his body. This doublet he wore above a shimmering pair of French, yellow hose, which in the recently fashionable Gallic manner showed the lean muscle of his leg most elegantly, and at whose strength every woman couldn't help but glance. And finally, I might say, the lily's gilding. At the hosiery's confluence thrust forth a spectacular and imagination-filling codpiece, as if an enemy's executed head were stored therein for subsequent re-animation at the brush of a feminine hand. The only trace left of the Cardinal of Valencia was his halo of crimson skullcap. He'd become a dramatically beautiful man, who well knew it.

"Lord Ludovico—the Moor—Sforza and Gian Galeazzo Sforza, the Duke of Milan, have thousands of loyal troops under their commands and enough gold coin to sink a fleet," Cesare said. "As well as the deep respect of Charles VIII. Charles would never dream of attacking Papa again if the Moor were Papa's in-law."

" 'Night is day's more pleasant sister,' " came from the Count of

Pesaro, who'd been patiently listening to my insults without comment until now. He stood just to the left, below Papa's throne.

Another damned filthy-footed proverb, I thought. Cesare and Papa, however, as if simply gushing approval for this sailors' hackneyed saw, gestured toward the aphorism. There he was. Count Giovanni Sforza of Pesaro, two sides of rolling blubber as wrinkled as a Pharaoh's mummy.

I'm being unfair. He was only thirty-five. He was fat only by comparison with Cesare, but an adolescent girl's opinion of a man's looks is ipso facto unfair, unless he's a god like my brother was. Giovanni stood for this formal occasion in full, noble armor, giving him the look of a cast-iron capon, orange feathers extending from his beaked helmet. Each time he gestured, his feathers twitched and he'd clank. To my utter surprise he'd arrived early the previous evening, June 12, 1494, with a clinking retinue of 120 or so heavily armed, unshaven, Pesaran troops, who'd stunk of moldy Asiago di montegrappa cheese, turned tocai friulano and spoiled scampi. No one had bothered to inform me I was even to become acquainted with such a *pulchinello*, never mind engaged to him. Vatican City had been driven into an uproar all that night by Lord Giovanni's retainers, who, being of seafaring Lombard coastal families, were the next things to standing octopi in every Roman's opinion. Even more so than cod-stinking Norsemen. These Lombards—carrying their great-grandfathers' handheld trebuchets, which slingshot skull-cracking glass marbles, miniature mangonels and chattes, chain mail, lame destriers, gonfalons, halberds, crossbows, pikes and broken-down ballistas—proceeded gaily to live up to their reputations by breaching the doors of the Vatican wine cellars and trebucheting the vintner between the eyes just after yesterday's sunset. They then guzzled themselves blithering drunk, spending the night howling like Adriatic albatrosses, sliding down the smooth Vatican banisters, horsebacking on their nags through second-story windows—taking the rare, Venetian-glass windowpanes with them—and gleefully raping any nun or altar boy and pillaging any purse they came across. Nine months later, in fact, there'd be a spate of fishy babies born to a number of the distaff Vatican staff, turning one of its cloisters into a nursery. A miracle indeed. The Palatines tried to control them, but the Lombards attacked them with all their antique weapons, broken wine casks, fists and teeth. To this day, if one looks closely, there are teeth marks in the wrist-guards and greaves of several of the senior Palatines. By midnight Papa had had enough. He got up,

fetched Cesare from his own apartment and burst with him into Giovanni's sumptuous bedroom suite.

"My Lord Pesaro," Papa shouted at the sleepy Giovanni, "your men are
berserk. You will please go outside immediately and control them. Or at
least put leashes on them."

"What?"

"Cage your men, they've gone out of their minds."

"Forgive me, Holiness," he mumbled. "Lombard soldiers are traditionally quite gay whenever they travel."

" 'Gay'? Don't you think this gorillas' rumpus goes well beyond gay?"

"Well, Holiness, not really. Not for Lombards. The Moor's soldiers
are all Lombards, and thank God—you know, that's why Charles
fears him."

But at that point they heard the screams of several nuns—some terrified, some ecstatic, from the courtyard below, women with whom the
Lombards were evidently being extremely jovial. Giovanni sighed resig-
nation, got up and he and Cesare left together. In moments they stood
on the steps above the courtyard, in which the bulk of Giovanni's troops
were in the process of inebriate chaos. Papa and I watched from the bedroom balcony above.

"Faithful soldiers," Giovanni cried, "it's bedtime."

The Lombards froze and turned to look up at their Lord Giovanni and
Cesare. Giovanni looked as if he thought the troops might kill him.

"And who are you to boss us around, you big coward?" one of them
slurred. These were the men who were to be my subjects? I wondered.
Better D'jem's turbaned assassins.

Many have rumored Giovanni was a coward, especially when faced
with Papa, but in my experience that was unfair. He was brave enough;
he was merely a gentler man and without blustering, faux-mannish
virtute.

"They're very drunk, you know," Giovanni whispered to Cesare. "I
think it's better we just let them alone till they pass out; it can't be long
now. How much damage, relatively speaking, could only 120 of them
cause such a big place?"

"But they've been drunk since they arrived in Rome and they've up
till now been obedient to you."

"Yes. But since sunset they've glugged themselves to the point they've
taken leave of their heads. They're Lombard seamen, you know, descended

from Ithacan pirates. 'Two-legged sharks,' we call them. Odysseus himself couldn't control them when they're this plastered."

"We'll see." Cesare walked down the steps into the courtyard, until he stood amidst the weaving soldiers. "I am Lord Cesare Borgia," he cried out so the courtyard's walls echoed with it.

"Are you indeed, Y'r Worship?" a Lombard drunkard brayed at him. "Shall I kiss your golden ass? Or would you kiss mine?"

Cesare's eyes circled the men around him. He picked out the one who'd spoken. He walked toward him, until he was a foot away. "Are you the captain of these pig-fish?" he asked.

"I am."

"If there's an ass to be kissed here, you ought do the kissing." Cesare paused, as the captain sneered and spat a moonlit, viscous spurt. "Do you think you could kill me, Captain?"

The captain grinned. "Why not?"

"I'll make a deal with you. If you can kill me, so be it. Howl till dawn, fuck every sister, fuck Mother Superior, fuck your own mother, drink till your tripe bursts."

"You want t'fight me, Y'Worship?"

"I'll make it easier for you." Cesare lifted his own gold-hilted sword from its scabbard. Every Lombard drew his in response, except the captain. Cesare then handed him the sword, hilt first, and the captain took it, swaying slightly. Cesare untied his golden night-robe and put the sword's point to his own chest, exactly over his heart. "This particular ass is the son of the Vicar of Christ, therefore grandson of the Lord of Eternity."

"Are you indeed, Y'Worship? Well, son of a bitch."

"Kill me, if you can." Cesare's face froze into something resembling a handsome icepick, his eyes utterly empty and cold as the Ninth Circle.

I saw from my courtyard window the captain blanch to a lunar color. Then with visible effort he summoned once again his courage and managed a wan smile. He wove, then his arm tensed with the determination to drive the point home. But as he did, I saw him look into Cesare's eyes.

"Go ahead," Cesare said softly. "I swear there'll be no punishment. All it requires of you is the simple courage to move your hand six tiny inches. The length of a big scampi."

The sword quivered. Then the captain regathered his grit and went once more to thrust. But instead he froze a long moment. He slowly lowered Cesare's sword, his body trembling and his smile dissolving all the while like an oozing icicle under my brother's gaze. I watched from my window, unable to breathe.

"Who am I?" Cesare asked.

"W-what?" the captain stuttered.

"Who . . . am . . . I?"

"You are Lord Cesare Borgia."

"And who is that?"

"The son of the Vicar of Christ and therefore grandson of the Lord of . . ."

"Eternity."

". . . Eternity."

"And what is the only proper attitude for horseshoe crab-bait such as yourself before such a man?"

The captain sank to one knee, falling sword clattering on the pavement. Cesare walked completely around the Lombards' circle. As he reached each "shark," the man would try to meet Cesare's gaze with all the bravado he could muster, but couldn't, no matter how drunk. He'd then drop to his knee before my brother.

When all were down, "Long live great Lord Cesare Borgia!" they cheered in a drunken din.

"Go to bed," Cesare quietly said.

All the Lombards got up as one and lurched off, mumbling happily, in the direction of the Vatican stables, in which they were now evidently content to be locked in by the bruised, bitten and exhausted Palatines. Giovanni, mouth agape, stared at Cesare as he walked past up the steps and back toward his own apartment. In my window it occurred to me again what Cesare had once said to Papa, many years ago, about the Vatican rats. That he could just gaze them into submission, that by looking into their eyes he'd make them so afraid they'd die. Cesare had just put a similar surrender into the eyes of a pack of drunken sea monsters. How long could it be—he was a grown man, if yet a young one—before he dropped the whole world to one knee?

"God Almighty," Papa whispered next to me on the balcony. "That boy's a Borgia. A young Octavian to my Julius."

"Or a Ptolemy to your Alexander?"

He frowned.

Two mornings later I found myself again before enthroned Papa, with brave Cesare and Count Giovanni of Pesaro, as well, in armor I'd found out he'd had to borrow from the Moor, who had hundreds of sets of all sizes made, as he'd gain and lose weight. There were again a few Palatines and this time a squad of moderately well-behaved sharks. I was eager to carry on with what I knew even at the time had been my naïve and spoiled performance. As I said, Giovanni wasn't really *that* old. And I knew half the Princesses in Europe had been married when they were my age, or younger, to rich or powerful men as old and well larded as that German burgher Saint Nicholas. But this was the only time I had the power, so I thought, to have a real impact on my fate myself. Papa was always so starry-eyed with Vanita, if I could just rouse in him the memory of what he'd felt like then, maybe I could get my way, put this armored blackmail off and marry the Sir Galahad of my dreams. A man like Cesare.

"If we were to wed," Giovanni that morning uttered in my general direction from inside his pullet's headgear. It was difficult to tell where the head within his helmet was exactly pointed. "If we were to wed, we might spend so much time abed, I may shed my excess inches in exertions. I may lose a decade in my exercises. I'll then be svelte and ageless as Helen's Paris."

Giovanni meant well. I sensed it in his tone of voice, which had at the moment an avian, slightly metallic echo. Unhandsome though I thought him, not a trace of arrogance nor spite accompanied that deeply mature voice, whose unassuming well-meaning, I confess, only spurred my immaturity to like him all the less.

"I trust you won't lose the critical inches, my Lord Pesaro," Cesare said, restraining a chuckle. "My sister will require those for bliss."

Maybe he was gorgeous, maybe a Cardinal shark-killer, but what a boor Cesare could be. The three men giggled like schoolboys at his small joke.

I decided to put a stop to their obnoxious titters. "So, you wish me to love a hog?" I asked them, looking straight at the bulging iron. "Riven between my upraised legs like a disappointed sow by this one's mushy pig-sticker?"

The trio's tee-hee choked dead. To emphasize my point, I switched my golden braid, which sparkled in the sun from the window with its own gold, as well as with a profusion of tiny sapphires, woven into its length. I put my hands to my waist, which I knew emphasized its slimness. I pivoted in my gown, also sewn with sapphires and cinched at the waist with a golden hanging belt in congruence with my hair. More sapphires, large ones, dangled from my ears and slender throat. Their facets glanced a rainbow of blues as I pivoted. My power was now fully formed—still feeling new to me in its virginal, but seductive, heat—of which I was well aware. Maybe Cesare had his powers, but I knew myself far from impotent. I'd the self-assurance that my body, my self, could kill a few sharks, as well, and I wanted to show these roosters its not inconsiderable force was only at their peril to be cackled at. But the barnyard wasn't finished with me.

"My child," Papa said, "romantic love, a thing of admitted beauty, but without use in itself, must subordinate itself to the Will of God. It's been so since Adam and Eve, naked in Eden, bowed to the Divine Will. They then clothed themselves in a cloth of marriage vows, throwing aside carnal desires that they'd lately had for one another's unlovely flesh. That desire, picked from the tree by Eve at the Snake's behest, had been their apple of banishment from Eden."

"Papa, that's a terrible mess of an analogy, and you know it," I snapped. "My mother and I are ashamed of you. Even a sophistical Benedictine drunk in an apple orchard would be ashamed to make it."

"Be that as it may—"

"In my mother's house, when I was a child," I went on, "you promised me the man of my dreams, as she had the man of hers." I glanced again at the friendly iron poultry. "Some dream."

"It's said, sister, the great Agamemnon was portly," Cesare said. "Perhaps the Count is another such."

"So would you have me another Clytemnestra and slice the Count's jugular in his bath?"

The room was deathly quiet, but for Giovanni's delicate, nervous clanking. Then it came. It started, as it regularly did, with foot stamping. Foot stamping with both his feet as fast as he could on the hollow wooden platform that supported Papa's throne, a savage drum sound. Then the screeching voice, which seemed to begin at his kid-clad toes, and vibrate from there throughout the rest of him, as if Gabriel's Doom's Day–announcing trumpet were played from inside a wet wine-bladder.

"I remember! I was there at Subiaco that day!" the voice of tantrum burst finally into syllables from Cesare's head. "The Holy Father promised you the man of *our* dreams! And we've dreamt of this fat Sforza!"

Giovanni's slight clanking increased, as Cesare's foot-stamping subsided.

"Cesare, please," Papa condescended.

He knew that was all he could do. Once a tantrum began, as in childhood, the only policy was to wait until it dribbled itself dead. Whether Cesare would react to any situation with preternaturally calm aplomb and self-assurance, as he had to the Lombards only two nights before, or whether he'd blow one of his many loosely screwed-in gaskets and embarrass everyone in hearing range always seemed entirely a random matter. I remember Papa and I sometimes betting on which outcome would obtain, but at least we knew an outburst, at this or that stressful moment, would be entirely unpredictable. So we'd wait. Giovanni clanked expectantly. I stood, braid and sapphires glinting. Papa sat, enthroned. Cesare vibrated like a sounding bar of gold.

At last Papa continued, "Lucrezia, We've sworn an oath to this man. Would you have Christ break His Sacred Word?"

"But Papa—"

"Love this man, and We'll love you more than ever I have before."

"Papa—"

"Refuse, and Our love for you may die as the Parable's seed died, thrown by the wayside."

A flash of fear and anger ripped through me. "As died your love for my mother?" I couldn't help it. All those years I never threw that in his face, but now felt just the moment.

I saw that had been a mistake, both because it only angered him and closed him off from any argument or even honest feeling of mine, but also because it hurt him, as I guess I'd meant it to. He turned his head aside, so we wouldn't see tears. I saw the resolve—the resolve I knew impenetrable—settling onto his shoulders. I'd seen him learn it at the same time and pace as he'd learned to wear his power. That damned resolve angered me, too, because I'd learned that all my feminine devices couldn't wriggle me through or around it. It was as pointless to strive against as God's Judgment.

"Yes. Choose, young Countess."

I gazed at him. Papa'd become stone. I looked at Cesare by his side; I could see the force of my brother's will to accomplish this alliance with Gian Galeazzo and the Moor, as if dripping from him all over the floor. Pesaro would evidently be his first conquest, taken by strategic deployment of my flesh. The bones of my neck felt wobbly and soft. I bent my head to all this inevitability, the same way Vanita bowed hers in the Basilica on Papa's coronation day.

"Here I am," was all I could think to say.

My father and brother smiled. Giovanni was so delighted, his helmet's mouthpiece looked suddenly to grin. Cesare rushed down the throne's steps, ran to the iron fowl, by now madly clanking with joyful, self-congratulatory guffaws, and tried to wrap Giovanni in his arms. But Giovanni in his armor croûte was far too well leavened for Cesare to actually encircle.

"Brother," Cesare nonetheless cried.

"My new son," Papa joined in.

"My new family," Giovanni clanked, turning to take the three of us in through his visor. "What a lovely bunch of Borgias."

I remember at least a month of wedding preparations. All the great ladies of Rome, an impressive group, gave me wedding parties, at which they duly showered gifts on me, each grande dame endeavoring to surpass the others in cost or rarity. Exquisitely woven brocades and tapestries were brought to me from France, Persia or the Holy Land. One, embroidered with a ferocious dragon like Moloch's pet, even had come on the Portuguese Black Ship all the way from the mysterious Japans. Taxidermied animals with curving eyeteeth from climates no European had ever seen. The ivory tusk of a water-borne unicorn, brought from so far north, it's said the sun doesn't rise there for months for Apollo's fear the cold will extinguish it. Chests of rare and costly spices and teas from beyond the earth's edges. Gifts of ivory, lapis, silver and gold. A huge living beast with a great horn for a nose. He was said to come from below the vast Sahara. This "rhinoceros" was as big as a cow, had skin like tree bark and was further said, by the aged courtesan who gave him to me, to be only a cub of its kind. The beast would gaze lovingly at me and twist his head as if a gigantic toddler, inquiring of its mother on the strange ways of the world.

"I pray you'll have babies as big and healthy," the old battle-axe cackled.

"But I hope with softer skin," I replied.

I gave the Palatines charge over him and they quartered him in their stables, where he remains their snuffing, loving mascot to this day. He's reached by now, I'm sure, the size of a dynastic outhouse. I gave the baby giant "Xerxes" for a name, because it went well with his dry, rough hide and sounded like the noise he'd make when content. Hundreds of gawking pilgrims to Vatican City visit him daily still. I also remember Papa presenting me on a balcony to the multitude below, Giovanni by my side. They'd gathered on a rainy Sunday in Saint Peter's Square. They roared approval.

"Ah, you see? They love me," Cesare said as he stood on the other side of my Count Groom-to-be.

"Cesare, that's for me," I replied in my soaked burgundy-cloth gown, embroidered with Arabian Gulf pearls. "It's for me and my soon-to-be husband, you overblown mound of conceit."

"You think so?" Cesare said. "Don't be an ingenue fool; no one cheers a silly bitch, unless he's fucking her." And he laughed. "Or maybe down there they're all imagining doing so."

"Cesare," Papa said. "I know you can't help it, but do try not to be a swine."

"You're right, Papa. I'm sorry, sister."

"Lord Cesare," Giovanni said, "the shouts are for her. They're cheering Lucrezia's future happiness."

I looked at Giovanni. Well, there was plenty of room for good in him. I recall the purchase of each and every item of my trousseau. I think all women do who marry young. A dozen tailors and three dozen Milanese seamstresses—sent by the Duke and Moor—flooded into to my apartment, even more than had before Papa's coronation. They'd brought cloth, piles of it, each bolt looking valuable enough to ransom a king. Besides cloth there was an enormous, dark brown, fur-covered skin the tailor said he'd turn into a coat, and later did. He said it was from the white summit of the world and was as soft as the hair of angels. I remember each moment of my first wedding day, less than a month later. I recall the exact instant I woke up, sun blinding me through a slat of my shutter. I mused that this was to be my last sunlight as a girl. I thought of Vanita, and the rest of the day filled with coming-and-going reflections on her. I was sad for her, never to have had such a day with Papa. Each person I'd pass would greet me with a knowing grin, as if I were about to encounter the most delightful surprise. Even the men—mostly Vatican priests—looked at me differently that day. None seemed capable of resisting an unabashedly dirty chuckle as he'd pass, men who'd usually bow to me like consummate courtiers. Something about a wedding day that cancels out all the usual rules of politesse and replaces them with the more honest ones of a frilly whorehouse. Praise be to God for whorehouses! All this sensual expectation had its effect on me. I began to anticipate the first moments of my husband's love with a physical, driving longing. I remember the Bride's Breakfast—just after cockcrow—with Cesare and Papa. I terribly missed Vanita. But father and brother looked and acted gloriously happy for me, kissing me constantly on my eyes and lips. As I think back now, I wonder how much of that was happiness for me and how much was displaced self-congratulation at the conquest of Lombardy and the acquisition of Sforza arms? I knew that was at least partly true, but by that time my anticipations and longings had driven all depressing thoughts from my mind. There was a moment, just as the breakfast ended, that I know was nothing but genuine.

Papa took me in his arms and kissed me again on the lips; I tasted the sweet breakfast moscato's alcohol on them. "You're as beautiful as your mother ever was," he whispered in my ear, our cheeks touching so I felt his hard, masculine brush of beard. "More beautiful." He kissed me once more. I could feel passion trembling through his whole body, vibrating into my mouth. "I wish these lips were hers," he whispered. "They look just like hers, the shape of them like the burst fig of Vanita's lips. Every time I look at you, I see my love. Every day of my life I've wished I could have twenty-four hours with her such as Giovanni is going to have with you today and tonight. Even at this moment, though it's damnable to think it, I want her. I want to have lain with her every night of my life. I would've led a happier one. Have I become evil, to realize that only now, when it's too late?"

I went to reply—God knows what I would've said—but he put up his hand. "No need to answer. I'm sorry; I've drunk too many toasts to you too early."

Preceded by Mambrino, the famous comic in velvet suit and golden cap, and announced by a joyous sound of fifes and trumpets, the groom's party moved slowly down the Via del Corso, past the Basilica of Saint Mark, through the crowds in the Campo dei Fiori, across the Ponte Sant'Angelo and finally arrived at Santa Maria in Portico, where I awaited them. As soon as we heard the groom's trumpets, Aunts Giulia and Adriana sent me out with Papa to stand on one of the loggia of the Santa Maria, overlooking Saint Peter's Square, so the populace could see me. The thousands of upturned faces bewildered me. What did they all hope to see? All I was aware of was a girl and her father. Was I sufficient? I certainly was as sufficiently dressed as my fiancé. I wore an ivory dress of Mesopotamian silk from Baghdad, embroidered with hundreds of table-cut diamonds, sewn in Milan into the shapes of Eastern desert lionesses. It had a mane-bordered train, held by a two-foot black pygmy girl from below the Nile's source.

"Who are you?" I asked.

"I'm the black virgin, Lady. I'm brought for you from Africa to hold your dress."

A virgin apostlette to bear my train. I most positively was a heavenly princess. The rest of the world strove to be with Jesus; this tiny disciple was enough for me. My dress was further embroidered with the gold thread that was so much the rage then. All by myself I felt like a moving royal barge. I smiled down at the rabble, as instructed. They screamed back.

I soon caught sight of my approaching capon. He'd dressed himself in a cloth-of-gold Turkish robe with a collar of rubies and pearls that he'd borrowed from the Marquis of Mantua. He reined in his horse and saluted me. I curtsied in return. My barge was so heavy that my legs wobbled with the effort to stand up straight again. Giovanni then dismounted and entered the Portico. Papa brought me indoors and scurried off to one of his throne rooms in the Apostolic Palace, the one with him worshiping the Risen Christ in Master Pinturicchio's full-length portrait. We waited till Papa was in place, then we all walked in procession to the throne room. First me, then Aunt Giulia, Aunt Adriana, then 150 noble Roman ladies, all of us led by Cesare. We entered the room, the Hall of the Saints. One by one, starting with me, each of the ladies kissed Papa's foot. Thus half an hour was passed in foot-kissing. Papa groaned at the pretension of it, but he was faking; he always loved pretension. Giovanni then entered in the cloth-of-gold Turkish outfit and borrowed collar. He didn't show any cowardice, he strode to his cushion, immediately knelt and kissed the Papal foot.

"*Pater Sanctus,*" he said. "I am Count Giovanni de Pesaro. I kneel before you, betrothed to the Lady Lucrezia Borgia, your heavenly Princess niece. I pledge myself and my lands to the service of Your Beatific Lordship for as long as my bride and myself shall live."

I was suddenly Papa's *niece?* Cesare leaned over and whispered to me, "A formality. Technically, the Pope is Christ and can't have had any children, as you know."

Everyone politely applauded, notably Duke Gian Galeazzo and the Moor, the Pope's new allies. Giovanni and I were to kneel for the ceremony on satin cushions before my "uncle." I remember the chanting of a hundred nuns as I was escorted to my cushion by the miraculously still-alive Cardinal Camerlengo Costa. I kept him more or less upright as we stumbled together down the enormous aisle, made of guests, his red silken vestments looking to have by then quite a bit more substance and color of life than himself. About a hundred nuns sang glory to the Virgin. Papa stood to officiate, surrounded by scads of formally robed cardinals, archbishops, bishops, priests and a hundred Sforzas, looking like starving vultures, of both sexes.

"This is a longer walk than to Calvary," Costa mumbled, halfway home, which I supposed at the time didn't bode particularly well.

I wondered which Station of the Cross I'd reached. The Stripping of the Garments? The Scourging at the Pillar? The Nailing to the Cross? Not the Stripping or Nailing, anyway; those would come later.

Cardinal Cesare, the witness, waited in the simplest black doublet and hose next to Papa, with an unwontedly, yet blessedly unarmored Giovanni. What was my brother doing in black? I wondered. Ah, well. That traitor. No clanking, perhaps, but Giovanni's rustling Turkish robes had enough sumptuous fabric to them to clothe several more modestly girthed men. We reached finally the throne. The Camerlengo handed me off to Giovanni, an egg to an omelette gourmand. We stood below and facing Master Pinturicchio's *Story of Susanna the Chaste,* in which Susanna fends off two old rapists. Was she successful? I wondered. I guessed so; otherwise she'd be "Defaced" or "Shamefaced" Susanna, instead, wouldn't she?

Cesare smiled, black codpiece rampant. Alexander smiled, arms raised like Christ, welcoming the blessed to Heaven. Giovanni smiled, looking happy as a pleased father of my rhinoceros. Nuns chanted to the Holy

Mother. I sparkled in my diamonds and wept to myself, remembering the joy Vanita had long ago taken in Roderigo's body and imagining how little I might ever take in the one next to me. When I stepped in next to Giovanni, I remembered from long ago my little girl's prayer underneath the table, that I'd be as happy and open, when this moment came, as the yew bride at the Wedding at Cana. I could hear some of Giovanni's retainers, still drunk, from behind me in the vast room. They were surpassingly gay, their Lord being "hitched up to a hot fish," as they never stopped phrasing it. I and everyone else smelled them from the crowd, their month or so in the Vatican stables having imbued them, in addition to seafood and rotgut friuli wine, with an unmistakable equine redolence, only partially dissipated by the clouds of frankincense. They were singing some Lombard wedding anthem or other under their stinking breaths—a ditty on the sublime joys of sodomy with pirates' wives and the revengeful plunder of Troy—in savage Adriatic counterpoint to the chanting nuns. A pair of unfortunate Palatines watched over each Lombard. The Palatines held perfumed hankies at their mustaches.

That night was the reception, a Borgia-worthy extravagance held in the vast reception room of the Apostolic Palace, the Sala Reale. Papa and Cesare wanted it in the Borgia Apartments, but the place was still a Lombard mess. Hundreds of guests flowed from indoors to out, sampling the exotic foods. There were 30,000 pounds of meat, a castle made of sweetmeats and a live pig, whose grunting, mad efforts to get free provided its own cruel entertainment, plus a flood of delicacies from all Italy. Thirty thousand pounds was much more than we could consume. The leftovers were to be distributed later to the army of poor outside, as was the wedding custom. The guests gulped the expensive wines from a hundred silver and gold ewers, throwing back, as well, some even stronger drink, the amber, throat-stinging tears of grain for the first time brought to Italy from above Hadrian's wild wall, as wild and smoky a drink as its Caledonian makers must be. There were dozens of servers, entertainers, musicians, a Commedia dell'Arte troupe, who gave a remarkably smutty and overacted performance of *The Struggle of Chastity with Love*, and singers, all plying their various instruments at once and mingling with the invited guests, and general noise loud as a battle. Scattered amongst the guests were many crimsoned Members of the Sacred College, their mistresses and bastards, plus oodles more miscellaneously colored prelates, most all with unofficial families.

I met the Moor. I whispered, "Giovanni, he's not—"

"Uncle Gian didn't nickname him 'the Moor' so much for his skin's hue as for the mulberry on his Arms and because he has the nigritudinous soul of the Ummayadic Saracen."

"Really? Is that good?"

As the Moor approached me, the way parted for him as if he were the Minotaur, maidens and adolescent men giggling in fear. I'd expected his skin to look sun-beaten, the color of Cordovan saddle-leather, and a great beak of nose, but he had a wide, turned-up nose, pink complexion and sandy hair, like a German or Englishman. He was even handsome. But his eyes did live up to the moniker. They were the black of bubonic pustules. When I met him, nonetheless, he was the embodiment of a courtier, as graceful and elegant as an Emperor's Chief of Protocol.

"My child, Aphrodite's entire body would glow pink with envy to meet you," he said. "Giovanni, thank God every day He's given you such an angel. And that dress! Like a ground of spring blossoms."

Duke Gian Galeazzo was a less graceful, clumsy adolescent. He came up behind me, stepped on my train, then the dress itself, spilling his Montalchino down my back, and belched. "Watch out, clumsy bitch. Giovanni, that dress is capacious enough to be worn by an expecting gorilla." He recovered slightly. "Oh, the bride. You're not the gorilla, are you?"

"Not a gorilla?" I replied.

"Not pregnant."

A stone pause, as all about us considered that.

"Nephew, don't be a pig," the Moor said, breaking the silence, and everybody laughed. He'd soon murder young Gian Galeazzo and take his title. I can't say I was sorry.

I kissed the Moor on his scarred cheek as I bid him farewell. He blushed. Everyone was drunk, dressed to the nines in whatever finery each could afford. Only a few of Giovanni's Lombard scampi were there. Cesare had beguiled most of them into the Vatican stables for the ceremony, but he'd provided them there a brimming cask of wine, a roast side of red beef, a hundred carp, forty loaves of bread, twenty-five street whores—whom he'd had to pay triple before they'd agree to service these "pox-ridden Pisces"—and a monstrous dessert of a cake, made with fortified malmsey and the Hesperides' golden apples.

Around midnight, a dozen drunken hours into all this orgy, Mambrino, the famous Pierrot, garbed, of course, all in white like a comical Pope with a painted vermilion tear and smile on his otherwise powder-pallid face, ran through our party. He was entirely heedless whether he'd knock to the floor trays, learned monsignors or even the occasional grand duke. Mambrino shouted, as he ran, "It is time, Lords and Ladies! Time for the bursting of the dam! The flooding of the estuary! It's time! Odysseus' sneaky, cramful horse is to breach the Trojan wall!"

All through the throng he ran, shouting and ranting. Everyone laughed in ribald anticipation. Then they rushed in an excited dither toward one of the halls that extended off the courtyard. From there they scampered out from the Apostolic Palace into the Santa Maria, just to the left of Saint Peter's, up the long, formal stairway and then raced down its upstairs hall, off which the many bedroom suites extended. As all this was occurring, Aunt Adriana and Penthesileia, a Lady-in-Waiting, hustled me through a back hallway also into Santa Maria. They brought me into the largest upstairs suite, one formerly used by Papa. Both of them and Aunt Giulia—giggling all the while—stripped off my ivory barge. They then removed my petticoats, stockings, bodice and other foundation undergarments, until I was naked as a whore, and told me to lie down. I insisted they leave me my necklace and earrings.

"I don't want to be completely nude. Clothed in sapphires is naked enough."

"Yet more perfect than perfect," Penthesileia said. "I love it."

I lay in the suite, as custom dictated, completely undressed beneath a white satin sheet on a marble slab pallet, brought for the purpose. I could hear the approaching noble mob. Next to me on the floor Aunt Giulia placed the red satin dressing gown, in which I'd shortly be reclad to signify my new state following the upcoming ceremony. The robe was traditionally bloodred, like a Spartan hoplite's cloak, so it might camouflage blood. Gold decoration tinseled both cloths. I was freezing. I felt as if I lay on the Queen of Denmark's catafalque, the cold of stone on my shoulder blades, ass and the backs of my legs. The crowd gushed into the room and quickly surrounded me, their tongues waggling, lolling and drooling in salacious expectation. From my Carraran bed I could see, as well, Alexander, Cesare and most of the Rome-based Sacred College, besides sundry dukes and courtesans. I remember particularly a tall Balkan Archdeacon, his hand resting on and massaging the behind of a shorn Armenian monk, a boy well known to be his favorite Anchorite. In graffiti the pair were commonly depicted in flagrante and labeled as the "Bogomil Buggers." They were infamous for fondling each other in sacristies before Mass, most enthusiastically before a *High* Mass. Doubtless something invigorating about an expectation of Gothic harmony. But at those High Masses the boy sang gorgeously as any angel, turning the general disdain for ecclesiastic sodomites to praising God for His Gift of this adolescent's song to us all, whatever its unhygienic inspiration.

From the hall, still more craned their necks into the broad archway to see me. I looked into Papa's and Cesare's eyes, just next to the pallet, as coldly as I knew how. I'd resisted the inclusion of this revolting custom with days of ranting and crying. I'd begged Papa and Cesare to let this particular cup pass, this damned custom, brought to Italy, it was said, by conquering Visigoths centuries before. Visigoths, indeed. I thought it as barbarous as a poet's blinding. I was sure even Giovanni's ravaging Lombards in their fishing barques could hardly have come up with a more revolting wedding ceremonial. But we civilized Italians had been bequeathed this Viking rite, doubtless created in some cave to entertain of an evening the heathens of whatever Hell it was in which Alaric's raping, murdering and loveless Visigoths had originated. But all my pleading had been for nil. The nuns finally sent me to Camerlengo Costa, who cackled me a learned disquisition. He was a known expert on the Seven Sacraments, their histories and all their attendant customs. He said Christians had adopted this one from the yellow-beard pagans to demonstrate to God, and to the witnessing members of the Body of Christ, that the Holy Wedding Vows had been fulfilled. Well, he admitted it had originated as a barbarian rite, stabbed into Europe by Viking spears; but it had been sanctified by centuries of Christian usage. We God-fearing, sophisticated souls kept it up not for the earthy and primeval pleasure of the show, but so there'd be no doubt the Sacrament had been fully entered into by virgins and loving husbands and to leave no doubt in future and before God's Throne that our marriage was legitimate. My ceremonially and publicly ruptured hymen would be a living document, as it were, subject to confirming, doubt-expunging decipherment by teams of experts. None thereafter could gainsay the sanctity of my wedding, either in this life or the next.

"Will I have a quim to examine in the next life?" I inquired.

"Let's see what Aquinas' opinion is, shall we?" Costa said, reaching for a volume of *Questiones Disputatae de Veritate.*

"You won't find the answer there," I said. "Try the *De Perfectione Vitae Spiritualis*. In it the Sacred Doctor says that for each noble body part there is a spiritual correspondence."

"So there's your answer," he said with a relieved grin.

"Is the quim 'noble,' do you think?"

"My view is that noble always is as noble does."

"Good point. Most enlightening."

His grin puckered into his toothlessness.

So here I was, ice-cold and naked, awaiting the present-day Visigothic sack of myself. I turned my cold eyes from Papa and Cesare and looked across the room toward someone else.

Giovanni. He was walking toward me. He was dressed neither in clanking iron, nor in his Turkish noble cloth—but in nothing. As naked as the day God made him. He was a sight.

"Mount the mare!" my guests and servants shouted. "Breech the wall! Burst the dam!"

"Onward Saladin to Paradise!" added turbaned D'jem from the back of the room.

All the Christians booed good-naturedly at D'jem's Islamic huzzah, but enjoyed it nonetheless. I now realized exactly and gloomily of what all those lascivious grins and dirty chuckles all day had been in expectation.

"Screw it to the sticking place!"

Everyone laughed again. Giovanni finally reached my bed. He pulled aside my white satin sheet, exposing my torso, which caused a momentary stunned hush of appreciation among our guests, especially among the professional women. He rolled upon me. He swayed a few moments, as he tried to locate the appropriate vessel. I must admit, I wasn't of any help. I was disinterested as a desert island and cold as a Scandinavian congratulation. He struggled on for a few more moments, until he at last found the portal he sought. Never in my young life had I felt a thing of less pleasure. Any unpleasant vision a maiden might have of the consummation of a moment of public sex didn't come close to the damp and chilly void this moment produced in me. I gazed once again at my father and brother, praying my glance might freeze their blood, as mine was freezing. But then I thought for a second of Papa in the *sedia stercoraria*, the balls-feeling chair. Could he have been any happier to go through that than I this? Why did he have to? He could've told them all to go to Hell. Wasn't it a sacrifice he allowed himself to make for God's Will and high station? I couldn't stop the pusillanimous watering of my eyes. Finally, to escape as a child might, as the child I still was, I closed them. I tried to remember Vanita, in a moment of her warmest pleasure, my father beginning to make love to her, a look of amorous and lovely transport on her face as she'd tug him into her bedroom with a laugh like a bubbling hot-spring. I tried, but I couldn't bring the maternal image to mind.

"Cassandra, daughter of Priam, has accepted Odysseus' gift-laden stallion!" Pierrot at long last sung out in exaltation. "The Greeks are within the city! The Argive Ithacan of many wiles has sunk his bronze-bright sword into Cassandra's bower!"

Papa led the intoxicated cheer. Pierrot then rang his Pierrot-bells, rang and rang them. All I could remember were those other bells, their chimes as a child at Subiaco frightening me so. Those bells that always announced the coming absences of my beautiful father and the wretched sorrows of my magic mother.

I remember some months earlier, the day we'd finally moved into the unfinished Borgia Apartments, I'd first gone into my new bedroom. There was no furniture yet, except the bed and a dressing table. On the dressing table I saw an onyx jewelry box. I recognized it. It'd been my mother's. I went over, trembling, and opened it. Inside was Papa's ring with its huge, hinged sapphire. Next to it was a tiny bottle of the blue powder I remembered went inside the ring to kill in a glass of wine. There was nothing else. What was this for? Was it a suggestion? A command? To kill Giovanni, I wondered? Or someone else? Who'd left it? Papa? Cesare? Vanita? It was too strange to bring myself even to think the obvious answer lay in the box. Had it been Vanita, come from wherever her Nymph's lair was to offer a daughter a desperate solution?

four

Giovanni quickly left to return to Pesaro, where he'd scads of bills awaiting him from the wedding. He sent immediately a messenger to ask Papa for a 5,000 ducat advance on my 31,000 ducat dowry. He and Papa agreed he should leave me for a "couple of years" to mature, because, they said, I was still too much of an inexperienced virgin, and shouldn't be expected yet to fulfill conjugal duties on a regular basis. He and Papa made me sick. I felt they should've at least thought of that before the Visigothic ransack. Having taken the public taste, I felt myself more than ready for "conjugal duties on a regular basis." The idea of those duties with Giovanni didn't do much for me, but he was my husband and therefore the proverbial dickie-bird in the hand.

The two-year thing didn't work out. Less than a year later Giovanni thundered back into Rome one morning, fully armored, with his usual escort of Pesaran madmen to reclaim his bride.

"Papa," I said to him that day over lunch. "Giovanni wants to take me home to Pesaro."

"No. You're a child."

"Not too much a child for a public deflowering."

"Lucrezia, please. That was just politesse."

"But I'm ready. I want to go."

"No possibility. Charles the Frank is still causing unrest; it's dangerous to travel. You don't want to stay here with Us? You don't love your father anymore? Or Jesus?"

"I'm a married woman. I belong with my husband. Charles won't attack me. He fears the Moor, who wrote to tell me he loves me like a father since meeting me on my wedding day."

"You have a father. Ourselves, lest you forget. You belong with Us, protecting you, not with some cutthroat Milanese mercenary of dubious ancestry." He glanced at my husband. "And don't you still find the Sforza capon old and fat?"

I'd told Papa of my "capon" impression. Now I looked up at him, moving my peas into the shape of an emerald necklace on my plate of *risi bisi*. I could see that resolve was just in process of settling onto Papa's shoulders. If someone didn't say something quickly, his decision would directly be writ on stone tablets.

"Holiness, it's scorching hot in Rome again this year," Giovanni said.

"A steamy Purgatory. And what has that to do with the subject?"

"The heat will defile the air. There will soon be plague in the city. 'There is no health in our flesh, no peace in our bones, because of our sins.' "

"Yes, Papa, it's been ten years since the scourge of 1485; it's time. You don't want pretty me to die of plague, do you, all covered with russet-black lumps? Do I have a temperature, by the way? Husband, feel me."

He did. "Maybe a touch." He smiled at the Pope.

On May 31, 1495, we set out for the Adriatic coast. We weren't alone. There were the hundred Lombards, of course, all riding just behind us in a weaving trot. They drank and sang all along the way their Adriatic folksongs that ought've only been sung while pirating Asian seacoasts or harpooning giant calamari. Behind the Pesarans were Aunt Giulia Farnese; Aunt Adriana de Mila; Giulia's Lady-in-Waiting, Juana Moncada; and another Lucrezia, Lucrezia Lopez, whom Papa'd insisted accompany me; and finally my Penthesileia. We were soon joined by Francesco Gacet, Papa's spy. Giovanni that day grew tired of this intrusive group, took our carriage's reigns from the coachman and quickly outdistanced everyone but the Lombards. We rushed the team through the olive tree–covered hills and walled castles of Umbria, then descended into the Marches and Duchy of Urbino. We cantered along past sun-cast meadows, edged with orange-crimson poppies, where now and then a raggedy shepherd could be heard playing on rustic ceramic pipes to summon his flock. I thought some of these tunes fit for great polyphonies. All my world began to feel bright and young and filled with promise. But every time I started to relax into myself, I'd look at Giovanni next to me on the seat, still trussed in his jangling suit of armor and starting to stiffen with rust at the elbows and knees. He looked old, fat and corroded. I told him so, as I thought of him in an act of love beneath me. I was a cruel bitch.

He caught me looking at him, I'm sure, like a harpy. "Lucrezia, child," he said, "a man's worth doesn't lie in his outward appearance or age, it's in his soul."

"Would you want to make love to an ugly woman, my Lord?"

"Well, no. I see your point, but I'm a man."

"Really, I thought you a gorilla, as your cousin Duke Gian thought me."

"I meant . . . a love of beauty is a part of the male soul, but not so much a part of the female."

"Really. Why do I not love you? Isn't it that you lack beauty in my eyes? No other reason occurs to me. Therefore I must lust instead after what my quite female soul cannot even grasp. Do I grasp the matter correctly?"

He didn't answer. I felt like the Thomasina Aquinas of good looks.

In a beautiful glade in the descending Apennine foothills, creation-green and with a sound of crashing water in the near distance, Giovanni ordered our carriage to a stop. We'd been touring since Rome so far for about two weeks and it would take us at least another seven days to get to Pesaro. A respectful distance behind us all the way still galloped and belched his hundred or so Lombard knights, day and night as sloshed as ever. At least their fishiness wasn't upwind. We started with a hundred or so of them, but before we'd finally arrive, their number shrank closer to forty, half or more having been knocked unconscious from their horses by assorted thick tree branches they'd whack into amidst their delirious, drunken gallops and left behind.

"How did they all make it to Rome in the first place?" I asked Giovanni.

"Oh, when we left Pesaro for Rome, I think there were two hundred."

Giovanni and I'd stopped so far at a few dusty country inns and Pilgrim Hospices, each of which Giovanni had found "romantic," "lovely" or "charming." I'd found each a far more fitting establishment in which to entertain pigs. At each one he'd arrange a meal for us that I'd let him know in no uncertain terms I thought revolting, comparing the simple peasant foods to my usual Roman haute cuisine. After some sickening peasant sausage or other, we'd retire to the six-legged-creature-infested accommodations available to well-born travelers, where he'd insist on carnal relations, much to my horror. There was little I could say about that, though I managed, nevertheless, to say quite a lot. After all, he was now my husband and I owed him by custom and Ecclesiastical Law the duty of my spread legs. To the during-and-after sex patter of hundreds of scurrying little legs, I thanked God not to have been born a pretty blond cockroach.

In a green glade that day the footman lowered our carriage's steps. Giovanni had been babbling on our journey east all day about some or other collection that was his passion, a cache of ancient copper and gold coins, about the Attic and Peloponnesian dates of whose manufacture he seemed to me ridiculously overinterested. I climbed down and rushed off in the direction of the rustling waterfall, which we could hear from the clearing. I didn't look back. I just wanted to get away, to be free, if only for a moment, of coins, fat, drunk Lombards, sex, bugs, salamis and, most especially, of him. As I ran through swaying poplars and weeping willows toward the sound of falling water, I heard him behind me, grabbing up from the carriage our lunch basket, which I imagined filled with more of the chunky intestine meats he particularly favored. Giovanni trundled from our barouche and rushed after me, huffing and puffing—so far, anyway, as a "rushing" was possible for such a bulky, metallic mass as himself.

When finally he caught up, I'd reached the waterfall. I was gazing into it, contemplating suicide, that way the young and love-wretched do, by leaping into its rock-bottomed ribbon. I was recollecting all the Romances I'd read by moonlight in Papa's library, in which the lovelorn maiden, forced to marry the ogre, takes the final plunge into the cold, clear stream near her castle and how everyone, having recovered her soggy, chrysanthemum-clad body, thereafter is so sad she's dead and blames him- or herself—the maiden's tragic revenge—for failing during her pretty lifetime to take better care of her romantic yearnings. I then segued in my mind directly into Agamemnon's speech over the dead Iphigenia's body, the grief-prostrate Agamemnon looking distinctly like Papa. In my imagining, Papa-Agamemnon, swaying slightly on his too-tall pair of white cothurni, spoke over my sopping carcass, his voice, I was gratified to hear, trembling and choked with tears:

Now is my omnivorous compulsion complete.
Behold my portly army, girt about by my overage fleet;
And with them all those adipose kings of Greece's
With oversized armor and Golden Fleeces.
They're too fat to sail to Illium's towers,
Far too old for sacking Trojan bowers,
Until, as the augury of lard-bottomed Calcas has decreed,
Fate was sealed by my girl's self-sacrificial deed.

Or something like that. Oh, in my own mind I loomed tragically a figure for the ages in dactylic hexameter. I then heard my particular ogre's stentorian breath behind me. "Why, by the sound of it, it must be Hannibal," I said. "Back in Italy with his elephant."

"Lucrezia!" He'd run all the way in his armor, carrying our massive lunch-basket. He was exhausted.

For a moment I panicked he'd die. But what would be so bad about that? I reasoned. I stood unmoving, my back toward him, my arms crossed, staring at the death water like some bitchy Antigone. Oh, I was most melodramatic. Downright Euripidean, I was thinking.

"My Lady," he cried again.

He sounded unwell, probably just enervated, but I confess to praying for a heart attack, as the large are prone to.

"What?" I said. "You wish to speak to me? To take our lunch? Stuff your face with revolting sausage? Then doubtless stuff me with your own?"

He sighed, not an impatient sigh, as my despicable, childish behavior warranted, but of genuine anguish. As in Papa's throne room the day this marriage had been sealed, there resided neither guile nor spite anywhere in Giovanni's armored vastness. I could feel his eyes on me; I turned back to him. He was breathing hard. I had a vision of him walking toward me again on my wedding night, on the marble slab. I shuddered.

He took another, especially deep breath. "My Lady, may an unattractive swine speak honestly to such an angel's dream as yourself? Or, if pork spoke the truth, would you lash him once more with your cruel tongue?"

That took me aback. I went to lash him, as he'd said, but another angel, the one who guards me, held my tongue. "All right, talk."

"Since our betrothal, and especially since our wedding night, you've treated me like the lowest rabid dog. I'm sorry, Lady, if I'm old for your romance. If I'm too gross a Lancelot for your story." He looked down at his portly armor like a surprised boy, unable to imagine how a thing has happened, though he's done it himself. "When alone, I weep the Almighty has made my unworthy flesh such an abomination to you. And that there is so abominably much."

"My Lord Pesaro—"

"Let me finish. People say I'm a coward and belie my Sforza blood, the blood of the Moor and the Virago Katerina, anyway. But they're not wrong. I'll never find the courage to begin again if you stop me." He paused. "I'm hardly a sophisticated humanist like your ladyship, but neither am I a fool. I know such a beauty as yourself couldn't love someone like me. I know I was forced on you. When your brother approached me, if I'd known you such an angel, I would've been too shy to come to Rome." He opened his lunch basket and began to spread out our lunch on the grass at my feet. I saw small roasted birds and a modest cask of precious claret. "But I did come, as the terrifying Moor and the Virago ordered me. And when I saw you—by the Blessed Virgin, a golden vision, waiting like rainbow's treasure—I couldn't help but love you. I can't expect you to love in return, Lady. But I beg you on my knees simply not to hate me. I'll be good to you, as an ugly, old coward can, and shall protect and serve you with all my heart and courage until I die, and all I possess will be yours and our children's. I think you will find my heart, and my estate, as large as the rest of me." He'd finished spreading out our picnic and gestured toward it. "Are you hungry? I roasted the truffled quails myself this morning, while you slept."

My arms fell slowly to my sides. I'm sure I looked the perfect idiot. He took off his orange-plumed helmet and laid it on the ground. His revealed face at once struck me the most soulful I'd ever seen. A face with a certain sudden and large beauty and a hasty youth. I stared at him in wonder. "Yes, my Lord," I whispered, in shock still at my discovery. "Let's lunch. It's past time. You look famished."

We both laughed quietly. We sat on the grass, me all the while looking at him. He turned his head away. I saw him ashamed still of the way he must've thought he looked to me. I kissed his cheek. The shame of that being the first kiss I'd given my husband I could feel coloring my face.

"I'm especially sorry," he mumbled, "for the 'Visigoth and virgin' ceremony at the wedding banquet. I know you loathed it. It's an ancient, vulgar practice, forced on young women by old men."

"My Lord, it's the custom in Italy."

We ate our picnic. The truffled capon was delicious, as if prepared by some Florentine master, the claret as fine as any aged Vatican cask might house. Afterward to the sound of rushing water, I stripped off all my clothes and threw them into the waterfall, a demi-, happier suicide, I thought. I undid, one at a time, the sun-and-rain-hardened straps that held his armor. I pulled it from him, piece by piece. I did the same with his undergarments. I bid him lie on his back on the soft green. I sat astride this sudden Lancelot and fucked him like Guinevere before God in His flowing Sunlight, to give him as much pleasure as my inexperience was capable of. His warmth felt inside me like a radiant benediction. I kissed him on his eyes and lips, as one might a well-loved child. Tears streamed down his face onto the green shoots.

"My Lord," I said. "You're crying."

"My Lady, all the better to see you now like an angel inside a rainbow of tears."

As I fucked him and afterward, lying on the grass, the small wind and cool mist from the waterfall playing over our skin, and then later as I climbed naked into the fall's chasm to retrieve my clothes, before strolling back to our carriage, I realized him the loveliest man I'd met in my life—all right, maybe excepting Papa and Cesare. That's wrong. I knew part of his beauty, unlike Papa's or Cesare's, was the unconditional quality of his loving. I thanked the Virgin for not letting my own childishness, pride and books' clichés deprive me of Giovanni. I thanked her for Giovanni's courage in confronting nasty little me. I congratulated myself on my reaction to his speech, my newfound maturity. How grown-up I'd become to have perceived Giovanni's physical unattractiveness only skin-deep. What a woman of the world I newly was, sophisticated enough to take pleasure in loving and making love with a man's soul, rather than only his body. Dante and Cicero, respectively, would laud me in verse and oration. Oh, I quickly became as self-congratulatory for the ages as I'd been previously tragic. But I did love Giovanni. His speech by the waterfall had spun me like a good spanking. Loving him was no girl's delusion. That was the truth; is still the truth. It may not have been a passionate love—oh well, I thought perhaps in time I'd learn that—but I loved him. He was the man most filled with simple, innocent goodness I've ever known, even today, after my subsequent raft of men.

We continued our journey east toward the Adriatic, fewer and fewer inebriated Lombard knights farther and farther behind us as we went. One night on a cliff we heard and saw the aunts' and spies' party, far below us and celebrating with a torch-lit and barbecuing calf under the stars. They lit a firework, which rose abeam our cliff, before exploding in a great, lustrous shower of fire-drops. All along we heard progressively fewer knights singing cheery songs of slaughter, illicit sex and revenge, as they galloped after us in the distance. We made love by a moonless, Milky Way–reflecting lake. Again in a public square in the

Virago's Forli after nightfall, giggling like babies. We stopped one day before a monastery of the Franciscan Order, at which Saint Francis himself supposedly slept. I learned on this trip that if one adds up all the sites in Italy at which the locals say Francis slumbered, one finds he must've dreamt away more nights than Methusalah's nine hundred years of nights came to in the Hebrew Testament. The Abbot of this institution said Holy Francis had received the Stigmata on a rock that was kept in this monastery's vaulted basement, a stone that Francis often used as a penitential pallet. On Mount Verna Francis struck it with his thick staff and thousands have been cured from the stream that flowed thereafter from beneath it. The monks had brought it here from Verna and the robins in the nest in an ancient oak above the site, the Abbot swore, were the exact same centuries-old robins to whom Francis had bid good morning while descending the peak from his sacred woundings. Francis, of course, is said to have been Stigmataed on nearly as many rocks as spots he slept upon, going to his grave with such a profusion of holes, he must've looked to Saint Peter like a wheel of pious Helvetian cheese.

The Abbot led the way down crumbly stairs and then left us alone in the subterranean chamber. He left us facing the rock, upon which, he'd assured us before he left, the Saint's sacred skewerings had occurred.

"Saint Francis received the Stigmata on this very rock," my Lord Giovanni said with a sacerdotal hush.

"This very apocryphal rock?" I asked.

He nodded.

"Would it please you to grant me a legendary screw on this rock, my Lord?"

He was aghast. "Here?"

"This rock moved Heaven for Saint Francis. Perhaps it will move the earth for us. At the least the Stigmata should lend a Celestial zing to the piercing."

Giovanni tried with all his Sforza-Lombard solemnity to keep a straight face, couldn't and burst instead into strangled guilty laughter. We ripped off one another's clothes as quickly as we could and did it on Francis' boulder. Stigmatic zing, indeed, and a most excellent fornication on the Vernal, holy rock. Noticeably more so than usual, though the robins' unremitting cheeps added a certain Franciscan, bestial aura.

After a week's further journey, we reached the stronghold of Pesaro.

As we approached the Lombard coastal rocks, I could see, after a short causeway, Giovanni's castle, rising into the sunset dusk. It was large; not styled like a Vatican one, of course, but of unfinished stone. I saw battlements, a moat and drawbridge. It was an antique, built, Giovanni said, by Sforza and Angevin ancestors to defend Pesaro from marauding Greek, Cypriot and Venetian pirates.

"It's said hereabouts that the locals are descendants of Odysseus' crew, diverted by Scylla and Charybdis and marooned here forever on their way home from Troy to Ithaca, which lies directly across the Adriatic," Giovanni told me.

Hundreds of cheering Argive peasants met us at the causeway. Benighted, Cesare may've said these people were, but their love for their Lord was written on every face I saw, even, once they'd sobered up, on the hungover knights' faces. Sobriety, in fact, appeared to fall upon them like a brick the moment their feet touched Pesaran earth. Each knight rushed up to one or another corvine Lombard crone and hoisted her from the ground into his arms. These ancient ladies with eyes of pitchblende and arachnid hands turned out to be the knights' mamas. Giovanni told me the sharks had sobered up so quickly because they were terrified of punishment at these gnarled, feminine claws, if their baby boys appeared drunk in public in front of the other mamas. Those mothers whose boys had whacked into tree boughs and been abandoned here and there on the trail to and from Rome—by far the majority—merely walked calmly away with no more evident sorrow than a lobster having lost a drop of roe. A group of fishermen put Giovanni and me in another rustic carriage, which they jubilantly drew themselves, as I was told was the wedding custom in Pesaro, and began to pull us toward Giovanni's castle, looming high at the terminus of the causeway.

Along our route high-spirited Lombards cheered, sang, hurled flowers and played rough instruments in our arrival's honor. The songs were sharp and robust, distinctly un-Roman. They spoke of earthy passions with lyrics as frank as I'd ever heard, except from the mouth of a priest or cursing ox-teamster. They spoke of the body parts of lovers, vendettas that killed a brother—his blood flying through the air—even morning sickness. But every song, however sad, was bathed in joy, with Lombard fog, love and the ultimate, unfathomable Mercy of God. At the drawbridge I caught my breath. The fortress was indeed huge, an ancient Norman monstrosity.

"It's rustic, ugly and fat, Lady," Giovanni said.

"Giovanni, it's beautiful. Promise me you'll rape me at least once in each room."

I could see hundreds of windows in its walls, each with a candle in it. Behind each window lay flickering shadows of a room.

"Many rooms," he said.

"So little time."

"I'll get started tonight."

"Right now."

Giovanni took my slim hand in his huge one. "I hope you're as happy here, Lady, as you've made me."

I kissed him a long kiss on his lips. The torch-bearing Lombards cheered it with a bright, musical roar.

The aunts and the spies joined us in two days and we all partied superbly on friuli wines, seafood and passion for a fortnight. The Pesarans were especially and decidedly mad for Adriatic scampi, their petite, crustacean mitts raised in prayer. The hard-shelled, mini-lobster bugs with their eye-poles and insect bodies were everywhere. Breakfast, lunch and dinner. Fried with fusilli, steamed in cipolini, boiled with rutabaga, inserted Hapsburg-style like multilegged berries into savory waffles and open-fired and stuffed in hollowed-out loaves of bread with hulking-great slathers of butter. For the first three nights Giulia, Adriana, Juana, Moncada, Lucrezia Lopez, Penthesileia and I walked post-scampi along the castle's leeward battlement and showed off our Parisian and Milanese dresses to the applauding peasants below. They'd clap politely for each Lady, until I came out.

Then they'd burst into cheers, whistles and shouts of "Brava."

This soon began to get on Giulia's nerves. "What are they so hot for you for, Countess Pesaro?" she crabbed at me. "Charles VIII had this dress specially made for me in Paris at the couture salon of the Queen of France. It cost more than this entire castle. You've nothing to compare with it."

"Some applaud the dress, Auntie," Giovanni said. "The rest applaud their own mind's eye."

"What the hell does that mean?" she asked, doubly irritated at the "Auntie" thing.

"The women applaud the dress. The ones whistling and cheering congratulate their own imaginations."

"What?"

"The men cheer not for the dress, but for what they imagine lurks beneath it."

"Hmf. Barbarians."

And that was the end of fashion shows.

During the seven hundred days I spent in Pesaro, I'd been for the first time in my life the delighted mistress of all I surveyed, a proper Liege Lady. Giovanni's subjects were all loving and cheerful as their Countess could imagine them being, barring the occasional shocks Eve's children are heir to. Everyone took beautiful care of me, as did my husband. His servants and subjects looked, as well, forever solicitous of our happiness, even asking me daily my opinions about everything from fish sauce to cloacal maintenance. No one since Vanita had ever asked for my opinion on anything, excepting now and then Cesare on how gorgeous he was. Perhaps, looking back as I write this, I wasn't precisely in a state of what some Provençal troubadour might call "passionate love," but whatever these moment-to-moment warmths were, I certainly felt a clear and deep reservoir of them. I felt them for Giovanni, for his windowed house and his dozens of ever-present, bubbling relatives—Cardinal Ascanio, Ludovico the Moor, Gian Galeazzo and piles more—as well as for our many subjects and dependants. I even began to feel it for his coin and medallion collection, which he spent hours over. He'd explain each to me, the panoply of history it had passed through in its journey through time. I began to understand why he was so enamored of them and I'd join him in his study, now fascinated myself, and we'd spend hours in the tower room he kept them in—it had a window, as well—making up fantastical stories for each other about the provenance of this or that metal circle. Had an unbelieving Caesar tipped the soothsayer with this one on the Ides of March? Had Cleopatra in her guise as Isis paid for the message of Marcus Antonius' suicide with that?

Over that year Giovanni fulfilled his oath to me in spades, made that surprising day by the waterfall. Of how many men in her lifetime or three lifetimes may a woman say as much? After we'd made love, and gazing toward the wave-rumbling coast, I'd pray in bed every night that

I'd provided and would continue to provide Giovanni as much content-ment as he'd gifted me. The only disappointment of our year was my failure to conceive a child; though, as the Virgin knew, we'd tried in every room, cabinet and back stairway in the massive place.

If anyone had ever asked, when I'd come to Pesaro, if I wanted chil-dren, I would've said yes in the way all young women—those not foreor-dained for the nunnery—have always answered yes to that question. I can't imagine a world in which there would be another answer possible for a female. . . . Forgive me; that was a lie. I *can* imagine it, but it's just such a harshly forbidden sin to write, my goose feather dipped in flight to dissemble. I can imagine such a world, now that I'm old. Maybe in future God will grant such a world's existence, as He's recently granted the New World's existence. If such a place is discovered by some Columba, it will be new as an eighth day of the week and will need brav-ery. At any rate, Giovanni and I imagined we still had years for children.

I regularly heard of Papa and sometimes Cesare from the many guests and relatives that constantly infested the place. In late 1495 the last out-post of Charles VIII in Naples surrendered to the Holy League of Papa's. The Neapolitans were delighted to get the House of Aragon back, since they, among all the people of Italy, are most noted for insta-bility and a love of daily revolution. Savonarola of Florence was hurling insults at the Pope in public, accusing him of all sorts of sins, notably lust—"the most carnal of men," he called Alexander. He also charged Papa with greed, paganism, mendaciousness, the worship of idols, mur-der and graft—the selling of cardinal's hats and bishop's mitres. So what? I thought; that's what Popes do. Sextus did it. Pius did it. Even Innocent did it. And finally thievery, calumny, bastardy—a pointless insult meant more for Cesare, who never minded being misbegotten, as long as he had enough gold—and simony as well as a collectivity of heresies, from being secretly a Templar to *Devotio Moderna*, with its overly close for comfort *Imitatio Christi*.

Papa didn't care much about Savonarola, Ascanio Sforza told me.

"Will the Medicis not toast me this quarrelsome priest?" Papa'd said casually over bruschetta to the Florentine Ambassador.

"It would help our lawyers, Holiness, if you'd excommunicate him."

And, of course, he did. So they did, subjecting Savonarola to the "Trial by Fire," in which he was burnt at the stake. The "Trial" part being that if he were truly innocent, the fire shouldn't burn him, of course. This

seemed fair and satisfied everyone, including the subsequently inciner-
ated monk himself.

The Pope went to war with the Orsinis, the powerful Roman barons.
Within a month he'd captured ten Orsini castles. The Sforza magnates
had joined the Holy League, delighting the Pope and enraging Charles.

During all this time away from the Vatican, the wide-open Adriatic
air and the presence of Giovanni allowed me a perspective on my previous life in Rome with Papa, books and Cesare. Pesaro reeked of finny
honesty and a kind of misty clarity I'd never known. There seemed no
Ninth Circle here. Nor duplicity. Nor adultery. No dissemblance at all. I
was the princess of contentment. I only wish I'd been able to carry
Pesaro with me once I'd returned to the City of Lucifer.

I recall one day in particular in those years. I was reading on a chaise
in Giovanni's great room. He had few books, but what he had were surprisingly good, especially the ones in Greek. He told me they'd been sal-
vaged from a ship of Byzantine pirates and scholars, who'd shipwrecked
below our castle, all of them drowned or killed by rocks or shark-men.
Bibliophiles and pirates? I wondered. The modern age is full of learned
men in the oddest places. As I was reading Pliny's account of the
destruction of Pompey, fire-belching Vesuvius reminding me of my
dragon tapestry wedding-gift that now hung behind me, I heard a com-
motion of sudden yelling and weeping from the adjacent hallway.

"My Lady!" a jagged voice shouted. "I must see the Countess. I beg
you, where is she?"

I walked quickly into the hall, where there were three of our servants,
who held by the ragged shirt a muddy peasant man of about sixteen
years. The moment the peasant saw me he dropped, as if pole-axed, to
his knees. Tears streamed down his face. "Please, my Lady, you must
come. For the love of God, you must come immediately."

"What is it? What's wrong?" Goosefleshing fear seized me. I was envi-
sioning my Lord Pesaro in some horrible accident, or assassination; they
were both common since the war with the Orsinis. "Has something
happened to my Lord Giovanni?"

"No, Lady," a servant said. "It's this man's wife."

I love you, Holy Mother, I thought, for not letting it be my husband.
"What's wrong?" I asked again. "What can I do?"

"Only you, Countess, only you can help her," the kneeling peasant
moaned. "Please, come now."

I thought to ask him why only me, but he was too distraught for reason. I tossed Pliny on a table, glancing at the boy again. I've just written he was "distraught," but that was hardly the word. He looked like a boy in Hell. Whatever his trouble was, these people had been sweet and good to me. He stood, turned and rushed away. I followed him. Outside our keep waited a horse and black mule. The horse was my own, Giovanni's gift. She was sidesaddled, traces in place, obviously waiting for me. The mule wore a thick blanket, which was all a peasant would commonly ride on. The weeping man hoisted me into my saddle then mounted his mule.

"Follow me, Lady. There's no time," he cried, and took off in a rocking mule-gallop toward his village I could see about a mile distant.

We reached the collection of huts. I heard a sound of a woman's screamings. I saw him hear them, as well, and he grabbed his gut, as if knifed. He dismounted, helped me from my saddle and rushed into the cottage he'd been heading for. The cottage was composed of compacted uneven earth and thatch. I followed him, the female screams assaulting me. For a moment inside I saw only black, broken by two pin-spots of early fall sunlight, creeping in through cracks in the thatch and moist mud. There were no windows. It might've been a bear's cave, but for the pin-spotted distaff of a spinning wheel. But as my eyes adjusted, I saw the object of his panic. There was something resembling a bed made of straw with a patchwork covering against the far wall of this tiny room, which was hardly larger nor better smelling than a stable stall. The floor was of pounded black dirt. There were damp aromas of that dirt, some kind of porridge and rotting straw that filled the room. Also the coppery stench of fresh blood. On the bed lay an unclothed woman, bathed in sweat, her long hair plastered with it to her thin face and neck, her belly round as the Pantheon's dome. I could see the muscles of her swollen abdomen pulling and contracting. She was in labor and each muscle twinge produced from her a scream as if from the victim within an Iron Maiden. Next to the bed stood another woman, older, tall, with a skeletal, pockmarked face. This older one was the well-known midwife of the village, of all the villages hereabouts.

"What's wrong?" I asked the midwife. "Why are you standing there? Help her. Help her deliver the child."

"I cannot, my Lady. I've done everything in my power and knowledge. The baby won't come."

For a helpless moment, I just stood and stared at Eve's punishment. "What do we do?" I asked. "Why did you call for me? Do something, woman. What's wrong with you?"

The midwife couldn't answer. She just hung her head, tears dripping to the earth floor. "The Blessed Mother has abandoned me," she whispered.

The woman on the bed then screamed again, as another contraction bit into her. The childlike husband fell to his knees, sobbing and hiding his eyes. On the bed the mother looked up at me.

She was perhaps twelve or thirteen, though in her agony she might've passed for fifty. "Cut me, my Lady. Cut me. Save my child. Let my child live. I beg you."

I was stunned. "But . . . I don't know how. I don't have the skill. . . ."

The midwife held a flint blade out to me. "Cut her, my Lady. It's the only way."

"I don't know how. . . . I've never . . . You must do it. You must know the skill."

"I cannot."

"Why?"

"To cut her is her death. This is Lombardy. For me to give her death will be my own. It's the unwritten law. Not noble law, but of the people here. It's been the law since times long before there was law."

This was mythology's hard blade. "But if I cut her, she'll die just as surely."

"But for you to give death is no crime or offense. All our lives are in the hands of our Lord and Lady. You may take them from us freely anytime it suits you, because they're yours to take or give. Cut her, my Lady."

"Cut my belly, my Lady," the naked woman pleaded once more. "I can feel my baby dying. Cut now, before we both die." She then reached out, tore the knife from the midwife and shoved it toward me. "Take it. Cut." Then she screamed again with another horrible contraction. "Cut, you timid bitch!"

I took the blade. "What's your name?" I asked her.

But pain was too strong to answer.

"Vanozza, my Lady," the husband answered. "My Lord Pesaro gave her the name. She once was his bed-girl. Her name's Vanozza."

I hesitated a second, stricken by this name, but realized half the women hereabouts were Vanozzas, as half the men, like her husband, were unlettered Aristotles.

The midwife took me by my hand that had the sharp stone in it. She guided it toward the naked woman's side. "Right here," she said, the knifepoint at the bulging skin. "The cut must be as long as a baby's head. You must go deep, to penetrate the fibrous muscle, but not so deep as to touch the child."

"Cut," begged the wife.

"Cut," echoed the husband in his sobs.

I cut, praying to the Virgin, and the woman opened to me like an egg-laden fish to the fisherman. She didn't cry out, but a stream of blood sluiced from her clenched teeth like hairdressing through a narrow-toothed comb. I saw the child's body amidst her blood and entrails. A daughter then emerged from her wound—like Athena must've from Zeus's forehead, it struck me. Then I saw within the mother a second child. This had been the killing dilemma. Twins are an often deadly blessing. I placed the first in the midwife's arms. She guided my hand to cut the cord. I reached into the butcher shop of the wife's belly. As gently as I could, I removed her second child, afterward cutting his cord. The midwife expertly cleared the two children's air passages and they began their new screamings, but these were joyous. The screams of life. We placed the two babies at their mother's breasts and they began to suck. On young Vanozza's face lit a sudden expression of such joy—like the Blessed Mother in the Manger, I thought—that I've never seen its like since. Vanozza closed her eyes, her brood giving suck, and she died. I watched the two children, as Aristotle touched them tenderly for the first time. I suddenly remembered that the great Julius Caesar had been born this way—Caesar, "the one who was cut"—never to know his Vanozza. I wondered if this son would one day be master of the world. Or maybe this daughter would be its mistress.

On April 1, 1497, a Papal Nuncio, a dwarfish Monsignor by the name of Lelio Capodiferro, looking vaguely sick and escorted by a white-and-golden-yellow-clad company of equally nauseous knights, carrying Vatican banners with Papal and Borgia Arms—white with Peter's gold Key

John Faunce

to Heaven's Gate and black with the red Borgia bull—had appeared on Giovanni's castle drawbridge, demanding my immediate attendance before the Vicar of Christ.

"Myself, as well?" Giovanni asked.

Lelio Capodiferro was a messenger Papa was known often to send when he wanted bitter news delivered suavely. But Lelio was to prove today there was an uglier side to that pretty tongue.

"Most definitely *not* yourself, my Lord," the tiny Nuncio replied in a voice bigger than himself. He was one of those men the Almighty evidently created specifically for the purpose of announcements to multitudes.

"The hell with Rome. I refuse to go to Rome," I said. "If Papa knew how happy I am here with Giovanni, it's impossible he'd force me back."

"His Holiness didn't equivocate. His command is under threat of excommunication for you both if you refuse."

"What's the matter? Why's he so insistent?"

"Your elder brother. He is dead. I am sent to tell you."

I felt an iron in my heart. "Cesare is dead?"

"No. Juan. The Duke of Gandia. He'd nine deep knife-wounds in his body."

I thanked the Virgin it wasn't Cesare dead, but I ran to the tower and wept for my stupid brother Juan, that fun, innocent child. I let the Greek and Roman coins dribble through my fingers onto the table like tears. They rang on the table's stone surface like a baby's silver playbell in a crib. Had the Caesar on this *denarius* a sister? Did she weep on March 15, 44 B.C.? Or did this Cleopatra/Isis at her brother, Osiris/Ptolemy's, murder by Caesar? Had she known Ptolemy as vaguely as I'd known Juan, a distant figure with a five-pointed crown? Did she place two of these coins on his eyes to pay Charon? Lelio'd told me the Orsinis were naturally suspected. Also the Moor. A dark-skinned, nobly dressed man with a hooked nose had been seen that night at the location on the Tiber, from which the Palatine Guards had dragged the mostly beheaded Juan the next morning.

"But the Moor hasn't dark skin nor a hooked nose," I wailed. "He looks like a German."

"*All* Moors are dusky and beaked," the Nuncio remarked.

"But he's not a Moor. That's just a nickname."

"Innocent III's nickname was 'The Wicked.' I think you'd agree he was more wicked than innocent."

Naturally Cesare was popularly suspect. Cesare'd been jealous of Juan ever since Papa'd made Juan the Duke of Gandia, banishing Cesare, or so he'd phrase it, to a jackal's life beneath a red hat. That jealousy had openly exploded when Papa'd given Juan the *Imperator's* Golden Baton of the Holy League, command of the so-called Army of God or, appropriating the old-time style of Templar Crusaders, *Militia Dei*. This baton Cesare coveted with his whole body and soul.

"Its gold was annealed in the blood of warrior Saints. It retains the power of their hearts and souls," he'd say with a fond smile and, *"In hoc signo,"* with a glance to Heaven.

A tear fell on one of my coins. I picked it up. It'd been burnished and its image flattened by a million fingers over its 1,650 years, but the outline of Macedonian Alexander's face was still unmistakable beneath the word ΑΛΕΞΑΝΔΡΟΣ (Alexandros). This took me to thoughts of Alexander VI. Papa. Papa'd always loved Juan intensely, a love Cesare'd resented all his life. Had it been Cesare who'd played Cain to Juan's Abel? I wondered.

"Cui prodest?" I was told Papa had asked the Sacred College of the murder. "Who benefits?"

"Caesar Augustus adulescens aureus," the Camerlengo had squawked, "the young, golden Caesar Augustus," giving tinny voice to what younger throats dared not whisper.

"Henceforth benefices will be conferred only upon him who merits them; We intend to renounce all nepotism," Papa answered in a momentary spasm of contrition.

The Sacred College burbled obligatory harrumphs of thanksgiving praise.

Was there a part a sister might yet play in this apocryphal drama? Meanwhile I stared out the tower into the dank Adriatic that lashed our castle's seaward wall. What was I thinking? The hell with Cesare. The hell with my impotently sentimental, girlish tears, self-pity and dramatization. Papa was the one who must be in agony. It must be terrible. His baby boy, dead, beheaded. Yes, I was fearful to leave Giovanni, but I wouldn't be gone long. Besides, to whom did I owe my Pesaran life? To Papa, who'd insisted I marry Giovanni Sforza, despite my romance-inspired, whiny objections. Two days ago Papa'd said Juan's funeral Mass, had fallen on the bier and wept, choking and crying out like a man in Hell before the entire congregation and again at the tomb. If it weren't for Papa—and Cesare—I'd have no Giovanni, nor loving Pesaran subjects; I'd not be anyone's Liege Lady. I'd have no home of my own. I had no time to grieve for the dead or for my own bitter, though temporary, loss of my sweet Adriatic lair. I had to get back to Papa posthaste. I imagined him wandering alone and wretched with a candle in his hand through the midnight and ghostly Borgia Apartments. I had to stop him.

Giovanni took me in his large arms, as he bade me good-bye. "I've a vicious premonition I'll never see you again in this world, beautiful girl," he said. "I'll die before Lucrezia Borgia's angel's rainbow arcs over the Adriatic again—"

"My Lord, I'll just be there until the edges of Papa's pain begin to dull. I'll be back in Pesaro in a fortnight, at most a month."

"Don't interrupt me. I've practiced this, and if you stop me now, I'll never find the courage to finish."

But he couldn't find his courage, couldn't continue whatever thought he'd rehearsed. It must've been pleasing, because I've observed ever since that the hefty tend to speak well. Or maybe it's merely in me to remember his words by the waterfall that picnic day. I've always longed to have his rehearsed farewell in my memory, to have heard it, to be able to call it to mind to soften this or that painful moment with the wistful smile of a more saccharine remembrance. But it's not there. All he could do was weep into his hands like a tubby little boy, the lovely bulk of him trembling and rolling with his grief. I stepped into my carriage.

"God be with you, my little stigmatized robin. I'll pray for you every day God grants me" had been all he'd been finally able to choke out, calling to me as my carriage wheels rumbled and crunched in their cloud of dark dust into my last Lombard dusk.

"God grants you? Stop it! And I thought *I* was a mass of self-pity! I'll be back before you know it!"

Next to me, driving the carriage, Lelio smiled. Soldiers from the *Militia Dei* rode behind us.

As I drove along the road west toward Rome with the Nuncio, we came upon a peasant man, who stood shirtless by the roadside. My God, I couldn't help thinking, he had the body of a Greek god. Giovanni's ancient Ithaca must've been an extremely interesting place to live in, while they were striking those coins. All those naked wrestlers and wound-up, platter-hurling δισχοβολοι—discus hurlers—lumbering around the place in muscular, olive-oiled perfection. What could it be like to be made love to by a man like that? I felt great affection for my Giovanni, but let's be honest. I fanned myself, pretending to be clearing away road dust, yet thinking, ah well, that I'd never find out. I prayed I could deal with whatever it was Papa needed in Rome quickly and get back home to my sweet, enchanting fatso, whom I'd rather see eat olive oil than rub it on himself. As I passed the Greek god, I recognized him. He was the widower husband of Vanozza, the twins' father.

He made a Sign of the Cross. "Christ's love be with you, sweet mother of us all," he cried after me into my carriage's dark dust. He held up a child in his arms to me. "One lives!" he shouted after me with a gruff, wet, Poseidon-like bellow. "We pray together at every bedtime you'll return someday."

Which lived? Had the boy, or had the girl? I'd never know.

"Kiss the child for me," I shouted back. "I swear I'll be back to see you all again."

But Papa," I now said to white Alexander, who sat on his Apostolic throne, "Lord Pesaro is the sweetest, kindest man under Heaven. He loves me. I couldn't do it to him."

A week of travel had passed since my good-byes to Giovanni and my Lombards. Cesare'd come to my Borgia suite as soon as I'd arrived at the Vatican and had informed me what was in the works since Juan's murder. I was to be married to Alphonso, Duke of Bisceglie, heir to the Prince of Salerno and nephew to Federico of Aragon, at the moment King of Naples and the Two Sicilies and one of the greatest and richest Lords in Italy. I was furious.

"It is said," Cesare finished dryly, "he's the handsomest man in Europe, present company excepted, of course." And he gave me his most sparkling grin.

"How can I do that? I'm married already," I said now to Papa.

"The mistaken marriage will have to be annulled. You will be declared *virga intacta*, due to Giovanni's *impotentia*. This match is far better than the one to cowardly Pesaro."

"And he's impotent, why?"

"Necromancy."

"But you, Papa, and half the Prelates in Europe saw Giovanni make love to me on my wedding night."

"That is what appeared to happen. Only God and Satan know."

"Plus presumably Giovanni and myself."

"Perhaps not even you two. If you call that event on your wedding night 'making love,' then I pity you. But the word is that Giovanni is impotent, because you've been married three years and he's not 'known' you yet in a biblical sense on account of curses cast upon the marriage by some French Hecate. *Quod non cognoverim*, Lucrezia. 'Because he's not known you, Lucrezia.' "

"On the contrary, I've found him quite demonstrably a biblical scholar. How many rooms do you think there are in the Stronghold of Pesaro?"

"I've no idea. Fifty, a hundred?"

"Two hundred eight. Giovanni's made love to me in each one of those. Some of them twice or thrice."

"It's said Giovanni might not be the only one to desire a divorce," Cesare said.

"Meaning?"

"Meaning Marino Sanuto—"

"That pimp."

"Yes, he's a pimp, but that only makes him the more reliable in this case. He says you've had your lover, Pedro Calderone, the Spanish faux-poet known as Perotto, murdered by Lord Cesare, myself, and dumped in the Tiber out of fear he'd sonnetize and publish the two of you. He says he had this information from the Amazon Penthesileia, Perotto's other whore and your Lady-in-Waiting."

"That's absurd. Perotto is Papa's servant and a numbskull. I don't sleep with the help. And I sense Penthesileia doesn't sleep with men."

"Quite. But people say it, I'm told."

God had sealed Giovanni and his people to me, I thought. I was happy with him and them. What business was it of Papa's and Cesare's to meddle? I wanted to rush to Papa and slap him till the cloud of him rained salt water and warn him not to mess with Vanita's and Roderigo's daughter or there'd be Hell to pay. And tell him to burn Perotto's corpse during a staged reading of *Incendio di Troja*. I fantasized Papa'd even like that, to see what a strong, thorny woman his little daughter had grown into on her Lombard beach. But shrewdly on Papa's part—and even wisely, it turns out—he instead left me to braise several more days alone in my juices. That stew didn't make me any less angry, but it did make me weak and weepy, adding more salty broth to the recipe. I kept thinking of Giovanni. I brought his face constantly to mind, the agonized twist it would take when he found out what was in store for us and he'd never see me again, just as he'd predicted. I thought of the baby-fat little boy or girl—or the twins—I'd now never have with him, and especially how he'd grieve over the death of that possibility. When I'd think of that, I'd cry bitterly. And the more I cried, the weaker I got. The weaker I'd become, the more easily I'd cry. And so on. I summoned the aforesaid Penthesileia. I well remembered her, since she was over six feet tall and swayed like a stilted carnival acrobat when she walked. I'd decided to chop her down if she gave me the slightest provocation.

"That's not true, my Lady. You couldn't have been a . . . whore of Perotto's, nor could any woman."

"Sanuto also says you were Perotto's mistress."

She gave a deep, long giggle. "Perotto was a well-known gentleman's gentleman, as I myself am a lady's lady. An unabashed homosexual. A match of the two of us could've only been made in Purgatory and I'm presently having too much fun with girls to be there. Perotto was *Sanuto's* lover. Sanuto spreads these rumors to drag suspicion and prejudice from himself to you."

"Thank you, Penthesileia. I'm grateful to know that. I mean about Perotto, not yourself."

"Is it all right in your service, Lady?"

"Is what all right?"

"What I do."

"Of course. What possible business is it of mine?"

"If you require a deeper understanding of the Sapphic path, I'd be glad to show you—"

"Don't trouble yourself. Not that there's anything sinful in it, except on a formal basis. I know many prioresses, bishops, archbishops and cardinals, Saints even . . . Is *that* why men hate Sappho's poetry?" I looked up, surprised to find her still loftily there. "Was Hildegard of Bingen a metaphorical inhabitant of Δεσβοσ? A Lesbian?"

"Our lay sisterhood says so."

"That sisterhood always hints everyone is. You may go."

She swayed out of my suite in her high heels like a sensual giraffe, practically caroming from the opposing walls of the corridor. By the time two of Papa's Apostles and two Palatines finally escorted me into His Holy Presence, I'd lost ten pounds from my already slight frame and reached the condition of a woman who's been Inquired into by the branding-irons of the Holy Office, ready to say anything, if it will make the crying stop.

My brother was by Papa's side, but no longer dressed as a cardinal, not even the crimson beanie. He wore a cloth-of-gold doublet, a matching Florentine cap, golden-yellow hose and boots with strands of gold down their shanks. He stood as handsomely as the rising sun when I came in.

"Cesare," I said, "what happened to your pectoral crucifix and ring?"

"I've resigned the Sacred College. I'm no longer Valencia. I'm Borgia once again."

"Have you resigned all charity for your sister, along with your red hat? I've done little but cry for two days since last you spoke to me."

"Lucrezia, sweetheart," he said, "this match is a hundred times one to impotent, gutless Pesaro."

"Hold your tongue of Pesaro, brother, or I'll cut it out. I've recently had practice cutting even larger things out."

"Forgive me, Lucrezia. But Bisceglie's uncle is the greatest Sovereign Lord in Italy, excepting His Holiness. Alphonso might well be his heir, assuming the appropriate relatives die first, which they will, trust me."

"I know all that. I love Giovanni."

"You'll be a first-rank Duchess," Cesare went on, "a Princess, upon the father's death. And upon Naples' demise, a Queen. Your sons of the House of Aragon will make history."

"I ought to fuck him for 'history'? What similar has history done for me? Giovanni makes me happy. He labors, would burst his heart, to make me so."

"A crone's joy," Cesare snapped. "Tending an old man's bed."

"Old man? He's thirty-seven."

"Don't you want a woman's love with a young man beautiful as Apollo? Alphonso is nearly as much a man to dream on as myself."

Oh, Cesare was still as conceited a pissant as he'd always been, I thought. But looking at him at that moment, I now confess, it struck me it would be a thing of undeniable beauty to have a man's body as lovely as that next to me one day. "I love Lord Giovanni in my way. It's not for you, brother, to judge our love."

Papa went to speak.

"Nor even for His Holiness," I cut him off. "Who's in my bed seems hardly a matter of faith or theology."

"You underestimate yourself," Papa mumbled.

I was neither furious nor shouting, as I'd been before in this room, when Papa and Cesare confronted me with unsolicited and undesired romantic plans. I was too filled with enervated sorrow for that. Sorrow still lingering from Giovanni's farewell. Sorrow at the thought of never seeing his sweet bulk again. Sorrow at the loss of his unborn children. Sorrow at the cloud of inevitability that seemed to be enveloping this room as if a dim familiar to the cloud of Papa. Sorrow at the edgeless pall of rumor that'd become part of my life. Exhausted, I knew what the outcome would be. I'll resist it, I was thinking. Thinking in the way the Inquired-into imagine they'll resist, when first stretched on torture's table. I knew I was lying to myself. I might fight this till the Last Judgment, but what would be would be. The mob will think me an adulterous murderess no matter what the truth, no matter what I do. It's as impossible to resist God's Desires as to deliver a child without pain or sorrow. Such anyway were my self-justifications for my weakness. I was about to give in. I can go to my Vatican rooms and at least and at last stop crying, I was thinking, when the stamping began. Then Cesare's wine-bladdery trumpet.

"Lucrezia! If you'll not consent, my enemies, who are many and powerful—the Sforza, the Colonna, the Medici, a dozen cardinals from everywhere, Charles VIII, the Venetians, the *Lupus Magnus* King of the Two Sicilies, for God's sake—will use the failure of this alliance to destroy me! The Moor will cut my head off as surely as he did Juan's; I shall be killed! I! My love for you, which has always been the closest thing to my heart, will vanish from the world!"

"Cesare, please." Papa sighed.

Cesare with golden, offended difficulty pulled himself together. What an obnoxious, deceitful child he was. But I sensed something else in Cesare. Inside his overblown speech had been a truth, as there's always an ironic snippet of truth in the ludicrous. As I looked at him now, nothing appeared in his perfect face but the most heartfelt sincerity and care for my happiness. It's Satan's honesty, not his overly vaunted lies that has eternally been his most dangerous weapon. Cesare really does love me, I thought. Oh, yes, he was thinking of himself with his plots for me. But mightn't he truly be thinking of Lucrezia, as well?

"Child," Papa said, "this is the right thing to do. You'll be happier in the end."

"Papa," I said, "don't do this."

"You've been with Pesaro for long enough to have a child riding a pony by now," he said with as much sudden gentleness in his voice as if talking to the six-year-old me, the way I remembered he used to. "Yet you're without child. God's Displeasure at a marriage always finds expression in a woman's barrenness. Alphonso's young seed will give you children."

Could that be true? I don't know, but it was, if nothing else, Papa's Trojan Horse to my Cassandra. "But Papa—"

"God's Will shall be done by Us for your own good."

Cesare smiled, happy, I supposed, that the Moor and the Great Wolf of the Sicilies would let him keep his head.

I bowed my head. But it wasn't to be that easy. By the icy damp last week of December of 1497, I lay below the main altar in the Sistine Chapel, stark naked on another freezing marble slab, my nipples knobby with cold as brass studs on a breastplate. It occurred to me I'd been naked at some point during every recent ceremony I'd been involved in. Once more I'd only a white satin sheet between the frigid morning air and myself. There were the customary, invisible nuns, chanting in the background to the Virgin. Or maybe to the virgin, I thought. Why do I never see those damned nuns, I wondered, at any of these ceremonials they're eternally yodeling at? I turned my head and could see a clutch of Cardinals, about half a dozen of them, assembled for obstetrical duty at the aisle's lower transept. In the middle of the flock was Camerlengo Costa, who'd survived—another stupendous miracle, praise God—yet more years of influenza-threatening decrepitude. He now looked a red-sheeted ghost. He was dithering, prevaricating. His ancient face wiggled in embarrassed seizures below his crimson hat, which were both the same color. The other Cardinals began pushing him toward me up the aisle.

"All right, all right, brothers," he complained. "Do not push. I know my duty. I am going. Why this unseemly haste?"

Haste? I thought, as he shuffled endlessly up the freezing aisle toward me. The Almighty has been hastier delivering Judgment Day.

At last he arrived at me. I looked up, he down.

"Lady . . . Lady Lucrezia Borgia," he dribbled out. "I have come to . . . to . . . to . . ."

"To what, Your Grace?"

"You know very well to what, young lady."

"Yes, but I want to hear you say it."

"*Quapropter?*" he gawped at me.

" 'Why?' "

He smiled momentarily, the smile quickly fading back to senescent bewilderment.

I had mercy. "Because it's part of proper ceremony, the saying of a thing, isn't it?"

He looked self-consciously toward the Chapel ceiling, scandalized I'd known what he'd said. He looked as if he were speculating maybe *"Quapropter"* was enough in itself to deny me virginity. "Um, well, yes, I suppose it is. . . . The saying of . . . whatever, I mean."

"Well, say it."

"Yes. Lady Borgia, I have come to . . . have come here today . . . in the Presence of God . . . and of my brothers . . . to examine . . . your . . . to perlustrate . . . to inquire into . . ."

"My twat?"

I couldn't have stopped myself from trying to shock him. I'd schemed for two days what I'd say to that purpose. The virgin's pitiful revenge. He was so cute in his granddad's robes and quaking fingers, all raisiny and anxious, but still trying to act Devil-may-care. He looked as if what I'd said had abruptly granted him a fresh century. I'd thought to shock him, but instead it was relief washing over his sagging mask when he heard me speak of my sex first, no matter the word. For men it's often not the thing itself they shy from—as I'm sure the Camerlengo never shied a speck of a moment from the actuality of some whore's organ—as it is for us. For men it's rather more customarily the saying of it.

"Yes!" he joyously yelped. "To catechize your noble kitty cat!"

"Well, inquisition away, Eminence," I cried. Also preplanned.

Finished with his sacred gynecology, he tottered back down the aisle toward his expectant brother Cardinals, all of whom had been front-row ogling at the "piercing of the virginity" ceremony at our nearly four-year-ago wedding banquet.

"Well, is she . . . ?" the Ascanio Sforza, still the youngest of the red-breasts, asked breathlessly of the Camerlengo.

"Is she what?" he replied, evidently having forgotten why he was there.

"Is she intact, Cardinal?"

"Is what—? . . . Oh, that's it. I remember. The pussy inspection." And he paused. "A miracle, brothers," he then exulted. *"Virga intacta!"*

The red flight applauded in pleased, though moderate, surprise.

On November 18 of that year at Pesaro and under threats from Gian Galeazzo and the Moor, Giovanni had signed a ceremonial *Confessio*, in which he stated he'd "known" me *"numquam,"* never, and on December 22, right before Christmas, Papa'd formally dissolved my marriage to Pesaro and absolved me of him and all I loved there. I wept. I then stayed with Papa in my Borgia Apartment while the contract for my next husband was negotiated. I saw Papa often, trying still to comfort him about Juan. But he seemed to have gotten over that or at least wasn't receptive to my attempts to soothe him.

"Juan's in Heaven, a rare thing for a Borgia," he'd say. "He's lucky. Who are We to question God's Will. We're fit only to accept it."

"I thought your will was a mirror of God's Will. You told me they were the same, didn't you?"

"The Father has said He is Our reflection."

An icicle ran up my spine. "Or was it your will alone? Did you then pray your inclination must be Christ's, while following your own desire? The Pontius Pilate method?"

"I could never wash my hands entirely of blame where my children are concerned."

"His Father did."

But was blasphemy a proof? Far from it. There were so many suspects; even odds-makers were betting against the Pope's guilt. All the other suspects had more compelling motives. Had Papa killed Juan? No, not possible. What would he gain? A baton for Cesare as the new *Imper-*

ator of the Army of God? What a nightmare for Papa that would be. Papa'd thought he'd seen tantrums from my brother before? What new Apocalypses from Field Marshal Tantrum, then? Might he amidst a snit invade the Holy Roman Empire? Or England? What Papa'd said about his feelings for his children—and his highly unwonted use of "I" in saying it—had a more unquestionably true ring, I'd warrant, than even the Father's Feelings for His Own Child, if He'd ever even expressed them at all. It was impossible for Papa to have killed Juan, I relievedly decided.

That night I put on a black cloak. I took my sidesaddle, a gift from Giovanni, made by his peasant leather-workers. I made my way to the Palatines' stables, where I located a beautiful filly, a black with a startling mane and braided tail, named Diana. I saddled her, climbed into the saddle and rode from the Vatican onto the Porta del Popolo and finally to the Via Appia, heading north. I rode to Subiaco. Not Subiaco exactly, but rather the Convent-Monastery of San Sisto. There I was met at the gate by a novitiate, a Sister Anne, who took me in immediately to see the Abbess, Reverend Mother Fortunata, who was praying in the Chapel beneath Saint Sebastian.

I walked up behind her. "Do you love Saint Sebastian, Reverend Mother?"

She turned back to me slowly and effortlessly as a pirouetting angel. "I pray to him. He's our principal bulwark against the plague, daughter."

"But in your prayers, do you love him?"

She blushed, though her eyes remained steady as a cloister's doors. "Don't all of us?"

"Naked Sebastian," I said. "My mother used to marvel at him. Do you know, Reverend Mother, why he's forever in such a sensuous pose amidst his agonized martyrdom?"

"It's his effort to brand the heat of what he's sacrificing onto his soul."

"Doubtless. He's hot enough to put his brand on any woman."

"Don't be irreverent, child. What may I do for you?"

"I'm persecuted, Mother, driven against my will toward a grievous sin of adultery. You may provide me Sanctuary, if you will."

"It's my duty. Come with me."

"I'm no virgin, Reverend Mother. You've no duty to me."

"Not to you, child, to the Blessed Mother," she pointed back at my mother's favorite Virgin. "Whose virginity was a sacrifice for us all."

It wasn't until that moment that I fully understood the meaning of *sacrifice*, used in a religious sense. Like many cloistered clergy I've known, Reverend Mother Fortunata was a milleniarist mystic, who took her apocalyptic view of history from Joachim of the Flower that this was to be not an age of renaissance, but of the great-and-final death, the age of the Holy Spirit—with whom Fortunata was intimately and daily acquainted—and of Judgment Day. She opined to me that Papa was the perfect Pope for such a Day. I begged off comment on that. She was also one of those rare spiritual nuns that seem not to walk through a convent's shadowy corridors, but to float, her feet never actually touching pavement. She hovered me to an empty cell, made the Sign of the Cross over me and left me to get some rest.

The following morning I went to the chapel once more, to pray to Sebastian and the Holy Mother. As I came in I saw a girl of ten or so, one of the bastard girls the convent regularly adopted and brought up, I imagined. She stood in front of Sebastian, in evident prayer, her small hand resting quietly on his arrow. She turned to watch me enter.

"Good morning," she whispered.

"Good morning."

"Who are you?"

I walked up to her, trying to smile, but filling for no reason I could fathom with shuddering nerves and unable quite to smile. "Lucrezia Borgia."

Her face fell. I now could see her face and legs wobble. She wasn't attempting a smile, but a scowl. "You can't be."

As I came close to her I was noticing this child bore an uncanny resemblance to myself at her age. The gold braid. The eyes the same color. I wondered if she had a bastard brother somewhere. How adorable, I thought. This girl can't believe her luck to meet someone as beautiful and famous as myself. I must be her heroine; she's made herself over in imitation of me. "And why can't I be Lucrezia Borgia?"

I reached out to caress her beautiful coif. I was wishing her my *own* daughter.

"Because *I* am," she whispered.

I froze. "You can't be."

I stared on. She must be thinking me an idiot, I imagined, instead of a paradigm. Was the whole thing possible, even remotely so? This place was a refuge for bastard girls; I ran through my siblings, trying to think of someone mentioning or even obliquely intimating such a child. I couldn't think of anybody. And why name her after me? Who in our family, if it were true, would have the iron discipline and motivation to keep such a gorgeous Gift of God a secret? And who'd determine to take the chance on secreting such a Gift just below a Borgian villa? "Who is your father?"

She grinned and proclaimed, "The great Lord Cesare Borgia."

Of course. Cesare, the ultimate secret-keeper. But was it true? I thought through the dozens of girls and women Cesare'd slept with. Well, *that* could be. And if I was the girl's model, maybe she just wished such a thing. "And your mother?"

"I've no mother. I don't need one. Papa said he and his gold are all the parents a little girl needs."

So it was true. Only Cesare could've said that to a daughter.

"He gives me gold, when I'm good to him. I'm good to him every time he comes to see me."

A shiver ran up my spine. I stayed at San Sisto ten days or more, almost two weeks. I spent every day with Mother Fortunata or little Lucrezia. I began to teach the child to read. She insisted on *The Golden Legend*.

I told her now she could read it for *him* the next time he saw her, because he'd be so proud of her.

"I can't," she said. "Papa says being good to him is the only thing that's good. Papa says written words are for hiding the truth and God gave them to us to hide our hearts in. He says they're like a cocoon with a dead, icky butterfly inside. Reading's bad, he says. He won't give me gold for reading."

I'd have to have a little talk with my brother. "I never thought my father would like me reading, either, but I think now he did."

"You mean Godpapa?"

That was creative, I thought. This girl could be a wordsmith. "Evidently."

"Papa says everything he says and knows he got from Godpapa."

"Not everything."

Speaking of "Godpapa," daily some or other cardinal-nuncio would come from Papa with an enunciation of my steadily more execrable excommunication and, following from that, how steady and daily deepening my descent into Hell would be, when the time came. I was far below the Ninth Circle of damnation—somewhere between the thirteenth and thirty-third—by the time the last Nuncio arrived. In the pitch dark of early morning, I'm not even certain what hour it was, the heavy door of my cell banged open with a sound like Giovanni's dropping drawbridge. Forcing my eyes open, I was drowsily certain that's what it was.

But I looked up at the entryway. "Cesare!"

He was armored, gold breastplate and greaves, iron gloves and a compact, gold-handled sword that made me think of the Roman *gladius* from Caligula's old Amphitheatrum Flavium, which we call the Coliseum.

He stepped to my pallet. "I've come for you, sister. My knight is here to fork your queen. Your time of games and nunneries is over."

"I've Sanctuary here."

"Sanctuary," he spat with contempt. "You wish Sanctuary from your own fate? Well, grow up, we all wish Sanctuary, but only get it in tales. And what is this terrible providence you seek Sanctuary from?"

"I wish to make love to the man I will. As will your daughter, when her time comes."

"What in the Name of God is so exciting about forking that whale?"

I couldn't help it. I giggled.

He went on. "My daughter is my affair. Leave her alone. You wish to desecrate your name. You wish to put ambition aside, the birthright of Borgia, and simper over some impotent fool, 'Oooh, I lub you, Gianni, Gianni. And I lub especially your widdle peasants an' their baby fishies.' We offer you a key to a throne."

"You and *Godpapa?*"

"Yes."

"If I can't love Giovanni, I'll become a nun like my mother and Mother Fortunata. I'll be little Lucrezia's mother, since at the moment she thinks she came not from a womb, but out of your purse. It's pleasant here and the sisters are kind."

"Now you want a habit of potato sacking? The girl of golden gowns and sapphires, who could wear better still?"

"Better still?"

"You could wear one day an Imperial diadem. In such a jewel you could whore before the world and none would call you naked."

"An Imperial circlet? What are you talking about?"

"I've prepared your fate for you. Don't be a coward. Marry your fate. Be who I know my sister is, Lucrezia Borgia, sister to Cesare." He grabbed my black robe from a hook and tossed it to me. "Put this on. *Tempus fugit.*"

I felt a wave of lust overcome me. But not lust for a man's body, but for Cesare's soul, the soul of a Borgia. I felt the rush of Cleopatra, when Caesar showed her the Roman Forum. I had to ride that wave. We rushed from my cell and down the main hall on our way toward the front door, which was open, as usual. I thought of the smaller Lucrezia, but decided to leave her behind to her own fate. Abruptly Mother Fortunata drifted into the hall's gaping, night-filled archway.

She turned to face Cesare. "Where is my Lucrezia going?"

"To do the Holy Father's temporal will," he said. "We've no time for this. Charles the Frank rides here to kill us both."

She had the bell in her hand, with which to summon the monks. "Lucrezia Borgia has Sanctuary here. She goes nowhere, be it the end of the world or an apotheosis of Frenchmen."

"I am Cesare Borgia! Do you imagine my intention is to harm her?" Cesare was trembling.

Fortunata went to ring the bell. "She has Sanctuary even from archangels."

"*Sanctuary from me?*" Cesare screamed in full tantrum. "I am the Seraphim's master!"

In a single round, yet stuttering two-handed gesture he grabbed Fortunata by her wimple and slashed his gladius through her throat with a distinct clink against her spine. The warning bell dropped, making a sound like the bell on a swooning cow. Fortunata slumped to the floor, groaning as she did. From her laid-open windpipe her groan emerged in a cloud of little pink bubbles like soapy ones little Lucrezia might blow on a birthday. I had a sudden realization that each globule must contain a bit of her soul. The crystal circles would float to Heaven, where they'd burst in the Father's Face, gore-staining His White Beard and Everlasting Mustache.

"Your Apocalypse of bubbles, Mother," my brother said.

Mother's blood-washed corpse had oddly little effect on me, but I gagged like a colicky baby at the sight of her incarnadined wimple. It was so bloody, the starch had washed out of it and it appeared nothing but a red bib. The wimple was where nuns wore the stains of sin, I always imagined, when I'd been little Lucrezia's age, as if their clothing were their soul. This before me looked a sudden incarnation of my childish fantasy, sin flowing over her in red surges. Cesare pulled me, stepping in her blood, over her body and outside. I could hear monks rushing from the Monastery to give aid, but it was too late. Cesare pulled me into a pathway, where waited two saddled horses. He literally threw me into my sidesaddle. As I gripped his arms for the toss, I could feel the muscles beneath his skin, like the cords from which they suspend bridges. Cesare lashed Diana with his horsewhip, and we were at a gallop.

We traveled the road south to Rome in the moonless dark, me at first praying I'd see my niece again and wondering what she'd become by then. Where was she now? Did she know about Mother Fortunata yet? As I thought of her, I remembered that all the time we'd spent together, I'd never seen her smile. Why? I sensed she knew something little girls weren't meant by God to know. What could it be? Could it be the difference between mind and soul? Was the answer really so depressing? But she wasn't allowed to read; would she realize there *was* a difference?

Cesare was in front. Without conscious prompting from me, Diana galloped to keep up with his stallion. I was rocking crazily in my sidesaddle, both from the motion of the filly's gallop and from my lamentation, which struck me in great choking waves. Sister Fortunata had affected me like a minor order of Vanita, caressing my cheek, trying to protect me in that Convent of San Sisto, below Vanita's Subiaco. I cried for them both. I cried for myself. Everything my life meant had turned to blood and air in that gladitorial cut. Why? What could it have meant? And what did it mean that I now rode with the killer? I barely knew Fortunata, though she'd become another Vanita in my mind. Another of Saint Sebastian's lovers? What had it meant about Cesare, or Papa? To have killed a Saint. To have martyred a Virgin. Did it mean anything about myself? It had happened in Vanita's cloister; was that relevant? Why hadn't Sebastian stopped my brother? Or had Sebastian become my brother? Those are the barely rational questions that must've been moving me. But at the time my mind felt like an agonized blank. In fact, at that moment I began to feel the agglomeration of bits I'd always called "myself" being scooped from me, as if I were a gelato tub, and plopped into a feathery cone. I thought of Marsya's dying cry under Apollo's scalpel, *"Quid me mihi detrahis?"* "Why do you cut me from myself?" Or as if my center were a winged hand I was pulling from a kid glove. As Alighieri's Canto says:

> *Enter my heart and fill it with your breath*
> *As you extracted satyr Marsyas*
> *From his skin's external envelope.*

I heard a hoot and looked up. A golden-yellow owl flew above us, heading in the same direction as we. I felt as if the central part of me floated up from my lathering filly—as Fortunata had floated in bubbles—and became the owl. Athena, I thought, burst from the skull of the god-king, remembering my childhood book that Cesare'd read to me about her. She was the owl of wisdom. Or was she myself? I was wondering whether I was the wise owl, when I recalled Capetian Philip the Fair famously saying the owl was a "pretty, but otherwise dumb, useless bird." To whom was I of use? I was pretty. If pretty is as pretty does, was I better than dumb, all my library's Latin and Greek useless— *nihil prodesse*, μη χραομαι—unable to halt for the blink of a bird's eye the pointless murder of a Saint? I looked down, my blond wings beating to keep up, and saw Cesare and me below, stallion and Diana galloping toward Rome. I tried to think, but all thought, all my vain intelligence, remained as if below me within my rushing, sidesaddled body. All I was, all my owl-soul, was a certain, warm clarity. An immediate apprehension without need of ratiocination or sensation. I closed my azure eyes. "Suppose your eyes were an animal," Aristotle said. "Sight would be its soul." I'd no need to see them to know their color. Nor did I need them to follow Cesare and me underneath. Rain began to fall in a downpour—as Hesiod would say, through great, gaping "holes through the sky," Zeus' bolts arcing everywhere round us in search of mistletoe. All I heard was blasting wind and barren thunder and all I smelled was its watery fall of empty, electric scent. I experienced, I was shocked to intuit, finally the distinction between mind and soul. I slept in darkness and flew through the god-lit rain.

Dawn's rays opened my predator's eyes. We were approaching Rome. All was bright. I'd been blown dry; the rain had stopped. We entered San Giovanni's Gate, an irony not lost even to my inarticulate soul, and rode down the Via San Giovanni in Laterano to the Via Papele, over Saint Elio's Bridge, past the Castel Sant'Angelo, along the Old Borgo and into Vatican City and Square, to the Apostolic Palace, Santa Maria in Portico and the Borgia Apartments. Cesare and I dismounted, she entering the Santa Maria and he the Apostolic Palace. My soul flew about the Square for an hour, until my body reappeared on a high balcony of the Santa Maria. She turned back for a moment and tall, wobbling Penthesileia brought her a small chair. She sat, facing the Square. My owl-soul dove down, straight for her breast, its talons extended, until they sank into my heart; I'd become the "sparrow in the talons of the gryphon," and I'd returned to myself, was whole again, as far as I was cognizant.

I sat in my new wedding dress on the morning-sunny balcony and awaited Alphonso the bastard Aragon, Duke of Bisceglie, Princeling of Salerno, my affianced and soon-to-be husband. Papa'd said Alphonso was to arrive today. God willing, though the first Visigoth had worked out surprisingly well, he'd not be another fat, old one. I gazed out at the Square through the gauze of my bridal veil like the yew virgin on the table leg. For no apparent reason, I anticipated happiness.

five

I didn't hear, see nor sense in any way his approach. Not his horse's clattering hooves, nor his blue-blooded, shouting companions and young Neapolitan relatives on red stilts, not even the polyphony of trumpet and drum players and cheering crowd of a thousand or more soldiers with roaring, slugless harquebuses and fluttering banners of the House of Aragon in his wake. My Parthenogenetic owl had long since winged shyly away in the withdrawing morning's mist. I didn't perceive my Lady-in-Waiting Penthesileia gasp at first sight of him from her naturally stilted height; though I'd sensed her at some point creeping onto the balcony and standing like a Lesbian Caryatid just behind me. I sat before her amidst the debris of my wise transcendence and twiddled my thumbs. I sang to myself over and over the same three insipid bars from a lullaby my mother for some reason used to sing Roderigo. As I'd used to when four years old, I practiced crossing my eyes and wiggling my ears, talents everyone at the time had found adorable. I hadn't lost the knack. I felt like the Vatican's village idiot.

"Madam, do you think he'll want a wife or the village mooncalf?" Penthesileia muttered in disgust behind me.

The sun shone high in the sky. I could feel it on my shoulders, forehead and in my lap. Then I heard him:

"My Lady! My Lady Lucrezia!"

The sensual world exploded upon me as if I'd been a deaf and blind girl, whose portals God burst open. Sky-blue popped wide as eternity. I smelled the vast, well-wishing herd beneath me, heard the guns, drums, song and trumpets. I tasted harquebus smoke. I felt my hair float back off my face in warm puffs of air, in which I picked up whiffs of Sangiovese di Romagna, I swear, from his breath.

"My Lady!" the tenor voice came again. "Lady Lucrezia Borgia, you are for me, are you not?"

What's taking me so long to find this voice? I wondered, searching right and left. Where the Hell has he gone? Why can't I find him? And he's calling to me; he must see *me*. But the only human shapes I spotted were pigeon-shat statues. I realized I was looking for him eye-level across Saint Peter's Square. He's not midair. Look down, simpleton!

"For God's sake, Madam, will you *look down?*" Penthesileia growled. "Do you imagine him a bridegroom for birds and bees?"

I jumped out of my chair and leaned over the balcony. "God grant me a Lancelot, but if not, at least not a fatso."

I saw a man on a white stallion. To his right and just behind the man, Cesare rode his usual palomino. Cesare's horse clopped a few steps forward to come abreast. He and my brother looked up at my loggia.

"Lucrezia!" Alphonso cried.

My tongue was too thick to act its part.

Cesare leaned in his saddle to Alphonso. "Is she not, my Lord, as beautiful as I reported in Naples?"

"She is. More so than I could've imagined. The Heavenly Father must've labored on an eighth and ninth day to create such a creature."

Cesare leaned again to Alphonso. "My father always said *he* did, actually. I've always thought of her as Trojan Helen. But from experience let me say you'll do far better with her if you act as if she's rather Minerva than Aphrodite. She's always fancied herself more an intellectual than the carnal fantasy she truly is. 'If she's smart, tell her she's beautiful; if she's beautiful, tell her she's smart.' Was it Aristophanes who said that?"

Alphonso side-longed a suspicious double-take at Cesare. Then, "Lucrezia Borgia!" he shouted back to me. "I've come to rescue you!"

I remained mum, still unable to find a voice, though on wobbly legs I'd begun a sort of Corybant's mime of welcoming excitement, hopping from foot to foot, my knees buckling.

"She's notably mute. For an intellectual," he whispered to Cesare.

"You'll find you appreciate an occasional dumb moment after a while."

Together they sat their horses at the head of the partying-on mob and gazed up at me.

"Madam!" from Penthesileia, "your tongue, engage it! This is your husband. He'll not pause forever. This is no time for pantomime!"

"Your tongue, swallow it," I snapped at her, and whirled back to Alphonso. "Rescue me?" I shrieked, my voice having the timbre of a parakeet. "From whom?"

"From whatever armored Arthur has you in his thrall! From yourself. From another single hour of unhappiness!"

He put his arm around Cesare. The two centaurs grinned up at me. They took my breath away. There was Cesare, the Apollo of golden-haired, red-bearded, golden-clothed beauty. But there also was Alphonso. He wore a plum-colored velvet doublet and light-blue hose, serendipitously matching his eyes. But he looked positively the Vicar of Modesty next to Caesar. He was clean-shaven; his brunette hair slouched in an arousing wave across his forehead. He had the body of an eighteen-year-old—as had I—like a slender δισχοβολοι*, especially turning that way in his saddle. His torso turned as if a Pythagorean triangle—wide at the shoulders, narrowing to nothing at the waist—its muscles in a tight torque to hurl the disc. He was the physical perfection of all my girlish fantasies. I prayed he'd find me his analogous female. *And he was distinctly handsomer than Cesare.* We gazed up and down at each other, enraptured. All could see my whole body shaking, my braid quavering, "like a lustful Maenad's," Penthesileia said. The crowd made a great roar and screamed approval for another quarter hour. Each and every poet who was there that day, and many who were not, have used the same word to describe our reaction to one another. It's become part of my legend, the word at the turning zenith of the arc of my story: *Fulmen,* "the Thunderbolt."

Papa moved *Carnevale* up to coincide with our wedding. Balls, banquets, games, bullfights and Plautine comedies provided nonstop spectacle, entertainments and parties, of which two—Ναυμαχια, *Naumachia* or "waterfests"—were held on boats and barges, floating over the stinking moisture of the Tiber. One float carried Penthesileia, my Lady-in-Waiting, portraying Glory with *GLORIA DOMUS BORGIE†* on the float's flank. As these fests progressed, oarsmen at the barges' sterns would ply here and there to accommodate this or that partyer's desire to party with this or that other partyer in another boat. On both *Noctes aquae* or "Nights of Water" a constant school of rowboats and dinghies

---

*Greek discus-hurler, a Greco-Roman scuptural favorite.
†Glory to the House of Borgia.

with sails slid like ducklings after swans around the barges. The boats dispensed food, drink and courtesans to bachelor men, and "courtiers" to similarly spinster ladies. One barge tipped over. All the guests in the foundered yacht sank like rocks from the rocks about their necks and the instantly waterlogged mooring of party clothes. But the servants had hooks ready. They stripped, jumped into the water, swam down to the drowning, attached the hook to doublet or gown, tugged on the hook's rope, and the servants above water hoisted the person up. The staff was expert at this. I was told that at the last wedding in which Ναυμαχια had been held, less than a dozen guests had drowned, unfortunately including the bride and groom.

"My love, you must sit down in your boat, lest a breeze think your dress a sail and blow you into the drink," Alphonso said.

"No one's ever drowned in the wretched little Tiber," I replied.

"To think the other bride came all the way from the Grand Canal to drown in the wretched little Tiber," the servant who told me said.

I sat down in my rowboat and refused thereafter to move. At both land and Tiber events every Aragon or Neapolitan servant, doddering grandma, unremembered thought-dead cousin and friend or acquaintance who might have an interest in the suitability or demeanor of a prospective Duchess of the House—or even Queen, God willing—spent most of his or her partying time vetting me. How many points allowed on a Ducal Crown? The same number as a Grand Duke's? And on the Royal? Which artists were acceptable to paint portraits of children in a duke's line? Was a Dowager Duchess or the present title-holder seated first at the execution of a relative consanguine to both? I didn't mind all their questions. Being on-the-block horseflesh was a small price to pay, if the gavel's final blow were to confirm I'd be the wife, mistress, Duchess—or only broodmare, for that matter—of my Southern god. The Vatican's palaces blazed torches that lit every fabric and jewel in the world on both female and male guests. The ageless sex war at the moment looked to be fought primarily by splendid victims of tailors and jewelers. Everyone of note within two weeks' horse, and many of little or no note, came to these parties, at which I found it easy to enact my duty of plastered-on, charming smiles, since I was already more or less floating like a snowflake through each and every affair.

But the most striking things to me about the celebrations were the gifts of an artist—two artists, in this case. On the seventh evening were the formal acceptances on both families' parts of the various wedding gifts. Earlier in the day Alphonso had signed the marriage agreements in the Sistine, with Ascanio Sforza and Cesare as witnesses. Thereupon he'd accepted my dowry, 40,000 ducats in gold, an enormous, but appropriate, sum, larger than that given at my first wedding. I was happy about the sum. It would make this marriage more real, more valued and valid in the world's eyes, than my last. Tonight was reserved for the "gifts of the heart." Vast piles of jewelry, ten pounds of pearls, a pound of emeralds, furniture, plate, gold- and silverware, more exotic animals, miles of precious fabrics and finally, the pièce de résistance, a gold, emerald-haired and naked statue of Apollo from Papa and Federico, the King of Naples and the Two Sicilies, and Alphonso's grand-uncle. The Apollo had his arms wrapped snugly about a platinum, naked and yellow diamond–haired Venus, their hips boldly alloyed together in a precious metallic act of love. It was difficult to discern whether the gasps of the guests resulted from the richness of the pair—three feet tall and weighing nearly a ton with a thousand carats of stones—or their unseemly, yet divine, encounter.

"*We* paid for the Apollo. He's solid gold." Papa stood from his raised throne to quiet everyone. "The Venus comes from Our brother Naples. He purchased the platinum."

Everyone aahed and applauded.

"And the amalgamation?" Cesare cried. "By whom was that done?"

Alphonso knelt on one knee and ran his beautiful hand slowly down the Venus' breast, flank and down her leg. I swear, I felt his fingers over my own breast, down my side and along the inside of my thigh. I shivered again.

He looked at me. "Lucrezia and I shall be the amalgam."

Everyone oohed pleasure and applauded once more. Alphonso stood; the time I'd been anticipating had arrived. He was to present his personal gift to me, as when my fat Giovanni had presented me with a silver coin with the face of Herod Antipas, said to be one of the original "thirty pieces of silver." What might Alphonso's be? How "personal"? My gift to him had been a Arabian vial of precious, myrrh-scented oil, which I trusted was sufficiently suggestive of the manipulation his body would enjoy, part by lubricious part, under my hands. I hoped for the maximum of intimacy from his also, maybe a scanty item of spun-gold lingerie to hug my breasts or a belt I'd seen of a tiny golden chain with a diamond or emerald every inch, to be worn about a bride's waist that she might still sparkle when otherwise stripped by the bridegroom.

Alphonso stood. He was on the steps to Papa's throne, just below him, just as I'd so many times seen my brother. He motioned to four men at the back of the room. They walked forward, two each carrying two richly framed paintings, each about three feet by four feet. They carried them to Alphonso, who motioned them to place them on the throne's steps, below the Pope, facing outward. They were life-size portraits. I turned gelid as their gazes struck me. These two stunned me the way an artist's evident genius would again and again in my life. I'd seen hundreds of impressive portraits, many in our Borgia Apartments. Just above me then on the wall was another miraculous portrait of myself in mural, *The Arts of the Trivium*, by Master Pinturicchio. I'd sat for the enthroned central "Rhetoric." But these two smaller ones from Alphonso stopped me cold. They were old, without as much color or chiaroscuro as is used now in the strictly modern style. Initially I thought the first one was Alphonso, until I met its gaze more closely. It was a picture of a young Lord, his brown hair long to just below the ear, just as Alphonso's. His face, the color of ancient, variegated ivory, had a sadness beyond terrestrial imagination. His nose was prominent and straight, almost Classical, lips pink with life, his eyes of deep, calm brown, all as Alphonso. But unlike the living man above me, these eyes were filled with remnants of some sublime agony, more like Papa's onlooking eyes behind them. This image looked to be of a man who'd mislaid his future and retained only a dead past. He held in his slim hands a hammer and delicately a gold ring with a single ruby. He wore a purple tunic, so dark it was nearly black, a chain of gold around his neckline. He was one of the most beautiful men I'd ever seen. As beautiful as my soon-to-be Lord's twin.

"Who is this man?" I asked.

Federico stepped forward, old, yet straight as a sword. "He's Our grandfather and Alphonso's great-great-grandfather," the King said.

"It was painted from life by Rogier van der Weyden a century ago," Alphonso went on. "His name was Francesco of Aragon. He was a great man, but only in ways troubadours once called a man great."

"Van der Weyden had the gift of the brush," I said. "Why does Francesco look like that?"

"Like what?"

"So sad. So empty, or filled with sorrow's emptiness. What's that ring on his hand? What's the hammer?"

"The ring belonged to my great-great-grandmother. He gave it to her on their wedding day. When this portrait was still wet, she'd recently died giving birth to Francesco's only son, my great-grandfather. Great-great-grandpapa built a tomb of marble and silver for her on the rim of Vesuvius' cauldron, where sulfurous smoke turned it Tartarus-black in a week. Stories say, every morning for thirteen years he'd climb on horseback to her tomb and pray alternately to the Virgin and to Hades for her return to life. A blasphemy, to be sure. When her coffin had been first placed in the tomb, it'd been nailed shut by undertakers, as usual. The hammer in his hand—you can see how big its claw is in the picture—supposedly is the one he took to the tomb to pry her coffin's nails loose, in case she awakened in panic. Many holy men, some of whom the Church has since declared Saints, as well as Archbishops and Cardinals, came to the mountain to pry him from his gloomy devotions, but all failed. Each morning for the thirteen years he'd climb alone the tomb's mount, only to return alone at dusk. Some of the more ignorant even went so far as to spread rumors of him engaging in pernicious, forbidden rites up there, trying to raise her dead soul and body from the grave with Satan's help."

I turned to the other portrait. "And this girl? Is this your great-great-grandmother?"

"No," Alphonso whispered. "No one knows who this girl truly was."

A sweetly striking ingenue confronted me, maybe sixteen years old, and dressed in a fashion long past. Her skin, unlike Francesco's, was as white and monochrome as the newest snow. Her face was rounder than his, with a high forehead and smoothly curved as an egg, as if no thoughts but ghostly ones could hatch inside. Her inklike hair was wrapped entirely on top of her head and covered with a black, tall cap, which cinched below her chin with black cloth. Her nose was small, the cleft chin weak and a touch receding, though pretty in a girlish way, as if it might've snuggly fit into a Dutchman's tulip. Around her neck sparkled a tripartite gold necklace, inlaid with black diamonds of a type unknown to me. I've never seen such stones in the real world. The skin of her neck and upper bosom was as unblemished white as her face. She wore a black dress with a collar. The preponderance of black in her picture was further testimony, if any were needed, of the painter's skill, since several have since told me that black, so superficially simple, is by far the most difficult pigment to master. Her cautious glance was sidelong, as if peering around Purgatory's black corner for a centuries-expected lover, as former paramours are condemned to do there. Her eyes glowed as darkly raven as her necklace's stones, with a scarcely earthly light.

"She looks like a creature only partly of this world," I said.

"She does look like a pale Lucrezia," breathed Alphonso.

"Thank you, my Lord. That's the finest compliment I've ever received."

"But nothing compared to the ones you'll get tomorrow night at the 'Visigoths Ceremony,' " chuckled Cesare.

"Cesare, don't be a boor," Papa said with a frowning glance, but plainly anticipatory of a tantrum.

But Cesare smiled, pleased with himself.

Alphonso continued, "The story goes that one smoky Easter morning Great-great-grandpapa Francesco was kneeling alone in prayer before the black tomb, as usual, when he looked up from his sorrow to find a nude girl, one he'd never seen before, standing above him on Great-great-grandmama's tomb, and framed by a looming corona of erupting fire. She was crown-to-foot wet with condensate that ran in blackish rivulets from her body. He'd always say her naked skin struck him as not immodest, but the natural fashion of a well-clothed *diabola*. No one knows what was said between them, or if anything was said. The legend is that the rest of her days she spoke not a single word. He wrapped her in his tunic and they walked down the mountain together, making love for the first time in a field of red blossoms near its base. He never returned another morning to the cauldron's edge, until the day he was put into the black tomb himself. He never married the girl, of course, because he'd taken an oath never to take another bride. But this girl came home with him, his companion of days and nights. She never seemed to age a day the rest of Francesco's brief life, only to vanish to God knows where the same day Francesco was himself entombed finally beside Great-great-grandmama. Moments after the funeral party left, Vesuvius belched, and tomb and contents vanished, evidently vaporized. Francesco's son, my great-grandfather, sent knights with this picture and a hundred-weight of gold for any news of her all over Italy, all over Europe. This picture was painted from life, or from whatever state this girl truly existed in, by the great bygone Master Petrus Christus."

I was as deeply in love as ever I'd be capable of. As any Borgia would ever be capable of; quite a lot, I knew, remembering Vanita and Papa.

As I went to sleep that night, I thought about Alphonso. His romance about his great-great-grandparents and the fairy-tale girl had struck me hard. I was moved that any man with such a blazing and virile exterior could speak with such feeling about an event so erstwhile and potentially sappy. I was unused to this. It was certainly unlike Papa. It was utterly unlike anything Cesare, who hardly lacked the imagination or rhetoric, could even dream of saying. It was even unlike sweet Giovanni, whom the story would've enraptured and who would've told it eagerly, but also would've concentrated far more on the history—with a long quote from Pliny's Pompeii letter, no doubt—and science of the long-ago events. Alphonso'd fixated on the people and their interior atmospheres. And he'd resisted defining or limiting these atmospheres for them or for me, but rather had opened them out for our imaginations to work on—the dead and the alive—like an artist, who imagines us the interior mask by depicting the exterior.

But was any of the art true? Or was Francesco's legend no more than a tale Alphonso'd heard from old Neapolitan wives? The King hadn't thought so. Or had he learned it, as his grandson had, as all families learn family mythology?

In the days before my wedding I thought about all that had happened to me in so short a time. I'd also begun to wonder, as foolish, overreligious young girls will, whether this happiness of mine might be a sin. I kept asking the Virgin, in dreams and otherwise, if such a sudden love for a second man—however strongly I trembled at the thought of his touch and however virginal the Sacred College might proclaim me at the moment—if this second love wasn't tainted with corruption and evil, especially when I thought of Giovanni's face, dissolving into his Adriatic mist, as he so bitterly waved me good-bye. It simply had to be sinful, didn't it, to cause so good a man as Pesaro such misery? After the second Ναυμαχια, the one during which the barge sank, these notions became an obsessive sequence of water buckets that I was throwing on my passion's wildfire. Giovanni's lovely face was a constant accusation in front of me. But listen for the Holy Mother's voice and pray to her though I might, I couldn't hear her answer inside, not even in Alphonso's usually inspiriting stories. This inner silence made me all the more unsure and desperate for an answer; even one I didn't want to hear. I knew the only way to get hold of a definitive reply was to confess, to bare myself completely and intimately in the little coffin. I decided to go do to the Sacrament immediately.

John Faunce

I went to my Holy Father's morning confessional, which he still held in the Sistine from time to time. Even the Pope is a priest, and not too grand to hear the confession of a soul in pain, no matter how humble or seemingly unimportant. I pulled aside the heavy maroon curtain, went inside, knelt and waited, listening to Papa's drone of penance and forgiveness to the previous particularly naughty sinner. My little window-grate slid open. I could see the outline in the shadows of Papa's white-laced beard, his white skullcap, glints of teeth and of Peter's Ring.

"Bless me, Father, for I, a child of Eve, have sinned, as have all her children." I began purposely in the old style, hoping to bring his old life to his mind. "It's at least a year since my last confession."

"Lucrezia—?"

"Papa, please," I cut him off. "Let's be just souls here without names. Let's you and I be truth-tellers in the Sacrament, not Papa and Lucrezia."

"Agreed."

"Promise me. Swear it on the Blood of the Savior that the Virgin washed from His Wounds with her hands."

I had to be absolutely certain. I had to know there'd be no agenda, even in *pectore*, that Papa might let skew his answers in favor of statecraft. I remembered his oath from my childhood, the most terrifying and strongest. No one, no Christian, nor even Judas himself, I imagined, could possibly break it.

He looked at me gravely. He frowned. "That serious?"

"Yes."

"We were sure this husband would be handsome enough for you. For God's sake, Lucrezia, he's so good-looking, I'd almost consider sleeping with him myself."

"He's magnificent as Lancelot; but that may be part of the matter."

He paused momentarily, evidently to allow implications to swirl around in his head. "Then I swear, child."

All right, then. "Father, is it damnable to love two men?"

I could hear the drip of Pascal candle, murmurs of previously confessed sinners. I saw a smile, a somewhat relieved one, come finally over his face.

"No, Lucrezia," he said. "It's damnable at the same time to *express* love to two men. . . . Which two loves, by the way?"

"No Lucrezia Papa, you swore."

"*Mea culpa*. Continue."

"My father and brother gave me in marriage to a man I hated, but came to love. I didn't think I could love another. But I was wrong. It happened so fast. I've known this second only a few days. Is that a sin? Is his beauty blinding me to my sin?"

"Oh . . . I thought before you might mean Cesare."

"Papa! What are you saying?"

"Nothing. Papa's stupid mistake." He thought a moment. "Why did you love the first man?"

"Because he was sweet and kind . . . and because my father and brother commanded me."

"And why the second? Didn't they also command this one?"

"Because my blood sings when he walks into a room. When I hear his voice or think of him."

"And do you know what a song like that signifies?"

"What, Father?"

Papa looked straight at me through the skeletal grate, a stab of sunlight striking his lips from a moth hole in the curtain. "It means this second is the Virgin's gift. She gives her gift, if at all, once in a lifetime. It *is* a sin to refuse the Mother of God. Take it."

This was precisely what I wanted to hear a priest say. But that, it hit me forcefully, was a perfect cover for it to be a lie. "Truly, Papa? You know God. You and He occupy the same Being, so to say. Is that God's true answer?"

"It's mine, anyway. Let God just this once speak for Himself, if He wants." His smile faded entirely. "It happened to me. The Virgin gave me once such a gift. I squandered her to gain a white cassock. The result is, I'm now His man, who walks damned in a pair of fisherman's shoes."

It had been true. As I looked at Papa's face, my heart cracked for him. It must've been true, the love I'd sensed between them when I was a child. I thought it right that here, in God's Sacrament, and now, just as his lost happiness was to devolve on me, had been the place and moment Papa could bring himself to reveal such a thing about himself to his daughter. He blessed me and began to buzz again the rite of forgiveness. As he did, Giovanni's precious face began to turn ghostly in my mind—like Francesco's sprite's must've once passed to spirit long ago, though a certain love of my rotund Lord will abide in me forever. Many have called Papa a great liar; he's often lied to me with painful consequence. But if I put all the deceits

of his lifetime in my heart's balance with his words during this one brief
confessional—so painful to him—then the scale tips so violently that all his
evils fly up to Heaven. Whatever Papa might thereafter do or acquiesce to,
even his fantasy about Cesare and me, no matter how horrible its effect,
without his surpassing wisdom and gentleness that confessing day I
might've never had what time with Alphonso I did. Or at the least we
would've spent it under a corrosive trickle of my doubts. I wouldn't trade
Alphonso's and my perfect time together for anything, not for Vanita's arms
around me again, not for a billion centuries in Paradise. As I knelt there, the
in-sewn jewels of my gown penitentially gouging into my knees, I couldn't
think of any words of Christ's that contained more love or simple, human
insight than my father's about the fisherman, damned on the earth, had just
had for me. Blasphemy to write, but I know it's true and I'm a truly blasphemous woman, anyway. Still in the booth, I talked to him about the portraits. There was something, I felt, otherworldly, even about the multi-
leveled paint of them, and I wanted to know, were they a bad omen?

"Did Francesco really pray on Vesuvius to the Lord of Darkness?" Papa
smiled.

"No, Papa. That was only rumor, started by the superstitious ignorant.
The young man's face I saw was a Saint's icon."

"Then the girl must've been a Holy Gift to Francesco, as this Alphonso
will be to you. What have I just told you about such gifts?"

And within days, July 28, 1498, yet again those background nuns chanting
away about virginity, hair shirts and the Beatific Vision, I strode through the
Borgia Apartments to the Hall of Divine Mysteries, toward an Altar with its
forest of lit, skin-tone shafts for a ceremony, whose unsaid purpose was to
sanctify lust. I wore another wedding gown, this one purplish blue with
creme accents. Saffron-colored diamonds covered it to such an extent, the
Camerlengo mumbled that I looked "like the night sky, rising toward bliss."
Behind me streamed my blue-and-white ermine hundred-foot train, borne
by the customary dozen virgins. Un-re-created ones, I think.

The Camerlengo once again escorted me to the altar and Papa. "There
you are, my noble young pus—"

"Thank you, Eminence, that will do," Papa cut him off.

I stepped into my place. Papa raised his arms, rolling his eyes at the Camerlengo's senile near-malaprop. The Pope began a Nuptial Mass. Cesare, naturally, was once again the witness. I remember at that Mass Papa leaning over his golden jeweled chalice at the sacred moment he was to turn the Merlot into the Blood of God. I wondered what it would've been like to wash my hands in this New Blood, as the Virgin had long ago in the Old. Would this red liquor cleanse my hands, or incarnadine them forever? I wondered if even the Holy Mother had remained a virgin after such a washing. Papa spoke directly into his chalice, first into the wine, then, as it transubstantiated, into the Blood. *"Hic est enim Calyx Sanguines Mei . . . ,"* he said. "For This is the Cup of My Blood." The servers rang their chiming bells and for a moment the fearsome bells of childhood turned to a sound of bliss. I remember Papa's phrase, the carillon lifting it up. I hear the words and angelus still, as if he's saying it still, as if they're being rung in the next room. They harmonize with his election bells. God's cursed me with a bell-filled spirit. Papa finally said, ". . . And by the Power vested in Us by God, We declare you one body, one soul. What Christ has forever bonded, no man shall part, save under dread penalty of Our eternal curse."

Alphonso grabbed me up in his arms and kissed me. With the touch, taste and cherry scent of his mouth on my own, a memory of Vanita ravished me, so strong a memory, I swear I smelled a whiff of Arabian perfume. Or was it the new Arabian oil? The scents were the same. Why did God bind our senses of scent and taste so much more tightly together than our other senses with our memory, like a vellum binding around a book of vellum pages? There must be a Divine Reason, hidden from us. But the Arabian lasted only a heartbeat, during which time halted in its long walk. Our tongues enwrapped each other's. Papa, the King of the Two Sicilies, and even Cesare began to chuckle together at our happiness. I remembered the great laugh of Papa's coronation. I looked at the ring Alphonso had placed on my finger. A gold band with a single ruby teardrop, like in the portrait. His great-great-grandfather's ring, or one identical. I'd become the Duchess of Bisceglie. I was to love my Italian god's body. The Laws of the Creator of the Universe had been diddled with to reaccommodate my lust and destiny. Borgia will had greased my rebirth.

In the same courtyard in which I'd consummated my wedding with Giovanni, another took place that evening for Alphonso and me. First there was a dinner, which Cesare had decreed a dish-for-dish renaissance of the great dinner at the 40 B.C. wedding feast of Anthony and Octavia, Augustus' sister. A meal from Cesare's dream-life, I couldn't help but think. He'd issued an order to the Vatican that he was to be in charge of all wedding plans. He was always fabulous at parties; I didn't argue. In fact, that ancient day Anthony and Octavia'd shared two menus, as we did, one for men, one for women:

Men's Menu

GUSTUM (A TASTE)
Beets with mustard
& Mixed shellfish salad
with Cumin sauce

MENSA PRIMA (1ST TABLE)
Pork stew with apples

Swan skin stuffed with forcemeats

MENSA SECUNDA (2ND TABLE)
Pineapple fruits
& flavored ices

VINI (WINES)
White: Ischia, Frascati
& Lacrima Christi

Ladies' Menu

GUSTUM
Fried anchovy patina
& Seasoned Melon

MENSA PRIMA
Stuffed pigeons

Herbal bread & cheese

Squid stuffed with veal brains

MENSA SECUNDA
Figs and bananas

VINI (WINES)
Red: Barolo, Gattinara
& Port

A Classical alphabet of Roman foods. The Ladies' Menu consisted of foods the ancients thought especially conducive to conception. All the utensils and settings were set according to *On Conviviality* by Giovanni Pontano in imitation of *Dido's Suicide Banquet*. I thought each dish tasted spicily of Alphonso's name, and couldn't get enough. I felt myself under Subiaco's table once more, love's aromas in the air. I'd become the Canaan bride at last. The air danced also with a million-noted snowfall of the motets of Josquin Des Prez, whom Cesare'd borrowed from Ascanio Cardinal Sforza, with all his up-to-date homophonies and cadenzas of polyphonies. I asked Master Des Prez how I could duplicate his music in future in Bisceglie, and he gave me three "scores," he called them, newly printed in Venice by Petrucci.

"Music is as readily put to paper today as poetry, my Lady," he told me.

Contrapuntal blizzards of oval dots. Why hadn't the Greeks such writing?

"The ovals are the sounds, my Lady. There are now whole books of such dots."

If more harmonious, at least the meal was smaller than it'd been for the hungry Giovanni, but there were still more than a thousand of each meal— mainly the stuffed swan skins and invulnerable cuttlefish that most found too frightening to eat—plus a dozen tuns of wines and a portly bear, cooked in its own skin, left over to cram and inebriate to vomiting and passing out the crowd in the Square. In any case, the same bejeweled guests ate it, plus the glittering Neapolitan suite—though the House of Aragon looked drunker than had the Sforza. The same entertainers and servants, same spectrum of churchmen. The same din. After dinner, the same three progressively drunker hours of port and Christ's saccharine tears.

"Lords, Ladies, it is time!" Pierrot finally squawked, running exactly as before through the throng. "Odysseus is come, girt for spoil, with his towering horse to breach the Trojan wall!"

Breach the Trojan wall? I thought. My chubby Adriatic Lord had long since battering-rammed every brick to smithereens. But everyone made again the mad Virgin-Visigoth dash toward the hall in which I waited, public testimony to my miraculously revirginated body. But miracles are never as the mob expects them to be and I wasn't stark naked, thank God for great favors. I stood in my diamond-encrusted gown and long train before the satin-draped catafalque, on which during the last such social occasion I'd endured such a clammy congress. Alphonso stood next to me.

As the guests surrounded us, I could hear their gasps and hundreds of whispers. "What is going on? . . . This is a scandal. . . . This marriage will never last. . . . And they looked so happy. . . ." And on and on in similar vein.

When the crowd noise began to subside, Alphonso raised his arm. "Lords and Ladies, all our guests," he shouted. Silence replaced the room's remaining whisperings, as if we were about to announce a death. "There will be no 'piercing of the virginity' this evening, at least not a public one." Scandalized hubbub filled the hall and courtyard. "It's a stupid custom, brought to Italy by invaders from loveless, cold lands without imagination. It's past time we end it." I'd composed that sentence for him; I'd stolen and edited most of it from a speech of Medea to Jason, by Seneca. Now more hubbub, this time confused and alarmed. "Also, I've learned it may cause my Lady embarrassment."

Shouts of "No! . . . Who does she think she is? . . . Introverted pervert!" Followed by still more hubbub, but changing gradually its character, beginning to sound even approving.

"In hopes you'll be satisfied of our love, however . . . ," I announced.

I took Alphonso in my arms and kissed him long and hard, his usual tastes and smells flowing into me as well as another momentary hint of Arabian. As we kissed, I hurled my flowers toward the mob, because it just felt the natural thing to do. A short, baby-fatty girl, fourteen or so, with black hair, in a forest-green dress, leapt into the air, snatched my flowers and held them aloft in triumph. The crowd cheered and clapped approval. If Giovanni had had a fourteen-year-old sister, she might've looked like this girl.

"Odysseus of the many wiles penetrates the Trojan wall with a mere kiss!" Pierrot shouted. "Cassandra accepts him with a flower's toss to a hoping virgin! A new custom!"

And that was the beginning of that. Pierrot kicked his heels in the air and rang his bells; our party recommenced. The feast finished with three masques on the subject of "The Apotheoses of Apollo and Aphrodite," supposedly representing Alphonso and me. They were prurient and delightful.

I'd wanted desperately to "honeymoon," this time with Alphonso. But part of the marriage contract he'd signed stipulated that we'd live solely in "Rome or its environs" for at least two years, so Papa could retain Alphonso's person, if necessary, as a hostage. Or as he explained it, "We can't bear to be without Our sweet girl again for a while. It would kill Us to lose you."

"But Papa—"

"Humor your papa. Remember Juan. Save Our life. We'll die if you leave."

"Just to Naples?"

"Naples is a cesspool. Enemies are everywhere. We will not risk you."

So a honeymoon was out.

I'd stayed as far away from Cesare as I could all during the prewedding festivities, the murder of Fortunata weighing horribly on my mind. For a while, anyway. But from the time Alphonso appeared beneath the balcony, arm in arm with Cesare as if conjoined twin brothers, it became increasingly difficult. And from the moment he'd met him, Alphonso *loved* Cesare. Every moment he wasn't with me, he was toadying up to Cesare. They were a natural fit. Both gorgeous. Both lusted after by all the women. Both swordsmen, horsemen and generally athletic. The same class, same sex. Similar physiques and turns of mind. Alphonso, of course, was nowhere near so overeducated a "humanist" as Cesare, but he did love that in others, especially my brother—and, I hoped, one day in me—always digging at Cesare, Papa or any of the well-known humanists at the Papal Court to spin him stories from Virgil. He also adored the Spartan injunction "With it or on it." He was a complete sucker, on the other hand, for Socrates' death scene with the self-knower's last words, "When the poison reaches the heart, that is the end." Alphonso burst into tears each time he heard it. So Cesare would recite for him the last two death-scene pages of the *Phaedo*, ad nauseum. After a week of my beautiful man going on and on about what a "Titan of kindness and intellect" Cesare was, and Papa cooing about how they'd become "Heaven's new Gemini," I found my anger at Cesare losing its courage, especially when I thought of Alphonso's possible reaction to my feelings. Any feelings, in fact, unfit to tell my husband I now thought unfit to have at all.

Cesare had come to us at the wedding feast during the figs and bananas. His softly placed hand felt warm and loving on my shoulder, massaging my party-stiff neck beneath my jewels. I remember at that moment wondering whether, after all, he'd been right in what he'd done. Or had he done it for me? I was certain he'd killed many enemies in his short life, for Papa or, unbeknownst, for me.

His hand on my shoulder, "Sister, I've arranged for your honeymoon."

"We can't honeymoon," I replied, chomping on my I hoped fecundating banana.

"I've sworn—" Alphonso started to add.

"Regardless, I've arranged one in detail, which I promise will conflict with no oath or contract. The two of you leave this evening, after the Visigoth ceremony. I've arranged a horse and carriage for you, sister, and a chariot for your husband.

"A chariot?" Alphonso asked.

"Most apropos, as you'll find out. Have you ever driven one, brother?"

"No."

"It goes just like a one-horse carriage, but you stand. It's very Classical. Very Trojan. You'll be Aeneas."

"That sounds like *ludus*."

"Good, brother. 'Fun' indeed. We'll make a Virgil scholar of you yet. It will be. I've arranged, as well, gorgeously romantic lodgings for you tonight, sixteen miles northeast of Rome."

"Sixteen miles?"

"Still technically *'sub urbe Romae'*—the Roman undercity, and well within the environs."

"As defined by?" I asked.

"Emperor Hadrian, who loved fixing boundaries."

"He'll do," I said. "How will we know how to get to the right place?"

"I've had road signs laid out. Follow the ones in Latin."

"Cesare, this is unexpectedly sweet of you." I looked at him. "Especially considering."

"And I'm honored to have a new brother so kind and considerate," Alphonso said, eyes awash in sentiment. "On to love in a chariot, like Aeneas. Thank you forever, brother."

"Considering what?" Cesare said with a grin, and turned back to Alphonso. "Don't thank me yet. You'll do so doubly in the morning, after a night's worth of Paradise."

Hours later found us on the road northeast, after saying good-bye to Papa, who wept as if we were on our way to Erebus, and farewell to the remains of the parties in Palace and Square. The one in the Square was much livelier, with drunks on stilts, bonfires and lewd, omnivorous sex. Alphonso indeed drove his chariot like an Aeneas. He loved it, constantly whipping the horse into charging off into the night like a loony Trojan into an Argive Circus. We kept coming on signs, as Cesare'd promised, giving the direction and distance we were to go on to our wedding-night destination. A dizzying array of charcoal-gray birds accompanied us all the way. They were tiny, smaller than my tiny fist. In the dark and chaos of wings I couldn't actually see any individual bird, but I could hear them, both wings and little cheeps, as they'd buzz by my head. The wings sounded like little scraps of vellum, rustling wildly in the breeze next to my ears, making the full-mooned night sound as if it were filled with the souls of abandoned babies. I prayed I might rescue one of those souls later tonight, and conceive a child. After fifteen miles Cesare's signs increased in frequency to a sign every fifty or so feet. We came upon a wood, and the road entered it.

"I think we've gone about sixteen miles," Alphonso said. "Maybe this is the entrance to where we're going."

"God knows. Or maybe Dante. You haven't seen a pale man in a hooded cloak, have you?"

"No. Who might that be?"

"Virgil."

There were no trees exactly, but rather a stand of giant shrubs with a clearly defined entrance-passage. We rode in. The passage between the hedge plants was so wide, the two of us could ride abreast. The shrub bery hallway went on for a hundred yards or so in a straight line, then made a turn. I knew from the myth of the Minotaur, always in a maze at least be consistent; we'd little choice, having brought no ball of string to trail behind us. So we went consistently left.

"The direction of the heart," I said.

For an hour we rambled through the labyrinth. Once we'd gone in, the signs had disappeared. I kept reminding myself that this was my wedding night. I should be making love to my husband by now, rubbing him with that oil. I reminded myself that I'd lost Giovanni supposedly for his failure to make love to me. I'd cut my throat if I lost Alphonso for the same reason, and again through no fault of my husband's. Why am I wasting a wedding night in this pointless puzzle?

Our horses were nervous, panicked by the end, prancing our vehicles in circles and pawing and kicking the ground and bushes or ripping at them with their teeth. Alphonso's appeared to me as if no longer a horse, though I knew it still must be, but like Laura's ghost-white hart, and he said mine looked the same to him. We had to keep struggling to keep them on track, assuming there was a track. Alphonso would hack at the branches with his sword, trying to cut a way out, but the bushes were far too thick to cut with a sword. As he hacked, the birds rose up out of harm's way like swarms of giant wasps, and he'd shout out, whacking them madly from his face and striking out at them with the blade.

The birds never left us. They'd settle in extensive clumps on the branches of the bushes around us, with a cheeping noise no longer like weeping infants, but a million newborns in Hell.

Thank God the birds lacked interest in me, even when I'd try to horsewhip them off Alphonso. But Ariadne's left-hand consistency blessed us. Finally we emerged through a leafy archway just like the one through which we'd entered. Behind us, the birds lofted up in a screech-ing swarm that for a moment eclipsed the moon. Together they made a sound like a lone soprano dragon. Alphonso and I cried out in fear and the horses bucked and whinnied, mouths bloody and sides streaming sweat. As we came out, an arrow-sign pointed down a low hillside, and we descended in a rush, both of us whooping freedom, to pull up when the slope flattened out. We'd wheeled onto a flagstone patio around a large pond or concrete pool. Around the patio were moon-shadowy statues of the dozen Olympian gods, interspersed with top-lit oak trees. It was dead quiet.

"Oh, thank you, Cesare! This is just the perfect honeymoon spot!" I shouted.

"It's more like something with Saint George from *The Golden Legend.*"

"You read that, too?"

"They read it to me. Where are we?"

"I recognize this place."

"I don't."

"Papa took me here once a long time ago, with Cesare. . . . We're at Tivoli, the summer palace built by Hadrian."

We could see looming palace walls all around us.

"Now what?"

We looked, but saw not a clue what we might to do next.

"Well, it's our wedding night," I said, trying my damnedest to turn my voice seductive, but it came out an appalled squeak.

"We're to make love here?" Alphonso squeaked in reply. "It's freezing."

"Evidently any warmth is to be generated by our intensity of friction. I'll skip the oil."

Alphonso giggled. So much for seductiveness. Then I saw the Guardian. Leaning against the largest oak was what looked like an ancient Roman Legionnaire. Even by the colorless moon I could tell he was all in gold. Breastplate, greaves, sandals, wrist-guards, cloth-of-gold skirt, cape and a golden helmet with palomino crest. But the helmet wasn't exactly Roman. It was Tarquin- or gladiator-style, so its gold closed doors hid his face. Of the face I saw only the eyes behind olive-shaped holes. "Who are you?"

The figure didn't answer.

"Who or what the hell are you, sir?" Alphonso shouted, drawing his sword. But his shout wasn't quite steady.

The Guardian drew a steel-bladed sword with gold hilt. "I'm the Guardian of the Golden Bough."

"Is that a fact?" barked Alphonso. "What the hell's that supposed to mean, if you don't mind?"

Crying birds still buzzed far above us.

"You're both dead. This is the Elysian Fields—"

"Well, that's a relief."

"—but you must fight me to the death before you may enjoy it." The voice came out with an echo, sounding like someone inside a helmet trying to disguise his voice. Badly. And there was that gold outfit. Who did we know that dressed in that kind of thing?

"It sounds very Etruscan," I whispered.

"Tuscan?" from my husband. "Are the Medici behind this?"

"Etruscan. None of this strikes me as if accountants did it."

"Why do I have to fight this Etruscan to the death?"

"He's not Etruscan. He's—"

"It's the ritual. That's just how it's written." The figure paused, the helmet tilted, as if trying to remember something.

"Cesare?" I said. "Is that you? If this is your little joke, I'll fight you to the death myself."

"He who tries to steal the Golden Bough must die by my hand and forgo Paradise," the Guardian said.

Alphonse glanced sidelong at him. "Didn't you just say we were already dead?"

"Oh, yes. But in myths the rules are very complicated."

Alphonso lashed the horse with his reins. Horse, chariot and charioteer launched toward tree and Guardian.

"Alphonso!" I cried. He was taking this seriously, and I was by now convinced it was only Cesare, pulling a little joke on me from *The Golden Legend*.

The "Legionnaire" panicked. He picked up his shield and held it up in front of him, but quickly realizing that would be feckless against two thousand pounds of rushing attack, he dropped it and looked madly about through his olive-holes. The oak was big; he ran around it to the opposite side, evidently hoping Alphonso would crash into the trunk. But instead he expertly steered horse and car to follow. Chased and chaser careened three times around the massive shaft, everyone yelling and the Guardian trying to stab at Alphonso behind him, but instead sticking ineffectually at the trunk with his sword. Alphonso kept swinging at the Guardian, but also kept missing, and would chop at the poor oak likewise, hacking off the sporadic golden bough. At last they stopped opposite each other at more or less the same time, both from exhaustion and because they must've realized how ludicrous they looked.

Uncontrollable giggles kept Alphonso from catching his breath.

The Guardian looked at us in a perfect mime of faceless, offended confusion. He sheathed his sword. "This is not at all how this is supposed to go. This ritual is hardly meant to be an exercise in making fools of each other. Haven't you read Virgil?"

That was definitely Cesare.

"Yes, *Cesare*. I have read Virgil," I said. "And I don't remember any farce scenes."

"Well . . . never mind. You ruined it." He reached down and picked up two twigs of yellowy leaves from a green, whacked-off branch of oak. He walked over to us and gave each of us a twig.

"Mistletoe?" Alphonso asked.

"The Golden Bough," I clarified from Virgil. "Jupiter's living fire from the sky."

"Come with me." And the Guardian strode in a snit across the patio, toward the dark ruin of the palace. "Follow!"

"What about the horses?"

"Sylphs will take care of them," he called back.

" 'Sylphs'?" asked Alphonso. "What are sylphs?"

"Little soulless demigods," I explained.

"I knew that. They're in Virgil, right?"

"Wrong!" exclaimed the Guardian, disappearing into the palace's arching maw. "Lucrezia, if that boy's to be a Borgia, educate him!"

"I'll educate *you*, brother," Alphonso cried after him. "Today was this woman's wedding day!"

We trotted after him into Hadrian's great villa of brick and gloom. Pitch-black ate us. There weren't windows or exterior arches; all lightless as Hades. I thought of my old Giovanni on that first day, as the only way to follow the Guardian was by his clanking.

"Not another labyrinth," I said.

"The darkness didn't last long, but turned only a hundred or so yards on into a bath of cozy candle- and torchlights from new chandeliers along the ceiling and sconces on the walls, as well as an ooze of glorious heat, feeling as if it were waterfalling up from the floor. The Guardian came to a large arch in the stone to our left.

We turned at the archway and followed him. The first thing I remember then was my eyes hurting and involuntarily closing the way they would at a sunrise unexpectedly glaring through a window. The hundred or so flames in the hallway had been replaced by several thousand that burnt in a tremendous chamber of luxury under a fifty-foot ceiling, its silvery chandelier with a hundred candles descending to eight or ten feet above the floor, upon which rested the central and defining element, a tremendous silk-, satin- and cloth-of-gold-covered bed. It had pillows on it the size of ten-year-olds, and corner-posts, like Odysseus and Penelope's bed, made of live oak trees, their crowns laced with lightning-colored mistletoe.

"This was the imperial bedchamber," announced the Guardian. He lifted his hand, and string music began to dance through the room from God knew where. He then motioned us to the bed, where we sat, wondering what next. He picked up two ewers, containing two golden liquids, walked over to us and poured them both into two Venetian-crystal goblets on the silver table next to us. "This is your 'honeymoon,' Lady?"

I knew that question. It was Saint George's to Guinevere, as she awaits Arthur on their wedding night, from *The Golden Legend*. So I gave Guinevere's response. "It's said."

Cesare continued the fairy-book dialogue. "I wonder if you appreciate what you say?"

As did I. "What do you signify, sir?"

As did he. "These pitchers contain the origin of honeymoons. You see, as I pour this one, it's honey. Honey of clovers and orange trees from Hadrian's—" in the *Legend* it'd been simply "Caesars"—"labyrinth." He continued from the book. "Now I add white wine, the sun's gift of itself, creating a sweet liquor. This liquor you both are to drink each day for one month, or lunar cycle, symbolizing the sweetest days of your lives together. The *'honey* for a *moon.'* "

"Where does that legend come from?"

"From mists of time." That concluded the *Legend*'s scene. "And it's no legend. Try it. Drink."

I did, and it was the most satisfyingly delicious thing I'd ever tasted. It had a flavor close to a sauterne, but with a chthonic, overflowing undertone, like a great Rhenish wine, but cloyless. Alphonso tasted, too, and on his face came a look beyond Giovanni's at first bite of a sublime sausage Bolognese. The Guardian took a candle and lit the fire in the ten-foot hearth. Dry, radiating warmth began to replace the succulence I'd been feeling for some time tumbling up from the floor.

The Guardian bowed. "I leave you to your lives," he called back on his way out. He passed under the archway and left.

"Guardian Cesare," I cried, "what do we do now?"

"You know Greek. Be philosophical. Remember Epicurus' *De Rerum Natura!* Seek pleasure! Imagine the possibilities! Figure it out!" And he was gone.

"Are you Cesare?" I yelled after him, but there was no audible answer.

We decided to keep the candles lit. Every time Alphonso made love to me that first night and for the month thereafter, thoughts of Vanita overwhelmed me. Of the pleasure I remembered her body taking in Roderigo. Of the way she'd call out his name, so Cesare and I'd hear her through her door. I knew I was in the presence of everything she'd once known, in the company of everything I'd seen in her, when even as a child I'd known that these feelings were what it would mean someday to be a woman. I saw and felt them all now in myself. Every emotion my child's heart had longed for, every troubadour's lust I'd dreamt of. Every Guinevere in the Grail of Lancelot's arms.

"You see?" I kept whispering to her. "I've become you at last."

This would inevitably fly through my head at utterly inappropriate moments; just as the Italian god sensually began to fiddle with me, for instance, and I'd collapse in giggles. Alphonso wouldn't stop.

As we drank honey and wine at the villa for the next month, this time me thinking *honeymoon* a most appropriate and well-invented word, we began to hear rumors of Cesare from sylphs—servants, actually, provided to us from Cesare's household. Military rumors. He'd finally persuaded Papa to give him a small army of Papal troops. Not to kill artists and singers, evidently, but to subdue cities, especially in the Emilia-Romagna, the old "Papal States" that had long since broken away from the Vatican to become little Republics and duchies. Papa'd charged Cesare to begin to bring Italy under the outright, political sway of the Holy See. Cesare was to become, having finished part one, the newly created Duke of Romagna. When I became the Queen of the Two Sicilies, he'd have part two. A solid beginning at long last, Cesare must've thought, to his destiny of conquering Italy and on to the world.

I think that must've been the time the vulture began to follow my brother and the stench of carrion that waked long and bloody behind his battles. This vulture flew above the field, as Cesare rode into the newly conquered Romagnan city of Forlì, in whose fountain I recalled making love to my Giovànni. The sylphs one day told me about the bird, which had already attached itself in his army's mind to my brother's myth, never to fly off. I've always imagined the vulture a Fury, or Eumenide, after the Greek similarly black-winged spirits of revenging, mythic rage. The Greeks were so afraid of them, they nicknamed them ironically "Eumenides," "the pretty ones," instead of by their real name, "the Erynnies," "the avenging furies," so as not to anger them. This one floated high above Cesare, who'd learned well from Charles. In its sight lay the dead, hundreds of them, before and inside Forli's gates. The city's survivors waited below, eyes averted and tearful for their brother dead. He watched the vulture's smaller, avian apostles, the black crows, alight on men's bodies and with sharp, yellow feet and beaks begin to sup. The Eumenide waited above, hooked bill watering, circling.

On the other hand I recall from that moon-long honeymoon the sound of a rivulet's bubbling water, a sodden, foot-deep avenue for ducklings and polliwogs. The next night, having guzzled honied wine till dusk, we walked along that stream. It flowed from the northwest, emptying finally into the villa's concrete pool. I remember I laughed when I heard a flapping whirlwind and, afraid I'd find the thunderhead of swallows, looked up with Alphonso to find, instead, thousands of cooing turtledoves, fluttering like giant Palatine snowflakes above us. They sounded not like dead babies, but like a chorus of laughing toddlers. Then somewhere behind the birds, far off, from behind the next hill or farther, we heard a crack, a popping sound. Then another, followed by a booming, sudden whistle. They were much louder than any man- or animal-made whistle could've been. A dozen-foot pyrotechnic of girandoles exploded bright as sunlight on the crest of the hill facing us, in blues, greens and vermilions. *A & L*—interlaced with fire—*OF ARAGON*, it spelled out across our horizon in blazing letters.

"Cesare!" I shrieked, hoping he was out there in the night's flames somewhere "Are you my guardian angel? Is it you?"

After two weeks of Paradise and sweet fireworks, Penthesileia on horseback brought me a letter.

"It's a matter of your lives and deaths," she said.

I figured, coming from a six-foot Lesbian, I ought be suspicious about that, but not ignore it. The anxious generally have God on their side.

"You read it?"

"Of course."

"How? The seal is still attached."

"In the Girls' Steam Room. We—"

"I don't want to know."

She curtsied hugely and left for Rome. I took it to Hadrian's bedroom; Alphonso wasn't there. Although it was paper, not parchment, it was rolled and sealed—and evidently resealed—with a wax crest: a Dragon in a Royal crown in process of eating a man. The paper told me it must be from someone unafraid of modernity, the wax that he was a nobleman. I cracked the dragon-seal, unrolled the beautiful Arno paper—it was three feet long, perfect and smooth with bloody fingerprints in the margins, written in an angular, thickly masculine hand—and began to read:

August 1498, from Imola.

My Dearest Sister-in-Christ,

A month ago we began to see the black Eumenide, hanging amidst the clouds above my city of Forli, as if the bird were a successful example of those machines of Master da Vinci's that he makes of dark animal skins and balsa in the form of giant bats.

The vulture we saw was following Cesare, your lying bastard brother, and his army. They attacked my city with an excess of slaughter and suffering far beyond the necessary, though I'm not one generally to shy from excess of blood. But this geyser of murder will give the lie to chivalry for a hundred years in Italy.

Afterward we looked him from the walls of our fortress' keep, the Rock of Ravaldino. We saw your coward brother, Cesare, riding across the dusty plain below, then rushing up into my palace grounds. But he had no compassion for me, the widow Katerina Sforza Riario, Duchess of Forli and of the same family as the Moor he dares not attack. I was once a comely woman, yet am still brave. I was in armor that day from head to foot, famous for my beauty and infamous for my bravery and strength-of-arms in battle, having killed hundreds of idols of chivalry with my own slashing steel. The world calls me "The Virago," in recognition of my worthiness to sit beside any Lancelot at Arthur's Table. But don't get the wrong idea; I'm equally well known for being no virgin, with children by a veritable titled squadron, dotting Italy from Aosta to Termini. I am as proud of that, my sensual appetites, as I am of my bellicose ones. I *understand from my cousin, Cardinal Ascanio Sforza, you must be likewise sensually proud. As regards that, Lucrezia, I have thought of you as my sister since you married cousin Giovanni. The night of your wedding to him, as I saw you in the Visigoth ceremony of sacred provenance, you seemed to me a honied melon, about to burst with bodily sweetnesses. Nor can I blame you for putting Giovanni aside, as Uncle blames you.* I would never have lasted as long as you did with such a mass of cowardly bacon. But never forget such a reputation as mine for sensuality may be your destruction. Take your pleasures where you find them, but keep them secret is my advice. The reputation of a killer is a good thing, for worms fear such a Lady. But that of a lover is perilous, for at their hidden center all men quail at a strong woman's love.*

The Eumenide and Cesare must've seen my dead knights littering my grounds like crushed strawberries-meringue over the walkways. The Eumenide doubtless imagined herself rewarded for her wisdom to have followed Cesare. She is cold; she is always logical. Revenge is always philosophical and cold. The Eumenide remains from time before time a soaring goddess of revenge. Cesare looked about the courtyard of the palace, until he saw the doors he'd come to open. The ones to my so-called "Ravaldino"—my dungeons and treasure house.

"Open those," he commanded.

Cesare glinted in the sun. He was mounted on a palomino, the traces, saddle and caparisons all gold and cloth-of-gold. I know his master armormaker from Toledo, since he's made a suit for me of ebony-plated ivory. He had perfectly crafted Cesare's metalwear, styled in the modern mode as if a suit of clothes from some Milanese tailor's shop, but detailed in imitation of an imagined antique Knight's of Jerusalem from the First Crusade. His palomino was enormous, bred in Denmark to haul harvested forests to construct Viking dragon-ships. The stallion had to be enormous, since otherwise he never could've held his colossus' weight of gold.

Two knights brought before him Katerina Sforza. I was covered in blood.

"My former Lady Forli?" Cesare asked.

"Lady Sforza," I said. "Yes, Boy Borgia?"

Cesare, who had all day been the image of the calm, unflappable conqueror, like me, the kind of field marshal men follow gladly through the

---

*I realized "Uncle" must be Ludovico Sforza, the Moor and now Duke of Milan.

Gates of Hell, suddenly went insane, a five-year-old amidst a whirlwind, the sort of tantrum that terrifies a parent, fearing the child will burst its heart.

"Forli is my name in this palace now," he bellowed, complete with eyes starting from his head, and feet madly splattering the bloody dust. "If you think the ugly Moor's cognomen will frighten me now, you're far more a little girl than I a boy!"

I was astonished but unafraid. I stared at Cesare's outburst, as if at some ingenuous Inca madman. "Perhaps, through the luck of the day, a rude boy with the chattering temper of a rabid squirrel might kill enough good women's sons to breach a city's walls," I said. "But such a bastard brat will find to rule wisely a far more difficult mumblety-peg to play at."

He punched me in the mouth with his mailed glove.

"Besides, I need no Moor. Even now I'd cut your balls off, if only they weren't so hard to find!" I cried, and I spat my bloody canine-tooth in his face.

His body still shaking, your brother regarded me. He drew his heavily jeweled knife and put its point under the shoulder straps of my breastplate. He cut them. "Let's play a game of Heracles and Melanippe, shall we, Duchess?"

"Have you the balls for it? I do," I said. "I do."

He cut my belt, thigh-pieces, my undergarment chemise. Finally he snipped my pantaloon. I stood naked in the sun. A creature of arousing beauty, the torturer later told me on the rack. Cesare placed the blade at my neck, outlining the route of my carotid.

"Having a chivalrous time?" I asked.

He sheathed the dagger and walked the steps toward the Ravaldino. "Bring the cunt," he said.

The two soldiers took me again under the arms and dragged me after Cesare, each on the way grabbing the occasional feel of the body of the Duchess of Forli and great Virago.

"By all means, bring my cunt along," I said. "I never go to jail without it."

Cesare's soldiers took me to my own torture chamber, where they stretched me taller than any of my husbands on the rack. The sensation is intriguing. One feels gentle pops of releasing cartilage within a lengthening Scylla of pain. Then he raped me repeatedly all the night till dawn, while I was stretched bowstring-tight. I was not surprised to learn your brother's fond of cavalry, since he is of a distinctly stallionlike aspect where he sits a saddle. In between bouts with me he'd arouse that equine member yet again by rolling, naked, in the large piles of Forli gold coins at the room's periphery.

"Fucking you is like notching my arrow in a taut crossbow," he commented.

"You're a boy," I said from the rack. "A boy needs his father. When Great Alexander dies, Borgia, you will have had your last arousal."

Your loving, illegitimate sister-in-law, if I may call you that, Vale,
Katerina
Deo Gratis Sforza Riario,
The Ravaged Duchess of Forli & Imola

Even after what he did to Fortunata, it hurt me to read such a vindictive story about Cesare, especially from a Lady with such an inelegant and bellicose writing style. Had these crimes become part of his myth already, to rape Katerina, the infamous Virago, upon whom many a myth's already been made? I hoped not. For safekeeping and secrecy I filed that letter in the library with the rest of the Vatican's general correspondence for A.D. 1498 I imagine it's still there, if any disbelieve or think I may've made her calumnies up. Cesare gave himself a Classical Triumph with all the trimmings on arriving back in Rome. He bore banners that said *"Roma Triumphans."* And others, *"Aut Caesar, aut nihil."* "Cesare or nothing."

But I wasn't a simple dolt, either. Was any of it true? I wondered. Or all of it? I was certain Cesare could let no sentiment stand in the way of victory. And that he'd let nothing keep him from branding the myth of defeat into an enemy's very bones, or the softest part of her body in this case. He'd therefore naturally seem as frightful to the conquered as Caesar must've to Vercingetorix. But the rest of it? I'd blushed on reading her comments about the mass that would characteristically rest behind his saddle horn. But the torture of a noblewoman, and rape? That felt utterly unbelievable. My brother, who used to read me stories about Guinevere and courtly love? Who always held Vanita and me in such respect? Who'd given me a wedding month of such legendary luxury? And the Sforzas, excepting Giovanni, were infamous for political intrigue and treachery. The Virago Katerina especially so. It's common knowledge that those husbands of the multiwidowed Kate could testify to that from their tombs. Or is common knowledge only common gossip? Had agents of Forli been the source of the plot that was only foiled by Cesare's uncovering of it and killing Fortunata to save us all, especially me? Even the Moor was said never to let his manly niece into Milan at the same time as himself. "There's murder in her every glance, knives in her smile," the most feared man of our generation often said. "She's grimmer than the Plague."

That's what I convinced myself of. In any case, I'd put the letter aside with dead Fortunata and all the other signs and warnings. But just to be safe, I sent a letter to Penthesileia. I ordered her to watch Cesare as closely as she could, but not, in any case, to be seen to be doing so. "It may be a matter of our lives and deaths" was my envoi just above my signature.

<hr />

At the time Alphonso and I had still run through a field in the vast Tivoli Gardens. A stream bubbled beside us, the one we'd looked across to see the eponymous fireworks of the other evening. We'd had a picnic lunch in this field and I'd thought of Giovanni and his truffled chicken by the waterfall. But during that day, after all Alphonso's and my time together in this beautiful place and as I brought to mind the phantom face of my fat, lovely, previous husband, for the first time I began to feel a final acceptance of all the hurt I'd caused him. I regretted it still—even Jesus' own Absolution could never expunge all my regret—but I felt, as well, an acquiescence. I realized in Alphonso's arms that even Giovanni, especially Giovanni, would wish me this happiness. That especially Giovanni would've understood this moment as a fulfillment of his waterfalling oath. Christ had been a good man; Giovanni had been a good man. Neither would hesitate an eye-blink or heartbeat, if a sacrifice of his own meant the redemption of one he loved.

After I'd made love with Alphonso in the blue-flowered fields, we stayed naked, because the sun was August-hot and the moist air, blown overland that morning from our sea, felt on our skins soothing as a steam bath. We ran hand in hand next to the stream through the pasture, the moving air washing the sun's heat from us with cooling luxury. The fertile loam squished between our toes. I watched my husband's beautiful muscles, clenching and loosening with his every stride through the blossoms, his chest expanding and contracting. I watched the lovely power in his sides that men have more definitely than women, when they breathe, the intercostal muscles, I think Galen called them. Against the blossoms he looked like another Hector in his perfect body, running along a baby shore of blue Scamander.

"Your hair's a comet's tail," Alphonso said, looking over at me.

I could feel my gold talisman streaming behind me like a Trojan helmet's mane, my breasts like a breastplate, moving in time with it. The field was filled with blue and wine-dark flowers. Their blooms reached our shoulders.

Joy is the swiftest of all God's winged creatures, zipping quickly as a hornet, buzzing through sun-warm herbs. After our designated month, it hardly seemed as if we'd been in Tivoli and its Gardens more than a day. From the Vatican library I'd brought Francesco Barbero's 1415 manual on marital philosophy, *On Wifely Duties*. It was all the rage in Rome since its fresh republication—many said it was a plagiarism of Plutarch's *Conjugalia Praecepta— with new illustrations!* It was distributed only in the Vatican. But what is plagiarism, I wondered, since all thought is creative theft, the Father having already thought all possible thoughts in every possible transmutation long before His Creation of the Universe? The new illustrations by an unnamed Dominican were profuse and imaginative well beyond the text, with the positions and attitudes most likely to result in pleasure, though it said the positions were merely aids to pregnancy. The Vatican censors had restricted its publication to the Vatican, where, naturally, no one thinks about pregnancy.

Alphonso and I pored over Barbero together in Hadrian's golden bed. Alphonso especially enjoyed the engravings, but I liked the articles. The volume pointed out that Alphonso should have the more perfect and acute climax, but that I might enjoy the more all-consuming and long-lasting ones.

"You do tend to go on and on," he said.

"And your attitude seems to be *'Tempus fugit'* when I'm the one having fun. I'm a lady that has intelligence in love."

The manual showed illustrations of the husband arousing the wife to prepare for proper conception, which is much more likely to occur, the text emphasized, if the wife enjoys a climax. It told him he should rub with his fingers my principal sexual locations and also prolong the act by toying with my breasts with his fingertips, tongue and mouth. He should kiss me long and strongly, lingering on my mouth and making sure to likewise excite the "area below" my navel, replicating intercourse with whatever came to hand without actually doing it. Alphonso hung that particular illustration on the bedpost. All this would make me ready for conception, the book said. After love Alphonso should apply to my sex a pomade of cotton, soaked in musk, gum of lada leaves—

"What's a 'lada leaf'?"

"It's like a rose. They use the gum in perfume," I said.

"I'll use roses. There're a million of them in the gardens."

—and several spices: rosemary, thyme, sage and minced parsley.

Most agreeable, as he insisted on crushing the rose petals on my nude body to manufacture the "gum."

Amidst all this visual and literary explicitness, Barbero tried to make his theme how men and women (in this case Alphonso and I) should rise above our goatishness and cultivate our "intellectualities." Was he mad? We were fucking like crazed bunnies by the time he got to the theme; too late to stop and rethink now. Please. Have mercy. The delights of dirty books and the best medical texts are ipso facto animal and shouldn't have to edify. Be a Greco-Roman; let pornography be pornography.

"I don't know about you," I said, "but after years with my nose in a book, I've already got enough "intellectuality.' "

We were in a lather by that point to graduate to the next chapter, which was "Exotic Positions." A chapter for circus acrobats. Most of them turned out to be more exercises in physics than in human biology. Alphonso and I tried about seventeen of them, because those were all we could figure out how to get into. Who can possibly twist one another into the *"Nodus Gordii,"* the Gordian Knot? The mere illustration looked spine-tingling. We favored most the *"Cave canem"*—Beware-the-doggie—and the *"Meretrix supra,"* the Whore-on-top that I'd done already to Giovanni by the waterfall without knowing its name. My God, that super-*meretrix* thing I'd always thought out of this world, but it hadn't half the savor in the rooms of Pesaro it had under these more effervescent circumstances. Alphonso was fond of one the text said was "Concocted in Muslim Arabia"—the man in the woodcut wore a turban and the woman a veil over her face—therefore "Mortally Sinful for Christians" and also therefore "only to be properly understood using Arabic numerals." The "LXIX," the section was labeled.

"How could Muslims have invented this?" I asked.

"Why not?"

"Won't the long veil render the whole endeavor nugatory?"

"Maybe she takes off the veil."

"But then wouldn't it be a mortal sin for a Muslim, too?"

"D'jem said Muslims don't have that type of mortal sin. Allah's a stickler about pigs, wine and female barbers but quite open-minded when it comes to the physical act of joy."

Time had flashed by, chapter by chapter, in a staccato and rapid passage, when what we wanted was the length of time it'd take for Achilles to catch Zeno's turtle in the Paradox. We'd made love to one another each day and night. I'd counted by the third phase 112 times so far in that single moon. We still wanted 112,000 more. The real number seemed hardly even worthy of Archimedes' overflow. But more importantly, I knew Vanita's body, were she then in Heaven, Hell or Umbria, sang with us with each variation. We made love with more passion than Hadrian could've ever expressed to Antoninous, however legendary their intimacy might've been. At the new moon we decided to stay on.

Cesare brought new honey and wine. "Don't fuck on too much longer. Papa is anathematizing to everybody in earshot that he wants his little girl back," he said. "The Sacred College is drafting a Bull for him to sign to that effect. So finish up your Dionysian orgy and come home, before he excommunicates us all."

"We've vowed to make it to 250 times," Alphonso replied. "Can't stop now."

At any rate, the key must've been either the *Cave canem* or the *Meretrix supra*, certainly not the LXIX, fun as upside-down cake though it may've been, because by the time we got back to the Eternal City, we'd discovered to God's glory that Barbero's pleasurable purposes for our acts of love had correlations indeed with the pregnancy purpose. I was upchucking honied wine each morning.

On March 29, 1500, after Cesare's victory at Forli, the Virago's tortured rape, Cesare's Caesar-style triumphal return and months of rapturous approval by Rome's citizens, there occurred a moment of history, doubtless ignored by God, of terrible consequence for every Italian. In Saint Peter's Basilica Papa raised his arms in the traditional embrace of the Body of Christ. He held the Golden Rose, a rose on a long, thorny stem, made of gold, rubies, and sapphires and given on rare occasion by Popes to someone they wished to especially honor or as a badge of some high office. He spoke to the assembled prelates, knights and lords, all in their best and most elaborate daytime outfits. "We do appoint Lord Cesare Borgia, Our beloved and gentle child, who has already brought the Holy See great conquests, many triumphs and much honor, to the Sacred Office and Title of Lord Captain General of all God's Armies, as well as to All the Benefices, Privileges and Rights thereto Appertaining."

Cesare bowed his head. He was kneeling in a cloth-of-gold toga with a purple border—the garb of a Roman Emperor—that fell to the floor, flowing down the altar's marble steps behind him. "Your Will be done, Holiness," he answered. "I humbly accept your glorious charge. I will kill, slaughter and ravage your own and Christ's enemies in their lairs, in their secret tents, before the eyes of their children and women, until blood runs a Noah's flood, overflowing the borders of this land."

Papa's breath was taken away. He leaned forward and whispered, "Cesare, a little linguistic self-control in public, please."

"Sorry, Papa. I've great enthusiasm for this work."

"Where did you find that little rant? It's quite well phrased, if inappropriate to yourself."

"It's partly a quote of Hannibal's to his elephants, partly my own improvements."

"You think to improve on Hannibal?"

"On everyone."

"We'll have to find you a pachyderm. . . . A quote? According to which author?"

"Livy."

"Interesting. We don't remember that one."

The Pope then readdressed the congregation. "May he one day slip on Our Holy Foot the entire boot of Italy, even as Aaron slipped on Moses' foot by God's Will the royal sandal of Amalek. Bestow on Our beloved son the boots of virtue and authority Joshua and Gideon wore into battle."

"Papa, who in God's Name is Amalek?" Cesare whispered back.

The Pope winced, slapping Cesare gently in the face with the Golden Rose—

"Ow."

—then touched him with it once on each golden shoulder and finally handed it to him.

six

For the next months in Spoleto I thwacked myself like a tennis ball back and forth between hilarious happiness and abject fear; happiness when I'd think of my coming child, fear when memory of that hut in Pesaro overwhelmed me, when I'd cut peasant Vanozza open and Aristotle had to watch me eviscerate her. I was terrified of the thought of twins, which the book had said were a result at the time of conception of too much and too avid sex. I thought I'd had enough in pursuit of this pregnancy to have sextuplets cut out of me. I didn't so much fear death as I couldn't picture my belly being slit open and my beautiful body destroyed—especially if Alphonso had to watch—without crying wretchedly. I saw with dreaming eyes my golden braid dipped in my gut's blood and strangling my beautiful twins.

I'd been sent to Spoleto by Papa and Cesare for my own education in the arts of politics, and for protection.

"Nine months of rest and idleness. When could be better?" said Papa, Marco Palmezzano's century-old *Virgin and Child* hanging just over his shoulder to the left.

I needed to learn politics and Papa thought Spoleto would be an easy spot to do so, since, as my brother pointed out, I might be "an empress one day and should know when and how to execute people and when not." I must've been a bad pupil; I executed only a dozen or so murderers, rapists and the infrequent heretic. Everyone thought rape an odd capital offense.

"Did you see that girl's fabuluos body? The people will revolt. You can't execute them for not being Saints," even Alphonso said. "It's a miracle she's not ravished once a minute!"

"Kindly don't talk like a Neapolitan slut-monger," I said, and he turned bright red.

Spoleto was a famously peaceful spot, removed from the dissension, politics and treachery of Rome, and on the other hand was close enough to the Vatican to get back there to its arms and soldiers quickly. Louis XII of France at the time was invading Italy much the way his dwarf Uncle Charles had, and we were close enough we could decamp immediately back to Rome in a day or two. Alphonso wanted us to take up residence at Naples under the protection of Grandpa Federico, an ally of Louis'. I at first agreed, but at our farewell dinner in the Pope's Privy Dining Room, Papa, tears falling onto his white cassock, persuaded Alphonso that the thought of a garlic-blooded Calabrese assassin attacking us during the journey—like what'd befallen Juan—was giving him shooting pains under his pectoral cross and down his left arm. Wouldn't we be far safer and better protected from harm, of whatever stripe, under the Pope's immense protection? Alphonso put up stiff resistance though.

"Are you a coward, only safe under Granddaddy's skirt?" Cesare cracked.

"My family fought with Charlemagne at Roncevaux. There's never been a coward in the House of Aragon since," Alphonso continued.

"Tell that to the Moor, Aragon's ally, who doubtless expected some assistance from Federico, before Louis and Venice stole Milan and drove him into Maximillian Caesar's Tyrolean arms."

"It wasn't Aragon. Wasn't it rather the coward Cesare who betrayed the Moor? Or wasn't that you, following Louis like a common poodle on his entry into Milan? For cowardice, I say look to yourself."

Both of them instantly stood, chairs flying back.

"Boys, boys," Papa said. "*Misericordia Dei.* Please, you'll upset Lucrezia in her condition. Be pleasant to each other."

"My sincerest apologies, dearest brother." Cesare smiled, but the grip on his pie fork definitely got tighter.

"No, mine, please," Alphonso growled, wiping a napkin across his lips like a first-time hunter, blooding himself.

But my husband finally gave in to Papa and we stayed in Rome. Papa had wept in Alphonso's arms, begging him to reconsider, until Papa's state, gasping for air, his hand over his heart and looking heavenward, became blatantly embarrassing.

"I remained firm," Alphonso said afterward, "until I could feel my shoulder getting wet from your father's blubbers."

Was Papa's emotion genuine? Was his fear of additional killers real? It's a fifty-fifty thing. I've nothing to guide me, except my own desire. I admit I still wish now, as I did then, that Papa did things because he loved me and would love my child, or at least did some things for that reason, at least some of the time. I chose to overcome my doubts, nag at me though they did. I choose for his emotion to be sincere and his angina actual. I chose he was afraid truly of Borgia-killers and loved my husband, although his policy—then still obscure to me—was simultaneously committed to destroy Alphonso along with his entire Aragonese dynasty. But in tiny part, I'm ashamed to admit, I well understood that policy as proper to a prince. My understanding may've come from my experience at Spoleto, where I'd learned that the best policy is rarely the best personal choice. Many's the time I'd let the rapist go and burnt the raped, because of a family's power or the populace's threats to resist. Not only was France repoised to subdue Italy, eviscerating the Pope and stealing all Cesare's recent conquests, but the Moor had also threatened that if Papa didn't immediately help him fight Louis, he'd convince Baz al D'jet, the Grand Turk, to attack the Vatican, something the Turks had dreamt on for centuries. Papa was desperate not to attack Louis at the moment, because he was simultaneously negotiating for Cesare to marry Louis' sister, the Princess of France, which would solve substantially all his foreign-affairs difficulties all in one Visigothic matrimonial swoop.

After that night Alphonso felt guilty about his little tiff with Cesare.

"After that amazing gift of the honeymoon, I call him a coward to his face and in front of his father? What kind of ungrateful hog's-breath am I?"

"I believe it was he who first called *you* a coward, and in front of your wife and father-in-law," I reminded him. And I was every bit as grateful to Cesare as he was. That time at Tivoli with its mythical Guardian, its Emperor's bridal chamber, wines, sylphs, foods, fireworks and love was the sweetest, most thoughtful gift I've ever had in my life. "But I also believe it was *I* who provided the sensual gift of *your* life, not my blowhard brother."

He laughed, but looked befuddled. "Well . . . naturally."

"I'm so glad we think alike on that."

But no matter. Alphonso set out to make Cesare his best friend and overdid it. He and Cesare went boar hunting in the Tuscan countryside with only halberds. A five-hundred-pound boar ripped Alphonso's leg open. The boar turned and would've killed him, but Cesare—observing that Alphonso's escort of Aragonese Knights could see the situation, but were too far away to give assistance—leapt from his own horse, ran between the charging boar and defenseless Alphonso and midcharge cut the boar's head from its body with a perfectly timed halberd slash. Alphonso joked about his leg wound that we should call him the new King of Ithaca and I thought of Giovanni, staring toward Ithaca from his coin tower. During Alphonso's ridiculous attempt at—of all things—jousting, Cesare knocked him silly from his horse, the lance glancing off Alphonso's shield and smacking him between his helmet's eyes. All as if we lived still in the days of Percival. Alphonso joked he was the new Knight of the Crumpled Countenance. He developed a sudden interest in Cesare's large fire weapons, those black powder da Vincian devices Cesare's Army of God rolled into the enemy to explode, turning men to sausage filling. The two of them had worked on one device all morning, when it took it into its incendiary mind just to go off for some reason known only to Hephaestus. Four men were killed, two troops of Cesare's and two Knights of Aragon. All four had been standing farther away from the thing than Alphonso when it burst. Cesare was absent the moment it went off, having excused himself behind a tree for nature's call. A malicious motive for that coincidence was more than I could bring myself at that time to think of or was one I chose not yet to usher into the field of my awareness.

Were Cesare's actions and apparent rescue intentions during these incidents genuine, as I believe Papa's earlier ones to have been? I thought so at the time. I'd yet little reason, I knew of, to imagine otherwise. Do I think so now, knowing what would come? . . . Please. I may be my needs' and wishes' obtuse daughter, but not their idiot. I'm sure all three incidents were arranged and purposeful setups on Cesare's part to kill Alphonso. On the other hand it took remarkable talent and balls to kill the boar. No one would've blamed Cesare in the slightest for turning away from, rather than into, the boar to save himself. Several brave knights, acknowledged as demons in battle and who've themselves faced a charging boar, have told me they fled at the critical second. But Cesare stayed, faced and killed the beast. Master Perugino, in fact, immortalized the moment of the boar's death for Cesare in a painting on canvas, which Papa thought a masterpiece, and in which Cesare reminded everyone of Ulysses.

🍇

This was also the moment the art bug bit Papa. The bug forever buzzes about Vatican City and has always especially liked the taste of Popes.

Not that Papa hadn't always had an appreciation for a fine piece of paint or stone—he hired Master Pinturicchio, after all—but he abruptly switched from interest to mania. His former obsession with his books, library and literary pursuits was replaced by an even stronger one for oily tints and marble. He was especially fond, as in his reading, of the strictly Classical, with no use at all for art of the unlit millennium between the fall of the Roman Empire and the thirteenth century.

"Dark Age trash," he sniffed at that thousand years of pigment and chisel. "Fashioned by men with zero confidence in their own capacities and who thought the world dominated by trolls and spiky demons, instead of by God, expressed in His Perfect, Supple Image, which is man himself."

But quickly realizing all the real Classical artists were for a thousand years shades in Hades, he latched on to alive ones, those in particular working in the strictly modern, neo-Classical style. He commanded every artist of that ilk in Italy to appear before him, where he'd grill each for hours on the minutiae of his craft, much to my fascination as well as Alphonso's desperate boredom and Cesare's oft-expressed itch to kill them. Papa's first art idea, of course, had been to hire Master Pinturicchio to paint the Borgia Apartments. His second was to redecorate the centuries-old, plain-stone interior of Saint Peter's Basilica, erected by Constantine, as well as to revive his former concept of repainting the ceiling and dull wall behind the altar of the Sistine. He gave Master Pinturicchio a pictorial audition for the Sistine, letting him paint *The Disputa*, centered around a full-length, life-size Saint Catherine in my Apartment, with Catherine modeled on me, her lovely head framed in a halo of golden hair. But Papa hated it.

"You're much better-looking than that," he complained.

Too bad, it was awe-inspiring and I thought I looked especially breathtaking in it. I used to gaze at it for hours. He went on to a fight with Master Bramante, his original Petrine architect, over Bramante's concept that the new Saint Peter's dome should be modeled on the one over Santa Sophia.

A barely-out-of-his-teens, bratty, bowlegged midget named Buonarroti showed up. This Buonarroti was hot as a harquebus all over town, because of some stumpy baby-Bacchus he'd carved with grapes in its hair. How original. He arrived before Papa covered with white chiseling dust, convinced him that Constantine's Saint Peter's Basilica, the most sacred church in Christendom, was an out-of-date piece of "Dead, Gothic,

Vandal junk" and should be "tossed onto history's holy garbage heap" and replaced, before any new tints were wasted on it. Papa was temperamentally receptive to this and I heard him mutter "Vandal junk" under his breath for days in agreement. This Michelangelo brought a model of his design for the new Basilica. A piece of madness. Michelangelo also consented, though he thought sculpting and architecture more fun, to be the one to fresco the entire ceiling and rear wall of the Sistine with new images, chiseling off the old, time-sanctified "shit."

"And what image would you put behind the altar, instead of the manure that's presently there?" Papa asked.

"The Last Judgment, Holiness."

"That might be nice. And on the ceiling?"

"I don't know. Something colorful."

"Um-hum. And how long will this new behemoth take to build, Master Buonarroti?"

"Not long, Holiness."

"How long a not long?" I asked.

"Oh, I could do one in not much more than a century, O Daughter of Sanctitude. I've developed a new way to construct the dome. Other architects would take vastly longer, you know. . . . By the way, I just started a new *Pietà*. You wouldn't like to pose for the Virgin, would you?"

"Love to." I smiled, looking down at my bulging abdomen. "But wouldn't I be unsuitable? I mean the 'Virgin' part."

"A hundred years strikes you as 'not long'?" Cesare said. "His Holiness is sick of putting off his completion of things. He must start now; he must finish tomorrow. Your proposed schedule assumes he'll live forever. I pray you're right, but I doubt it. God created the universe in a week. A man and woman create a child in a flash of lightning, isn't that true, Lucrezia? I can never understand why you artistic faggots take so long."

"God's never been picky about His finished product, my Lord. And even those old-fashioned, horrendous cathedrals with spikes and uncouth beasties took five hundred years, you must be aware."

"The hell with Saint Peter's. How long to do the Sistine ceiling thing?" Papa interrupted with an annoyed glance at Cesare. "We'd like to finish something while I'm alive."

"In Eternity's face? An instant. No more than twenty years."

"We're sure I'll live that long," Papa groaned. "And what would you charge? We mean for the Sistine, not the new Saint Peter's."

"Hard to say, Holiness. I'll need a big scaffold, pigments and a hundred tons of gesso at, let's figure, a half-dozen ducats a ton. And tint; that roof's going to take a dung hill of color for the paint. And there's my time, which don't go cheap. But only for you, I'll cut the price on that . . . let's figure twenty percent." From his leather purse Buonarroti pulled an abacus, which emerged in its own little cloud of white grime. He began madly shuffling beads, which squeaked dustily. "Let's see. Twenty years on my back—oh, yes, we're all whores for art—ten hours a day times twenty years times three hundred and sixty-five days per year, minus Holy Days of Obligation . . ."

Cesare leaned forward from behind and whispered something into Papa's ear.

"You've given my son the impression you're a man of young men's back doors, Master Michelangelo," Papa said. "Is this so?"

The artist had indeed had his eyeballs affixed to Cesare's shapely rump through most of the interview—utterly ignoring beautiful me. I'd chalked it up to my pregnancy.

"Why, yes, Holiness," Bounarroti replied. "But many artists of the Classical world, the period of the greatest art, devoted themselves to the immature male posterior, its perfect, sensual circularity a concrete expression of the geometrical beauty of the cosmos and therefore of significant aesthetic interest."

"Are you being ironic with Us?"

"Certainly not, Holiness. My work is never ironic. In fact, I was considering the worthiness of your son's posterior for a marble re-creation."

"My dead ass in a *Pietà* with my sister?" Cesare sniggered.

"I find it an inspiring example of the genre. You're a climber of Helicon, where the Classical Muses live, Holiness, and I'm a climbing Classicist from the tips of my fingers to the end of my pecker." I looked at him in surprise; he nodded toward me. "No offense meant, Lady Lucrezia."

"None taken. I was unaware they lived there. Calliope and her sisters."

"Lucrezia is also acquainted with peckers, I think, to which her swollen condition testifies," Papa replied. "We personally are of the opinion that lust is no sin, but believe like the Greeks it's a Gift of God. So whatever lust He implants in us for whatever revolting objects, including, I suppose, Classical bottoms, must've been put there for some or other Sacred Reason. *Mysterium Dei*. Our cardinals and theologians always excoriate Us for this opinion, but if you saw some of the objects of their own affections, you'd wonder."

"How broad-minded and Christian of you, Holiness," Michelangelo piped happily.

"Of course We're Christian. We're Christ."

"Naturally."

"And, Classicism aside, what you engage in on your own time is none of Our business, Master Buonarroti," Papa continued. "On the other hand, We don't want the ceiling of such a sacrosanct edifice as Sixtus IV's Sistine to wind up encrusted with colorful fantasies of your perverse persuasion. We don't want to look up one day to see some stark-naked God the Father all covered with homosexual muscles, his universe-engendering pecker dangling about for all to gawk at and cavorting with some mathematically and perfectly butted Adam above the Sacred Altar.

"What a concept, Holiness."

"And all this male overexposure looming above the floor, upon which Christ's Vicars are elected. When We die, what Antichrist might the next Papal Consistory elect, voting in such a faggots' museum? They might even choose that vulgar Visigoth, della Rovere."

Master Buonarroti's previous happiness at Papa's liberal ideas about lust turned, when he heard those opinions didn't extend to his art, into an affronted and put-upon hissy fit, foaming at the mouth and foot stamping, to which Papa from his years with Cesare was somewhat indifferent. Michelangelo screeched on and on about his lifelong devotion to the Classical Muses and about how much the Florentines had liked his nude *David*. He then yammered about how we three were tasteless, untutored Philistines and about how he himself was so dedicated to his craft that he'd learned it by sneaking into cemeteries at night and cutting to ribbons the recently dead for the aesthetic purpose of seeing how the Almighty Artist, the First and Greatest of all, had miraculously designed their insides to work. Papa was as patient with this tantrum as he'd always been with Cesare's, but Buonarroti finally stopped when Papa calmly reminded him that such dissections of the faithful were capital offenses, since the cemeteries' residents, once Holy Mother Church housed them there, were meant to be as pristine as possible on the Day of Jesus' Raising of the Dead.

"So kindly shut up," Papa snapped, "before We let Our son of the Apollonian fundament have his way with you and roast you to a neo-Gothic crisp in Saint Peter's dreadfully Romanesque and old-fashioned Square."

But after thinking about it, Papa, as usual, decided to prevaricate and let some successor tackle the Sistine and Saint Peter's projects. He further determined that having Master Buonarroti constantly puttering about the Vatican would drive him crazy.

"We need two screeching Cesares like We need another Crucifixion," he said. "And his new Saint Peter's? Too dull. Though maybe I'd like it better with statues on top."

No one will ever hang such a titanic dome as Michelangelo proposed above such a titanic opening as he designed, anyway. If Buonarroti were educated in the ancient writers, he'd realize this. Marcus Agrippa's Pantheon is acknowledged the greatest dome allowed by the physical Laws of God. But like most artists, all his awareness stopped at yesterday and he has a mad desire merely to be eternally plunging ahead. Papa gave up the new Saint Peter's and Sistine ideas, then switched his aesthetic ambitions back to the Borgia Apartments. Everyone thanked God.

The Holy Father levied a one-time tax, a "Special Penance," to be taken from the benefices of cities in Cesare's new Duchy of Romagna, starting with Forli, specifically for the purpose of raising cash for the decoration of the suite of rooms Alphonso and I'd now moved into. I tried not to overburden the towns with expense. They complained bitterly and endlessly, anyway. Every day some legate was crabbing to Papa about what a spoiled spendthrift I was. How about wood instead of ivory for this or that piece? Dutch pewter instead of Castilian silver? Did it have to be lapis lazuli? Couldn't it be cerulean seashell, instead? It's so much cheaper. And on and on in this shortsighted vein. They pointed out they could no longer field armies to defend Mother Church, my decorating expenses were such a drain on their treasuries. I asked what the hell they needed an army for. Weren't they vassal states, now part and parcel of the Holy See? Hadn't my brother's forces expunged their army and only spared their whole town from being burnt to the ground at my request? Their former ruler, Katerina Sforza, was presently Cesare's guest in a cell at the Castel Sant'Angelo. I suggested perhaps they'd like to talk to Cesare about their paying for the new Saint Peter's, instead of our puny

Apartment. At each pronunciation of "Cesare," I'd get my way, their faces twitching and draining of color. But I shouldn't complain; they wound up doing their duty by me, even if dragged to it. I tried to decorate our rooms in a manner less formal and forbidding than most of the Borgia Apartments. I think one would find them so to this day. The thing I was happiest about in the new place was a dining table the Camerlengo gave me. He said it was made in Cypress. It reminded me of the one beneath which Cesare and I'd played in our mother's apartment. This new one, like Vanita's, had also scenes from the Life of Christ carved into its legs—the Wedding at Cana and the Child Jesus in the Temple. Though it didn't have Peter's crucifixion nor Paul's SPQR headsman's block, it was close enough to make me smile when I'd sit down to a meal.

My white Holy Father now sat in Alphonso's and my Apartment in a large receiving room with a newly installed, malachite mantel, carved to re-create a fireplace of Hellenic Alexandria. A squad of Knights of Aragon, sent by Federico and now interspersed with Palatine Guards, ringed the room. Alphonso and I still dressed in purple, my gown of Japan's silk embroidered with yellow diamonds in Eastern designs. My husband said, when I'd first put it on, that the purple silk, allied with the stones' sunny sparkle, made the skin of my face and throat appear as fine as a Seraphim's belly. Alphonso's doublet was purple, too, as were the bandages still wrapping his leg from the recent boar attack.

"We urge you, My son, to resign your title and cede it to Our Captain General, your loving brother, Cesare. We say this out of love."

Papa sat in the seat of honor by the malachite. Alphonso was across the room from him on a Byzantine love seat below a lunette of musical cupids by Master Pinturicchio.

"Holy Father," I cried, "are you cuckoo? Resign his title? His father's and grandfather's patrimony, the Kingdom of Naples and the Two Sicilies?" I was stunned, not yet even angry; Papa's suggestion had been so absolutely absurd.

"Child—" Papa started.

"My title, as well?" Now I was beginning to recover, anger moving more strongly into my voice.

All cynics say a title is a venial thing, and perhaps it is to those who've never had one. Alternatively, I'd point to the many men and women now thought great who willingly died for such venialities. After a short possession, my present title of Duchess and future one of Queen seemed as important and not-to-be-betrayed as the qualities they were supposed to body forth, the pride, language, honor and word of the Neapolitan earth and people.

"Has Beelzebub addled your brain?" I asked Papa as politely as I could. "Have you been struck in the head by the gaming racquet of the Grand Turk? Has senility, God forbid, cut loose your mind from its anchor?"

He sighed. "We shall provide you both with excellent substitute titles. Cesare has suggested you shall be created and henceforth known as the Prince and Princess of Pesaro."

"Pesaro?" We'd have to live in Pesaro. When I next saw Alphonso in that coin-strewn castle by the sea, would I see sweet Giovanni's weepy, portly ghost bleeding from the walls?

"We'll send Giovanni somewhere nice. He's never been much taken with governance, anyway, and his uncle, the Moor, is no longer of any use to anyone."

"And we shall do what in Pesaro? Lord it over fishmongers and stinky fishwives in mud huts? Have you ever met a Pesaran? An odor of turned scampi announces them ten minutes before they arrive."

"You once loved it there, you told me. And besides, Pesaro, like Monaco, has a future, We think. And We're ineluctably right, you know."

"You're always right? Who said so? God, I suppose?"

"It's a doctrine We've set the Curia to work on."

"I thought you were going to give up on that 'infallibility' nonsense."

"At the Curia's urging We've rethought Ourselves. Who was I, the Curia asked Us, to tell Our Better Half He's wrong? We are the Christ's Vicar. Is Christ ever wrong? Ipso facto: *quod est demonstrandum*. That's the abridged version, of course. The formal proof, being drafted by the Curia, is four hundred Latin pages long. So far. We despair of its being completed in Our lifetime. You once claimed to love Pesaro, are We right?"

"I love another now."

Papa leaned back in his chair and thought a moment. He bit his lip. He looked into the fireplace. His shoulders settled into that decision-mode as they used to. He bent forward and looked at Alphonso and me with a pinch of melancholy. "The Sacred College thinks this Pesaran set-tlement—"

" 'Settlement'?"

"—settlement most merciful. The House of Aragon, your son's and Our unborn grandson's House, has made plain its sympathies with Louis of France and his evil intentions toward the Church in Rome, headed by your father. As heirs of a sworn enemy, a more suitable disposition might well include death for you both. I've dissuaded the Curia and Holy Office from this by pointing out Our eternal devotion to your unborn child and that over Christ's Vicar's dead body will you be burnt, Our grandson still within you."

I was by now pacing back and forth. The knights and Palatines were looking worriedly at me. Alphonso hadn't as yet made a sound. He was sitting, still astonished, a look of abandonment and betrayal having entirely taken possession of his face, just like the one I was apprehensive to find on Giovanni's ghost.

"Is Cesare behind this?" I asked Papa.

"It's Our idea."

"Which is only rhetoric to avoid my question." Had it been "our" idea, as in Papa's and Cesare's? Or "Our" idea, as in Papa's and God's? So I asked him precisely that.

"Ours," he muttered. "But We've determined, whether it is His or not, when the right of the great individual outweighs other rights, such as rights of state, family or inheritance, we will have reached the Borgia Paradise."

I grumbled, "The 'great individual.' You mean my lying brother?"

"If he lies, We lie," he snapped. "But speaking of rights, the Holy See could provide a Papal Tax rebate to Pesaro," Papa said.

"For what?"

"A rebate would allow you both to turn the somewhat godforsaken outpost into another pearl of the Adriatic. Perhaps Pesaro will become a not-so-perverse Venice under your practiced and humanist governance. A reborn Athens."

"Athens? You're patronizing us again."

"The new Pesaro will sing your praises for a thousand years, as Athens sang of Solon."

"And I'm to be the Alcibiades of this foggy, sunless Republic?" Alphonso mumbled. "Condemned to wander the streets of my wet El Dorado with the mark of Cain braised onto my forehead, having sold my name and family for a momentary flash of happiness. But it will only be momentary, won't it, Priest? Your true son, your Borgia Nero, will come to kill us all in the end, won't he?"

Papa turned his face away, as if struck. He was starting to bend. I saw it in his eyes, his cassock increasingly wrinkly. I saw him begin to understand that while he might actually accomplish his purpose—more likely Cesare's—to accomplish it required too high a price. "Lucrezia, We do this only out of love for you and your husband."

"I think we'll refuse."

"It's for your own good."

"No," I replied.

"It's God's Will."

"Whose will? Is it yours and that Divine Doppelganger's within you? In that case, I don't care if He Inquires of me personally. Or is it Roderigo alone, preyed on by the cancer of his own desire?"

"Lucrezia, please, child—"

"No," Alphonso said.

"No."

Papa sighed, got up, made the Sign of the Cross over us and glided whitely—he was beginning to be fat—from our Apartment. We'd kept our identities and were still ourselves.

In the corner of my eye I saw the Knights of Aragon and the Palatines surreptitiously smiling at our stubbornness and little victory. What had that terrifying warning been about? Papa'd never spoken to me that way before. I couldn't even imagine such thoughts vis-à-vis myself in his head. Had he just threatened to kill Alphonso and me? Such a "consummation" seemed beyond the pale of political necessity and must've rather fallen from some Aeschylean nightmare. I felt a thrill of fear; my hands were shaking; my eye stung from a droplet of sweat. But as I stood there, the wondering also hit me, whether all the things in my life that my girlish passivity had led me to—leaving Vanozza and Subiaco, my first marriage with the iron poultry, seeing Fortunata murdered, fleeing Subiaco a second time, not reading books for all those years, a hundred others—would've required from me only a firm enough "No!" in order to have avoided. This questioning should've made me feel powerful and more self-assured than before, but instead angered me for all I'd put up with that maybe I hadn't had to. The anger then turned to confusion and a sense of being adrift in a squall. I realized that the two foremost things over the years God's Will had forced me to—my precious time with my coin collector and my honied Paradise with Alphonso—were joys I'd most definitely have said no to, had I been left to decide for myself. Who had been the instruments of this Godly Will? The same Papa who just threatened my life? And the same adored-and-adoring brother from whom the threat originated?

✿

On All Souls' Eve, I'd gone to bed late, after witnessing a grand parade of costumed madmen and -women in Vatican Square, celebrating the Holy Dusk, during which God in His bottomless Mercy gives a night's respite and release from Purgatory and sometimes Hell—and their various tortures—for countless millions of souls. We watched from my wedding balcony as thousands of the living, masquerading as dead, danced most devilishly about a hundred-foot obelisk of fire. They called for the dead—symbolized by the towers of swirling smoke—to remember them, as they were remembering in return, to help them, to cure disease, blindness, pox or plague, to give them a new brother or sister, husband, wife, child, or just a surcease of pain. I wept that so much misery, so much pain and desire for such little, simple things were displayed before me for Father, Son and Holy Ghoul to ignore. I cursed God for not providing His Children with these little gifts, such everyday nothings for cosmos-creating Him to do. I considered us, Papa, Cesare, me and Alphonso on our high balcony. He'd given us so much, vastly more than any of these. More than the shades of millions, floating tonight on each wind of the entire world. Why is so much not enough for us? Why do we desire with such world-destroying passion the few trifles we imagine we lack? I cursed myself for my hollow and pompous censure of Our Lord. I shuffled off toward bed. My heart was cold.

I woke just after midnight, a whole new body of pain inside me I hadn't felt before. I rested in a puddle. I reached out for Alphonso and grabbed his shoulder.

"Alphonso. It's starting. I'm afraid."

"Of what?"

"Roderigo's coming to kill me, to cut us from our future."

"Roderigo who?"

"Roderigo and little Vanita. The second of them will kill me."

"What are you talking about? Who are Roderigo and little Vanita?"

"Our twins! I'm giving birth, you blockhead. Do something!"

Alphonso rushed from bed, knocking over, I remember, every side table and lamp in the room, looking for his codpiece for cover. "What do I do? I'm a man!"

"Really?"

"I know nothing of birth and babies. Should I get a knight?"

"And he'll what? No men with knives! Get the midwife, for God's sake."

"Where?"

"She lives in the Hebrew ghetto. The guards know the place. They'll get her."

And he rushed off, barefoot, hoseless, to find a Palatine. I heard Sister Angelique scream in the hallway, "My Lord Bisceglie! Cover that thing with a pantaloon, *please!*"

"I have none, Sister."

"Here. Veil it, at least!"

But after three hours of my writhing and feeling as if my back were breaking, no one could find the midwife, and the doctors all claimed to be specialists and didn't deliver babies.

"You don't want to see me midwife myself," I cried. "I only know one method, and it isn't pretty."

Alphonso was in a rage. "I swear to Christ I will kill everyone here if a midwife doesn't appear in two minutes!" And he drew his sword and wounded an armchair.

Papa was no better. "And I will excommunicate anyone he kills, just to be sure you go to Hell!"

"Papa," I gasped, my insides seizing. "It's All Souls' Day. Nobody goes to Hell today; everybody gets out."

A tall, thin figure in white stepped forward from the cowering group at the room's edge. "I know the midwife's craft. My first lover was the midwife all about our estates. I used to follow her everywhere. She taught me her secrets."

Penthesileia.

An enormous hubbub of "Lesbos," "the Spartan gymnasium," "the child will be a catamite" and such like tumbled through the room, with Papa and my husband the loudest voices.

"Penthesileia?" I whispered, and understood in a second how quiet real power can sound, when the room's cacophony transformed at my slight sigh to deathly silence.

"Yes, Madam?"

"You're not embroidering your past, are you? It's not as if your experience is from helping your cats, is it? You can really do this?"

"Yes, my Lady."

"Then get to it. I comfort myself with the thought that you couldn't be as inept at it as Cesare. And Papa, get everybody else the hell out of here; it's like a Venetian fire drill in this room."

"But Lucrezia—" Alphonso objected.

"Especially get the father out," Papa said. "Fathers are a curse. I always was."

She didn't lie. She was a sorceress and fairy godmother. Her hands, having lost her lover, kept hold of her lover's craft. She repositioned me, showed me how to breathe properly, and in half an hour my child sluiced from me in a gush of agonizing pleasure, Alphonso said, "like a mermaid's child into the Bay of Naples." He wasn't twins, the Blessed Mother be praised. He looked at first somewhat a scraggy daemon of Donatello's, but after a night at my breast, he detached a wingless, buttery putto à la Giotto, a freehand hexagon of perfect circles. Meanwhile, Cesare had been banished with the rest by Papa and was nowhere to be seen, even in my imagination.

"Born on All Saints' Day," I said in his long trip down from Penthesileia's arms to mine and then to my breast.

"Not *another* Borgia Christ," Penthesileia cracked. "I'll find a manger." She adjusted the tip of my breast, so the child could feed properly, during which I caught her eyes glittering more pleasurably than strictly a midwife's ought. In fact, that seemed true of her whole midwifery, though it may've been simply delight in the nativity.

On the morning of November 11, I was carried down in my bed—covered in red and "Alexandrine" blue velvets to the chapel of Santa Maria in Portico. In my full-length mirror, as we went by, I looked pale, but with a vague, ethereal loveliness that I attributed to motherhood, because really I felt like a cracked and abandoned egg. An atmosphere of giggling attended the Apartments and palace: halls hung with Catalan tapestries, arrases and lined in Turkish carpets, silk hangings from the staircases and at the entrance. Modern art and Spanish antiquities combined in baby-blue anachronism.

"Lucrezia looks a Beatrice from Dante's Heaven," some Cistercian Abbot whispered.

At the set hour we all adjourned to the Sistine through the connecting side door. There awaited us various Borgias and dependents, including Papa, Aragonese relatives, Katerina Sforza, the Imperial Governor of Rome and the rest of the sumptuous College of Cardinals. Sandro Botticelli's diaphanous *Daughters of Jethro* and Master Perugino's *Handing Over of the Keys* looked down on us like musical intervals in crystalline spheres of space and time. Over the far wall behind the altar, where Buonarroti had wanted to put his *Last Judgment*—I thanked the ghost of Sixtus IV we'd passed on that horror—hung a golden banner with a Roman Tribune's dais against it, draped in gold brocade.

The austere Cardinal Carafa baptized my son with water, he said, "of Neapolitan virgins' tears" from a crystal cruet. "Roderigo, *baptizo te in nomine Patris et Filii et Spiritu Sanctus,*" Carafa intoned, and the usual, unseen nuns' chorale blasted out an echo-soprano *Gloria.*

Papa beamed, his face marinated in his tears. I saw him mouth the word *Roderigo* with Carafa. Cesare served as godfather, at Papa's insistence; Katerina Sforza, at my behest, as godmother. I laughed to myself at God, thinking what a pair of godparents these two should make. Cesare, as usual, betrayed not a speck of the rainbow of ironies he must've sensed arcing over him and Katerina.

"Do you renounce Satan and all his works?" the Cardinal asked them on behalf of little Roderigo.

"I do," Cesare said.

"Most of them," Katerina said, followed by a scandalized hubbub.

I imagined the great rapist-murderer having red horns on his head and a pointy tail, standing next to his infamous, ravaged Virago.

"I do," the Virago finally repeated, as I imagined the blood of thousands dripping from her hands, which held my baby.

But in the same thought as the ironies of the moment, I was stunned at the simple, blessed beauty of it. Roderigo's cry as the Water of Salvation glissaded over his forehead. The Holy Chrism, winking colored light from the windows, as he'd blink his eyes. The look of startling tenderness on the faces of rapist and murderess, as they looked down on my tiny Christ child. I shifted slightly in my sumptuous pallet and there she was, standing behind her father in the cloth-of-gold gown and an emerald and diamond tiara, both of which I'd worn at Papa's coronation. It was little Lucrezia, as unhappy and forlorn as ever. But her presence was a quite literal revelation. Had Cesare publicly recognized her? Had Papa?

When I smiled at her, she scowled, shifted, and hid herself again behind her voluminous Godpapa.

Little Roderigo moved with us into our Borgia Apartment amidst what I might honestly call a "family" for the first time since my days below the Life-of-Christ table. I lived in unalloyed happiness for eight goo-gooing turnabouts of the Vatican Square's moon—goo-goos on the parts of the Vicar of Christ and the Duke of Bisceglie, as well as tiny Roderigo of the Vatican Hill. Over the months my faith in the Triune God underwent a complete rebirth. My Stoic cynicism of Halloween disintegrated. As I nursed Roderigo at night in the silhouette of Constantine's Saint Peter's, my anger at all Three of Them rose off me and away like a father, son and holy ghost of larks. I felt the same way I once had under the table about the whole Blessed Triangle: the way I imagined my baby must feel right now for the Father of bounteous creation, the Son of mercy and love and the Holy Spirit of Infinite Mind and who dances on the walls of Plato's cave. The Father had created Alphonso and Roderigo for me. The Son had given me the love I bore them both and they bore me. The Holy Spirit had lit my soul with the knowledge of what these loves mean and that the universe, from Throne of Heaven to Ninth Circle, is wholly of that same Living and Loving Substance.

The night of July 15, 1500—that it was the Ides of July I'm sure didn't escape him—Cesare hosted an intimate dinner in his rooms at the Castel Sant'-Angelo with only forty diners—including a few cardinals, other prelates and assorted whores. Once inside Hadrian's mausoleum we all climbed down and up labyrinthine stairs and passageways, leading from the helicoidal central ramp—we Romans love simultaneously to sense both the nearness of Heaven and a certain proximity to Hell—to Cesare's maisonette, carved from the solid masonry of the great drum. In excavations masonry had been found from Hadrian's ancient temple of Venus that was carved *"URBS AETERNA,"* "the Eternal City," which everyone said proved it'd always been so and not merely the Church's idea. The Pope also attended this dinner with Aunt Giulia, although I regretted to hear from her that Papa was gradually jostling her out of the Papal bed. But the party mostly comprised officers of Cesare's. He had rooms in the

Borgia Apartments, of course, but at this time used his maisonette in Sant'Angelo as his "headquarters." All forty of us easily fit around the solid-gold dining table in Cesare's dining chamber, his triclinium. He'd modeled the room on the one found in the excavation of Nero's *Domus* of gold around 1485—the scene of the spectacular debaucheries that Suetonius and Tacitus wrote of. The table had been forged for him in Frankish Arcis-sur-Aube, where tons of molten gold had been heated to fluid and then poured into a vast, table-negative of reinforced, hardened clay. The table cooled for a year, required a hundred men to lever it even an inch and had been carted over the Alps on a gigantic sled, drawn by a hundred of Louis' twenty-hand Percherons. It had been craned with da Vincian tackle into place in the dining room at a point in the maisonette's construction, when the outer walls were not yet finished, the mansion's remainder replaced thereafter around it.

Hadrian's Tomb, now Sant'Angelo, had sat for centuries, guarding the entrance to Vatican Hill on the shore of the Tiber, all the way across Vatican City—a carriage journey away—from Saint Peter's, the Belvedere and our Apartment. Cesare's new place had been crammed and jury-rigged into the tomb in the style of an empire-era Roman patrician's home: multistoried around a central, roofless courtyard below, with a large reflecting pool and the maisonette's rooms arranged around that opening. But it had, of course, every newly imported convenience and embellishment. Cesare loved modern technology. He'd turn into a delighted child when showing off to guests his indoor plumbing system, an elaborate affair of terra-cotta piping with little blue dolphins on it that he said had been brought for installation in his "little *praetorium*" from the isle of Crete, where plumbing was famous for being the only surviving artifact of the civilization of King Minos. A few learned exegetes have even suggested that Minos' Minotaur-enclosing Labyrinth was in reality a mythical retelling, corrupted by time and repetition, of a tale of lost souls in the Minoan sewers. Besides the table and plumbing, nearly everything else in Cesare's palace was of—what else?—gold. The chairs, cloth-of-gold wallpapers, the frames on his gleaming plethora of mirrors, the dinnerware, plate, goblets, were all of gold, with the occasional vermeil thrown in, I supposed, for Socratic moderation. Cesare's many servants, while ladling rare clarets, Burgundies, black fish-eggs, known as "caviars," and golden sauternes, were dressed in costumes of gold fleece and hooves in imitation of the god Pan and goddess Diana.

Another Diana sat at the room's periphery, naked, but for golden triangular and round spots of sheep fleece, daintily affixed to sex and tits—all the men leered over how they might be attached—with beeswax by the Vatican's apiarist.

"Doesn't beeswax melt from body heat?" the Archdeacon of somewhere or other said to her with salacious expectation.

Diana strummed her golden harp in either questioning reply or a closed deal. Cesare sat at the table's head. He was dressed all in gold. Gold in this case fashioned in an exacting imitation of the fully geared battle outfit of a Hadrian-era Roman emperor. Gold breastplate, wristguards, greaves, sandals, purple and cloth-of-gold cape, attached by clusters of amethyst at the shoulders, and a myrtle-leaf gold crown above his golden hair. Alphonso, still in customary navy blue, sat next to Cesare in the "seat of honor," opposite Papa, on Cesare's other side. I'd dressed in a simple black Parisian gown with ruby accents. Cesare had placed me conspicuously in the "Lady's seat of honor" at the foot of the table, opposite himself. All the other guests ranged around the great Apollonian oval.

Cesare always threw a terrific party, and by midnight the dinner had been a rousing success. He'd placed everyone next to someone he or she actually enjoyed talking to, such a rarity that when it happened it could only be genius. The food had been wonderful; French wines overflowed beyond everyone's satisfaction. The most recently brought-out dish had taken everyone's fancy, the whole table by then well soused. It followed the frozen dessert.

"The pièce de résistance," Cesare announced in his abominable French accent. "Saved to *le fini*."

Which from his mouth sounded more like "lou fanny." A Diana and a Pan brought the *pièce* out on a golden tray and placed it in the table's center. It was brain, an intact one, an exceptionally difficult dish for even the finest cook to do well, since when not prepared by a master it's susceptible to a texture like squamous jellyfish. But Cesare had promised us his new French *chef de cuisine* couldn't create anything less than a *chef d'oeuvre*, or "chief dove" in his dialect. When the brain emerged, it had cloves stuck into its crinkly surface and was surrounded with exotic mushrooms, all laved in a Madeira sauce. It smelled like a meaty vineyard, filling the room with a blend of aromas as vivid as the sharpest memory. But it was so large, none of us could remember ever eating a calf's or sheep's brain this size.

"Lord Cesare," a Cardinal said. "That must be from a cow the size of a baptistery."

Cesare smiled. "It's from France."

Everyone else appeared satisfied with this explanation. But the more I glanced at it, the odder it struck me. I thought, as well, that the calves' brains I'd seen had always been smoother, not so covered with swirls and indentations as this one. I'd a horrible thought that perhaps this wrinkled organ might've one day envisioned within itself the Florentine *David* inside a tall block of marble or had composed some well-known, Provençal love song. Or maybe it previously resided within the helmet of a recently defeated Lord or Lady of some city of Cesare's conquest. Does white Burgundy go with soul?

"Brother, by any chance has Master Buonarroti or any of his friends passed away recently?" I asked as ingenuously as I could. "Is Katerina Sforza still with us?"

"No. Buonarroti's gone to do another piece of marble for the Florentines," Cesare replied. "The Virago was alive and squirming last time I checked."

"Oh. Good," Papa said. "He likes Florence."

"Everyone likes Florence," volunteered Alphonso.

"Except the Florentines, under the thumbs of Medici swine," Cesare said.

"Perhaps you'll pen Doctor Medici a death certificate," Papa punned.

Everyone laughed at that. I couldn't think of a tactful way further to ask about any of my imagined Lords or troubadours. I skipped the brain. Alphonso skipped it, as well. Just at that moment one of the Pans began to play a song on a clef of bells that were arranged on three strings, strung on a lyrelike frame. The bells made me think of Subiaco. I wished this were Vanita's yew table or that she'd been here to see us. She would've been so proud of her children, one becoming a great Lord, his sister in love and a Duchess, maybe one day a Queen in love with a King. She would've missed her Roderigo, but now I had another Roderigo.

But as Cesare and everyone else gobbled brain, all the way from the table's opposite end I heard Cesare's alcohol-slurred voice beginning to rise substantially higher than necessary to address the person to whom he was talking, Alphonso, just next to him. "Beloved brother, my spies have told me the Papacy seeks your life and Sicilian kingdoms."

"Cesare, don't be an ass," Papa said. "Think of Lucrezia's and Our feelings."

This all naturally sounded so interesting, the rest of the table quieted and chewed less eagerly, to facilitate eavesdropping.

"Let him try to take them," Alphonso replied, glancing at Papa.

"Brother—" Cesare started.

"He'll find a warned Aragon more difficult to overcome than Juan Borgia, relieving himself a river."

I looked carefully at Papa. He flinched not a muscle.

"Say something, Papa," I said.

But he only smiled, as if granting his indulgence for boys to be boys.

"The French are famous," Cesare went on, "for their finesse with the fair sex. If I know them—"

"And well you know them, especially their *mesdames*," I interrupted, which produced not the tension-abating guffaw I'd hoped for, but barely the slightest titter.

"I know them well. They won't spare a woman's breast their knives, if they perceive her an enemy." Cesare looked first to me then to Alphonso. "You should think of my sister, Aragon."

"I think of little else, Borgia," Alphonso said, "but my wife."

"I'm happy to hear everyone is thinking of me," I said. "Why don't you think further and stuff further thoughts down your throats."

From Cesare's point of view I knew this was going badly. I detected a tremor just below one of his eyes. Alphonso was also beginning to get upset. He loved my brother, especially in light of all the time they'd spent together since the wedding, but Cesare was going well over the line of Φιλαδελφια, of *Philadelphia*, of brotherly love, with this conversation.

"I'm a man of great power," Cesare said. "Commander of a great army. I'm far more fit to defend my sister than either of you children."

Alphonso ignored the "children" crack. In Cesare's voice I'd heard a smidge of vibrato to match his eye's flicker.

"That's doubtless true," Alphonso said. "But I and my knights will lay down our lives to protect her readily as a baby might lay down an unwanted rattle. They're each as ten other fighting men." He looked calmly and straight at Cesare. "Any fool stupid enough to test them will find my grandfather's seen to that."

I was wishing we'd brought some Knights of Aragon tonight. Cesare's body was beginning to subtly shake. I well knew what was coming. I sent a fast plea to the Virgin, praying it wouldn't arrive, but knew I was too late. I shot a look at Papa, but he pretended to be occupied with cerebrum.

"It's the Will of God," Cesare said, "that my sister be safe. It's God's and all His Heavenly Host's Will that I accomplish her safety by becoming King of all Italy, including Naples and the twin Sicilies. It is the Will of God's Vicar that I accomplish her safety by becoming Emperor. It is the Will of God's Vicar's son, myself, that I accomplish her safety by now becoming the Duke of Bisceglie and inherit the Kingdoms of Naples and Sicily, saving countless lives without need of messy conquest."

The breaths of all the other guests came silently and without motion as those of entombed Lazarus. Even the fleecy servants had frozen, the only sound Diana's harp and the bells, which were both engaged, I recall, in a particularly insipid, faux-Claudian ditty.

Alphonso looked at me, then Cesare, straight into his twitching eye. "It's God's Will, I'm sure, that Lucrezia be safe. But I, by God's Grace, not you, Cesare Borgia, am Prince of the House of Aragon, while I live."

My brother turned back to him with a trembling smile. "While you live?"

"I live today, a condition you haven't the balls to alter."

That was a purposely baiting and untrue thing to say. Cesare, if nothing else, most certainly had balls. Cesare's eyes began to roll back in his head. His sandal-clad feet started to stamp on the marble floor. A noise began to come from him, as the raped Virago must've told him, such that if a squirrel could scream, this would've been the noise. He abruptly rose from the table, his golden chair flying and clanking to the ground with the force of him. He picked up his full gold wine goblet in one hand and brain-laden plate in the other. He hurled them down the length of the dinner table's golden oval. They skipped into and smashed any number of antique Grecian crockeries. Vintage wine covered a whore's cleavage with claret far more expensive and three times as old as herself. The plate, as well, splattered gray encephalon on the pectoral cross and red cassock of one of the Cardinal Deacons. Cesare turned to Alphonso, my brother by now screaming in his golden rage, his sandals a drumroll on marble floor.

"You call yourself a fucking husband? You're nothing but a simian shit-merchant in noble cloth! You loudly claim to love my sister? You feign swooning and twitching before her like Pyramus before some well-worn, secondhand Thisbee? And yet you give not a shit for her, nor for her child, which you could only give her with my help in the seduction!"

With a dissonant, horrible chord and twang of broken string—Diana had been so alarmed and upset, she'd given her G-string an overpluck—the harp ceased its wretched jingle and two out of three of her fleeces fell off. The bells lost their voices. The rest of the table was by now frozen into a stone frieze of a dinner party.

"Cesare, we're not having a little tantrum, are we, now?" Papa asked the whole frieze of us.

I prayed Cesare might be finished.

But far from it. "I'd kill you for a dung-eating snake if you weren't my brother! But for my sister's sake, for whom I've more love in the crack of my ass than you do in your entire putrid body, I swear I'd cut your semen-sucking throat myself and throw your corpse in the Bay of Naples!"

"Cesare, don't be common," Papa said.

"Common, Papa? I am the least common man in the world!" Cesare grabbed up the cloth-of-gold tablecloth. He gave it a great yank. Soup, pasta, Bordeaux, sauterne, floating island, brain and fish eggs smashed to the floor and all over the guests. Cesare was standing, Caligula Augustus, glaring and trembling like a madman at Alphonso. I was thinking Cesare a babyish, overblown asshole, but I confess I felt also sorry for him. He looked such an utter ass in his towering rage and emperor costume. I knew from seeing a thousand versions of this over my life that he'd been no more able to control his absurd mania and mouth than a Sudanese giraffe is able to be short. I asked the Virgin to help them. To help Cesare control himself quickly and apologize or replace his tantrum with blessed calm. To help Alphonso recognize my brother's disease for what it was—a personal curse—and bring himself to forgive his brother. Alphonso sat immobile for a moment. He watched Cesare but looked oddly peaceful. Not like the frigid calm of Cesare's other self, but composed as an April breeze. This struck me better than I could've hoped. Alphonso fiddled idly with a fastening on his doublet. He put his hands on the table and calmly stood, Papa patting his shoulder. Forget this Cesare in front of you, I said to Alphonso in my mind, and remember the one that faced the boar and saved your life. As if in response Alphonso looked not as if he were about to strike Cesare, but to hug him. Oh, thank you, Virgin Mother, went through my soul.

"We judge apologies to be in order all round," Papa said. "In fact, We issue Our verbal Bull to that effect."

The frieze cracked a doubtful set of grins.

"My Lord brother," Alphonso said serenely as a meadow. He looked at Cesare and smiled. He looked at the Pope and they both smiled.

This remarkable manly forbearance and self-control of Alphonso's was having a softening effect on Cesare. His tantrum was beginning to wane, his eyes returning to normal. The whistle of his breath's wine-bladder slowed and softened. His stamping ceased. But in a single, abrupt motion Alphonso grabbed a jeweled golden carving knife from the goose on the table, which as in a magician's trick was the only thing that hadn't budged an inch with Cesare's tablecloth yank. He simultane-ously grasped Cesare by his emperor's breastplate and hoisted him above his head. He then smashed him, facedown, onto Louis' dining table, his nose whacking with a crunch into the goose's bones. Alphonso slightly pivoted, holding Cesare, and slammed the carving knife across my brother's throat. The other guests now leapt, gasping and shouting, from their golden chairs, backing and shying from the fight, now that it was dangerous. Two of Cesare's soldiers, Brutus and Cassius, drew knives from little scabbards, but dared not interfere. The implication of these knives was clear. If Alphonso killed Cesare, these soldiers were to kill Alphonso. The blood from the knife at Cesare's Adam's apple began to drip along the blade and into the caperberry and blood-orange dressing of the goose, as if the final tableside ingredient. I thought of Christ, the stab in His Side, bleeding at first Blood, then a watery nothing.

"No man in a thousand years has spoken as you have to an Aragon and lived," Alphonso said in a guttural whisper. "Least of all to my noble father or grandfather, men whose misdirected piss you are unfit to lick up."

Cesare's eyes were those of a terrified child, of a bully who's been struck back, beaten to the ground and getting what he deserves, but who can't understand why he deserves it.

Alphonso went on. "The thought you will take with you to Hell, brother Borgia, will be that you are not manly enough garbage to break this thousand-year precedence."

"Merciful God, spare him," gasped Papa.

Alphonso's knife went to kill him. I saw the blood coming faster and screamed. I ran from my end of the table down its length. I wrapped my arms around Alphonso, grabbing his hand to stop his blade from cutting deeper.

"Remove your arms," Alphonso said. "I'm sorry; he's dead."

"Alphonso, please, I beg you." I could feel Alphonso's beautiful muscles tensing all the harder. "He's a pig. He deserves to die. He's lost control like this since we were babies together."

"Someone should've cut his throat when you were babies together, and spared me the time and trouble."

"He's beneath contempt, but he's my brother."

"Were he James, the Brother of Christ, I swear—"

"My mother vanished from my life. If you kill my brother, it will be like losing her again. Like losing myself. I beg you."

"Honor demands he die. From their graves all the Aragons' honor cries for his death. Your own honor and our son's demand it."

Papa knelt in the wine and table-scraps, bowing his head. "But God's love forbids it, which cancels all. Please, my boy, I beg you on my knees; let my son live. Just for tonight. If you feel the same come the sun, kill him with my blessing."

Papa's rare and humble use of "I" and "my" hit the whole room with a balm of humility. "Just for tonight" also should've worked, a gamble of Papa's that by morning young men's passions would've inevitably cooled. But I felt the muscles of Alphonso's arm clench to ram his knife home. Papa'd failed and I was the only one that knew. It was up to me. I had only one feminine card left, the Queen of Hearts, and only a second to play her. "Don't you love me at all? No one who loves me could kill my mother's child, no matter what the cause. That you love me pleads he live. Please, Alphonso. I beg you. Listen to Papa. I beg you before God, before the spirit of your boy. If you kill Cesare, I swear I'll become Medea; I'll kill our Roderigo, and tonight!"

That was unfair, and my child's death, I pray to Christ, a bluff. But then, haven't all women been a hundred times in each of our lives in receipt of the unfair? This teetering arrangement between men and women was a bargain struck outside Eden's gate. Shouldn't each side be free to spend, when it will, what capital it's left? Should anyone begrudge me what small, feminine advantage I could take from the con-tingent facts of Creation, from Eden tipped against me? Alphonso looked at Cesare. Brutus and Cassius, to whom Alphonso had paid not a whit of notice, poised at last to take action.

"Alphonso, he's your brother, too," I whispered. "Cain had cause, but his regret was endless."

"As was Jason's," Cesare whispered.

Alphonso paused. I saw decision flop over and click inside him. He leaned down and whispered in Cesare's ear. "Remember, Borgia, each minute and moment of the rest of your overblown life, that every tick-tock is Alphonso of Aragon's gift. Not a gift to you, but to your sister. That you draw each breath only by her grace."

Alphonso removed the knife. I saw blood run down its gutter and I burst into childish tears. Cassius and Brutus relaxed. The other guests politely applauded with relief. The claret-bosomed whore took me in her arms to comfort me and I smelled Vanita's sort of Arabian on her, making me cry all the harder.

"*Gaudeamus Dei!*" Papa shouted from the floor. "We rejoice in God!"

Cesare rolled over and sat up. He breathed deeply. "Thank you, sister, for this breath."

The guests laughed, if somewhat nervously. Cesare and Alphonso were still looking at one another. Cesare picked up a cloth-of-gold napkin. He began to wipe gleaming goose grease from his face. "I apologize, brother," he said. "You would've been well within your rights to kill me. I think myself the Calydonian Boar, when sometimes but a Parma ham."

All laughed but me. I made a silent ejaculation of thanksgiving to the Virgin. But as I did, a flash of knowledge struck me, the whore's Arabian still circling. It hadn't been the Virgin, or even the Trinity. It had been Vanita, and Alphonso's little Roderigo, who'd saved Cesare. I'd invoked their names to Alphonso to sway him, and Cesare lived, when only a miracle could've kept him alive. Only the dead can answer prayer, and my baby surely lived; my sagging exhaustion proved it every morning. So my mother must be dead, I thought. I burst into more wretched tears. I'm sure everyone thought me mad.

Cesare put his arms around me. "I'm sorry, baby sister. Please forgive me. It was my devil; plus I'm drunk. Think of me as a little thunderclap. I sound dreadful, but in a measure I'm at rest."

I laughed, myself, which felt so good after all this. The little bells and Diana's harp resumed. She was now missing a string, which rendered her chords oddly Syrian. All the guests once more applauded and looked to see if any remaining brain might be edible, but it all looked like mashed strawberries and cream. The fleecy herd of Dianas and Pans started to straighten up. As they did, Cesare rubbed his neck with his palm, where the knife had cut him. He looked at his hand. It dripped blood. His eyes rolled slowly back into his head. He fainted dead away into Alphonso's and my arms. We carried him to his bed, where after fifteen minutes or so he revived and came back to his party. I wondered, staring at out-cold Cesare, if this was the one who'd bested the Adriatic's two-footed sharks. Was this the hero that hadn't flinched before the rushing tusks? It occurred to me that it's only other people's blood that excites men—no matter how otherwise fierce, their courage vanishing at first sight of their own. Women are the opposite. His lying there led me to wonder with how many women Cesare had slept in this bed. What is he like in the act? Any actual love in it, ever? I then considered what he'd said and done earlier tonight with Alphonso, of the push Papa had undertaken with Alphonso and me to make us cede our titles and lands to Cesare, of the moments of the boar, of the joust and finally of an exploding cannon, Cesare behind the tree. I thought of all those things differently than I'd ever before. As they wound and rewound, I found myself in a labyrinth of Cesare. There was no way out but to follow the truth. He was trying to destroy us. He was after the Aragon lands, name, honor and gold. He wanted my husband's life and, God curse him for a pervert/murderer, even perhaps my child's. All the contingent facts and feelings that had emerged since my last retreat from the truth bound themselves into a book with chapters and a plot suddenly in the midst of God's writing this fresh scene about a dinner party—in the dialogue between Alphonso and my brother. Unlike little Lucrezia, Cesare's exquisite daughter, I'd always loved words and trusted in them. Only scratched now into words did I believe in the fratricidal power and intent of my Father of Lies. Behold Lucrezia, I mused, Abel's wife. I was afraid of my brother for the first time in my life. I feared my father, as well, though I couldn't quite connect the two apprehensions. A new world began to open like a nightshade's purple hood to Lucrezia Borgia.

I imitated a shy mouse, retreating by myself into a golden corner in another room and turning over private thoughts for the remainder of Cesare's party, even after he'd recovered from his faint and rejoined the trailing-off festivities, when the Pans doused most of the candles and guests began to sample the varied after-dinner mensae of one another's bodies. I tried going back into the dining room with the others, as any proper Lady would've, especially in my role of honorary hostess, but couldn't. I failed when I attempted to tell myself there was no real proof for my suspicions and that my brother's and my shared blood cried out for more proof than surmises. I failed, even when I tried to tell myself my mother would damn me for thinking this way. Finally, other guests began to solicit me.

"Is something wrong, Lady Lucrezia?" an Archbishop said. "Cesare and Alphonso are asking for you."

I turned abruptly. "Go away, Excellency. I need to be alone just now."

By the looks on their faces, he, his mistress and teenage catamite were empathetic, assigning my antisocial crabbiness to the earlier brawl.

An hour and a half later Cesare bid us farewell in the drive. He had a cloth-of-gold napkin tied round his neck to stanch his goose-knife wound. He was damnably charming in his boyish guilt. He could still make me laugh. The power of humor in human affairs is nowadays vastly underestimated by philosophers and artists, who assume each melodramatic circumstance inevitably surrounded by melodramatic everything else, as if real life were by Euripides. I'm certain Aeschylus and his Greek impresarios were right to intersperse the tragedies of the Oresteia—Agamemnon, Libation Bearers and Eumenides, all as fearful and piteous as tragedies get—with ribald farces on the same subject matters.

"Brother, we were all amazed you didn't bleed molten gold," Alphonso said. I could see in his face he'd forgiven my brother.

Cesare smiled. "Perhaps the scar will be golden."

Alphonso and I went clattering off in our carriage with driver and footmen. As we made the corner, putting Cesare's entryway out of sight behind the great circle of Sant'Angelo, I saw my brother turn and speak to a servant. Then Alphonso and I were alone.

"Maybe it isn't true," I muttered.

"What isn't true?"

"I could be wrong, couldn't I? Maybe he wishes me nothing but well, when he's in his right mind."

I hadn't until then mentioned my suspicions to Alphonso.

"It's extraordinary, this brother-sister thing you two have. There's nothing like it in my family. We all just straight-out loathe each other, so nobody's ever surprised. And we never set knives at meals. Thank God you and your father were there. I would've killed him."

"Ummm. Maybe you're right."

Alphonso and I banged noisily on in our blue carriage's Tiber-side way on our little post-midnight ride under the moon. Out the window it looked like a painting in the river.

"That's the idea," I mumbled. I half slept, dreaming both of my new suspicions—the new ways these suspicions would now require Alphonso and me to rethink our lives—and of how romantic Diana's image looked, reflected in the water.

Alphonso kissed me, but I was too far gone to respond. "What's wrong?" he asked.

"Nothing."

"Nothing? Don't patronize me."

"I'm thinking of the moon and Cesare."

"Not the moon and me?"

"He's dangerous."

"So am I."

Then inside our coach I heard the coachman tighten the reigns on our four horses, the iron-rimmed wheels sparking to a stop.

"My Lord, my Lady," the coachman shouted from above.

I heard our footmen scrambling across the coach's roof. I felt our horses buck and prance in panic. We looked outside. A gang of young men had stretched itself across the street next to the river, either blocking us entirely or sending us into the Tiber. They looked like boys, really, but I remember thinking immediately the word *gang*, because their look and demeanor were only of a gang. If they'd once been boys, they'd long lost the air of such creatures. There are thousands of these gangs, curse Lucifer, that prey in cities all over Christendom on the unsuspecting, on each other and the unlucky. But rarely do they make an attempt on a nobleman, as they were doing tonight, since the retribution for that can be swift, hard and often not worth the money. The bourgeois or clerical are more likely to carry cash—jewels are too easy to trace and therefore undesirable—since the truly noble can pay with credit and their word. I knew these boys must've been well bought to undertake this risk. But by whom? It took me little imagination to answer. They drew weapons. Some had swords nearly as large as their owners, some knives.

"Stay here," Alphonso said.

Alphonso went to exit the carriage, but before he could, the gang flew on it like a nest of asps. I heard screams and then saw our coachman's head—I recognized his just-married, always-hungry expression—rolling in the street. I heard and saw the bodies of our footmen, cut to horrifying pieces, dead on the cobblestones.

"Stay here," Alphonso shouted again.

"Alphonso—" But he was gone.

"That's him! The one in dark blue!" the gang's leader shouted as Alphonso hit the pavement, drawing his own sword.

Alphonso leapt at the gang's relatively large leader. I saw sparks of steel. Alphonso fought the leader for perhaps two further sparks, by which time the entire gang had surrounded him. Our dead servants had bloodied several of the gang's weapons and they dripped red. The gang paused only a second. Then they rushed in to kill my husband. I screamed. I jumped from the carriage. I ran at them. I jumped at the largest, the first back I saw. I grasped him from behind by the face with both my arms and hands. I kept screaming like Lilith into his ear.

The killer spun, trying to get me off. "Get this bitch off me!"

He slashed back at my eyes with his knife. I had hold of him still by his head. I felt for his eyes with my fingertips. I gouged them out, digging my manicure into jam-filled sockets. They felt rich, creamy, for a moment like the warm goo of one of Vanita's hot pie fillings she used to let me help her bake.

"My eyes!" he screamed.

Another immature devil swung his sword hilt at my face. I felt pain and simultaneously saw a bright light. He hit me again, in the jaw this time. I had a memory flash, real as my cracked molar, of Cesare when Vanita slapped him after Roderigo left Subiaco. I felt his shock and surprise, as I now felt my own. Was this somehow Cesare's revenge for that? I hoped not. I hoped that too venial for even Cesare Borgia. In the street by the Tiber my blood tasted in my sporadic mind specifically like the glop of Mama's cherry pies. Again, again they struck me, until my consciousness began to cluster inward and wander to my fingers. As I gloried in cherry creaminess, I let go, my body striking the pavement.

"My eyes. My fucking eyes!" I heard my victim moan from somewhere as distant at that moment as the mountains of the moon.

Another began to kick me in the stomach. Again. Again.

A third intervened. "Don't kill the bitch! Don't kill the fucking bitch."

I saw Alphonso, running from the side. At the run he plunged his sword into the head of the kicking beast, just at the soft spot where jaw connects with skull. Alphonso's blade broke with a metallic snap in the beast's head. He dropped to the ground, a puppet with strings cut by the foot of sword still sticking from his noggin. I reached over and took the knife from his dead claw. I scrambled from the ground and jumped the wolf closest to me, the one I'd already blinded. I faced him. I brought the knife up and cut his throat, I felt his tendons twang like snapping bowstrings with the knife's draw, his voice box, midshout, caving in with a noise of trampled trumpet, blood gushing warmly over my hands and down my face and cleavage. They say it's more difficult to kill while looking into the victim's eyes. I can testify that this one was easy while peering into his eyeless skull. It felt as warm and satisfying as removing my little girl's pie from the oven.

But the abrupt deaths of two of their number had some sort of aboriginal effect on the survivors. They all leaped on Alphonso, his arms, his legs and torso. They dragged him to the ground with their gross weight. The moment he hit the pavement they all slashed and stabbed repeatedly at him. I howled. I rushed with my own knife at the pack of hacking flesh on top of him. But the leader turned and saw me coming. He struck out at me with his sword, hitting my hand. Agony and shivering paralysis shot up my arm. I couldn't hold the knife and dropped it. Weaponless, I rushed back at him. I put my arms around him to attack him frontally. I bit his head, feeling hard cranium under my canines. He screamed. His filthy ear was now the only thing in my view, my teeth my only weapon. Oh, God, I wished I were only half the virago Katerina Sforza was said to be. I took the ear wholly in my mouth and bit down, as viciously as I could, shaking violently my head. He screamed again, his mouth just next to my own ear. Two gang members then turned on me from Alphonso. They struck me with the hilts of their swords. And again. Again. Again. I slithered to the ground from pain and fading awareness. I turned and began to crawl toward my motionless husband. Crawling, I still had the leader's disgusting auricle, dangling from my mouth. I tried to spit it out, but couldn't. It clung to my lip like a sticky, red-bee honeycomb. My pain and woman's party dress made it difficult even to crawl. As I hands-and-kneed, I could hear the pack chatting above me as they watched.

"What should we do with the bitch?"

"Golden boy told us not to kill her."

"Go'den boy?" I slurred at them, midcrawl. "What go'den boy?"

They didn't answer, but I knew.

"You wanna kill her anyway?" another said.

"I don't know about you, but I ain't doing nothing that guy didn't tell us. He was scarier than your dead mother."

A grumble of disappointed agreement.

I reached my husband's body. I collapsed on it. The blood, this red, was all I could think of. It gushed from him like miscarriages from a hundred wombs. I saw a white of bone, a glisten of internal organs. I knew I had to stop the red. I had to stop it. I took my hands and placed them over the strongest spurts to stop them. I pushed in to stop the hemorrhages, but they flowed back out through my fingers.

The blood surged from him, undiminished, like water from the Dutch boy's dike. I pressed with my hands, arms, with the side of my head. I put my mouth over a flow from his chest, but the red filled my mouth so fast, I gagged away.

"Remember me." I called as loudly as I could to Alphonso, though I'm now certain what felt a yell was only a longing whisper. "Remember that even in Heaven no one will ever love you the way I do."

"But she's a real piece of ass, isn't she?" a little prick said above us.

"A pisser."

"Remember me," I whispered again to my husband. "If you forget my voice, remember my body, the ways it loved you."

"When she's aroused."

They all giggled.

"You're not likely to forget her, are you, Petey?"

Petey? The one whose ear still clung to me? The Alpha-claw, Petey? Do such creatures have names? Even so far as familiar nicknames? I was stunned. Had some mother held this little Satanic brick to her breast, baby Petey, the way I had Roderigo, and whispered sweetness into that vile ear pit? Had he tried to bite her nipple off with his sharp-gummed toothlessness? If Roderigo ever turned into another Petey, I could happily turn Medea.

"Petey'll always remember her," another emphasized.

"Petey's in love. He always liked it rough."

All giggled, except, I guessed, Petey, who held the bloody hole where once he'd sported an ear for a woman to whisper into.

"You'll remember her, won't you, Petey," another said, chuckling. "Every time you hear something?"

Sniggers all round, except from Petey. If one more asked grotesque, shit-headed Petey if he'd ever forget me, I thought . . . but quickly realized there was nothing I could do.

"What harm could a good fucking do her now?"

"She's all loosened up. She's probably hot for something long, meaty and hard."

"Or short, fishy and squishy, in your case."

A big laugh, but the joke for a moment gave me a spark of relief. At least it was a change of subject.

"A thorough fucking would only be the usual for such a lusty cunt."

"It's the only excuse for her to be alive."

Giggle.

"Why else create a woman that looks like her?"

Snigger.

"She dresses like a whore. Everybody in Italy's already had her, anyway."

Twin giggles.

"Including her papa and the golden faggot."

Chuckle. Guffaw.

"The red-hatted farts will just con God to turn her into a virgin again. What's the difference?"

"Or her papa can bless her back into one every time he fucks her."

A particularly animated, that's-a-good-one snigger.

"She'll still be alive. He didn't say *not* to fuck her, did he?"

Which was followed by an utter silence more terrorizing than could've been all the giggling sniggers of every adolescent lizard in Hell. What happened in the next moments I'll not write on bright vellum. Not in the peace of recollection, not in Hell nor Purgatory, nor whisper into God's ear. Suffice it to scribble that the beasts and birds of prey in nature's butchering menagerie in no way visit upon one another the bestiality or high-spirited cruelty that the potential Saints of this world visit upon fellow limbs of the Body of Christ. All those human ferocities, as we happy, Christian lambs believe, may be canceled out, if only we savagers spend but a conversational moment in a darkened booth or croak at our death's twinkling a trite ejaculation. As this unwritable happened, I heard still-spreading blood dripping into the Tiber. I prayed Alphonso's life might flow from here to *Mare Nostrum*. In the waters of our Roman Sea, at least, I asked God that he be spared the company of such cold-blooded demons as ourselves. There a soul could find peace.

I remember the Tiber, red, sparkling and voiceless in a dawn light, as we lay in the street. I saw customary bits of garbage in the gutter across the cobbles. There also was our coachman's head, sitting upright, one motionless eye glaring at me, the other closed in a grim wink. His pupil, lit by the rising glare of sun, was unirised black. I remember the light, spraying down from Heaven, as in artists' paintings of dawn. I remember thinking I'd never see any beauty in eyes or those paintings again, but that in future I'd regard eyes as the things that see Hell, and dawn light as the adjective of the morning's dead. I remember my husband's lifeless body in my arms and not knowing how long we'd been that way. Time was dead. Or have I been here forever? I wondered. Have I died and gone to timeless Hell, Lucifer's skyless, dimensionless planet of this gore-stinking light? I remember larks' songs and with them the chorus of my own crying, my throat rough and sore from hours of it. My face felt as if it might fill a room, as if it would burst with swelling. Then I recall the sound of iron-shod hooves, first distant, then clanging on cobblestone next to my head. I tried to get up, to locate the hoofbeats and see where they came from. But I couldn't raise my head. Nor could I raise my body. I was glued, coagulated by his blood, to my husband, cemented in the middle of a dark red, frozen lake of him. Could it be possible a single human body could hold such a lake of maroon? If I could only raise my head, time would tick again; Alphonso might rise from the dead. In his blood we'd become one of those monstrous twins that emerge from the womb, allotted by God the ultimate intimacy of parts of one another's bodies, two to move or not move as one all their lives. I remember looking at the headless body of our kind coachman, at our dead, always prompt and cheerful footmen. All they'd be prompt or happy about now were their holes in the ground. I recall our horses, forlorn by the side of the road, looking as if guilty to find themselves alive. I saw horsemen pull up. Three immediately dismounted and ran toward us.

"My Lady! My Lord!"

"Oh, my Christ," another cried. "I've never seen such blood!"

When they reached us, the only way I could acknowledge them was to move my eyes.

"My Lady, you're alive!"

Alive? What is alive? I mused, but couldn't stay for an answer. "He's dead," I moaned. "The Virgin's gift is dead. . . . Look what they've done to him. . . ."

The Guards leaned down. As gently as they could—it was difficult, because of the glue of blood, and I resisted them as much as I could—they lifted me from Alphonso, as I'd once ripped a Caesarean child from a peasant's womb.

"No, no, leave me . . . leave me to my Lord . . . leave my Lord to my arms . . . the world's blue flower is dead."

They led the dead girl that was Lucrezia away.

"I have to rock him in my arms three days and nights, till he wakes with Vanita. . . ."

A fourth guard dismounted, looking to be their captain. I recognized him. Across his face was a tiny scar, as if from a woman's nail. He walked slowly to Alphonso's body. He bent down, again slowly, and appraised him. He appeared the sort who'd seen many dead in his time, his face a bumpy rock. He took his gorget, polished to a military, mirrorlike surface, from around his neck. For a moment I couldn't understand what he was at. He took the gorget and held it to my husband's face. I remember seeing the captain's body go tense as wire as he held the gorget. He looked up.

"My Lady!" he cried. "It clouds! I see breath!"

Only then did the Virgin reset God's earthly complication. I remember riding frantically in the morning's wet atmosphere into Saint Peter's Square in our coach, now driven by a Palatine. I recall the captain's breathing behind me inside the coach. I praised God to be in a coach with two men breathing. I remember four mounted outriders. Why hadn't we these giants with us last night? I asked Heaven. Because you, yourself, thought them unnecessary, the Virgin spit back. It had been I, the idiot-blond, phony, damned ingenue in her posh, slutty party dress who was responsible. We rushed through the column of pillars, each named for a Martyr. I saw Papa waiting on the steps of his palace. Papa, Papa, thank God you're here, I thought. Thank you for being true to me. Thank you at least for not deserting and betraying me, as your son has. Thank you for remembering. Oh, Christ, what have I to tell you? Is there anything in Dante stranger than what you'll hear from me? I'll confess it to you in our library, so we can take out our Sophocles when I tell you. Perhaps we can employ his verse to begin to understand. It's going to hurt you beyond imagination, as I'm hurt. But think, when I say it, how much I love you. How much Vanita loves you in eternity.

With pacing Papa were several cardinals, nuns, priests and Knights of Aragon. Our carriage reached them and stopped in a dusty rumble. The outriders dismounted. The drivers leapt down. Papa ran to the carriage, freezing at its door, as if frightened to open it. "Are they . . . ?"

"They were savagely attacked, Holiness," a Palatine said.

Papa crossed himself. "Where?"

"On the road by the river, Sanctity."

"In the Vatican?"

"Yes, Sanctity. We took so long because we never thought anyone . . ."

"Of course not." He made a Sign of the Cross. "Near Sant'Angelo?"

He knows, I thought, or at least suspects.

The captain continued. "Lady Lucrezia looks bad, but I assure Your Holiness she's all right."

"All praise to God."

"But my young Lord is very grave. He may die at any moment."

"God forbid."

"He's lost more blood than I've ever seen a man lose and live."

The knights opened the door and lifted me from the carriage. There was a brief scuffle between knights and guards over who should take possession of us.

"Let Aragon take them," Papa said. He opened his white arms to me. I walked to him and allowed those arms to encloud me. At that moment I loved Papa and let those arms surround me with as much cloudbank of comfort as they'd once, when I'd been little. None of this blood was his fault, was it? The knights then rushed back into the carriage. They gently plucked Alphonso from it and removed him. He was inert, a rag doll, looking dead as Wednesday's Ashes. The captain must've seen my reaction and felt compassion. He removed his gorget from around his neck once more and held it to Alphonso's mouth and nose.

"You see, my Lady? It still clouds. The cloud is life."

"You have a hundred gold passports to Eternity, Captain," Papa told him.

Alexander again made a Sign of the Cross over Alphonso, whom the knights were carrying up the steps. All the cardinals and priests made Signs of the Cross. The nuns blessed themselves in response.

"Bring him to our Apartments. Hurry. Gently," I said, removing myself from those white Papal arms.

Papa put his hand on my shoulder, the hand with the Fisherman's Ring. "Who were they, child?" he asked. "Were they French?" He paused and looked away. "Were they Cesare's?"

I felt muscles shiver at the back of my neck. I looked at my hands. They were still covered in my husband's blood. In my hand I saw Cesare drowning in that blood. "What difference does it make?" I said so all the prelates could hear me. "It was God's fucking Will, wasn't it, Papa?"

I took my hands and placed them on his cassock's white front on either side of his pectoral crucifix. When I took my hands away, the cross hung between the two bloody images of my fingers and palms, like a third thief.

"But know, Papa, that if this husband dies, I shall curse God—" I circled my gaze around at the assemblage of cardinals and priests—"and curse all who execute His Will, to my dying breath."

I could see the pain in Papa's face, as if I'd carved new lines in it. The Cardinals and priests all blessed themselves in horror. I was sorry for what I'd said. I'd hurt Papa, when he wasn't the one I'd wanted to hurt. Some have said Jesus wasn't the one the Jews wanted to crucify. I hoped Papa'd understand I'd lashed out only because I'd had to lash at someone. I'd try to explain it to him tomorrow; there was too much to see to now. I turned back and continued up the steps after my husband.

Several hours later, I went to the Hall of the Mysteries of Faith. Papa was there with a clutch of monsignors and abbots. I took him by the hand and pulled him from his throne.

"Lucrezia, what are you doing?"

"Come with me, Papa. I have to talk with you this minute."

I led him through and past the Apartments, to the library, opened the swinging doors and we went in.

I turned to face him. "Papa, Cesare tried to have Alphonso killed. He's the one who hired the assassins."

"Child, you're—"

"It's true, Papa. And this wasn't the first time. It was Cesare, wasn't it, who talked you into trying to get us to cede our lands and titles to him? Wasn't it Cesare?"

"It was Our idea."

"You've kept saying that, but in this case you don't mean yours and God's, do you?"

Papa just looked at me. From what I know now, he was dissembling like mad at that moment, but at the time his face struck me only filled with pain, fear and disappointment. He looked as if he were unwillingly admitting to me a truth that he couldn't say. That I was right, but that it was too mortifying for him even to think, for all of our sakes. A masterful manipulation.

"Lucrezia, if what you say is true, then it's beyond evil. Are you absolutely sure? What proof do you have?"

"Proof? What proof do I need? I need only have an uncooked brain to think, since we returned from Tivoli, to know all I need know. The assassins said a 'golden boy' put them up to it."

"A group of hired murderers refers obliquely to some or other 'golden child'? That's our proof?"

"Didn't you hear Cesare last night with Alphonso? He straight-out threatened to kill him."

"And likewise did Alphonso him. Yes? And in what state was Cesare? Did he say it calmly, as Alphonso did, or was he in the Devil's madness, set off by your husband?"

"Mad as Hildegarde."

He looked at me. "But *I* need proof," he finally said. "I am the Supreme Pontiff. Aristotelean reasoning to a proof is insufficient these days; I need proof palpable and definite as a stone. Something I can pick up and taste. If this is true, I'd have no choice. I'd have to have your brother taken to a place of execution. I'd have to have him stripped naked and whipped. I'd have his manhood sliced from his body to be burned before his eyes, his gut cut slowly opened with a white-hot blade and his bowels drawn from him by a horse."

"A palomino?"

"That sort of vindictive irony becomes no one."

"Fratricide becomes no one."

"Do you know how long a human bowel is? Can you imagine how slowly well-trained horsemen may draw it from a human body? Are you sure beyond Inquiry at the Throne of God? Is this what you want? Tell me; I'll do it. Swear to me you're sure on Christ's Blood, washed by the Holy Mother from His Body. Swear to me in those words and I'll do as you ask."

"Papa—" was all I could get out.

"You can't, can you?"

I couldn't answer.

"I love you, Lucrezia, no matter what you ever say to me. We'll keep your suspicions secret in Our breast. *In pectore.* If there comes a moment of proof, We'll do as We've described. But for now, We command you to let it go. And command you further, until We all have proof and the time is right, not to reveal Our suspicions to anyone else, not even Alphonso, if God grants he live." Papa made a blessing with his hand, evidently to encourage God in this secrecy, as well. "It would be unfair, if you turn out to be wrong. If you're right, it would serve to warn your brother and allow him to thwart Our justice."

"And how should the stone taste to satisfy you for proof, Papa?"

"This is such a deadly serious crime. Only confession will satisfy Us."

"Confession? Think of what my brother's done. Think of him. Will a man who could do that offer a confession?"

"With God's Help, all things are possible."

I rolled my eyes. "Even with Christ holding him by the hand or kicking him in the ass, such a thing is impossible for Cesare, and you damned well know it."

"Then only swear to Us the oath We've asked for and We'll execute his punishment."

"Papa, this must be your responsibility, not mine. It's for Vanita's sake you should do what's right."

"Vanita? Then make to Us another oath, if you don't like the first. Swear to me, straight into my eyes, that you're positive it's what your mother would have me do."

I tried. I couldn't.

He smiled. "No, it isn't. It isn't me, is it? It's not my responsibility, is it? It's *Lucrezia* Borgia's desire you must be sure of. Not Roderigo-the-elder's." Papa kissed me on the lips; he looked sadly into my eyes. "If what you say is true, don't despair. We'll protect you, as long as you're within the Vatican. We won't have a husband of Roderigo's and Vanita's child killed in Our City. Keep this to yourself and you'll have revenge one day. We swear it. We are never wrong. Our power is a matter of Divine power. Its righteousness cannot be assessed, nor its scope grasped, nor its majesty understood with the logic of Aquinas, the charm of Democritus or even with the passion of Lucrezia." He kissed me again. He turned and left the library. "What have you been reading lately?" he called back, as he passed from view behind shelves of Cicero.

For a few hours before and after that conversation I'd planned to remove Alphonso and the baby from the Vatican immediately. Papa was fallible—the Curia's tract be damned—and God only knew how Cesare might cross Papa, as well. But where to go? Remove them where? Back to Tivoli? To Pesaro? Or Naples? All three of those involved miles of dragging wounded Alphonso on a bumping pallet over mountains, rivers, swamplands and where the few good roads would be unguarded. He could reopen a wound. An attack could be at night. Worse yet, Cesare was Liege Lord by now of most of the ground between here and anywhere in Italy. Could I hire a ship from the Port of Rome and escape over the Mediterranean? To where? To whom? To Naples? Or had Cesare bought Grandpapa Federico? All it would take would be to turn the Sicilies' gaze from our ship for an hour. To the Ottoman Turk or into the hands of North African pirates? Both of those would love to have the Pontiff's daughter, grandson and son-in-law to trade for God knows what. Maybe they could get Spain back for us. In fact, the son-in-law would only be a bonus. In my head I could hear them. "Why don't we just kill him and do a cleaner deal for the bitch and brat? We can sell Aragon's corpse to Louis; he'll pay a ship of bullion for it." No. Leaving by land or water was too dangerous. For one moment I'd an idle speculation of having Master da Vinci fashion us one of his mechanical birds, but quickly abandoned that idea, since the second I had it I envisioned us crashing headlong into squat Janiculum Hill. Better we stay here in the Vatican. At least we'll be under Papa's protection. He's been informed of Cesare's treachery, at least, so he won't be taken unaware. He'll guard us. He's got more power than any king or emperor in Christendom. He'll prepare the Palatines. The captain that rescued Alphonso looked like he could retake the Holy Land all by himself. And not just temporal power. Papa will mobilize the Angelic host to fight for his grandchild. It'd almost be worth it just to see. The illuminated, winged billions, plunging from the sky, banners of the Seraphim aloft at their fore-edge. Moses, eat your heart out. Thou shalt not covet thy neighbor's Lucrezia. Nor kill her Italian God. Plus we've all those Knights of Aragon here; we couldn't be safer in a Ναυμαχια, a waterfest in foot-deep shallows of the Bay of Naples.

fter returning to our Apartment from the Vatican street's blood, an affinity with the Virgin I'd never before experienced overwhelmed me. In a thousand paintings they take Christ from His Cross. Saint Joseph of Arimathea accepts His Body, takes Him and lays Him on a stone pallet. The Virgin then washed His horrifying Wounds and the crusted Blood from Him with her own hands. She wrapped Him—naked from her cleansings—in the fine linen swaddling bandages, used then and now to enwrap the just born and dead. The Palatines and Aragonese Knights brought Alphonso through the Hall of Sibyls to our Apartment. They laid him on our bed. I cut his clothes from him. At first I tried to cut them with a pair of the sisters' scissors, but that proved as useless as cutting a leather cuirass with my fingers. Trying to cut the doublet, I found my Lord's clothes so crusted with dried blood as to feel like the suit of armor he'd worn jousting. I could only remove his clothing by carefully hacking with Alphonso's Damascus-bladed sword, whose edge a squire daily sharpened so to the point that if I laid a lilac petal across the edge, the petal fell in two of its own weight. I thought of Cesare's earlier tablecloth-pull from his golden table and fantasized whipping the clothes from Alphonso so easily; but that was fantasy. They came off with a horse-gluey, raspy noise. Each inch by inch, though I knew he felt nil, tortured my mind. I laid him naked on a pure white sheet. I washed his terrible wounds in warm water from the kitchens with my own hands. The wounds in his torso looked like lips, the edges of the cut skin revealing fatty layers and little upsurges like bunches of reddish-white grapes, or teeth forced from the cleft. I wrapped him in fine linen bandages. As with the Virgin's, my boy had the most terrible wound in his side. As with the Virgin's Boy, one of the Roman jackals had plunged an iron into his palm, a quarter stigmata. I felt so bad for the Holy Mother to have had to touch His Body, His Wounds in this manner; to be Immaculate even in Conception and still not be spared the agony this cleansing gave rise to in myself. As I washed him with bowl after warm bowl of water, the caked red began to dissolve and peter from him like sand castles from a red beach. I felt again so bad for Mother Mary, who'd had to do the same thing for the Christ. I felt in a way grateful, as she must've, that Alphonso hadn't his conscious mind. If he'd been aware, his agony would've been unimaginable. Had it been even worse for her to wash a son's wounds than for me to cleanse a lover's? Had both boys lost their souls, as well, and descended to Limbo? Alphonso, like Christ, absent mind and soul, looked now to be nothing but a ruined object. When I thought of that, I heard Roderigo crying in the next room. I went to him, saw he was safe and bowed my head in respect of the Virgin's suffering. I wondered if the prostitute Magdalen helped with the washing of His Wounds? Some say the Magdalen was a lover to Jesus, as we all should be. I fed my little Roderigo and returned to my husband, my linens and astringents. But I tried to push thoughts of the paramour Magdalen aside. Though thoughts in themselves have never felt to me sinful—and this was my husband—some covetously bodiless angel might see them as blasphemous. I was unsure and wanted no irreverence of mine interfering with any balm his guardian cherubim might grant Alphonso.

But blasphemous thoughts kept willy-nilly wrapping about my mind like a winding sheet, as my hands roved with their warm water and life's fluid over his naked body, whose wounded beauty aroused and still arouses me. I couldn't help thinking of my mother cleansing naked Sebastian in the Subiaco Chapel. I tried to stop my thoughts, but couldn't, and reflected that thought is like this bloody water, never pure or unclouded, always stained with life, penetrating, seeking its own level no matter our intention or attempts to caulk its flow. Wasn't the Christ a man like Alphonso? Didn't He live and die as one, as Alphonso had and may soon yet? Could He have been a man and never, not even once, have loved a woman? Would then He not have died half a man, and an ignorant one, having experienced only parts of human life, but never desire, nor desire's fulfillment and warmth? This led me to think of our lives. Was Alphonso's only purpose to die and mine to grieve forever after him, Paradise snatched away? I thought from there of the First Lovers' loss of Eden. Had they lost it by their own sin, as the Bible says? Or had a small-minded God, jealous of a sensual happiness together that He'd never know, snatched it from them? Many times in the Testaments it's said that He's "a jealous God." His excuse for retaking everything he gives, for even our death, furthermore seems to be our sinfulness, deriving from the Original Sin of a certain woman. All right, perhaps that woman in Eden led Adam into temptation, but it had always seemed to me so ludicrously easy for her. Is Genesis' message simply that men are self-indulgent and easily persuaded? If I'd been the Christ, I never would've let God the Father kill me, without having touched Alphonso. The Greek and Latin gods, all bastard progeny themselves, made love to us and one another so frequently and with such abandon that many ancient commentators have said their sexual lubricity was the primary function and attribute of all proper divinity.

Alphonso under my hands, it gave me sinful pleasure to imagine the Magdalen with Christ's Organ in her mouth, as I washed the blood from Alphonso's. I imagined she brought Him to momentary paradise, the little death. Was it blasphemous to imagine the living Christ, engaged in this manly pursuit? Could He have walked Golgotha's long, agonizing walk so willingly, knowing His own Father had denied Him even a small taste of the Magdalen's love, a fulfilling of what it means to be the Son of Man? Denied to Him, of all the most complete and perfect Man in history or possibility? To say so is to have it both of two contradictory ways. On the rhetorical inhale to claim He was a man like all the rest and while exhaling to deny Him the simplest manhood. When I finished wrapping Alphonso in his long bandages, took my water-warm hands from him and my lust for him began to cool, I finally could put these thoughts aside. I regarded them as having been only the sort of hysterical confusion to which the generally more lubricious female spirit is prone as a result of her owner's Briseis' heel for passion.

Just after dawn the next morning, July 16, I gathered together into our bedroom the Aragonese Knights and Papal Guards assigned to Alphonso and myself. Because of my conversation with Papa and because of his command to me, I knew I shouldn't tell them my suspicions, but I'd let them at least know there impended terrible danger here and their swords should be kept drawn for it. I ordered them all to wear full armor from now on; mail and plate should be their daily and nightly uniform. I told them to kneel in a semicircle around unconscious Alphonso's bed. I placed Alphonso's sword, forged in Barbarossa's own foundry, in its ivory scabbard on the bed, where it would lie in ménage with us for the next weeks. I dressed simply in a floor-length black gown I'd had in my closet for a year without coming across its right occasion. Sapphire designs covered it, embroidered in the shapes of old-fashioned swords of Araby.

"Swear it," I said.

The knights and guards looked about. "We've sworn long ago, Lady," one said.

"Swear it again," I replied, trying to appear as imperiously a modern-day, stiff-lipped Eudoxia as possible without her whoreish subtexts "I want to hear each of you swear it. On the Savior's Blood." I turned to the guards. "And all of you, as well. I'll have none enter this Apartment but have sworn."

"We shall swear what, Lady?"

"On Christ's Blood," I said, "which the Virgin washed from His Wounds with her own hands, that you will allow no suspicious man, nor woman, child, dog, nor even bird, nor dumb stone enter these rooms."

They bowed their heads, swords held before them. "We swear it to the death."

Two weeks of eventless sickbed torture passed, for me, anyway. Alphonso moved not a muscle; out cold, not an eyelid flicked. Doctors came and went, including two sent by King Federico: a surgeon, Galeano da Anna, from an ancient temple of Aesculapius on Vesuvius' flank, and Clemente Gacula, a physician of the Order of Saints Damien and Cosmas, Patrons of Physicians. Alphonso suffered terrible fevers, which one day raged, gave on the next a false hope of cooling, then raged once more the third. I laved his body continually in cool water to drain away his heat. Each time I bathed him, my loins and mind burnt with his heat. With each washing, another layer of Lucrezia Borgia felt burnt away by his skin. Each time it heated me in desire's furnace, then his nonresponse plunged me into cold, annealing water. Each time I came away harder and sharper-edged than the last. I asked the Virgin if this pointless heat was a sin. She answered in a dream that it wasn't. She said it was more like the healing Passion of her Son and if I offered those feelings to God for the purpose of Charity, they'd be received in Heaven in the nature of a prayer.

I could give Alphonso no nourishment or water. And although daily his wounds seemed healing and less terrible than they'd been the prior day, I noticed what a stunning wraith he was becoming, a young Desert Father with a snakeskin dryness about his mouth, his bones beginning to stick out. This lack of bulk could only make it more difficult for him to fight his infections. At night I'd post a fully armed guard and knight outside our door and a dozen more inside, who'd sleep on the floor around our bed. I'd open wide all our windows. I thought the clerical and medical warnings against God's Night Air patently ludicrous. If night air were poisonous, would the Holy Spirit have had Christ draw His First Breath of it? I'd get into our bed and take off all my clothes. I knew I should be naked, because I sensed my cool skin would be a medicine and palliative for Alphonso, as I knew his would be for me, were I so injured. I'd lie down next to my swaddling-clothed husband, my swaddled tot in the next room, take him in my arms and gently rock and sing to him. I sang a love song that, Mother Mary told me, Vanita used to sing Cesare as a child. The sleeping knights and guards never stole so much as a glance at my nudity. Not yet, anyway.

Papa had come into our Apartment on July 21 to confer his Apostolic Blessing on Alphonso for his recovery. Papa sprinkled Holy Water from the Grotto of the Holy Sepulcher over him. He drizzled some especially on the worst of his wounds. He enchrismed Alphonso's lips, ears, mouth, forehead and his sex, hands and feet—all the origins, or "occasions," of sin—with oil from the Mount of Olives. He granted him a Plenary Indulgence and touched the Bread of Viaticum to his dry tongue. He kissed him on his chrismed lips. I've no reason to doubt these actions of Papa's any less genuine or sincere than were his words with Cesare. I believe Papa wished his enemy death—as an enemy—while wishing him life as a son-in-law. He then went into the baby's room and spent half an hour dandling him. Little Roderigo the whole time screeched pleasure, as I once had in those thick hands. After Papa left, he further employed the power of Peter's chair to aid my husband. He sent a delegation of cardinals to Turin to command the Sacred Shroud of Christ's Body be brought to Rome. The Turinites packed it, arguing and lamenting, and brought it in a procession of five hundred chanting prelates and virgins down Italy to the Vatican. Six snow-white horses drew its silver and gold carriage. All it passed fell to their knees and faces before it. In every city, town and village every bell tower rang choruses of metallic joy. Many miracles occurred in its wake. An old, crippled woman suddenly walked as any girl, having only lifted her head to see its coach pass. A leper was cleansed, having but crawled to lick the dust over which its gurney's wheels had trundled. A blind man saw, having only heard its progress, and ran from the place, near Siena, bawling of God's sudden Light. Some say miracles are only results of human belief's power on our own bodies. But as the philosophers agree, if two things have the same result, they must in their natures be the same thing. "By their fruits you shall know them." If our belief in Him has the same healing result as a purposeful Action of His living Deity, then our belief, and His Being and Life, must be of the same manifestly existent substance.

Once in our Apartment, six Italian Cardinals unpacked the Shroud before me, unfurled and hung it in its transparent monstrance in a window in our bedroom. I had placed a brass pail with a rosebush beneath the window weeks before and now it looked as if the blooms had become the repositories of the ghostly blood that must've drained from the shadowed linen. In the daylight the cloth had no more substance or effect than an ordinary, stained Roman shade. But at night the moon's light, shining through it on the nights the moon shone, threw shadows of the naked Crucified God over Alphonso's person. As I looked at it after sunset, I saw the distinct Umbra of the Sacred Body as clearly as a sun-cast shadow. I saw the Wounds, the Blood, the gentle, Semitic Features, the imprint of the Crown of Thorns that Pilate had pressed with iron rods into His Skull, all outlining Alphonso. How was this startling Image made? Could It have been somehow faked, the nails' Wounds not in the Figure's Hands, where everyone thinks they truly were, but in His Wrists? This evidence aside, I decided not. I knew the Shroud as real as Divine Grace, because only Resurrection's Light could've made such an Image. No paint could, no earthly artist's hand could form such a potent and affecting Likeness of God, but only an aesthetic facsimile, the shadow of a shadow. The Wounds on it bled into our dark a Dream of God's Sacrifice. Surely Resurrection's shadow now fell softly on and enwrapped Alphonso as it once had Him on His three Days' and Nights' Journey into Hell. I prayed my husband would rise from his particular Purgatory as surely as He once had. But Alphonso had already been wherever he was traveling much longer than a 3:00 Friday afternoon to an Easter dawn.

Alphonso at last regained consciousness. It happened the night of August 8, during my song. At first I hadn't even noticed. I'd been singing, rocking him, and looked down to find his eyes open. My song zinged violently off-key and segued into a muffled scream, thinking Alphonso dead. But the fevers had stopped a few nights ago; how could he have died? Had the Virgin been so cruel with her gift as to pretend to restore it to me, only to snatch him away again? I touched him. No, he was warm. This gave me strength to look him again in the eyes. His pupils contracted as he looked toward the moon through the Shroud. My insides leapt.

"I'd like a chicken, please, stuffed, with crispy skin" were the first words Alphonso had spoken aloud in weeks.

"Alphonso!"

"What?"

"A chicken?"

"Is that a problem?"

"I'd expect a man, unconscious so long a less punctilious wife would've buried him, to have prepared some compliment as a thanks for saving his life."

"I'm hungry. Your singing always makes me hungry."

"That's not the compliment—"

"And thirsty. Have that Atlantic of a bathtub of yours filled with cold water. I've been dreaming of drinking the whole thing. And chicken. The smell of chicken, the crispy skin, a wishbone, sizzling wings, steaming fat, chicken livers. I dreamt of cold water and hot chicken parts."

I handed him the bowl of warm water I'd planned to bathe him in. "Start with this. It'll be better on your gut than cold."

"How long have I been asleep?"

"Twenty-three days. Why does my singing remind you of chicken?"

"What's my sword doing in our bed?" he asked, instead of answering.

"I was planning to stab you with it if you woke up saying the wrong thing."

"What's the dirty sheet in our window?"

"It's Jesus' Shroud. Papa caravanned it from Turin for you."

"What for?"

"To heal you."

"It took Jesus' laundry hanging in the window?"

"Even He was hardly enough. The doctors were sure you'd die. Everyone was, except me and Papa."

I scrambled from the bed to go to the kitchens for a capon. But at our bedroom door, I turned back to him. "You were dead, but the Virgin gave you back to me. Swear never to leave me again."

"I won't."

"On Christ's Blood?"

"Yes. Any oath."

"Washed from His Body by the Virgin?"

"If you like that one."

"I like that one."

"Then I swear that one. But Lucrezia, I'll be old someday. All of us have to leave someday."

"If you're very, very old, stooped over and entirely non compos; if I've died already and if you're daily miserable at my tomb like your great-great-grandpa—and no naked and attractive ghosts for you, by the way—only then do I release you from your word."

I left, as happy as I'd ever been in my life. I went to the kitchens, where I grabbed him the biggest of the hundred resting, steaming birds.

I slept badly the night of August 10, 1500, which was a moonless one, the sky black but for a dim dusting of God's Saints, who are the stars. I spent that night waking and drifting off once more every few moments to chase the ending of whatever reverie I'd been engaged in. I kept hearing noises from the floors below, but being at best half awake, never really exiting from dreaming and desperate to let my dreamy narratives play out, I ascribed the sounds to dream. The last dream was of those floors below. On the ground floor in our apartment's palace a Palatine Guard slept in my nightmare on a stone bench by a downstairs arched entranceway. His friend, a Knight of Aragon, was awake. The knight sat upright at the bench's other end, sword unsheathed and resting on his lap. They were both armored in darkness. Only with the ectoplasmic dark's covering could what followed have followed, in dream or life. Without sound a long knife slid from around the marble corner to the guard's throat. The knife then cut, nearly severing the head. The head fell forward onto the Palatine's chest, but still attached by a single tendon, stayed there. The knight thought he heard something. He turned to look at his friend. In deep shadow everything seemed all right, the guard peacefully sleeping with his chin resting on his chain-mail shirt.

"If you sleep like that with your chin on your armor, your stinking breath will rust your shirt," the knight said, a well-known wit amongst his fellow soldiers.

The knight thought he heard the sound of a flowing, thick liquid pouring over something with a syrupy, plinking sound. I heard it, too, and woke up, listening for it, then plunging back to sleep, where I saw the lone tendon snap from unwontedly bearing the head weight alone. The guard's head rolled down his torso to the knight's feet, and stopped, staring up at him, and me, and looking wide-awake. The guard's eyes blinked once.

"Lucius!" the knight gasped.

"Nightmare." Lucius' lips formed the single, literally breathless word.

Lucius' eyes opened wide with death's vista, faded and emptied. Sword in hand, the knight leapt to shout warning to the rest of the palace. But before he could utter a sound, a dozen men in head-to-toe black were on him with knives and swords, carving him as if to hang in a butcher shop's window.

I dreamt a Monsignor, well known by all who worked or lived in the Vatican, walked along a blackened hallway. He moved slowly, palsied with age, and had his present duty because he was too old to do anything else and too proud to do nothing, the kind of sin of pride Christ forgives without a moment's thought. He'd been at one time the foremost expert in the world on Lucifer and the geography of his netherworld. It occurred to me that the world of dreams, such as the one I was in at the moment, was also thought part of the Satanic empire. It was his duty at night to check our hallways for burnt-down candles, and he was doing so. He reached wobblingly up with his taper to light a new one. At that moment he must've sighted the black-clads coming toward him. He turned to cry out, but his skull, at eye level, was cut horizontally in half with a sound like an axe through an unripe pumpkin, and he fell. I didn't awaken.

I floated after the black-clads like a ghost, as they entered another hall, the archway leading to the section of the Apartments in which were our rooms. I wondered how they didn't perceive my dreaming presence? Weren't we of the same substance? On the walls at that time they would've seen a charcoal cartoon for a planned fresco of the *Rape of the Sabine Women*, if there'd been light enough to see such a black outline. The black-clads must've turned the corner into this short hallway. No candles were lit there at the time, a burnt-out pair still awaiting the old Monsignor. There was neither any window, so the hall was black as pitch. The black-clads could only see the dimly gleaming helmet of a Palatine Guard. He appeared to be moving, rather urgently, back and forth. The black-clads wondered what he was doing. No matter. They raised weapons, rushed forward and stabbed the guard repeatedly to death, placing their hands over his mouth to keep him from crying out.

But suddenly, "Soldiers! Soldiers! Help! Mercy! Help! We're under attack!" the nun cried—no dream—and with her cry I awoke.

Half in and out of nightmare, I realized she'd come previously, of course, under a sort of attack, being made love to from behind, leaning over and bracing herself with her hands on Saint Sebastian's hips, by the just-killed guard. In the dark the black-clads hadn't seen her.

But the guard's and sister's tragedy had given away the black-clads' game in the real world. Little further point in their silence, either. So they erupted into a great battle yell, at which I sat straight up in bed, wide-awake. I had heard the yell, and now their immediately subsequent charge in a chain-and-plate mass toward the end of the archway, leading directly to Alphonso and me. I heard another knight and guard killed just outside our bedroom. As they smashed through our double doors, I'm sure my former black companions heard another, answering battle cry from inside our dark bedroom. The black-clad avalanche burst into our chamber. Inside our bedroom, the nun's scream, of course, had woken *everyone* up, followed by the black-clads' battle cry. All about Alphonso and I had slept the armed Palatines of Papa's and Knights of Federico's. We had a dozen troops in toto. When some heard the nun, they leapt to their feet. For others, surprise was so complete, they hesitated, stunned, and didn't spring up until the black-clad yell. No matter, there was only a second between them. The guards and knights crossed themselves. They picked up shields and swords and prepared in a flash to die.

Without prompt and some at one moment, some the next, they shouted a battle cry of their own. "God save!" it started clearly, all together, only quickly to shuffle off into martial, cacophonous din, as if they called out still within my late dream.

Then the black snowslide from the archway, the bursting down of our doors just from its weight. Black Knights were in our bedroom barely moments after we opened our eyes, without interval for even a breath. I looked up. Twenty-four shapes of nothing but moving shadow and glints of steel. White flashes of eyes like evanescent snowflakes. It was difficult to see anything at all, the dark was so powerful. A moonless night, it was without even God's protecting Turin Shadow. Only starlight's dimness illuminated the room. I looked over at my husband. I saw him reach to try to unsheathe his sword, still lying between us above our only modesty of linen sheet. But he could only scream and fall back. For a second I accepted our deaths, sending prayer we'd at least arrive upon Judgment at the same terminus. The Holy Mother then sent me in reply a message of what to do as clearly as she sent my former hallucination. I jumped up—modesty be damned, which turned out to be the brilliance of her plan—and stood on our bed above Alphonso, straddling him. After all, he was the object of my protection.

"So!" I cried.

Everyone in the room for a long moment solidified like mandrake roots at the dim sight of me, whitish flashes of all the eyes glued to me. Starlit, I'm sure all could see at least the naked outline of me. I reached down and grabbed Alphonso's sword, to which he'd given some barbarian Teutonic name—Freya's something-or-other. I pulled. It rang from its off-white scabbard with its own distinctive melody. I stood and brandished it above my head. It was German, elegant, but extremely heavy; I had to hold it with both hands. I was terrified and trembling. I'd no idea what to say or do. But then I felt a surge of power moving abruptly through my body and mind that re-created me Judgment Day's naked Archangel.

"You've come from my brother to kill us?" I cried, the words simply happening in my mouth without volition of my own. "Is he joking?" I then let go as bloodcurdling a laugh as I could come up with, as if I were the curtain's demon in a Holy Mummers' play. "He'll learn it will take a far more cunning and far greater number than you to kill *this* Virago!"

The room was silent. Finally a voice I didn't recognize whispered, "That's the sexiest bitch in the world. Look at the pair on her, for God's sake."

Two of our dogs for some reason then let go with an interminable-seeming—but probably only three or four seconds—fit of deep-throated barking.

I gave my own bark. The entire room, as if it had been until my cry another parted Red Sea, suspended midair by the Elohim, crashed together in an ocean of battle. And this was a terrible battle. The clashes of steel, the snaps of bone, the cries of the suddenly wounded and dying, the scattering of teeth like unlucky dice and gushes of blood-geysers. I'd never seen anything like this yet in my life, even by the Tiber. If this was an example of that great male preserve, the waging of war, which has been always the main mechanism by which their superiority over us is supposedly demonstrated, then I welcome them to it, for they're baboons and morons. I knew from all the faces around me that if a genie of D'jem's had offered any of them at that moment a magic carpet exit from this horror—even a dishonorable one—he would've jumped on the rug without a tenth of a thought. I'm sure this look is the face of all men in all battles. I began to see our Papal/Aragon side was losing. The opposing sides were reduced to eight of them and six of us. We were losing incrementally, but it was happening. I thought I had to do something. I gathered my courage.

To bolster that courage, I let fly an ejaculation. "Holy Mother of God and Queen of Mercy, let me kill this prick."

I leapt from the bed and stepped in front of a black-clad. Even in the dark I saw his bloodstained face abruptly drain of battle passion. My naked body refilled his eyes with skin and desire.

"Allatri," I said. He had that long-dead Archbishop's look about him. "May I sit astride your lap, please?"

He smiled giddily. Why are men so vulnerable to the sight of us? We love to look upon a naked man, at least an attractive one, but the sight doesn't paralyze us, snatch from us our brain. It must be a thing God's given us, this look of a Lady's vellum that sends our brothers to Hell for a mere glimpse. It was that way, anyway, for this one. While he gaped at my breasts, I stuck him hard in the throat with Alphonso's sword, and he fell to the floor, never having raised a finger in his own defense, red life rushing from his throat as fast as it'd doubtless rushed to his procreative organ. He'd been handsome, but in moments he was a twitching thing, no longer worth even a glance. I turned to another and drove my husband's sword into his unsuspecting black back. He crashed to the ground. For a moment I was ashamed of myself, being reminded of all the French Romances I'd read, in which it's always the evil knight's tactic to strike from the rear. But guilt passed quickly, because I saw every one of the dozen, still-alive warriors second-by-second shattering each of those inane Romance rules without a thought. Men never tell a woman that, either. To listen to them go on and on about it afterward, one pictures battle a rather well-regulated tournament of scrupulous, if eager, rule-minders, when its reality is more an all-mutts-rabid dogfight.

My killing of the two brought the melee back to equilibrium at least. Six to six. I leapt back on our bed to guard my husband. But death followed death quickly, swords mowing both sides' fighters like Master Bosch's Scythe of Eternity through piles of the wretched. There were soon only three fighting pairs remaining. Then there were two. Then one. A blue-clad Aragonese Knight fought the black-clads' leader. They fought savagely, open wounds and blood covering both their bodies. In one strike both swords snapped at the hilts. They fought on with knives, no longer with even an illusion of chivalrous combat, now that swords were gone. They struck me as a pair of desperate, vicious rats, fighting to their deaths in some gore-clogged gutter. The Knight of Aragon finally received a paralyzing knife thrust. He lay on the floor, steel protruding like a sharp crucifix from his abdomen. He was looking up at me, unable to move from pain, awaiting his deathblow, which was delayed momentarily by the mad, lightless search the black-clad leader was conducting for another sword with which to deliver it. The knight was only a boy. I began to lift my sword again to help him, as I would a dying dog, but the deathblow was then delivered expertly by the other to the side of his young head. The black-clad leader looked up at me. He was exhausted, dragging his newly enbrained blade on the floor. He began to move toward Alphonso and me with weary murder in his eyes. He swayed, breathing like a worked ox, right up to the edge of our bed. He stopped. He glanced at Alphonso's form beneath its linen sheet, then back at me. I thought I'd do the same to him as I'd done to the other. I'd dazzle him a moment with my body, and while he was distracted, I'd stab him. I wiggled my tits at him in what I imagined as literally titillating a way as Cleopatra might've offered hers in the Nile's heat to Caesar.

He smiled. "Jiggle your melons all you want, girl; I'll not salute you. It's a boy's body that's Heaven for me."

The black-clad raised his sword to strike at Alphonso. What's sauce for the gander is sauce for the gander-who-would-be-goose occurred to me. With my foot I kicked off the bedsheet from over Alphonso. The black-clad saw his naked body. The leader's eyes went wide. A smile widened across his face. He hesitated only a moment.

"Ah" was all he said.

But time enough. As he vacillated, I swung Alphonso's Hanoverian razor down at an angle from right to left at the leader.

I was sure I'd hit him in the shoulder. But he simply stood there, not moving and apparently unhurt. I was sure I'd felt the sword strike, but nothing was happening. I saw no blood. I saw no pain on his face, no wound. He was staring still at nude Alphonso.

His eyes flickered unwillingly to me, as if hating to leave my husband's body. "You deceitful cunt," the black-clad whispered. "A cunt is Lucifer's cesspit."

And starting at his left shoulder and ending at his right waist, with a massive slurping sound the right side of his body slid away from the left to the floor. The left fell in the opposite direction. I'd cut him diagonally clean in two.

"Good attack," Alphonso whispered from the bed. "That's two tournament points easily." He tried to laugh, but couldn't.

His laugh struck me so anomalous, strange and otherworldly, I questioned if I might be still asleep. I swayed for a moment, hearing nothing but the blood rushing through my ears. I sat to keep from falling and touched Alphonso just to assure myself that here and now weren't some other there and then. They weren't. The nightmare was over. In my head I could hear Alphonso one future day, regaling buddies with stories of my tits, mingled with the merriment of all these skewered internal organs now before us. He and his friends would all laugh and laugh, especially at the leader's last, hateful comment and my halving him in legendary Lionhearted revenge, but "like a girl." But such fantasticalities are the Will of God, as are dreams and nightmares, not to be questioned by us here below. Our dogs all jumped, yelping, onto our bed and began joyously and furiously licking Alphonso.

"Oh, yes," he murmured, stroking the lickers hungrily as if to feel their life was denouement's punctuation. "And you guys were a big help, too."

We looked about us. Twenty-five dead bodies. The blood was ankle deep. There were twenty-four dead men and my beloved Sweetlips, the white—now red—setter. I looked at the Shroud in the window. There was no moon. It looked no more than a dingy Roman shade. But Alphonso, the still skinny and suffering Duke of Bisceglie and Prince of the House of Aragon, about whom all these others were doubtless testifying before Judgment's Throne at this moment, was very much alive. I sank to my knees and thanked the Blessed Mother for this congregation of death. I hadn't a doubt this cold flock was a blessedly benign exchange for my one lamb. Cesare had sent child assassins to kill Alphonso on the Tiber road. They'd failed. Now these fresh assassins. I was beginning to think we were invincible, under a Divine Safeguard. What else but a supernatural fly in Cesare's ointment could explain such miraculous escapes? Could explain my dream that slipped with no segue into life? Or was all this Papa's uncanny power, bending time's will on our behalf? What next from the Ninth Circle?

"How's Roderigo?" Alphonso asked.

I rushed into the next room and looked down at him. He gooed at me and wiggled his arms and legs. His baby-fuzz had begun to look like hair.

"Well, that'll put hair on your head," I whispered, noting I was sounding like Katerina Sforza, as I picked him up.

Had his hair changed just tonight? He was towheaded; he'd be a Borgia. What of Alphonso's heritage? Who ever heard of a blond Neapolitan? I picked him up and brought him to his father. I prayed to the Virgin I wasn't some modern Andromache, handing a reborn Astyanax to Hector.* My white quill wrote a half a page ago it was Satan who fooled me. That was a Ninth Circle lie of my own. It was and would be, as always, my own desire.

A week's peace passed. I never let my vigilance flag. My friend Elizabetta Gonzaga, the Duchess of Urbino, wrote to me—"But don't quote me," she added—that according to chitchat Cesare had received Louis' ambassador, who told him that his Gallic Majesty wanted this "Aragon bungle of yours brought to a conclusion." Everyone was now afraid of Louis, terrified of a prospective repeat of his Uncle Charles' failed invasion in pursuit of the Kingdom of the Two Sicilies, now ruled by Alphonso's Aragon family. Louis still claimed it by virtue of his descent from the thirteenth-century Charles of Anjou. But what sort of "proof" against Cesare was an unquotable, ambiguous, thirdhand report of a rumor? Besides, the Duchess of Urbino was unreliable. Elizabetta hated Cesare for two causes: first, because she was petrified he'd attack Urbino and Mantua, where she held her famous humanist court, and second, because for brilliance, cruelty and bad taste in painters, she was just like him. Papa would justifiably laugh at me if I presented her letter as evidence against Cesare. During that time my Lord Alphonso showed so much improvement that a Hibernian Archbishop,

---

*Astyanax, Hector's son, was thrown to his death from Troy's walls by the victorious Greeks, as Andromache, his mother and Hector's widow, looked on.

who I could hardly tell wore a skullcap because his hair was so red, began lilting of "miracles of the Book." Flesh began to crawl back onto Alphonso's bones and color into his face and eyes. Each day I felt more confident he'd eventually recover completely. Scars tracked all over him like *Viae Dolorosae*, and there remained that most terrible, jagged and still draining Golgotha in his side. That only partially closed wound retained the power to wrench him sideways in his bed with pain and was what most concerned me. As long as an unhealed gash remained, likelihood lingered his infection could recur or the wound reopen. Its forming scab had stayed angry red and I saw how deeply its roots sank into his body. But I'd removed the rest of Alphonso's bandages, and if nothing else, that dead-Lazarus look he'd had since July 15 finally was abating. There were simpleminded people, I began to hear—some even humanist prelates in Vatican City—who behind our backs hinted Lord Alphonso's dramatic recovery resulted from witchcraft, saying he'd sucked the living substance from those around us that night and had gobbled their escaping souls. Rumor—the wing-footed Mercury of lies—also gives birth to the protean world of sea monsters, dragons and talking Pisces with blond tresses. Those who believed such outlandish fibs had brains soft as cow-flops to swallow such wen- and wart-encrusted wives' tales—nearly everyone, in this case.

I further began to hear whispers of other vicious tales, dim rumblings in the Vatican's corridors. Rumors about myself. I'd hear murmurs from around a corner that stopped the instant I'd turn that corner. I'd see scrawled graffiti about me in Italian, as I'd pass in a carriage a wall under the Bridge of Saint Elio by Hadrian's Tomb, a wall for graffiti since the Roman Republic. It included one-line reports of Crassus-the-fireman's pyromania and a caricature of Dictator Felix Sulla's *ferula amoris*, his sceptre of amorous punishment. The graffiti about me—literary and graphic—soon multiplied to every Roman wall I'd go by. At least the Vatican's were daily scrubbed free of them by Jesuits, ever vigilant against all inaccuracies but their own. I now rarely left Vatican Hill; I never crossed the Tiber. As Dante demonstrated, Italian is a most expressive language, especially when its subject is love or the force and degree of the writer's loathing. There's no other language in which the word for "whore" bursts so spittingly off the page, tongue, or is loaded with so much masculine contempt. In others it's even a soft word, a soothing sound. Scrawled accounts and vivid diagrams of carnal relations between Cesare and myself appeared in spastic mural. Even between Papa and me and in poses more hair-raising than anything in Barbero, although I'd seen these before in centuries-old graffiti of fourteen-year-old Messallina with sixty-year-old Claudius. Myself and a horse or bull. Myself and a dog. Myself and the by now gigantic Xerxes, my wedding-gift rhinoceros.

"Why do they say such things?" I asked Papa one morning in confessional.

He thought a moment. "Because they're jealous of your beauty and greatness."

"But why does jealousy have me in a beast's embrace?"

"Because in the minds of jealous, small, sinful people such stories rip the great from our God-given, exalted station and render us another clutch of low sinners no better than themselves, pursuing fleshy, quotidian pleasures like every common sinner. Do you know what hyperbole is, Lucrezia? Do you know what it's for?"

I nodded.

"That's all these stories are. Hyperbole. The dogs, horses and even myself or Cesare are nothing but envious storytellers' rhetorical, sinful embellishments."

"But doesn't that imply a truth to embellish? They frighten me."

"Frighten you how?"

"I'm afraid they'll metamorphose over time from story to history, like Pope Joan. Each time one is repeated, each new one I see on a wall, it's as if a thing that can't be true becomes truer."

He laughed. "Like Ovid's myths?"

"Yes."

"Well, you're a true Borgia, at least."

"Why?"

"The rabble fear today's gossip. Only the great fear history."

"But all fear the Judgment of God," I said.

"Don't fear it. Be a Borgia. Be like Cesare. Create God's Judgment for yourself. Relieve him of the burden of it."

"How do I do that?"

"Create Him."

"I can do that?"

"The soul strives to become God; and this is our Divinity. Your brother strives terribly. It's why I love him; he's not an innately lovable man, you know."

"I didn't know. And what's Cesare's God like?"

"Cesare."

"I don't think so, Papa. I think you're his God. The God Alexander."

"Alexander the Father? Cesare thinks he's the Son? Is Lucrezia the Holy Ghost?"

"No, I'm the Virgin."

His laughter filled the confessional. I imagined it shoving out all our sins through the cracks.

I continued, "But will this graffiti and gossiping grow their way into history, Papa? My history for my children one day to read in books?"

"At worst they'll become myth, but they'll remain untrue forever. Deucalion didn't survive the Flood, Noah did. You don't think Alexander the Great really fucked his horse, Ox Head, do you?"

I laughed. "His horse, Ox Head? Wasn't he in love with that horse?"

"Βνσεφαλοσ, Bucephalus, Ox Head. It's a shame women can't read Greek, because the irony of mythical names is always so much more trenchant in Greek."

The condescension in that statement tore at me like the young Spartan's fox. Go on, I thought to myself, say it. What's he going to do now? Make me unlearn Greek? Say it.

So I did. "You mean like the Ψμενιδεσ, 'the kindly ones,' Πριαπνσ, 'tender of the pear tree' and Ιφιμεδια, 'she who strengthens genitals'?"*

"Lucrezia?"

"Don't ask."

"We won't. Although innately omniscient, We don't really want to know. . . . But We're proud of you. Greek is an exquisitely rare jewel, when worn on a woman."

"Proud of me? But you used to forbid . . ." I was crestfallen. My knowledge, held all those years in fearful secret, hadn't even the small effect of angering him. He was happy about it!

He went on. "But do you think he fucked Ox Head, Greek-style or otherwise?"

"I hope not."

"Well, all the 'histories' of his time say he did. And how would he accomplish such a daunting performance? He'd have had to be Alexander the Preposterously Great. Can you just picture Master Buonarroti's sculpture of that?"

*Eumenides, Priapus, Iphimedea

He gave me my Penance. I rose from Papa's coffin-shaped confessional, as I often had, with a much lighter spiritual step than the one with which I'd entered.

Master Pinturicchio looked up another morning at Alphonso from his beautiful painting of Saint Sebastian that I'd insisted on. "My Lord, you look . . . alive, for a change."

"Master, it's gratifying you've stopped thinking of me as a still life."

He continued to paint our Apartment. He was now nearly finished and our entire suite swarmed with glorious reds, blues, yellows and skin tones as well as with his magical way of combining Grecian perfection and order with Christian Faith, as personified in that Saint Sebastian, with his body of Apollo and yet the face of Jesus' younger brother. All were done with glowing, palpable, almost biologic warmth. Our walls had come to look to us blasphemously like a better Creation than God's own.

We awoke the last morning of those peaceful weeks, August 18, 1500, before dawn, as we were accustomed to, the sun not yet in the sky to burn off the damp. We'd often lie next to one another and listen to a pair of birds, nested and cooing somewhere in the cypress-filled courtyard outside our window, and we did so that morning. But for this aurora there was no cooing, but rather the chicks shrieking like an ensemble of Furies. Papa used to tell me cypresses only appeared in Italy after the defeat of Mithridates by Lucullus in 73 B.C. He'd tell me larks were the slaughtered military band of Lucullus' army. They sounded just like centurions' pipes, or so people used to say. My husband and I'd watch "rosy-fingered dawn" move across our sky, before we'd send a nun to fetch a light breakfast. But that morning I'd decided to make our breakfast myself. After bidding good morning to the guard and knights waking themselves around our bed, we dismissed them to their own breakfasts and other duties, the night's dangers having passed. I slipped on a robe and made my way down through the shadowy palace to the titanic kitchens. There I found a gaggle of chubby nuns, already hard at work.

"Do we have truffles?" I asked.

"Yes, my Lady," one answered, opening a drawer the size of an empress's hope chest, filled to the brim with precious white truffle. "The pigs have been generous this year, praise God."

"Of all His Creatures, only man and the truffle-pig go to Heaven," the fattest volunteered. "Without truffles, why have such a place?"

"Don't women go?" I asked.

That sent them into a gale of giggles. "Of course, girl. What would the men do for joy without us?"

"Do we have eggs?"

"Eggs? My Lady? Do we have eggs?" they howled, smacking their dough boards delightedly with suety palms. They thought each of my questions more and more hilarious, giggling on for several moments at my red face.

I made the truffled eggs French omelette–style. It took me half an hour, because I had to start the omelette over three times, from destroying it every time I'd go to fold it into its proper, Gallic shape and it'd come out looking like a yellow flop. The nuns thought those were a scream, too. They jabbered on and on with mutually exclusive omelette instructions as complicated as the instructions must be for the erection of the planetary spheres. I finally created an actual omelette. The sisters plated it, sprinkled it with a sprig of chiffonaded basil and gave me a tray and a "B"-engraved spoon. I took our breakfast back up to our bedroom, where Alphonso found the omelette delicious. I was pleased and shocked. He said he'd never had truffled eggs before.

"Don't they have truffles in Naples?" I asked.

"My father hated them. He loved saffron and said there was room in the world for truffles or for saffron. But not both."

"A sweet, fat man once told me by a waterfall that to make another a truffle dish is a sign of love."

"And did he cook you truffles? Or you him?"

That caught me unprepared and my stomach momentarily fluttered at being caught, so to speak, with another man. But a quick review of my conscience told me I'd nothing to hide. "I loved him. I always will. But the way a girl might love an old, fat, well-meaning man."

"Someday I'll be old, fat and merely well-meaning."

"I doubt it. I doubt 'fat and well-meaning,' at least."

"It may be."

"Then I'll love you anyway, but still in the way a virgin girl might love Lancelot."

He looked moved by that. He took my hand. "It's been a month," he said. "A long time for Lance-a-lot to do with none at all."

"None of what?" For a moment I was a simpleton, staring at him, my eyelashes atwitter like a vestal pigeon's, suddenly finding herself perched on the erect part of an antique roadside herm. At last, thank God, it hit me what he was talking about.

"B-but Alphonso," I muttered, ingenue pigeon still. "Isn't the pain still too piercing?"

" 'Piercing'?" he shot back. He scratched his chin and mocked me, pretending to be a philosopher, wracking his brain over some particularly abstruse question. "Now, where have we heard that word before?" Then he feigned the philosopher remembering the answer: "Ohhh, yes. From the Visigoths."

As if the sophist grabbing at the epistemological solution, he reached up to the neck of my robe. It was a flimsy, Parisian wedding gift from my brother and shredded away with Alphonso's insistent rip as easily and completely as any theoretical conceit yanked at by an ape. He smiled. He picked up the omelette plate. With his other hand he crumpled up and plopped my gown on the olive-oily plate and tossed the two of them out our window. He winced as he threw.

"My Lord!"

I jumped into his arms. I ignored his pain. He kissed me and rolled over on me and conjugated my *amo-amas-amat-amamus-amatis-amant* for the first time since that wretched night by the Tiber. The Virgin didn't lie, nor had Vanita. They're true Matriarchs. They're faithful to their daughters and sons. Everyone involved couldn't completely ignore his pain, however. At various moments of particular passion, I'd hear a sharp "Ow!" But then he'd chuckle. "Love hurts."

We made ecstasy for the next hour. I thought of Tivoli and knew every day for the rest of our lives we'd make love like this. The dawn sun grew with each pleasurable thrust of him, rosier and more sky-filling. Christ's Bones were golden lights in the window.

Near the end of our hour of lovemaking, during which the sun had risen, Cesare stood at the foot of the outside steps that led to Alphonso's and my Apartment, having walked completely around the place. These steps climbed to the principal entrance on the opposite side of the massive palace from the larks' cypress courtyard. Dawn had by then withdrawn its pink hand and left only its disc in a blue sky. The larks had flown.

Cesare looked up at sixteen armed Knights of Aragon and Palatine Guards, who stood on the steps above him, the ones I'd dismissed before. On their own initiative they now guarded this entry.

"I'm sorry, my Lord," a Knight said. "My Lady's forbidden entrance."

"To me, you half-wit?"

"To anyone, my Lord. At any time."

"Do you know who I am?" asked Cesare Borgia, as if there were another who dressed like the Golden Calf.

"Yes, Lord General. I'm sorry; we've sworn an oath."

Cesare's eyes went funny. He went through his accustomed five- or ten-second buildup, climaxing in his customary colossal outburst. I doubt this particular tantrum was exactly his usual uncontrollable gift of Satan. More likely it was at least a partial dell'Arte farce, Cesare well aware what effect it would have on these simple men.

"I am Lord Cesare Borgia, Captain General of the Army of frigging God!"

"Yes, m—"

"I am the Son of the Vicar of Christ, thereby Grandson of the Father Almighty, the Emperor of the Cosmos! On this earth I am the winged Coequal of the Archangel Michael! I have a terrible, swift sword!"

"Yes, my Lord, we're sure you—"

"Do not interrupt me again, you dung pellets, or I'll have your voice boxes for my cat to piss in." Cesare had begun to recover himself, the doubtful tantrum running its theatrical course. But he was unfinished. "But more importantly than any of my other titles," he roared, "for your purposes, I am eternally my sister's well-loved and loving brother!"

The knights stared at him, not daring to speak.

"And you have no answer to that for your better, you ill-mannered blobs of sunstroke?" Cesare snapped.

"Yes, your Grace—"

"Then what is it? Do you imagine in your wildest dreams that your oath against 'suspicious men'—which I personally commend you for keeping so diligently—or perhaps your oath against 'suspicious stones,' includes such a person as me? If you do, maybe I should command your testicles yanked on by rabid marmots, till you awaken from this slumberous delusion!"

For myself, Papa or even for some cardinal to witness an eruption like this one, phony or not, from such a powerful Lord as Cesare, from a man who'd killed entire cities and removed regions from God's map, was one thing. For these plain souls it must've been an awesomely frightening spectacle, as my brother had meant it to be. Then, of course, within Cesare's screechings was also one phrase of unmad, undeniable logic. He was truthfully my well-loved and loving brother.

The knights all looked at Cesare, at each other. "We're sorry, your Grace," one said.

"That's better. Now stand aside and let me pass."

"We're sorry, your Grace, but we've sworn an oath. No one may go in. Not Christ Himself."

"We apologize, your Grace. Would you like one of us to go inside and ask our Lord or Lady?"

"We're sorry, your Grace," the third said.

While doing their best to calm Cesare, the knights were steeling themselves for another rage and resigning themselves to die. Any second Cesare might summon a company of his own, or an entire battalion. They were willing to die, if necessary. But the tantrum didn't reappear, which relieved them. Cesare watched them, eyes filling with nothing. After a few moments the knights felt a wintry tickle at their skulls' bases. Cesare watched on, morning heat playing down. The knights abruptly remembered oaths from their past that had turned out wrong to keep. They thought of Charlemagne's oath to Roland not to return unless Roland sent for him, and thousands died without purpose. Anthony's to Caesar not to come to the Senate on the Ides of March. They began to shiver. They wanted to run. Their tongues and lips started to feel dry and cold. They tried to look into the sky to reassure themselves the sun remained, but couldn't. They couldn't move their eyes from Cesare's. I will not let him pass, all sixteen doubtless thought. I will stay my post, until I die or am relieved. No force in Heaven or Hell can make me break my oath. I swear it. I swear on the Sacred Honor of God.

They stepped aside to let Cesare pass up the steps. He walked through the same long ground-floor hallway in which black-clads killed the nightmare guard and his Aragonese friend. Today it was bright. He turned corners; he mounted stairways. In the passageway in which the ancient Monsignor saw his last candlelight, Cesare saw another Monsignor—as it happened, also an expert, though unretired, in the ways of the Prince of Darkness.

"Crush Satan, your Grace," the passing demonologist said. "You're looking fine this morning."

"I strive to crush him with every thought and deed, Monsignor."

Cesare strode on. He walked up to the sewing room, where the nuns who taught me to sew sat. The sisters were sewing again, this time while eating their favorite penitents' breakfast of cold Scots oat-mush with cups of "coffee."

"Good morning. Have a cup of the coffee with us, your Grace?" the eldest called to him. "The beans are just arrived from the Indies."

"No, thank you, sisters. The coffee gives me gas."

"It will drive the sleep from you, my Lord."

"I'm wide awake, thank you, sisters."

The second eldest then leaned forward and whispered, "By Our Savior's Fundament, sisters, that's the handsomest man in creation."

The circle cackled assent.

"Shame on you, ladies," Cesare called back, walking on, "for such a carnal thought."

What shall I imagine were the thoughts that ran through my brother's head on his long walk? Did he dream of empire or think of the earlier Caesar and his glory and fate? Or were his thoughts simpler? Of himself and me beneath Vanita's carved table? For years I've wondered what occupied his mind on his walk toward myth through those most beautiful corridors in the world, past the mural of the *Myth of the Bull Apis* and under the vault of *The Mysteries of the Faith*. But I can't imagine it. My imagination, my dreams, all my soul's familiars, when they approach that interior moment of my brother's remembering, run finally dry of him.

I've pieced together the facts of Cesare's walk from my imagining and from people who were part of the events, but the information is now easily obtainable in common gossip, where it's doubtless transmuting, as Papa said it would, into God-knows-what bogus historical hogwash. When Cesare arrived at the *Lunette of the Musical Cupids* and before those magnificent doors, he hesitated not a second. He swung them open and walked into our bedchamber, where he stopped and stood just inside the entrance in the cupids' shadow.

"Good morning, sister." Cesare said with a warm smile. "Brother, I've come to take back the gift of my breath."

"Good morning," Alphonso said.

"A day with a lovely promise," I added, panic vibrating my voice. Papa be damned. I cursed myself inwardly for not having told Alphonso my suspicions about Cesare.

Morning sun streamed in through our opened windows. Alphonso and

I lay under silken ecru satin, in each other's arms, having just finished lovemaking. My hair was an absolute rat's nest, a dead giveaway. Turin's Shroud had turned Divine once again in last night's shadowing moon, but was now so bright with Apollo, it had emptied of Christ. We'd no earthly idea what Cesare was talking about, undertows of our passion still sloshing through our bodies. I couldn't remember seeing Cesare this early in a morning since we'd lived in Subiaco. Seeing him so now gave me pleasure amidst my fear. The pleasure was a momentary reincarnation of those mornings with Vanita and Roderigo, before those long-ago morning bells. As the sun now glanced from the white marble floor to strike Cesare's body, he appeared to me the golden goblet—the fabric of his clothes, his shouldered shape—with which my parents toasted one another that last morning, both drinking their Tuscan red from it in the same swallow. I was terrified of him, but loved my memory of him.

Cesare walked slowly to our bed's edge. The closer he came, the more like a painting, gentler-looking and less frightening, he became. He then knelt on both knees below us. He looked up into our eyes. A tear rolled down his face. He appeared the saddest, guiltiest little twelve-year-old boy. I thought of little Roderigo in the next room and that I should be nursing him.

"I've a confession to make to you both," Cesare said, as if it were to be the sheerest agony to force it out. " *'Tempus est ut praetermittantur simulata nostra.'* "*

"A confession of what?" I asked. "And of what counterfeit?"

"Of ambition. The monster that killed Caesar has almost destroyed Cesare."

"Ambition for Aragon?"

"In part. My ambition's had terrible consequences, has caused me to commit unforgivable sins against you both. If you wish to make them public, I'd not blame you; I'll not stop you. I'll admit my sins in front of everyone. I'll go to the place of execution with a song of thanks. I'll whip the bowel-puller's horse forward."

"Cesare—" I began. I was about to cut him off. I wasn't really sure if this was bullshit or not, but it was so painful to hear him say it in such a prideless, self-demeaning way, I wanted him to stop. He was the Duke of

---

* "It's time to lay aside our counterfeit." Dante Alighieri, *La Vita Nuova*

Romagna and future *Imperator* of the World. If he were telling the truth, I'd bless God's Grace forever, but let's be off with this cringing Borgia god.

"Cesare," Alphonso said instead, "what did you do? What could've been so depraved?"

Cesare raised his eyes. "Papa called me in to him. He confronted me with Lucrezia's suspicions. They've become his, as well. He shamed me. He held up the evil in my soul before my eyes for what it is, for what it's done to me, for what it still could do to us all. I'd always thought the evil in me a Macedonian sort of drive, an ambivalent adjunct to greatness, but it isn't. It's lower than shit and I've become its slave."

"Lucrezia's suspicions?" Alphonso said.

"It was I, brother, that hired the assassins. The ones in the street and the ones that came here. They were all mine. I did it to gain the Sicilies, then Italy, and thereby the world." He then began to cry openly, as if he were trying to stop the choking and tears, but couldn't. "I beg your forgiveness," he bawled, and bowed his forehead to the floor. "I beg your forgiveness, brother and sister Aragon. I beg our mother's forgiveness before God."

Alphonso looked stunned, but unsurprised, and I the same way. Cesare wept on the floor. I've never in my life, before or since, heard heartbreaking crying like this.

"Vanita loved Lucrezia," Cesare choked out. "But no one could love Cesare."

"Cesare, I love you. Papa loves you. All Italy loves you."

"The mob pretends. You fear me. Even Papa now fears me *in pectore*."

"Cesare, that's not true; you're crazy."

He took out his gold dagger and handed it to me. "You think I'm wrong? Prove it. Kill Cesare; kill him now, while he's crazy. It's the loving thing to do. If you wait till I'm sane, I'm sure to go to Hell. Do it now; God forgives the insane." He turned his head to bare his throat. I saw the healed stitch of scar from the goose knife.

"Forgiveness first," he said, "then death. Do it. Don't you dare doubt even Vanita'd have you do it. I've spoken to her. Haven't you? She said to me, 'Let her kill you, before you kill her and the child.' Didn't she tell you? It's easy. It takes only a second. Saint Peter won't have time to write it in the book of your soul. Even the Virgin will forgive you in a finger snap for such a beneficial evil. I'll send you absolution for it from Hell."

There it was. A confession more than enough for Papa's proof. It was impossible; he never could've said it. But here it was. I reached easily down and put the blade across that upturned throat with its carotid rhythm, just above the scar line. I imagined the red gushing down Cesare's gold doublet, how lovely it would look, its coppery scent so satisfying. But the longer I looked at the scar, the whiter and more softly pitiable it appeared and the weaker I became. The longer the throat lay open, the less I wanted to cut. I put the blade exactly on the scar. The moment I did so I thought of SPQR on Paul's headsman's block, of Cesare and me together beneath the table and of my chess set and red rocking horse. I remembered the Wedding at Cana. I wanted to go back. Before the bells. Before ambition. Before Fisherman's Ring and library.

I chose the table. I chose to think Cesare was weak now and powerless from guilt and shame. Checkmated. I had the confession. If he attempted anything from now on, I'd go to Papa with it. I'd have the palomino walk out Cesare's gut along the cobblestones. *I* had the power now. I felt safe and chose love. I chose my brother to be the youth beneath the table. And of course, that's exactly who he was.

"Cesare, I'm sorry that piggy Alphonso ate the whole omelette, or I'd give you some," I said.

Cesare blinked at us. I handed the knife back to him. He took it and returned it to its sheath.

"It was excellent," Alphonso said with a smile. "You should try a truffle omelette, brother. It's a sign of love."

Cesare smiled, looking still like a little boy that's received a soothing pat, when he thought to be slapped. "Thank God. Thank you, brother and sister. You won't be sorry, I swear to you." He stood up finally. "Let me leave and come in again. Let's pretend none of my evil ever happened. Let's pretend I've been a bad, but am now a good, loving Cesare."

That was so boyish that Alphonso and I both laughed and Cesare joined in. He turned and walked out the way he'd come in. He waited under the Lunette about ten seconds, then came back, as if returning for the next round of hide-and-seek. He paused in the doorway's shadow a moment, then took a step out of the dark, and I saw his face clearly and his eyes. My body went physically cold and slithery as if suddenly inside an eel. I knew for the first time in my life what the drunken Sicilians saw in the courtyard. Or maybe what the boar had seen the stride before its beheading.

"Fuck eggs," Cesare said. "What presumptive bitch are you to forgive the Divine Cesare Borgia? Fuck forgiveness, while we're at it."

He calmly walked across and carefully pulled closed our tall wooden shutters, opened onto the cypress courtyard. He even closed the one over the Shroud. Sunlight still penetrated, though only in occasional bright blades. Then he closed the door to Roderigo's room.

"What are you doing?" I asked, fear drizzling all the while down my spine.

"I've thought about this to its cold bottom," Cesare said, his voice a vibrating icicle. "I've grappled with it and torn my soul apart over it more than you'll ever know, more than I could describe in another *Inferno* or *Purgatory*. Part of me shudders at even the thought of it. But in the pit of my thought and pain, at the end of all my love for you, Papa or Vanita, everything my life is, has been or will be requires this of me."

"What are you talking about?"

He reached inside his golden robe, taking again the knife. It was covered down its hilt with table-cut diamonds, rubies, sapphires and emeralds, arranged in the shape of an eagle. Running toward us, he raised the knife above his shoulder. He leapt at us from the floor onto our bed. In a trice he was on top of my husband. One hand clasped Alponso's throat; the eagle's talon poised in Cesare's other hand above Alphonso's heart, only kept from entering by reverse resistance, Alphonso's hand clenching Cesare's wrist. The blade's tip was just at Alphonso's nipple. I tried to reach for the sword, but it was now trapped beneath them. I began to scream, to call for help, to call the Palatines, our knights, the sisters, any nearby priest or brother, but God's Will dictated at that moment there was none, no one else within sound of my voice except my baby, who I heard begin to cry. I grabbed at the knife, trying to wrest it from Cesare, trying to pry its point away from my Lord's chest, but couldn't budge it. The male strengths being exerted by both had the knife as if welded to its quivering intention. As I pulled, it cut me repeatedly. My hands quickly became so slippery with my own blood, I could no longer hold it. I pulled at Cesare's body, its muscles as definite and hard as the Appian's archaic wheel ruts, at his golden clothes, at his hair. I started to bite him as savagely as I could, on the shoulder, on the arm. He cried out in pain, but kept pressing the point toward Alphonso.

Alphonso and I were naked. More blood kept flowing from my cut hands. An image formed in my mind. I know it was a terrible sin, but I couldn't stop it, any more than Noah or Deucalion or whoever-the-Hell-it-was could stop the rain. In my mind we seemed a strange, desperate ménage à trois. But I confess our threesome was oddly attractive to me, an unbidden, nightmare daydream. My dream was manipulating my desire. I pictured myself closing the Iron Maiden's lid on Cesare. An iron box, tapered like a coffin in the shape of a large woman or of an Egyptian mummy's container. Inside the box's hinged front door are attached iron spikes, sharpened by the Inquisitors to razor points. I closed the iron door, the spikes sinking into Cesare's gold doublet, into his face, his gut and sex. I heard his muffled screams from the Maiden's interior. I saw his tormented face in her spiked window, one spike into his eye, another in his throat's scar. But these were only momentary fantasies. What was real was Alphonso in agony and how difficult it was for him to maintain his push against Cesare's golden spike with the attending pain from his still-healing wound. I've no idea how long our struggle went on like this, minutes that felt like days, a little Purgatory, with the abyss waiting below and nothing above.

I saw Cesare see something and then a flicker of understanding in his eyes. He yanked his hand from Alphonso's throat, the one not holding the knife, and reached down with it to Alphonso's bare side. It's a demonstration of Satan's power that for a half moment I imagined him reaching toward my husband's sex to pleasure him. But he wasn't. He was bent for the wound, the angry, unhealed one in Alphonso's side. He ripped the bandage off. Alphonso let go a gasp. Cesare reached for the wound itself. He tore it open, deep scab and all. For a second I could see clear to Alphonso's whitish rib. Then my husband's scream. Then the blood from the newly reopened wound like a burst sluice. The splashing red began to cover everything, Alphonso's and my bodies from neck to knees, the bed, Cesare's gold clothing, our three faces. Alphonso continued to scream. Cesare then regrasped the knife by its eagle haft with both hands. He arched himself over and pushed down on its pommel with all his weight and strength over my Lord. With the new agony of his open side it became impossible for Alphonso to maintain the reverse pressure.

"Remember me in Hell, brother," Cesare murmured. "I'll join you there someday. We can hunt boar again in its forest of holocaust and piss fire together on one another's corpses."

Me screaming, Alphonso screaming, Cesare yelling encouragement to the knife, the blade sunk finger-breadth by leisurely finger-breadth into Alphonso's heart, slowly as the creation of a little girl's row of knitting. I saw Alphonso's pupils blank. His screams abruptly ceased. His reverse pressure stopped, Cesare and I collapsing on him, pushing the hilt to his chest. My husband's eyes were wide open. I'd become, in a moment, the Dowager Duchess Bisceglie.

For a long, hushed moment—the only sounds those of Alphonso's still-flowing blood and Cesare's and my breathing—what had happened was beyond my capacity to believe. I stared at Alphonso's dead face in uncomprehending, denying emptiness. But then came his final exhale's delayed, interminable rattle, which cracked my denial. Without a sound—his second death had put me beyond screaming—I attacked Cesare. With my closed fists, red with Alphonso's life, I pummeled Cesare viciously in his face, his body, his face again. And again. I lunged at his skin with my own knives, my well-buffed nails, now praying my fingers would become the Maiden's spikes. I left deep gouges. I felt his face's skin rolling up underneath my nails. Blood beaded up on his face like ten ruby bracelets. The rubies led me to his sapphire eyes. I went for them. Blind him, I was thinking. Smear the sightless, blueberry-marmalade of them into his golden, bloody hair. Then ram my sticky fingers in his mouth and let him taste the sights he'll never see. I saw terror on his face at the thought of blindness. He reached up and grabbed my wrists. In a single, double wrench, he twisted my hands behind my back. He rolled on top of me to pin me down, my hands pinioned behind me. I felt Alphonso's sword beneath me and tried to grip it, but couldn't and only cut my hand again. I was in the still spreading, red-liquid mass, Cesare on top of me. I struggled. I bit at his face, missing. I almost ripped free, but in a few more seconds of sloshing skirmish Cesare got control. We looked into each other's blood-covered faces.

"Yes, he's dead and I'm Aragon-to-be. You and I are doubly consanguineous. And I'm now little Roderigo's father," he whispered, when I'd become so exhausted I could no longer fight him. "I'm as sorry as you are, Lucrezia." He paused. I could see him summoning up the deepest dregs of his sincerity. "I loved Alphonso, too. He was my brother. But my sister's the cause of it."

I spit in his eyes, praying the spittle would turn to acid.

"Why do you spit at a brother, who loves you?" he whined. "Loves you more than himself."

I spit acid at him once more.

"What greater love could a man have?" he asked. "Than to wear the Mark of Cain before Christ's Throne for you?"

"Christ's Throne? What could you possibly have to do with Christ or His *Sedia*? You'll never see Christ. You'll carry an archbishop's crozier in Hell."

"This was done for you."

I was stunned. I had one of those dream-instants as if falling from a tower, in which a soul flips back through its entire existence, guilt-ridden and searching for that lost moment of its responsibility. I summoned up in a heartbeat all our sibling lives together. No such instance, no such sisterly sin, not even a near one. Or was it my Original Sin had cursed me out of my awareness, when I'd done whatever it was? Were all we Eves responsible for our lovers' murders? Because it'd been ourselves who'd tempted our brothers and fathers to sins of our flesh?

"From your mouth comes only lying ooze," I said. "You'll someday shepherd those damned for treachery. They'll cry out to you for a single sip of truth and you'll lie to them. You've said nothing to me but lies, since I was at our mother's breast."

"The Borgia power in Italy has doubled in the last five minutes. It's now a power greater than any since the earlier Caesars'. That's no lie."

"The *Cesare* power has doubled. I see the creamy pus of lies dribbling over your tongue. Does it taste as loathsome as it looks?"

"With the Two Kingdoms' land and gold in Borgia hands we'll destroy Louis, the *Serenissima* and the Moor within the year. Our father, as well as I, will be Kings of the World."

"We? Who 'we'?"

"Our family. Papa, you and I. The House of Borgia."

"You killed my beautiful Lord for that? All things of Aragon were already in Borgia hands. My hands!"

"Since you were five years old, you've refused to learn that what some slut like Vanita or you holds counts for nothing. It's the Will of God the Father."

"It's the will of shit-eating maggots like you."

He smiled. "I remember you used to sneak into the library at night. You thought you were so cloak-and-dagger, but I knew you were going from the first time you did. How do you think I was waiting for you that night, when I explained to you how to subdue the world? But I loved you so much, I never told Papa. Did you understand anything you read there?"

"Better than you."

"Did you read Suetonius' *Lives of the Twelve Caesars*? I did. I've taken all the attitudes it says are conducive to a Caesar. Ruthless. Cold. No

sentiment in policy. Quick to strike. Slow to mercy. All the virtues sim-
pletons call satanic. I've made each my own. I've absorbed the wisdom
in his slim duodecimo into my veins. In all the several lands I control I've
had it proscribed and I'm burning all copies and translations. But I've
memorized it. I shall be the lucky thirteenth Caesar. Shall I recite a few
partes I've especially *selectae?*"

"Please don't trouble yourself, brother."

"You don't believe me?" he asked. "And you? Papa will be a new Julius
Caesar. The *Novus Pater Familias.* I'll be Augustus—"

"Or Caligula."

"And you'll be an Empress. At my side you could become another
Theodora. Maybe you'll ghostwrite a new Code of Laws like she did. Of
course, we'll have to put my name on it, like Justinian did on hers. No
one will bother to read a book scribbled by some dizzy pigtail."

"With your name on its spine, we'll shelve it under the *Codex of
Duplicitous Shit.*"

Cesare laughed at that. "Whatever it's called, you'll be an Empress."
He then gestured at Alphonso's body with his head. "Instead of a lowly
Duchess. This has been our plan, all done for you, since you sucked
those nipples you say you loved so much."

"*Our* plan?"

"Papa's and my own." He gestured again toward Alphonso's body. "As
for your husband? He was a good man, wasn't he?"

I couldn't answer, much though I wanted to spit a reply. Papa's plan?
Papa's and Cesare's? It was the only thing that made sense, the puzzle's
critical piece to fit the other thousand. Was this the hammer's whack at
the nail through my hand? Presumptuous to say, but like me, not until
that moment could He have understood what His Sacrifice entailed.

"A Caesar to Cesare's Brutus," I spit my answer finally at Cesare.

"Then Alphonso's in Paradise as we speak, happier than even such a
miracle as you could've made him. What better could I have done for
him? You'd just fucked each other, hadn't you?"

I didn't answer.

"You look it. I could tell the moment I walked in, your hair like a rat's
harem. Your child's in the next room. You already have a chip off
Alphonso's old Aragon block to love. I'll grant the tyke a dukedom of his
own, a Naples or Forli, if you like. The boy will make history. I'll treat
him like my own son. I'll adopt him. The Prince of the World. He'll be

my heir, my Tiberius Cesare. All you'll be missing of Alphonso will be his prick." He glanced at Alphonso's bloody sex. "A relatively minor loss."

"Are you even a human being? Could we have come from the same womb?"

" 'Blessed is the womb.' " He lifted himself slightly off me. He looked down at my body, smeared with blood and sweat like a heap of pliable obscenity. I'd always thought my beauty the Virgin's gift, but it's just the same her curse. Many women, who've undergone it, have told me rape happens not because we are procreatively attractive to the male animal, but because authority is the true aim in forcible love. In the same manner those same women will say a dog will enforce his rank through gestures, superficially resembling, but in intention nothing like, the act of love. I'm not certain if this is true. No dog—leaving graffiti and hyperbole aside—has ever fucked me. Human rape seems a more complex matter. I'd felt him—as he'd talked on and on with his endless explanation concerning his becoming the new Augustus and how my husband, the love of my life, he'd murdered to serve me—all that time I'd felt his self-regard swelling. This physical manifestation wasn't, I'm certain, because he was finding me increasingly appealing, but because he found himself increasingly so. With each point he'd discover himself more irresistible. With each prediction of his glorious future and genius, he'd discovered himself more and more charismatic and desirous.

"A minor loss, as I said," he said again, continuing his revolting thoughts on my husband's dead sex. "And one easy to replace with a bigger and better."

He kissed me full on the mouth. I tried to resist him, resist that insistent, frigid salamander of waggling tongue. I spit, or tried to. I gagged. I tried to bite the damned thing's head off, but it was too slickly viscous. And it bit back. I feigned I was about to sicken and vomit into his mouth and he finally pulled away. I looked up at him. His eyes went funny. His wine-bladder began to fill with noise. I could feel his feet, unable to stamp, begin a kicking drumroll on the bed.

"Do not resist God!" he shouted at me. "We're each other's destiny and I love you! God put us together for a reason. You've always resisted it, but you know your love for me is the truest secret of your body, mind and soul. From the time we were young you've known us fated for this, from before you were born. Stop fighting yourself! Stop it, we are God's Will!"

"Fuck God's Will."

But instead of what I'd anticipated and seen a hundred times before, he smiled happily, as blissful and innocent as any little boy over Granny's best cookie. For a heartbeat his boyish smile, the one from our days beneath the table, had even the power—a fairly magical one, considering my circumstance—to turn him attractive in a bloody sort of way. I suffered desire. I recognized at the moment that was the most mortal sin I'd ever commit, my passport to the Ninth Circle, frozen *per omnia saecula saeculorum* under the thousand miles of Hell above me. That moment's ghastly titillation makes my reputation as "the most Evil woman on earth since Eve" not undeserved.

But immediately he was up on his knees. He ripped off his gold robe and doublet. He reached down on himself and tore off his vermeil codpiece and hose. The only good thing about this sudden undressing was it freed both my hands. With a shout I struck out for him again with my nails. I wanted to rip him. I wanted him mounted on my wall on a wood plaque the way a huntress might display a stag's head.

But I wasn't the hunter and only could flail momentarily at him, as he twisted, feinting and batting my hands away to avoid my claws, while continuing to strip himself. "I'll castrate you, Cesare, I swear, you lurid garbage."

"Will not, will not, will not, and I'll fuck you first."

"You're so good at this, I think you must be practiced at it."

He grabbed my hands again. But as he did, he began to giggle, evidently at my "practiced" remark, which I'd meant an insult to his manhood. The giggle turned my stomach. But then there flew into my head another moment in the lives of Lucrezia and Cesare Borgia. Cesare then had held me to the floor under the carved table, himself above me, while he giggled, just as now. I recalled so much pleasure. I recalled giggling myself, until my ribs ached with the funny happiness of it. I now began to giggle once again. I confess it. It was doubtless a sin and I knew it, but I did.

"Cesare, do you remember the table?"

"What table?"

"The one with Christ's Life and Peter and Paul on different legs? The one in the triclinium we ate at in Mama's house and you played chess with me underneath? We were always happiest there."

He looked straight into my eyes. "There was no carved table in Vanita's house," he said. "The house was modern; there was no 'triclinium.' We always ate on that faux gold bench beside her big window.

Mama would sit at one end, Papa at the other. We'd sit in the middle. I never played chess with you. I was older and riding real horses, not chess pieces. Mama always asked Papa to buy her a table, but he never did. We ate on the bench that faced the bells."

My sinful laughter stopped like a shot.

"You're dreaming," he went on. "All your life's been spent dreaming in fantasy palaces, until you've turned your memory dreams into history in your head. Because your whole life has passed like a little girl's fancy, a princess' castle in the sky, do you imagine real life is nothing but that? There was no such table at Vanita's," he said again. "There were no yew carvings anywhere of Christ's life, nor of Peter or Paul."

The most precious and first memory of my girl's life. He'd thrown them on the Inquisitor's auto-da-fe and burnt my pure memories of him and myself. Stolen them from me. Stolen us from me. Raped me of them, even as he made to rape me. But had they been fantasy, as he said? And all my life thereafter?

To rape a woman's spirit of its joy is far more dreadful than any rape of her body. It's to fuck her soul out. Cesare abruptly stopped his small laughter, as well, now naked enough for his purposes. I cried out. I turned my head and eyes away from him to gaze at Alphonso's lifeless face. At his morning-shadow's stubble. At the open, lilac-blue of his eyes. I wished him alive to protect me, to tell me there'd be no "piercing of the virginity" today, no matter the custom, no matter even the Wills of God and all His Cardinals, Bishops, Archbishops and every male power in Heaven, earth or Hell—let them all rage contrary till the Universe cracks—if it would upset me. But what was that he said about the carvings in the table?

"Did I say it was a *yew* table?" I asked in a little-girl voice.

"How else could I know?"

If it weren't yew, he couldn't. But he did. I remembered the white cloud of Papa, telling a little, golden girl that God would never let such a bad thing as the Papacy happen to a red-dressed sinner like himself. That I should just let him go that morning to his Sistine vote and not worry. I recalled how a short year later he'd trained me to trick Satan and Allatri. I impotently crossed my fingers behind my back, while my brother still held my wrists over my husband's bloody, trapped Freya.

I became then an unclean spirit; my flesh melts away with weeping.

eight

In Naples King Federico, sobbing over Alphonso's death, which he said God alone was liable for, cut a sardonic deal with Louis XII. Federico would live, as would all his remaining family. He'd go into exile in France and receive there substantial property. Meanwhile Louis would split the Two Sicilies with His Catholic Majesty Fernando—Alphonso's cousin—the King of Spain. The Valois Crown would get finally its Sicilies back from the House of Aragon after hundreds of years and a million dead Italians.

"It took those hunchbacked frog-eaters a dozen generations," Papa cracked.

Of course, that meant baby Roderigo of Aragon was disinherited. And hadn't it been a circumstance quite like this one that had caused this long bloodbath in the first place?

"Oh, it's always something," Papa replied.

Alphonso was interred the evening of the same August 18 Cesare'd killed him, in the obscure pocket church of Santa Maria della Febbri. Della Febbri was so near Saint Peter's and so insignificant that, had Papa built Master Buonarroti's proposed basilica, the whole of della Febbri could've fit inside the new Sacristy. Hardly a marble tomb in clouds of mountain sulphur, attended by mute angels. They jimmied him into a crypt on Febbri's side wall that'd been carved out for some not-yet-dead Poor Clare Mother Superior of the fratri-, patri-, and matricidal House of Baglioni of Perugia. Whoever she was, she yet floated down dim bloody corridors. On Papa's order the guards imprisoned our knights and tried to prevent me from attending Alphonso's funeral—"to spare Lady Lucrezia's and the Child of Aragon's feelings," the Papal Bull said. But I went, although Papa didn't. The Archbishop of Cosenza, Francesco Borgia, the son of Callixtus III and my uncle, wore the tenebrous chasuble of the "Mass on the Day of Death or Burial"— or "and Burial," in this case—and presided over the lickety-split obsequies.

John Faunce

Besides the Archbishop's Server, I at first saw no one else I knew there, except Cesare and six of his soldiers, the pallbearers. Six gold plinths to bear an ebony-wood coffin, containing the body of a Neapolitan god of love.

But on my way out, I saw Cesare's little Lucrezia in the back of the church in the shadow of a statue of Veronica. What an unattractive spot, I was thinking, for God's portrait on her snot-rag. My niece, on the other hand, had become a strikingly attractive young woman, just as her little girl's appearance had foretold, and she now looked just like me at her age of about thirteen or fourteen, when I'd married Giovanni. Like most young women she wore too much makeup and her hair was too preciously done, but she was elegantly dressed in the same diamond-lion dress that I'd worn the day Giovanni'd come to Rome to bargain for me. I wondered where she'd found it. Had it hung still in my Borgia Apartment's closets, arranged according to the year first worn? She'd had it retailored and it clung too close to her thin nymphet's body; she'd a golden braid just like mine, and a single pink diamond the size of a Merlot grape on a plain silver chain around her throat. My lions had shrunk at a tailor's hand to glistening lion cubs. But not a speck of gold anywhere. I stopped by the Veronica next to her kneeler. She rose, glaring at me with the same disappointed fury on her flawless face that she'd always shown in my presence.

"Little Lucrezia?" I said. "I didn't know you were in Rome. I'm so pleased you took the time to come."

"I came as soon as I heard, Aunt Lucrezia. I've been at the Sisters' House in Subiaco. I'm so sorry about your Alphonso. Everyone knew how you loved him; it's a legend already how you took care of him and brought him back to life. It was sorcery. And *so* romantic."

What an utterly, beautifully girlish thing to say! I thought. I wondered if she read Romances. I hoped so for a second; then hoped not. "Thank you, little Lucrezia."

"I'm not 'little' Lucrezia."

"*Mea culpa, mea maxima culpa.* You were the last time I saw you."

"Papa told me how you fought for Alphonso by the Tiber. He said you were an Athena with that blade and a Fury with your claws. He said he wished I could be like that for him one day. He said, though, that only the real Lucrezia could do something like that and I never will." Midway through she started to cry and sank to her knees below the Veronica. Her face declined into in her hands. "But he's always said stuff like that."

I put my hand on her head and stroked her hair as tenderly as I could, while still not feeling much tenderness toward anyone alive, but it didn't help her. Had Cesare compared her disparagingly to the myth of me all her life? No wonder she always regarded me with disgust. So by now in her head there's no distinction between me and the paragon she can never become. Here it was before me, an example of history walking, how it braids with a new story so easily together. Her crying got much worse each moment. I looked for a priest or nun—wailing this forlorn seemed their sort of *cruciare*, to deal with—but by now there wasn't a soul in the church, but Veronica, we two glum Lucrezias and a muscle-bound mason, who was slathering plaster by the bucket over Alphonso's tomb-in-the-wall. I felt the mason was applying his freezing-wet plaster to my chest.

"What did you say?" I asked. "About my nails?"

"By the Tiber? With knives, nails and finally with your teeth. How you fought the gang. Didn't you?"

"Yes. But my little injuries could've come any one of a jumble of ways. How would your father know how I earned them?"

She raised her head. I was relieved to see she'd stopped crying and now swabbed the residual water-drops away with a gorgeous sleeve as if once again disgusted at my adult thickheadedness.

I gestured toward the wet-plaster tomb. "None of this is your fault."

She swabbed at her eyes again and cried out inarticulately. She jerked the sleeve away and I saw blood from a lion-cub's diamonds dripping now into her eye, which only augmented the look of fury on her face. I thought of the Virgin, weeping tears of blood.

"Don't you know anything with all your years and Greek books?" she raged back so loudly and suddenly, the mason dropped his trough with a tremendous, slushy boom. The first thing that struck me was that phrase "all my years." I felt like slapping the little monster, but she kept on.

"Don't you know why your Alphonso's dead? Don't you know why we're all about to die? What's wrong with you? Are you deaf and blind?"

An auditory ghost of her father cut through my head, something about an ivory palace, something at San Sisto. I mumbled it to myself, but couldn't recall or reply.

"Because your brother wants *this!*" She grabbed her braid and jerked it out of my hand and in front of her pink stone for me to see. "It's what your whole life's been about. Don't you know *anything*? He wants golden Lucrezia. He says Godpapa promised you to him, when he was young, but broke his word and gave you to men whom you couldn't love like you would've him. No one else is good enough. 'You're only a silver girl,' he tells me. *'Lucrezia's* the only one golden enough to really love me,' "

"Cesare—?" I fumbled, but she'd already cut me off again before the second syllable left my mouth. I could tell by the cadence this was a speech years in preparation, with each gesture, breath and inflection rehearsed to brittleness. Its story had been written, rewritten and over-written again a thousand times in her version of her own Lucrezian *Confessions*, each comma and verb-tense debated over and over, and its rhetorical impact, I knew she thought, mustn't be bobbled for an instant.

So I let her go on, and on with it she went. "I say back to him, 'But *I'm* Lucrezia, Papa. Aren't I really loving you?' He only frowns and says, 'Not really.' And rolls away to fondle some gold knife or other he's enamored of that day. I even fail to be the scholar you were, because I can't cram enough conjugations into my paltry, evil-twin head. *Amo, amas, amat,* I love, you love, he-she-it loves, but not for the likes of me!" With her other hand she reached out and took my own braid. "He needs her, golden Lucrezia, he thinks, to be a whole man. But he can't have her, because, he says, God-papa's the only one you love. I've prayed all my life for the strength to cut that old hypocrite's fat gut open, but look at me. Small, weak, stupid."

"You're small, but you're lovely; you're just as much a Lucrezia Borgia as I ever was. Killing hardly made me my father's daughter."

She looked back up at me with a curled lip of disgust. "So Papa tries to re-create another you and fathers me on some gorgeous, blond slut or other of noble blood. Even I don't know the bitch's name; I *hope* at least of noble blood. Anyway, I disappoint and turn out only a poor proxy, 'without the requisite passion or intelligence,' he says, 'I don't know, something not in the same sense . . . golden about you,' only a faint sim-ulacrum, evidently, of the real, twenty-four-carat Lucrezia Borgia. I think that thing with Katerina Sforza was him trying to do it again. He mightn't have seen your looks in the Virago Sforza, but he definitely saw enough fire. Maybe he'll have Master Buonarroti fashion a forty-foot statue of you in gold for to worship and he'll be happy."

"If you knew how Cesare felt about Master B—"

"He can stick it in the middle of Vatican Square instead of Cleopatra's obelisk. And that's why we're all going to die. For a gold statue of you. To make Papa feel better. That's all. Good-bye, my Lady Big Lucrezia, we must have a glass of Tuscan red sometime together in Hell."

That last was the punch line. I knew an adolescent punch line as well as anyone; having delivered at least a hundred at my Giovanni. "Little L—" I started, but she put a hand firmly over my mouth the way I might over an ill-mannered brat's.

Her voice softened, sounding again ten years old. "Please forgive me, Aunt Lucrezia. I didn't intend to say any of this to you today of all days."

She stood up and marched from della Febbri, the outside doors shuddering on their springs like Scylla's boulders, banging behind her and flashing della Febbri's interior with alternating lights and shades. I knelt and prayed under my breath to Alphonso and Giovanni for an answer to her gaudy accusations. I didn't question their veracity exactly; they were too outrageous not to be true and beyond the competence of a girl her age to invent, even if she hated me and was as talented a rhetorician as she'd seemed. But what had she meant by "all my Greek books"? I knew it couldn't be an idle phrase and I ran through all the Grecian stories and mythology I knew, but couldn't find any to fit the Borgia case exactly. Electra and Orestes? Only just a bit. Athena? Athena and who? Zeus and Io? Who's Io? Me? Whoever thinks I'm to be mythologized as an alluring cow should think again. I admit the notion we were all involved in some reawakening Greek tragedy or retelling of some story in Ovid's *Metamorphoses* was blackly flattering to my overread ego. I recycled that thought and decided that she must've meant we Borgias were engaged in writing our own myth, neither Greek nor Latin, but a new, Italian one. Like Dante. Also flattering in a morbid sort of way. But what to do about it? What's our denouement? I prayed we'd reached at least the last act or Canto XXXIV. I was no Euripides, nor was Papa or Cesare, but I thought one of us, probably a woman for thematic balance's sake, ought finish the manuscript, and quickly. Otherwise it would become, like a drama by poor, overly sincere Seneca, long-winded to the point of never-ending. And what role would this fresh, ingenue Lucrezia have to play, besides her well-wrought monologue of amazing, if belated, exposition? Clytemnestra? No, I thought, that's *my* part. Clytemnestra's played by the leading lady, whom I figured by now I'd matured into.

But Rome never lingers for a funeral, only a good meal, so its mills of rumor buzzed on. Correctly, for once, it spewed forth the gossip that Cesare'd done Alphonso's murder, but that Papa was too scared of his boy genius these days to act. Papa went along by not denying the tale; he even repeated to the Venetian Ambassador that claptrap about Alphonso firing his crossbow at Cesare, implying the murder was a mere, and only natural, revenge. People began calling me *La Infelicissima*, the Unhappiest of Women, formerly an agnomen of the Good Friday Virgin.

On September 30, 1500, in his palomino-drawn chariot and trailing golden traces, Cesare rode below Papa, me and a clutch of church dignitaries and their girlfriends, as we watched him exit the Eternal City's gates along the newly renamed "Alexander Boulevard," once again in command of the Grand Army of God and of less-grand Mercenaries, to the exultant cheers, thrown white and yellow roses and music of a multitude of joyous well-wishers. He was on his way to subdue whatever free pockets of the Romagna were left. Not many. He'd become officially, by Papa's hand, in addition to his many other titles, the Duke of Romagna, which he'd been calling himself illegally for more than a year. Below us marched his archers, then harquebusiers with their shot-and-powder squires, and after them infantry and cavalry. But by far the largest contingent of Cesare's army was his magnificent assemblage of engines of war, for which he'd become justly renowned throughout Europe. The captain and creator of this wood-and-iron Trojan Cavalry was Leonardo da Vinci, the now old, hirsute ruin responsible for that constipated *Lisa* and tasteless *Last Supper.* A squad of mounted trumpeters preceded this senescent finger-painter and flunky, blowing up an introduction worthy of an archimagic orchestra. German and Swiss mercenaries of sundry war-specialties made up the rest of Cesare's total.

"Castles and all fixed fortifications are history," Cesare'd proclaimed, when years ago in the library he'd detailed for me his retro–Roman Empire. "Artillery will win modern wars." "What the hell's artillery?" I inquired at the time. He'd shown me a piece from his lead soldier set, but it looked like nothing but a tiny leaden penis with yellow wheels for balls and—masculine vanity aside—I couldn't see how such a thing would knock down fortifications. Before me now was the answer. These monstrous, ugly cannon—exactly what I'd expect of da Vinci's workshop*— were new martial toys, grown huge enough to batter down walls to satisfy the yearnings of such a mad child.

---

*Everyone knows he's not half the "Universal Man," he delights in calling himself on all occasions, that Leon Battista Alberti was. Da Vinci's generally overrated and once referred to myself as "merely pretty." How would he judge such a thing, that grizzled homosexual?

"Half cannon . . . quarter cannon . . . saker . . . falcon . . . falconet . . . half culverin and culverin," Papa recited as each iron squadron went by.

I'd been more than justified to shiver in the library that night. Before our time, war was a courtly game. Few deaths and scant blood. Honor was satisfied, and nearly all returned to their families. During our lives, since Charles, however, it's become a grinding abattoir, as beautiful soldier-boys die in their hundreds of thousands, ripped to pieces by ball and grapeshot. Many say war will soon become so horrifying that we'll abandon it for good. I'm not amongst them. The war-is-fun boys, who tell us constantly they hate war the most, because they most suffer, bleed lies from their wounds. They love it to death, say what they will, and their contemplated wounds for them are romantic and even erotic. They'll abandon war's slick joys only with the last casualty on Meggido's Hill.

Every artillery officer in God's Army rode a palomino; one or more mounted horses or teams of bullocks drew each artillery piece. All the foot soldiers and cavalrymen wore gold-plated armor, as opposed to my brother's solid gold. The engines' caparisons, wheels, barrels and the cloth of the men's tunics were yellow, a lesser complement of Cesare's cloth-of-gold. His army looked, as I'm sure Cesare hoped, like a host of moving sunlight, marching from sun's disc to sun's death like Apollo's militia. When I examined the soldiers more closely, however, and observed what manner of men strode beneath the armor, unlike their *Imperator,* they were of a common, military order, or even less. Men crippled or one-legged, one-armed, earless, one-handed, one-eyed, toothless, snoutless, one-toothed, jawless; faces covered with the appalling blemishes of Aρησ* and Mars, intermingled with beardless, unmarked and yet joyous boys on their denying way, I prayed not, to a similar cosmetic. They looked like the Army, respectively, of God's halt, lame and naïve, who forever enlist themselves to hoist great men to their great and destined empyreans.

My still-perfect brother dressed in his golden Roman Emperor suit and rode just behind his personal guard of savage, blond *Landsknechts,* whom he'd purchased from the Elector of Bavaria. He wore a wide, supremely confident smile on that face that I knew still scarred from my fingernails. But he'd touched his face up for this occasion with enough whores'

---

* Ares.

makeup—doubtless borrowed from last night's slut; or from his daughter, Lucrezia. From the holiday-dressed thousands on hand, it appeared as if every inhabitant in the city's history had turned out to send him off. He was everyone's young hero. Gaius Julius Caesar couldn't have been more pleased if this had been his triumph of 1,550 years ago, assuming, of course, that Caesar's march would've been returning from victories instead of on its way to presumed ones. The real Caesar would've told Cesare a *triumphus before* battle would tempt the gods; Cesare would've told Caesar *his* modern Roman renaissance wasn't so bashful and further that *his* God in the Judean desert had previously proven Himself beyond temptation. This parade also lacked the naked slave with blazing slips of parchment following the Classical Triumphator and murmuring, *"Sic transit, Imperator, gloria mundi."** But what now would've been the point? My brother was certain *his* glory would never pass. Cesare did wear a myrtle-leaf golden crown just as Julius and Nero had. As befitted an *Imperator*, he was the last of his army to ride out of the city. We Lucrezias stood on the balcony with the best view, set aside for Alexander and his suite, and watched the exiting procession. I wore a gown of imperial purple velvet, edged in tourmalines, as Papa'd commanded me to wear something brighter that day than my widow's black and Cesare'd ordered I wear something befitting an empress. Little Lucrezia was in a cloth-of-silver gown, a belt of diamonds at her waist and choker about her neck. Her silver cloth was nearly transparent, with nothing worn beneath. The outlines of her body—each crevice, swelling and color differentiation—shone out like the Nymphs' all-but-nudity in Sandro Botticelli's magical *Springtime* that he did for Lorenzo the Magnificent's cousin.

"Good God!" Papa said when he'd first seen her, his eyes nearly popping from his skull. "A siren of Venus! Child, you look something like my Lucrezia once did. Are We related?"

She didn't answer. I had the distinct impression he'd never met her before. But maybe it was only he hadn't seen her for such a long time. And then there was her body, which I hoped he'd never seen quite *that way* before.

On the balcony, as Cesare paraded by below, I looked to catch his eye. I'd assumed he'd try to avoid my look from guilt or shame. Foolish girl. He gazed with rheumy eyes right into my soul and bestowed on me that

---

*"As swiftly as this flame, Field Marshal, pass all the glories of this world."

dung-eating smile he reserved for adoring soldiers and servants, maiden aunts, dissolute bimbos and other fools, who loved him without reservation. Nearly everyone, in other words, except his daughter, at whose lambent translucence he scowled, as if the sister- and daughter-fornicator had abruptly discovered himself some sort of born-again Pietist.

As Cesare came into view, the Pope applauded, visibly swelling with pride. "Cesare looks every inch a second Caesar," Papa observed.

"Suetonius writes of twelve Caesars, Papa. Is this the thirteenth at their table?"

He looked at me questioningly. "You must admit his artillery shines like the field guns of angels."

"Angels fell."

Papa was upset with me for saying that. I didn't give a damn. In public he couldn't do much about it or even chastise me, so he just stewed in his sacrosanct juices. I could hear his now-huge stomach sourly rumbling. By parade's end he'd forgotten. I hadn't told Papa, of course, of Cesare's confession, nor of any of the other events in the bedroom, nor anything little Lucrezia had confessed. To what purpose? Everything must've had Papa's sanction or at the least compliance and I now had zero belief Papa would fulfill his promise to gut my husband's murderer and my rapist in Vatican Square. Cesare, to great, mourning fanfare, had announced that Alphonso died of complications of his Tiberside wounds. A speck of truth. He told everyone Alphonso'd risen from bed to kiss Cesare good morning and when he'd hugged Alphonso back— admittedly too lovingly—a vessel must've burst somewhere and my husband dropped dead into Cesare's arms without further ado, greeting kisses undelivered on both men's puckered lips. And I'd thought *I* might be a dramatist! Immediately after that proclamation Cesare added an Aragon Crest to the Borgia Bull of his emperor costume, to further pronounce that Cesare Borgia was now presumptive heir to the Two Sicilies and therefore, I suppose, my father-in-law's son and my newlywed husband.

Or, as he'd mentioned, "Little Roderigo's new Papa."

"I'll slice your balls off first and feed them to you," I dryly commented. "Be careful not to eat dollops of mozzarella in future."

He thought that was funny.

Cesare's smiling glance at me from horseback felt like him stripping me naked once more. It wasn't that frigid look I'd seen in the bedroom, but it nonetheless had a queer lividity, as if ice were stroking bones beneath my hips' skin. I moved my eyes heavenward to escape his, discovering to my shock *I* was the one to feel guilt and shame. Why? I'd done nothing wrong in that hideous bedroom. Had I? The murderer is a sinner, but is the murdered's wife? Or will some say the sin was mine? That my sluttish beauty propelled the murderer beyond blame from my moment of origin? I prayed to find in the sky some angel of retribution, some new, womanly Archangel of Bethlehem to cut him from his celestial Pegasus. For a moment I saw nothing in the sky but Apollo's disc and a single puffy cloud—white and small—in an odd, spinning-wheel shape, like the one I'd seen in the corner of the pregnant peasant's hut in Pesaro.

But then I saw something else. It emerged from behind the spinning wheel's unmoving spokes, a black, slowly flapping dot, so tiny in the distance it must've still been miles off, over Ostia from its direction, the Port of Classical Rome, where the immigrants Peter and Paul once berthed. As I continued to look, I made it out. The pulsing smudge was an Υμενιδε, an Eumenide, a Fury. The angry bird I'd prayed for. An ugly bird of lovely Putrefaction and Settling of Scores like some skeletal Argive crone, come to sniff Cesare's progress, I hoped, and descry him to his end. The black vulture was so many miles off, I could've easily been wrong. It could've been a day-flying owl—I knew there were such things—large hawk or ancient Roman Eagle of Victory, come to oversee the gold legions of the new Caesar across his new Rubicon to gloat over fresh empire. But I doubted it. This chick seemed older, foreign, scrawnier, darker and Greeker than any Latin Victory, of an age and place before Rome or Macedon. Before even Athens. Mycenaean. A pet of Clytemnestra's. This thing looked unlike Nike, but like what Nike might see, were she to look too long for her reflection into the bottomless depth of Δηθη, of Lethe, the Pool of Memory. I prayed it might be. I knelt in the loggia's sun and prayed an *Ave Maria* for that in Greek, tasting blood as the Greek sounds cut my tongue. I prayed to Vanita through the army's passing. I prayed to the spirit of my mother for this sweet Vengeance to strike against Cesare and even more viciously against Papa, the sire of all this misery. I smelled a trace of Arabian and thought my mind beginning to lose itself in so much and so long wishing. I turned my head to find little Lucrezia kneeling beside me, watching as well the black, downy goddess. No one else on the loggia commented or had even noticed.

As Cesare himself at last passed by, the noise from the crowd rose, rooting, applauding, whooping, cheering. I thought I'd vomit. I stood and waved jauntily. I considered leaping off the balcony and ramming something from Hephaestus' furnace up his palomino's ass, but restrained myself. Instead I brought the other Lucrezia to the balcony's edge with me and presented her to Cesare, my arm around her thin waist. Cesare blanched white as his palomino's tail.

"Eat dung, Cesare, you two-faced fuck," I murmured through my smile.

Little Lucrezia leaned into me with a smile. "What was that, my Lady?"

"Did you say something about Cesare, child?" Papa asked.

"You heard me." I grinned to them both.

Since Alphonso's murder, I'd been the perfect Borgia. I hadn't objected a word to the official myth of Alphonso's death. I'd beamed—sadly, of course—at Cesare's accession to my husband's former titles and perquisites. I participated in all the gaudy preparations for my brother's new campaign. I heartbrokenly enthused when he came at night, not to rerape me, but with maps to boast of brilliant battle plans.

Cesare now tipped his hand papally at the crowd. They went wild like a thousand giddy automatons. "I shall salt the earth behind their walls!" Cesare shouted to his rabble. "We shall drown every last Virago in tears and blood!"

Scipio *Italicus*, my butt. I smiled on. They loved him. Even in little Lucrezia's eyes I saw that telltale gleam of love, pride and desire that once were in mine at the sight of Papa or Cesare, no matter they were deserving of it or not; this love that God the Father gives women willy-nilly for some man or other, to ensure the future of His Divinity.

Papa immediately decided to place me once again on the marital auction block, while I retained maximum added value.

"You're still a girl, or almost, you're fertile, as Roderigo's proven, and you're rich. We want you to sit for a new portrait, so We can circulate it amongst those We think might make you a sufficient merger."

"By whom?"

"An avant-garde painter's caught Our eye. He's barely eighteen and as fashionable and naturalistic as tomorrow, which will doubtless please you. Bartolomeo de Venezia. And pose nude like you usually do—"

"I usually did because Alphonso liked it."

"—and wear lots of jewels. We don't want you to look too easy-on-the-purse to your suitors. Bartolomeo, unlike Bounarroti, is a healthy young man and will delight in nudes with jewelry."

I wanted to object to the whole process, but couldn't speak further. I just stood below his throne and cried. Papa came down, held me in his arms and kissed me on the lips. He made tch-tch noises and instructed priests to offer hundreds of Masses for Alphonso's soul. Since they only did that for dead people, I cried more. The auction went on. Various and sundry negotiations began, including Cesare's idea, Louis de Ligny, royal cousin of Louis XII. Serious runs were also taken at Ottaviano Colonna and Francesco Orsini, both of rival ancient Roman Baronial families, and both of which Papa'd hated and had fought with all his life. My beauty, as reflected in de Venezia's lewd painting, was the Holy See's historic opportunity to mend relations with one of the families and destroy the other. Ottaviano was also Duke of Gravina. I was still a prize, maybe more so of late as Cesare's sister than as Alexander's daughter. I resisted them all, especially Gravina. I loathed him, because he was so full of pushy macho that he'd room for no other character traits. When Gravina demanded to know why I'd refused him, I held the point of Alphonso's sword to his stubbly Adam's apple:

"All my husbands have been unlucky," I growled at him. "I fear the same for your Lordship." A pinprick of blood flowed from his hillock of larynx. "You see how bad luck stalks my husbands?"

He, his soldiers and clerics rushed in a clanking and swishing dither from the Vicar's and my presences.

Papa finally settled on another Alphonso. Alphonso d'Este, the heir of the Grand Duchy of Este, capitaled at Ferrara. This Alphonso was the eldest son of the musically cultured, notoriously tightfisted and feared Ercole d'Este, the reigning Grand Duke, and Eleanora of Aragon, his alarming wife, Duchess and the daughter of the former King Ferrante of Naples of bloodthirsty memory. On being introduced to her, the hair on her head rose in writhing tendrils from her scalp, giving me the impression I was making the acquaintance of the Gorgon.

"Through you my dead and living husbands are nearly consanguineous," I chirped gaily as I curtsied at the base of Eleanora's throne.

She raised a writhing eyebrow, looking something less than thrilled. "But my Alphonso is alive. To date."

"So far he must be lucky."

She made a gutteral sound of umbrage, I imagined quite like one from headless Medusa in Perseus' hand.

But d'Este was one of the great Houses of Europe, and so well able to provide protection to me and my progeny, present or future. Este was an *ancient* House, unlike one of a Sforza, Gonzaga, Medici or Borgia, therefore providing me with the protections due true and, in their case, well-fortified nobility. Also the city-size d'Este Castle at Ferrara was six hundred miles from Rome, and I wanted nothing more than to get myself eternally and as far away as could be from the hummocked city and all the pain and sorrow it now symbolized for me. I thought I'd cut my throat myself rather than relive that Tiberside street again. It was agony enough just to enter Alphonso's and my old suite. I could only do it because of the beautiful, clutching bundle of him I'd find inside, waiting to nurse. When I posed for da Venezia, I thought of my Alphonso and me in bed, which I'm sure contributed to the painting's eventual wanton effect. I'd laughed at Papa and posed half—at least—nude, which didn't seem to bother the d'Estes, although Duke Ercole proved himself in the negotiation cheap enough for both of us.

He'd point at the portrait. "A clothing allowance? In the picture she looks clothed in music, which is enough for any woman, for my money."

"Such a lovely euphemism for 'naked.' Ercole, you're a secret wit," Papa'd say. "The damned portrait's not meant to be realistic in a financial sense."

"And my son was so hoping it was."

"That painting shows barely half her charms."

"And how would you know that, Holiness?"

"The artist told me. He's a mannerist and strict homosexual, you know."

"He is not, Papa."

"And how would you know?"

The negotiations lasted more than a year, but were finally settled. On February 2, 1502, I was remarried in ceremonies and with gifts meant to reclothe me in a more "matronly" manner than in the picture. This included two hundred gold and pearl sewn blouses and velvet dresses; brocades; satins; more materials with filigrees of gold and silver; hems of beaten gold and sleeves with pearls and rubies; embroidered violets made of diamonds and sapphires; a coat for Ferrara's more northern weather that cost 20,000 ducats, enough to have bought Forli, rape included, I quipped to Cesare; a ruff for 15,000 ducats and a hat at 10,000. It all made my first two weddings look like a tinker's nuptial. Matronly is in the eye of the one who pays, I decided. The great d'Este crown jewels were placed around my neck.

"She looked an ideal galaxy of multicolored suns," the poet, my beloved Platonist and *arbiter elegantiarum* of Tuscan, Pietro Bembo, wrote of me, and sang me many a "blazon," comparing me, part by part—breasts, eyes, mouth—to objects of inanimate, Greco-Roman beauty, pink marble, sapphires, roses—bust, eyes, lips—making of me more of a rich, exotic spectacle for gazing on than any flesh-and-blood woman truly is. I didn't mind, but they were coldly far-fetched, too precious in form, and thereby aroused in me scant passion.

At my entrance into Ferrara a Nuncio, Pellegrino Priscanio, the so-called "new Cicero," greeted me in *falsus*-Ciceronian Latin, *"Habuit Petrus Petronillam filiam pulcherri; habet Alexander Lucretiam decore et virtutibus undique resplendentem. O immensa Dei omnipotens mysteria, O beatissimi homines** . . . and on and on for the typical Ciceronian multipage harangue. Ercole's famous chorus bellowed a prearranged antiphon to each of his rhetorical flourishes, the whole audition well beyond Plato's fourth subdivision of flattery and lasting an hour in the cool sun.

So I married Alphonso d'Este. I was shocked when I first saw him. I suppose, because their names were the same and they both had Aragon blood, I expected a man something like Bisceglie. This Alphonso was a decade older. I could tell he'd once been handsome, and his build was still erect and strong, but he'd a gut and fanny like an Austrian cardinal's. He'd have to be strong to move at all in his weight of filigreed armor. But he wasn't handsome anymore and the pecuniary expression of his face was only exaggerated by a Stygian weeping willow of mustache that at first made me think a raven had alit on his upper lip, its wings extending down each jowl. He'd no use for fun or any emotion, but devoted himself to forging cannons, his favorite pastime. He was also fond of the potter's wheel, before whose girlish spinning he looked ludicrous.

His manner was abrupt and crude. He frequented brothels; though I

---

*"Peter had a very beautiful daughter, Petronella; Alexander has Lucrezia, radiant with all grace and virtue. O unfathomable, almighty mystery of God, O men most blessed . . ."

couldn't imagine why, he was so dull in bed. He'd no interest in any of the arts, not even in his father's music. He had palsy and his behavior seemed strange. He'd often be seen walking nude through the streets of Ferrara in daylight, followed by bands of screeching, giggling children. A husband at this point imagining himself an unhorsed Godiva would've been fine with me, if he weren't so defensive and characteristically humorless about it.

"Like Alphonso of Bisceglie, I had a legendary great-grandfather," he told me, brought home as naked as he'd been born by his mummy, the Gorgon. "He favored an occasional nude walkabout for a healthy liver."

"Did it work?"

"Niccolo d'Este was his name. Niccolo once discovered his bastard son, Ugo, my great-granduncle, sleeping with Niccolo's wife at the time, Duchess Parisina Malatesta, of the blood-soaked Rimini Malatestas. He beheaded both wife and son. Duke Niccolo then decreed that *all* women in the d'Este lands accused of adultery be in future beheaded without Right of Appeal. The law remains to this day on our books."

"How romantic."

D'Este looked at me skeptically. At that moment I decided I couldn't call him "Alphonso" anymore. I'd call him "d'Este" instead. He rather liked it.

The night before I left the Vatican for Ferrara I went alone to the Sistine. I'd decided to take little Lucrezia with me. I figured more than enough Borgia evil had happened to her that she deserved to come. It'd been late, past midnight, only two candles lit. I sent an ejaculation of thanksgiving to the Virgin that she hadn't permitted Master Michelangelo to destroy the old beauty of the Sistine's ceiling and altarpiece; the new Perugino murals were tacky enough. I begged the Holy Mother to take care of little Roderigo, as the d'Estes wouldn't agree to let him come north with us. I should've then refused to marry a d'Este, but had already taken the oath of betrothal to the Virgin. Any other saint—or even God, under the circumstances—I would've gladly double-crossed. I begged little Lucrezia to look after him and she agreed.

"Lucrezia, We'll take good care of the tyke," Papa'd said earlier that morning.

"That's what I'm afraid of, Papa."

"He's Our namesake. We'll create him a duke. You'll have a duke for a father-in-law, husband, brother and son, as well. You'll be duke-happy. Or he'll be cute with a little red hat on his head. A miniature cardinal."

"I've already had two dukes as husbands, who made me happy."

"But, as you said, those were unlucky."

"Are you lucky, Papa?"

"I am. Most Borgias are."

"I now have a Pope for a father. Long ago I was happy with him. His luck may run out, as well."

"The way you look at me, child, when you say that, sounds approximately a threat."

"Don't make him a duke or cardinal. Don't create him anything God hasn't already; just let him be what he becomes on his own."

"Are you crazy? My own grandson and namesake?"

I went directly to little Roderigo, held him in my arms, and cried for days, after which I left both Roderigos at the Apostolic Palace, nonetheless. May I be damned to Hell once again.

I walked little Lucrezia up the Sistine aisle that night, until just below the altar. At the silver altar-rail I stopped, as women always must. But I wanted to get closer. I stepped over the barrier. No lightning struck me down, no angel with anathema's lance barred my way, both of which pleased and rather surprised me. I pulled my niece after me. I prostrated myself and then her like priests at Holy Orders on the steps leading up to the altar. At first I was silent, then began to weep. I cried like the lonely, damned whore I'd felt like that morning with Papa. I'm not sure how long I cried, but my eyes and shoulders ached before I stopped. I reminded myself of Cesare, blubbering for forgiveness below Alphonso and me on our bed. I looked over at my niece. She'd stopped crying, as well, but there were two small puddles on the red marble steps beneath where her face had been. Had she, so young, as much reason to weep as I? We turned over on our backs. I was breathing deeply to calm myself, when I saw above us God the Father, the pictorial, imaginary version of Him, anyway. He sat in Romanesque splendor on His Throne with His grisly Beard and stern Glance, His Feet resting on the world. His Hebrew Prophets surrounded Him, as well as His twelve-winged Seraphim, each aflame with love of God.

"I've never asked You for anything," I said.

"Nor I," little Lucrezia added.

"Liars," He called down. "You've asked and received a million graces in your short lives."

I moved my eyes to the Christ, to the Word made Flesh, with His gentlest of Eyes, his soft, brown Hair, attractive Whiskers and Gash in His Side like Alphonso. He held up his wounded Hands, as if for our scrutiny. Saints stood about Him, showing Him and one another, as if in competition, the wounds of their corresponding martyrdoms. "And Your Will has been to take everything good, everything divine, from me."

"Lucrezias, mother and child of Lies," replied Our Savior. "I've given you everything. I've laid the Kingdom of the Father for you both of all women upon the earth, but you choose not to see it."

I looked at the yellow-beaked white Dove, the Paraclete, the little Clump of Feathers, who symbolizes the notion that there's no sight, no sound, no thing at all that can be seen, heard, touched, or whispered of, that migrates even near God's Knowledge and Love. "So until this present moment, Little Lovebird, I owe You and the Rest of Your Trinity exactly zero."

"Each sentence you say is a negative tautology, the equivalent of Our saying, 'This sentence is false,' " the Dove chirped with a metaphysic of scholastic cheeps like nails across a writing slate. "Your debt to Us is infinite."

I looked then at the Virgin in her crowned *Maesta* manifestation and ultramarine vestments beneath the Almighty Throne. Her arms reached out in a gesture of comfort and love, interceding with God, pleading with her Son, with her incestuous Lover and with the Pimp Dove for the souls of all, men and women, the saved and Hell's Lucifer alike. I thought of Vanita.

"Holy Mother of God, Vanita's daughter and granddaughter speak to you. Let us make an of overdue feminine touch of history. Christen us your priestesses of vengeance. Make us the unspoken-of Eumenides of the Vatican. Let us kill Papa. Let us send Cesare to damnation at last."

We heard the Blessed Mother whispering Penelope's words from the candles' flickers:

> Or has she wed some other prince at last,
> The highest Lord amongst them?
>   "Surely, surely,"
> My patrician mother answered at once, "she still waits

John Faunce

In your painted halls, poor woman, suffering so,
Her life an infinite hardship like your own,
*Wasting away the nights, weeping away the days.' "**

What did she mean? Was it my answer? Certainly didn't sound like one. Had the Holy Mother read Papa's library, too?

I stood up and went to the burning candle, from which the sound of her voice had emerged. It was near fully burnt down, thick as a chalice, the bowl a lake of molten wax below the filament. I turned to my niece, closed my eyes and poured the wax slowly over her forehead, until the bowl was empty, then ripped from her face the hardened tallow.

"Ego te baptizo," I whispered, *"in nomine matris et se."*† I heard the wax sizzle her skin.

"I feel nothing," she said.

As we walked from the Sistine of God's Election, I knew she'd baptized us, Lucrezia and Lucrezia, then washed her hands of us like Pilate at his balcony. We were reborn. All our prayers were finally our own. We were both alone. We'd become Virgin Euphemisms of Vengeance. We were glad. We'd become Father Cronos' vengeful girls, the ugly crows of retribution. I wanted no other being, Divine or otherwise, to share in the exaltation we'd feel from the ancient feminine ceremonials we'd vowed one day to perform. I knew Vanita was with us and was us. We were the same mind and soul. I still didn't know the difference.

An hour later we sat in the library at the same table I'd sat at long ago with Cesare and his maps. The huge library table was carved with inlaid scenes from the conquests of Macedonian Alexander, which I'd oddly never noticed before, even during Cesare's lecture to me on the subject. But in addition, on the top someone'd recently carved a relief map of Italy. It was brand-new, with all borders drawn to include Cesare's conquests. I searched for Ferrara. There it was, almost halfway between the *Serenissima* and Florence, five hundred or six hundred miles from Rome. Not within his Duchy of Romagna, but within the d'Este domains. I calculated how long it would take by coach or horse to get back to Rome. Too long. I'd never get there and back undetected, when my time came for revenge.

---

*The Odyssey, Book eleven.
†I baptize you in the name of my mother and myself.

250

"I'll do it," she said. "Tell me how. Just let me do like a Borgia."

"Why?"

"I want finally to be recognized as a Borgia, my father's daughter. And let there be no mistake afterward Lucrezia was responsible."

We walked from the library through the long, painted halls to my old suite, and went inside. I checked baby Roderigo and Little Lucrezia held him. They looked a Madonna and Child of Perugino's one-time assistant, the divine Raphael. I went to my makeup table and picked up the wooden box. I took out the ring and its blue-green poison. Little Lucrezia's eyes glistened with desire, as she tried the fit of the great sapphire on her ring finger.

"It's perfect."

"Swear to me you'll write me when it's finished. That the news will find me, wherever I am in the world."

"I swear."

"Swear on the Blood from Christ's Wounds, washed from His Body by the Holy Virgin's own hands. Swear it to me, little Lucrezia Borgia."

She looked at me, as if she'd out of the blue discovered me insane or dead. She flipped open the sapphire with her thumb. "I swear it. On God's sticky dripping-wet Blood." She smiled.

Once in Ferrara I found that being the Duchess d'Este, or Duchess d'Este presumptive, anyway, was not as fun or safe a thing as anticipated. My marriage agreement stipulated I'd be granted 12,000 ducats a year for my living expenses. At first my father-in-law tried to give me 8,000. I raged at this. That would force me to dispense with some of my fifty Spanish servants or some of my already-ordered wardrobe purchases.

"How dare you, my Lord Father-in-law! This is barbarism!"

All right, maybe *barbarism* was a smidgen hyperbolic.

"My Lady, you just got enough clothes for wedding gifts to outfit the army of the Grand Duke of Muscovy for the next century. How many serving women do you need, for Christ's sake?"

"Fifty. And have you ever seen, my Lord, the army of the Grand Duke of Muscovy?"

"Have you?"

"No, but I met his ambassador once. They dress in shabby wolfskins and hats like dead ground-squirrels."

Ercole picked up my 12,000-ducat sable earmuffs with the dia-monded headband and shook them in my face, "*Squirrels? Are you mad?* These are the muffs of an empress!"

"But it's cold here," I bellyached. All right, maybe I'd become a bit spoiled, clothes-wise.

Ercole denied me, until Papa began to send Bulls to the d'Este castle threatening excommunication. The Duke wanted to know if he and his city were to be damned for Eternity for insufficient earmuffs. When the Ferraran Town Fathers heard of this, they ordered Masses said for my "lovely ears" and sent the Archbishop of Ferrara to beg and beguile the Duke in my favor.

"My Lord Duke, we beg you on behalf of my Lady Lucrezia's dia-mond earmuffs to restore her funds, lest we lose our souls."

"She's already got the world's finest earmuffs. And that's just what I've always suspected, my Lord Bishop, were in your wallets. Your souls."

So the Duke finally agreed to restore 10,000. He only raised me to his promised 12,000 when Cesare's armies brushed against the d'Este southern borders six months later, kidnapping some buxom d'Este noblewoman for my brother's personal use.

Alphonso II, as I said, wasn't so hot a lover, either. There'd be no Tivoli, nor even Adriatic, this trip. On the other hand, he was reasonably attentive. He technically fulfilled his conjugal obligations, all right. But as I'd look up at him, he looked like a man engaged in a patriotic duty.

"Duty?" I said to him, above me.

"It is my duty, as you know."

"I'm an infamously stunning woman. Famous body, famous eyes, face, teeth—of which I lack only one molar—and hair. And to gild the lily, I've a particularly gorgeous brain. I speak Greek, after all, though I properly restrain myself from advertising my multifarious accomplishments. Duty? I've never been so offended in my life."

"You speak Greek?" he grunted, his eyes rolling back.

"Πανυ καλωσ. Very well, thank you."

"Because some lover taught it to you? Your brother? You imagine Greek rouses a real man? Produce me an heir. That's the only thing will render you attractive in the d'Este Household."

"Get the hell off me, my Lord."

He was unable that night to continue. He accused me of being a "lascivious succubus and notorious slut." He brought no joy to bed with him, nor anything at all creative or daring. In fact, the only position in *On Wifely Duties* he liked was the one on the first page, which the text called the "Position of the Propagation of the Faith to Uncouth Peoples." He'd leave d'Este for long periods to inspect this holding or that, or to check the fortifications of this or that fastness. He was the perfect heir for an elderly ruler. I began to notice other men; there were dozens of them in and out of the gloomy, redbrick hulk of the Castle Destense, whose towers, battlements and dark shadows brooded over Ferrara. I decided I should take one as a lover; all duchesses had one, including my Medusan mother-in-law and that bitch Isabella. At first I thought I'd take Ercole Strozzi, the humanist, but then I met Pietro Bembo, the poet and son of Bonofacio Bembo, the infamous theologian. It was the combination of theology with the poetry in his soul that must've led to his perplexing writings. Soon after he wrote me a letter:

My Dearest Grand Duchess d'Este,

There is no treasure I could value more than the lock of golden curl you gave me yesterday, which you might courteously have lent me earlier. My wild misfortune has not such power over me to prevent, while my heart beats, the fire in which Lucrezia and my destiny have placed me, from being the highest, purest fire in the breast of a lover. The nature of the spot in which the flame burns will make it blaze bright and hot, and the flame itself will cast so much light that it will bear witness to the whole world.

In Inestimable Affection,
A Poet

A trifle overwrought maybe, but undeniably passionate, and the very antidote, I thought, for the dutiful. At the same time I'd a knock-down fight with screaming Isabella d'Este, my sister-in-law and wife of Francesco Gonzaga, the Marchesa of Mantua. She raged on and on to her daddy, the Grand Duke. Her husband, Francesco, just stood there, yawned and diddled his daisy boutonniere.

"Her clothes are better than mine!" she bellowed.

"No big trick," I said.

"She gets more money than me!"

"Less than I deserve, but I admit more than you're worth."

"You bitch! Go back to the Eternal City, and take up blowing your brother's and daddy's piccolos where you left off!"

I looked at Francesco Gonzaga. "At least they've got piccolos worth blowing."

"Oh, don't you dare think I've no piccolo," Francesco lisped. "I can pipe a veritable motet," he said, glancing at Isabella. "Can't I, Mummy?"

"Mummy" descended at that into apoplectic gibberish. Aha! I thought, another bag of tantrum. Francesco yawned again. The Duke rolled his eyes and nodded sagely. My husband, her brother, turned violently and backhanded Mummy in the mouth with a sound like a smith's mallet into a hoof. Oh, yes, this was a family I could relate to, all right.

Within a month of his letter, Pietro Bembo was all over me to such an extent and causing such gossip amongst the Ferrarrans, I could bear the suspicions no longer. This, combined with my conflicts with husband, mother and father-in-law, Isabella d'Este and sundry other d'Este famil- iars, made me decide to seek out a convent, in which to take a peaceful sojourn away from them all, but still within d'Este protection. On the Ides of June, 1503, I set out in the rain on a litter, borne by two white geldings—perfect, I thought—to explore the available sanctuaries. We visited San Lazzaro, Santo Spirito, Sant'Antonio and the church of the Olivetans at San Giorgio. I despised them all. Every one had knockoffs of paintings, sculptures or murals, whose originals decorated the Vatican, any reminders of which I still fled. Finally, about the first of July, we arrived at the Chapel of the Poor Clares at Corpus Domini. I went right into the chapel, froze and took a deep breath. There he was. The exact Saint Sebastian as in Subiaco's chapel. Same arrows in him. Same chamois-polished bum. Same bloody little rills. Behind Sebastian, look- ing down at him and me, was precisely the identical Virgin Mother, who was the matching blue to the one five or six hundred miles southwest. A blue-veiled memory invaded me of the young Priest Roderigo Borgia, with the expectant and hopeful Vanozza Cattanei. She seduced him, and how much joy he brought her. In my mind they made love again beneath the Saint Christopher, who was likewise in this sacristy. I stepped, felt hot and started to faint in my fifty-pound dress with its whalebone corset, but caught myself on Sebastian's arrows, snapping one off. I knelt and began to pray.

My prayers had the same unfortunate effect they'd had just before Fortunata's murder in Subiaco. I couldn't help but imagine they might've once had the same effect on Vanita, or might yet on little Lucrezia, that they'd inflicted on the unlucky Reverend Mother. I can only ascribe it to something about the atmosphere and infectious love of the convent, but I also began one morning to forgive in my heart my wretched d'Este relatives. They were themselves. They never represented themselves as being otherwise and they could hardly help being so. This penny-pinching duty that they were all so enamored of must be the manner in which great Houses are maintained, I reasoned. Our Borgia extravagances and self-aggrandizements must look to them not like the deserved and virtuous "magnificencies" our ranks deserve, but as if arriviste, nouveau riche, gauche and other Gallic belittlements. Louis of France was their French Letter vis-à-vis Rome, wasn't he? You should learn to be just like a d'Este, the Blessed Mother hinted to me with a wink of sunlight, as I went to kneel before her at matins.

"Blessed Mother, that seems a lesson well beneath you," I said. "Isn't Grace made of love and generosity? My other mother always told me so."

"Perhaps it's time you forgave Roderigo and Cesare. I would guess even your mother has," she whispered inside my soul. "The Pope and his son, like the Father and His Son before them, have chosen to be themselves, as well. They love you and have the most overwhelming ambition to make you an empress. Is that a sin against you? Judas had ambitions to make my Son the Savior and Lord of the Universe. Was that a sin? Judas had to betray Him to the Crucifixion to achieve *his* ambition. That turned out well. Wait till the denouement to damn. Wait for Eternity's Judgment to sentence them to Hell; then decide. My Boy did. Now Iscariot sits not in the Ninth Circle, as in the myth of Dante, but enthroned at Jehovah's Left Hand. He's almost made a Quartet of the Trinity and hosts of archangels sing praises of him to the last of the Heavenly Spheres. Think of your father and brother as Vicars of Judas, if it helps you forgive."

I tried. I emptied my heart of blood to forgive them. I felt Sebastian's arrows searching in my gut, but I couldn't forgive. So I tried at least the Virgin's second choice: to suspend judgment. I failed at that, as well. But what choice did I realistically have? I was there in Ferrara. What could I do tomorrow or in a thousand tomorrows? What had she meant, "Isn't it time"? Alphonso hadn't been dead that long; didn't I have a right to anger? Even to hatred? Was I to shrivel back into an absolving cocoon? And what? Let Cesare have me again and kiss him the French Kiss of Peace? Papa, too? Or could I take a carriage to Rome and stop little Lucrezia, before she struck? But she'd her own sins to commit, as Judas had, and who was I to deny her a destiny like his, as the Blessed Mother'd described it? And then what for Cesare? It doesn't matter, because he'll kill me first. The Duke won't let me go. None of these arch-suspicious d'Estes ever would. What, and give back that prodigious dowry they'd bickered a year over? Not possible. I was here forever. They watched me like a new crown-jewel. So that's where I left forgiveness and retribution. At least until I became the Grand Duchess. I was impotent to alter the course of either mercy or revenge; after all, it was God's Will now—one or the other—wasn't it?

The day after this acceptance of my Sin of Omission, July 31, 1503, my gelding ferried me back to my red Castle d'Este. Bembo came at once to see me. I was still dusty. I threw him out, much to his weeping and gnashing of teeth. Then August 1503 fell like an anvil on all the Borgias like the matador's sword. And it fell quicker than I—six hundred miles from the scene—had any idea of. On August 21, Pietro Bembo came running in the portal of Castle d'Este. He was yelling so as to alarm everyone in the place. He came up the stairs to my husbandless suite. D'Este was off to town, dressed or not.

"Lady Lucrezia! Grand Duchess, my Lady! Evil tidings! The Curse of God has fallen on the whole world! Lucifer's great wings have blotted out Apollo's disc!"

Well, he's a writer. Who else better to hyperbolize? I mused. I knew him engaged at the time in composing his *Lovers of Asolo*, partly based on me, and I imagined from his anguish some quatrain or other wouldn't rhyme in proper a-b-b-a. He rushed into my room, scattering servants and Ladies-in-Waiting. He knelt, bowing his head, and handed me a letter. Oh, no, I thought, not another love letter. Does it have to be in front of the servants? It had "Her Imperial Majesty, Lady Lucrezia Borgia" on its front, instead of "Lady d'Este."

I cast my eyes skyward, and opened the packet. "If this is your work, Bembo, I'll have you burnt in an auto-da-fé of love-sonnets."

"It is not, my Lady."

Within it he'd written nothing. A blank sheet. But wrapped in that sheet was another letter, thick, a packet of several pages by its bulk.

"Master Bembo?"

"I had it from a Venetian contact, my Lady. She made me swear to bring it to you as if I rode on Satan's wings."

"From Venice?"

"From Rome."

"Care of a Venetian whore?"

"A émigré courtesan, banished from Venice by the Doge, her best client."

I opened the packet. The first page of the enclosed epistle was crammed with prose. I recognized the curlicue, feminine hand at once.

August 20, 1503

My Dearest Auntie, the Grand Duchess d'Este and Empress of the World, Your Imperial Highness Lucrezia:

The last time I'd seen Duke Ercole and his Duchess, they looked ram-rod pictures, respectively, of elderly andante and a mythical gryphon. I wasn't the Duchess yet, or an empress, except in Cesare's fantasies. Had little Lucrezia turned on me and wound up now in Cesare's camp?

I'll soon be called the wickedest virago ever to walk under a sky. I'll kill Papa, the Empress' brother. I'll become Electra, without Orestes. I'll be the new Brutus Iscariot. I'll be a myth, Auntie Lucrezia, just like you!

But to the matter.

I went to your Borgia Apartment on August 8, after learning Cardinal Adriano Castellesi da Corneto, the "red pedophile," had planned to hold a luncheon al fresco for Godpapa, my father and the Curial Cardinals in his beautiful Monte Mario vineyard outside Rome on the 10th of August. Maybe someone would be alive now who's dead, if only Godpapa'd said *the simplest "Vale"* or given me a quick blessing of his hand or a kiss. In your room I checked to see if the jewelry box you'd left me was still on the dressing table. It was. And the ring inside? There, as well, with the vial of blue-green, powdered* aqua tofana.

So *aqua tofana* was the damned stuff that killed Allatri, though I've never been able to determine what sort of poison that is or its chemical makeup. How did she know its name? Doubtless from her father, who's likewise executed many an enemy that way in his time.

The day, August 10, came quickly. The sun glared in an empty, ultra-marine sky. The red guests and their courtesans assembled in the vineyard, whose green vines stretched hectares into the distance up to a hill. A table had been put up at the near edge of the vines. The table bowed with food and decanters of red wine from the Cardinal's vineyard. Lute and tambourine players were there, performing quietly, as instructed. Food and wines were piled high.

Godpapa, on his throne of honor, surveyed everything like an Alexander ought. His throne sat up on a little platform. Next to him was a small ivory table with a plate of his favorite pork and his wine goblet, a golden chalice with inlaid rubies. I could see him drink cup after cup, like a man intent on getting drunk as soon as God allows. I sat and tried to engage my own father in conversation. He looked at me, cursed me for attending uninvited, then got up, turned and walked away, as if I were a common whore.

"You've nothing to say to me?" I called after him. "I am not who you imagine; I'm your least *common whore."*

He didn't answer, but kept walking. I wish he'd answered; but so many prelates had arrived, I lost him. I stood next to Godpapa. I was dressed not in any of my usual dresses, but in another gown, borrowed from your Apartment closet, the one from Naples with white diamonds woven into its length in the pattern of an erupting Mount Vesuvius below the waist. Each of my breasts showed itself now a rounded flash of magma. The sunlight sparkled the many crags, peaks and mountain-climbers. The climbers' yellow diamond flag was the Papal one. I wore a white diamond necklace of yours and earrings. My waist is thinner even than yours.

---

*"Hello"

Thinner than mine? I laughed. This Lucrezia, I thought, has a more active dream-life than the real Lucrezia. I remembered the dress well. I had to admit she'd look breathtaking in it, though I couldn't admit she'd look better than I had. But why isn't she getting to it? What's she waiting for? Had she failed? The letter-sheets by now rattled in my hands.

After three hours of winey fun it was five o'clock, according to the vineyard's ancient sundial. Everyone, but me, was drunk. Happiness was on the verge of that tiny, subtle turn it makes at parties from drunken to wine-debauch. All these people would be sick tomorrow. I made my way across the patio to Papa, who sat with his Frenchmen. I leaned down to him.

I said, "I have to get ready for my dance. It's at dusk. Are you ready for it, Papa?"

"Dance?" he growled.

Like me, he wasn't drunk at all, God be cursed. His gaze cut me to my soul, as he turned and the setting sun hit his gorgeous eyes.

"I'm going to dance for you, Papa, the way she used to do."

"The hell you will. You can't dance like Lucrezia. Like a goddess in only a rainbow."

Even the French Bishops were scandalized. I thanked the Holy Mother that Papa'd never consented to introduce me to most of them.

"You think not, Papa?"

"You couldn't seduce a drunken priest with every charm in your quim."

Across the patio Godpapa was very drunk. I'd been leaning over to talk to Papa and I now realized the Pope was transfixed by the sight of my derriere.

"And you, Priest? Can Lucrezia dance for you?"

"Ready as Hell, child," he shouted.

I'm not certain, but I think he mistook my younger, firmer end for your elder, slacker one.

So I'd been reduced in her mind to the elder of two ends? But *slacker?* I'll strangle her, I thought.

I walked off toward the vintner's little house. Once there I ripped my dress and undergarments off, my stockings. I stripped to my opaline skin. I took a basin of warm water, stropped my razor and carefully shaved myself at Venus' mount and under my arms. I wanted to look as much a child as my shape still allowed. I wanted to be the dream of the long-ago child I'd been for Cesare Borgia. The dream of you, the only woman he or Godpapa ever truly loved.

One of them also once loved Vanita, I thought, but there's no way this girl would know that. This read like Allatri's long-ago dream and mine, of the little girl Alexander sent to him. That little girl had taken the baby steps to our present Hell, little Lucrezia. Shaved and naked.

I looked at myself full-length in the vintner's copper pig platter. Your perfect skin covered my body, I thought, or was it mine covering yours? I don't know, but that silken skin, our Virgin Mother's gift, was a sight to tempt the Lord God of Hosts. He made Adam in His Image. Was this Divine icon before me His?

No? Maybe *that's* what His oft-expressed pique has eternally been over, I thought, as I read. Maybe it's this feminine corporeal frame—the only thing in the Universe denied Him, after all—of which He's been so relentlessly jealous through the Testaments.

I prayed to the Virgin that I be seductive as the snake in the tree. I picked up the seven pieces of gossamer cloth I'd brought, and wrapped myself in them and only them. I looked at myself again. Perfect as the Whore of Babylon on her opening night. I left the vintner's and walked in my bare feet the gritty pathway back to the vineyard's drunken feast, your father, brother, Cardinals and assorted Ladies of the Dusk, with whom I identified and feared to disappoint.

I strode onto the patio next to the ongoing orgy. I motioned everyone to back away from me, and they did, leaving me amidst a circle of tall cypresses and shorter sinners. But as they moved, they all gasped and shuddered at the sight of me.

"Oh, my God!"

"The woman has finally lost her mind."

I smiled agreement.

"I always knew she would."

"Since coronation day and she cried and spoiled it for everyone."

"When thousands laughed at her."

"What the hell is the whore doing?"

"A whore and daughter of a whore."

And on and on in similar veins. Whom did they think they saw? I stood in the patio's center in the seven gossamers. The silks hung on my torso, leaving my legs bare and covering my upper body; so you could say I was clothed, but how well and in precisely what was a matter of viewing angle or debate. I wanted both to reveal myself and leave even more to the imagination. I glanced at Papa. He wouldn't even look at me. I went to Godpapa below his throne. He looked enthralled as a man on his wedding night.

I curtsied. "Holy Godpapa," I announced. "From the biblical story of John the Baptist just before his infelicitous murder, a Dance of Seven Veils."

"On with it, child," he slurred. "Hell awaits."

The Pope beamed, swaying and taking another swallow from his goblet. I made the signal to the musicians. They began the prearranged perpetuum mobile allegro. I nodded at the Pope, then at Papa, and began to dance, out-of-time and slower than the music at first.

Eve colors at the thought that one of her daughters—descended from a lady who seduced Adam with so lofty a cock-tease as the Knowledge of Good and Evil—could reduce herself to such a wiggle.

I'd danced this all my life for Papa's pleasure alone, though he was too shy today to even glance. I was sensuous, but tried to be graceful as I imagined the Virgin being, if she stripped in Paradise to seduce the Trinity.

It's written that during Classical days and nights such dances—a woman stripping to her skin for an audience—commonly took place even in the most patrician of palaces, even at Nero's Golden House. But such as hers hadn't been seen in Europe for ages, not since the old gods' deaths and a more priggish Cult's Triumph.

I released my indigo veil, and it fluttered to the floor like spiderweb. Cardinals gasped and cried out. The music played on. I stripped the green veil. The violet. With each curtain gone, excitement grew and I felt more of the poison of those years of Cesare Borgia oozing from me, the breeze off the grapes evaporating it. The little audience began—Cardinals, your *father, whores and Archbishops; all but my father, Cesare—to cheer at the loosening of each silk, at the fulfillment of each promise. The Pope roared from his throne as each lost color exposed more of me to the dusk and eyes of his son. As bits fell away, I knew our power was growing. Beauty reached from our body and skin, as if some exquisite instrument of the Inquisition, to grip all about us by their private desires. Beauty is curse; beauty is blessing; beauty is weak. But beauty first is power. Remember that, Lucrezia, my little Empress, because, as your brother always told me, it's the first thing a woman forgets.*

I knew the happiness of the Grand Inquisitor, the knowledge that he's irresistible and no power of earth or Heaven can stand up to his curiosity's fire while he performs his painful rummage. Your papa's rapture grew with everyone else's. The red veil. The shadows were deepening. The orange veil. The guests were nearly mad, Godpapa apoplectic. The violet. Everyone but Cesare.

I removed the seventh veil, the blue one, keeping it fluttering in my hand and throwing by now a lengthening, rivery shadow. I was bare. I thought of you again, for whom I did this. For a moment I posed motionless in the cypress shadows and let the men feast their eyes, especially that white cloud on his throne and his boy rapist. Our Virgin's gift stunned everyone. Finally Papa turned, but only his head, to look. Our powers moved through the sunset like a Passover Angel. I walked to Godpapa's throne and stopped inches from Alexander VI, his mouth having dropped slightly open. I'd a flash in my mind of honeybees, taking up residence in there as they used to in the hive at Subiaco, the queen offering Mass on his molars, her barbed lonely angels buzzing from his voice box with hymns of themselves.

I sat in his lap and looked into his eyes. They rolled back in pleasure. I smiled. I took his head in my hands and kissed him full on his lips, my tongue moving through them, over those offertory tables, exploring the Baptismal Font of his mouth, tasting sweet with his port wine. I took the blue veil and draped it over one of my naked breasts. I took his hand, placed it on that breast and kissed him.

I remembered Vanita placing his hand on her perfect breast beneath a slender spiderweb of fabric so many years ago, when she'd bid Papa her last family and familiar good-bye on his way to this damned, white-clouded, black-hearted Pontificate. I felt my heart should break. But it didn't. I was having too satisfying a read, and literature never yet broke a woman's heart.

But I wasn't entirely naked. I'd worn your ring. As our kiss went on, I moved my ringed hand—out of the sight lines of all, including my father— over the wine goblet. My thumb flipped the trapdoor open by its tiny gold hinge. I emptied the blue-green aqua tofana *into his red. I flipped the infinitesimal tombstone shut. We emerged from our kiss. The guests breathed again at last; no one had dared during our embrace.*

"A cooling sip of wine, Roderigo?" I asked. I reached for the goblet, picked it up and swirled the liquid.

*I said, "*Hic est enim calyx sanguines mei," *as I reverently handed it to him.*

The Cardinals gasped again—Cesare only laughed—at my ultimate sacrilege.

"For this is the cup of my blood," I translated, thinking of you, my brilliant old Latinist. My new and womanly Testament.

He smiled and continued the Consecration's words in Tuscan. "The Mystery of Faith, which shall be shed for you and for many unto the forgiveness of sins." He paused, and said, "You never knew Latin before, Lucrezia. We believe We disapprove. Greek is sufficient."

He went to drink his wine, but his eyes abruptly narrowed. His hand froze in the air on its path to his lips. He looked into the wine, then up at me.

"Woman," he whispered, "I remember a moment in a room with a little girl."

"Do you?"

"She was so pretty. She gave an old, wrinkled priest a cup of wine. He was about to drink death. My beautiful little girl, a seductress and murderer."

I laughed and traced a wrinkle on Alexander's cheek with my finger. What would he ask?

"Both my children were so beautiful," he said. "Just the touch and sparkle of Lucrezia's hair was a miracle. My children were Gifts of God." He paused again, looking over at Cesare, as if remembering something again, then once more looked into his goblet and asked, "Is this another such moment? Another such cup? Could it be?"

"It's only a cup of port, Roderigo."

"Swear it."

"Has Lucrezia ever lied to you?"

"No. You're the only person on this earth who never has."

"You've forgotten little Roderigo. Nor has God lied to you. But you've lied to us all a thousand lies."

Pain cut across his eyes. "The hell you haven't," he said bitterly. "He and you both. You both do nothing but lie. The cup. Swear, as We asked."

"I swear, Holy Father. It is wine."

He grasped my thigh hard at its apex. He put his lips right to my ear. I confess now, I was at that moment warming to him, to his hand, as all say you did. I could feel the old man's power uncoil, beginning to overcome my own.

"Swear by Christ's Blood," he whimpered, prompting me. "By His Blood that the Holy Mother washed from His Wounds."

Reading this letter then, surrounded by Ladies-in-Waiting and with Bembo at my feet at the Castle d'Este, I could feel Papa's expectant breath once again on my cheek. His hand and body were fevered, this heat giving me the oddly same feelings in my body that my first Alphonso's had once produced in Hadrian's gardens. I wondered whether it'd been too late for the touch and grip of Papa's hands to overcome little Lucrezia now, as they might well have done me. If she allowed the poison in the chalice its destination, she'll become a killer and liar forever. All good people will avert their eyes as she passes by and glare the Sataness in the back, to avoid her Evil Eye. I knew I was right. Stages will creak with it. Troubadours will sing of it and poets in aesthetics and forms unknown to us now will promulgate it. This will all happen, even though none see the green poison drop from her ring into the cup and even though none can prove her a murderer to a legal satisfaction. If the stories say it's even she. What if stories intervene with stronger, more poetical motives in the storytellers? Motives like a perfect denouement or satisfying αγον, agon, conflict of characters, or pity-and-terror. Couldn't anyone for that purpose say it wasn't she, but myself? Aren't I too far off in mythless d'Este for that. And if they do, anyway? Let them tell whatever yarn they wish, I thought. Let them scribble till they fill the walls and their fingers bleed, as long as they fill them in Italian. In fact, they did; as Master Sanizaro would have my epitaph:

Here in her grave lies Lucrezia in name, but Thais in truth:
Daughter, bride, daughter-in-law, and poisoner of Alexander.

Let them sing. Let them write books and melodrama. The hell with it. I'll become the bitch for the ages, if the Muses like. Or my niece will. Or both of us. Classical literature is full of twins and there's always at least one evil one to damn them both. "The Bitches of Death." What matter which of us?

I looked the Pope right in his eye and swore. "It is wine, Godpapa."
"And only wine? Nothing else?"
"It is a chalice of wine. Nothing else."
"Sw—"
"I swear by the Virgin's bloody hand," I said.
He smiled back at me. He downed the wine in a single swallow. He beamed. He was happy. I admit to pride.

As I read, I was proud of her that she could make him so, as I once could.

His other hand still held the veil to my breast. He whispered. "I can feel you still rising charmingly beneath the silk. Lucrezia, just like Vanita. You're as beautiful as she ever was," he continued, his breath at my ear. "More beautiful. I feel as though I've died and gone to Paradise, to be with your love again."
"Not yet," I replied.

I crumpled the page in my hands, which blew, for some reason, a wisp of Arabian scent into my face. Had little Lucrezia worn Arabian? I didn't remember that. I burst into tears, fell to my knees and wept like a dog, sniffing the air for more of the letter's myrrh. The sun had visibly moved in the sky by the time I could get back to my little Lucrezia's letter to finish it. And what had he meant, "just like Vanita"? Was the girl confused? Or Papa? Or was that rumor in the air already, willy-nilly, as I'd thought it would be, and little Lucrezia'd just imagined he'd said it?

The next morning everyone who'd been a guest at Cardinal Castellesi da Corneto's vineyard, except myself, was ill. Godpapa was far sicker than anyone. On the 12th he got worse, He lay aflame with fever in his Apartment. Father was in a panic, rushing here to there, making his plans

*in case Godpapa died. I knew how fearful he was, when he threw his
whores into the street.*

*On August 14th doctors bled the Pope for fever. He recovered. On the
16th he had a relapse. On the morning of the 18th he heard Mass and
took Communion in the Sistine, afterward feeling very poorly. As night
began to fall, he went back to the Sistine to pray. He fell while stepping
through the altar rail. Could our ultramarine Virgin have slashed his legs
from under him? Guards and monks laid him on the Sistine's altar, where
after a quiet hour he died in I-Am-What-Am's bosom.*

*His body began to swell and blacken terribly and immediately, both
symptoms of poison, though they will doubtless give rise to endless stories of
demonic possession or of the Holy or insane seeing Satanic familiars, flapping duskily about his corpse. Deacons took the body to the chapel of Santa
Maria della Febbri, where your Alphonso lay three years past to the day,
the day we met, cried and committed ourselves to this. They tried to fit
Alexander into a coffin, but could not. His corpse had swollen to twice its
previously corrupt bulk and blacker than any Moor. Two gravediggers
finally dropped an anvil on it repeatedly from the choir. Accompanied by
great gasps of escaping gasses, Roderigo, the Godpapa, finally subsided into
his Eternal, Borgian Box.*

Your Loving and Affectionate,
Lucrezia Borgia the Younger

When Cardinal Ippolita came to Ferrara to tell me of Alexander VI's
death, I went mad with grief again—or rather, feigned so. I dressed in
black moiré with a ruby-and-tourmaline pattern in outline across my
midriff of the Mount of Olives, where Christ wept.

"Life on earth is fundamentally hopeless and vain," I said to the Duke
d'Este.

He agreed wholeheartedly. "This is not news to a man with a spendthrift and capricious daughter-in-law," he replied.

"Stop crying," my husband said. "It's irritating."

Pietro Bembo took a deep breath and recited:

> *He's flown to Heaven asaddle the black Borgia Minotair*
> *To join Scipio Aemilianus of Spain, his forebear,*
> *And his namesake, Great Alexandair.*

"Forced rhyme is so irritating," I said. "Don't be irritating. The lot of you."

Absent Papa's power Cesare was now a dead man and well knew it. He tried to put it off by getting the French King's choice, Cardinal d'Amboise, elected the new Pope, but the Italians wouldn't have another *Monseigneur le Pape* after the century-long "Babylonian Captivity" at Avignon, and he failed.

"We wish no harm to Cesare Borgia," said the new Pope Pius III, "but We foresee that he will come to a bad end by the Judgment of God. We forgive, as We forgive all sinners, the man or men who hasten him to his overdue reward."

The compromise new Pope—a Piccolomini and nephew of Pius II—was old and sick, elected for the express purpose of dying soon. The dreaded Colonnas, Savelli and Orsini rushed back to Rome to reclaim all their properties and rights. In Umbria, Gianpaolo Baglioni and the Vitelli clan took up arms. In Romagna, Piombino, Urbino and Camerino revolted. All the cities of the Romagna soon joined them in war- and fun-loving treachery.

Cesare's shiny new empire disintegrated in a devious wink of Clio's eye. He fled south toward Naples, where the "Black Ladies" of the House of Aragon awaited him: Queen Giovanna, widow of Alphonso II; Beatrice, the ex-Queen of Hungary, against whom Alexander VI had forced a Bill of Divorce in favor of King Ladislaus; the young Queen Giovanna, widow of Ferrandino; and finally Isabella d'Aragon Sforza, widow, at Cesare's suspected behest, of the Moor. They sold him, at Louis of France's bidding, to His Most Catholic Majesty of Spain, who sailed my brother to a Spanish dungeon and promised no one'd ever see him again. But Cesare escaped with the collusion of the King of Navarre—an Aragon!

He joined Navarre's armed forces as a hired commander. No, Navarre wouldn't let him call himself *"Imperator."* Stragglers from his former Army of God would daily stumble into Navarre's camp, looking for their erstwhile Caesar, and finding instead a forlorn Cesare, they could hardly credit this the same man they'd known. Their impressions weren't much improved by the ravages of syphilis that had turned the face of Apollo into a face of Anabasis, his beautiful skin a mass of bleeding boils and boiling scabs. But many joined Cesare, anyway, and I'm told he began to regale his troops nightly by campfires with tales of his future reconquest of Byzantium from the Turk and receiving by the Golden Horn the diadem of Βασιλειoσ, the Eastern Emperor. I also never found out, nor ever asked, if I'd been mentioned as Βασιλεια, or Empress, in his new and glorious Greek myth. He wove his last mythical skein on the evening of March 10, 1507, though others say it was April 18. Little matter. The next day he led a small corps of his tarnished golden cavalry against the forces of Viana, which Navarre was besieging. A hundred yards from the walls stood a Vianian force of infantry. But it was tiny, no more than six or seven infantrymen.

Cesare yelled, "Forward at the gallop!" and led a charge of fifty of his horsemen against them.

But the infantry didn't move, not a single one ran, budged or even turned his head. As Cesare's horses approached the line of them, he realized this infantry squad wasn't of men, but of boys. He raised his hand to stop the charge.

The Count of Viana appeared at the town's wall. "We send out our children to face you, O imperious and vain-glorious Cesare Buttfuck," the Count cried. "Even our children no longer fear you, now your fat papa roasts in Hell on the spit of his poisonous daughter! We'll next send our little girls out to slice off your manhood, you whoreson rapist of patricidal sisters and unsightly cows!"

Cesare turned in his saddle, outraged, and reordered the charge. At the moment his cavalry was to make contact with the Vianese squad, the whole line of them placed their shields in front of themselves and fell backward, their entire boys' torsos and heads now beneath full-grown shields. Cesare should've recognized this tactic from the Spartans' battle at Thermopylae with Darius' Persians, which I know he'd studied in detail, and should've remembered its result, if he didn't turn at once his cavalry and circle back to reface them. Darius hadn't done that and the day's result had been 25,000 dead Persian cavalry to 13 Spartan infantry. Cesare, as had Darius, galloped over the prone infantry, the horses unwilling to step even on the shields, and was forced to ride up the rise behind them, in this case leading to Viana's wall. By the time the cavalry had galloped up the hill, horses and riders were exhausted, a number of them killed by mechanical spear-throwers from the Vianese walls and the boy-infantry had risen, their slaughter of horsemen ensuing. The boys stabbed the knights in their backs and cut the horses' throats or tendons, the cavalrymen falling, to be sliced to ribbons by the boys' minikin swords and knives. The boys then cut Cesare from his knights like wolves cutting a ram from sheepdogs. Cesare drew his sword and fought them a few thrusts and parries, until one landed a lucky stab to Cesare's wrist, shattering it. He could no longer hold the sword, and faced them with only his gold, jeweled dagger in his wrong hand. They leapt on him and dragged him to the ground by sheer weight. They stabbed my brother over and over with their swords and knives. They destroyed what remained of his face with the pommels and hand-guards of their weapons. They then stripped him naked for the crows and rats and left the Caesar of the World under a projecting rock in a mass of blood and his own butchered innards. They brought his liver on his sword in triumph through the gates of Viana, finally to be fought over that morning by a pack of dispossessed dogs.

Before that forgotten, stupid, meaningless skirmish outside the walls of Viana, he'd spent every moment since our father's death running for his life. He was thirty-one years old when he finished. His end was less grotesquely ignominious than it might've been, since at the time he was riddled with syphilis to such an extent he would've soon succumbed to its putrid molestations. I thank God daily I never saw his beauty savaged.

His sword was later returned to me in an obsidian case, on its hilt two gold reliefs: on the obverse Saint Peter, hanging upside-down on his Crucifix; and on the reverse a Borgian bull of rubies with the face and studious dome of Paul, his horned head twisted onto the headsman's gold block. On the block's side, in large, diamond letters, was the legend SPQR.

The same Amalfian contractor who'd installed Cesare's Minoan plumbing had put in my tremendous bath chamber in my d'Este suite, following Ercole's death and my accession to a Duchess' throne, with all its rights and cash, in 1505. It had high, vaulting windows to allow sun to flood in. It was still extraordinary in those days to have a room devoted exclusively to the bath. In this, as in so many things, I never was fashion's slave, but its Empress. I'd had the room especially made, constructing it of the finest gray, blue-veined marble with silver accents—no problem since my accession. I'd placed rare seashells here and there, pieces of oddly shaped driftwood and various taxidermied fishes, starfishes and octopi. My idea was to create my own little Bay of Naples. I lay in my bath one morning in 1509 in perfect peace and thinking of the Satanic bloodbath that was at the time consuming Italy at the behest of that drunken prick Pope Julius II, the former della Rovere, Papa's electoral enemy and savior. My bathwater had been heated to the degree that its steam rose all around my body, the tub in the shape of an enormous scallop shell that Alphonso d'Este had surprised me with from Alexandria.

"A good investment," he'd said. "I haggled those Egyptians down twenty percent."

A half dozen of my Ladies-in-Waiting were clustered about, washing me, my back, massaging my neck. I smiled peacefully.

"Master Botticelli?" I called.

"Yes, my Lady?"

"Are you nearly done, Master?"

Master Botticelli had asked if he could paint my portrait, as many asked over the years. I'd wanted an equestrian one on a palomino, with me all in black leather. I'd fantasized that might start yet another fad. Or in the same dress I'd worn when first I saw Alphonso. But when Master Botticelli heard of my famous bathroom, he'd asked to see it.

"Oh, my God," he said when I first showed it to him. "So much water! That tub! My Lady, I've an inspiration."

It's always wise to allow an artist to follow his Heaven-sent insight, instead of one's own. A work dictated in detail by the client tends toward stiffness and cliché. If you want a picture of your child and the artist sees the child's puppy and exclaims, "That's it!" let him paint the dog. It will be a more touching memento of the child even than the most flawless representation of the infant itself.

"Are you nearly finished, Master?" I asked again.

"Just there!" he cried, dabbing on a final ultramarine splotch. "It's done, my Lady."

"Any longer in this bath and I'll come out a flounder."

I arose from my bath. My Ladies-in-Waiting rushed to dry me with wonderful fluffy "towels" like cloth clouds, gifts from the Sublime Porte to Papa that I'd instructed Penthesileia to steal for me after his death. I hadn't felt guilty; the mob stole everything from his Apart-

"How was this done?" I asked my Lucia.

"Cesare left monies in his will to care for her."

"Where was she found?"

"Subiaco."

"I'm a nun now, as I began, if you can believe that."

"I can believe it, a virgin again at last and living with Saint Sebastian." I walked to her, knelt down and put my cheek to her breast, and with the touch of that skin I began to attain the Grace of peace and forgiveness.

My life is a myth, though as I write this, its public mythology has long ceased, praise the Virgin. I've long since become, as I portended, the immortal and legendary bitch-patricide. Della Rovere's doggerel scribblers were at it before Alexander's rigor mortis set in. Everyone said it'd been Lucrezia Borgia who'd poisoned him at the vineyard luncheon. I'm amazed Pinturicchio hasn't made a mural of it yet in the Borgia Apartments, a naked myself pouring the poisoned chalice of red down Papa's throat, as he tears with one hand dramatically but impotently at my mighty, envenoming forearm, his other on my bared breast. That I'd been six hundred miles away didn't halt calumny for a beat of a queen-bee's wing. Nor did anyone dream there was another Lucrezia Borgia might've done it, not even those who were there. Even the relatively few that knew of little Lucrezia's existence didn't know her motive, her true double relation to Cesare. It served them additionally for me to have done it; myth feeds most gratefully on myth, as they well knew from biblical stories. She's disappeared from history, never having been mythologized at all. She's my unseen shadow, my soul, as it were. Her name is a footnote or single line of text in works about Papa, Cesare or me, or even of the Borgia family.

Vanita went back home with Roderigo, my strapping boy, three weeks later. We had a wonderful time while they were in Ferrara, and we still write each other—in Italian—every week. I insisted Vanita have her portrait done, but she hated it, since by the time it was painted her long beauty had deserted at last her face and body.

She burnt it. "There goes the crone," she said. "Up in smoke in the fire-place. Her wattles are burnt from posterity now, and only *Ars gratia Artis*. Good riddance."

I sent little Roderigo and his grandmother after that visit back to Subiaco, for a loving life, I trusted. When saints walked the earth, angels came and took women and their sons by the hand and led them from damnation. Perhaps they will again. All the angels we see nowadays, of course, have flapping wings on trompe l'oeil ceilings. But if fortune smiles, we are still led from the Ninth Circle by a hand put into ours. A child's hand, the hand of a toddling Master of Them That Know.

Two years later I finally did my d'Este duty and gave birth to an heir, Ercole II, in 1508 and have since become beloved in my émigré city. When I held the tiny swaddled bundle and watched him grasp at the air and me as if, like any proper Borgia, he wanted to acquire everything, I was satisfied in a way I hope I never shall be again. I prayed he'd be like me, like *Lucrezia* Borgia, and neither like the men of our line nor the d'Estes'. I prayed his grasp would be for all the love and softness the world offers him and he'd not be enslaved by gold, power or mythic expectation. I hoped both my sons would stay children beneath the table. In fact, I sent Roderigo, my firstborn, Vanita's carved table for him to play under at Subiaco. I also sent him Bisceglie's sharp sword, because a man has to be a man. I know he'll have the Borgia beauty; he has it already. I hope it'll be a blessing to him, not a curse. "Borgia," our family aside, is only a spondee, a pair of empty syllables, though recently I've heard a certain deadly poisonous and newly discovered mushroom from the New World has been named the "borgia plant," which I've no doubt is an expression of the toxic mythology that will continue to grow for-ever around my family and me. Roderigo Borgia was his grandfather, and that's who he resembles. I also *finally* found out if the soul and mind were one or not. The Lateran Council of 1513 declared the unity of mind with soul heresy and anathema. I guess I oughtn't pay any mind, from that day on, to the facts of my life I've written here. I wouldn't want to commit a mortal sin and condemn my soul—leaving my mind free to wander where it will—to the Ninth Circle.

One more word on the mythosophy of the Borgia reign. During those times in which corruption and artful liars flourish most, like those of an Alexander VI or a Cesare or an Αλεξανδροσ of Macedon or Caesar—years of great birth or rebirth—we're kept in constant motion and emotion. We relish then the motions and emotions themselves, as well as those joys and geniuses, which are turbulence's natural throw-offs—the blind Ομερ, aristocratic Dante, dusty Buonarroti, Machiavelli, Cesare, Mehmet the Great and the astonishing Columbus of Genoa—"*Hic monstra sunt*" "Here be Monsters" at the edge of his old chart, where he'd find instead the New World. Such men, all Titans, were mountains of Κοπροσ, of *Excrementum*, of bullshit. Climbing those mountains, our minds then acquire new energies and enlarge their powers and subtleties, both satisfying our inborn, acquisitive desires and preventing unnatural ones that grow like sprouting putrefaction in indolence's rot. Strike these monumental liars from our histories; God will deprive us of action and pleasure, leaving nothing but dull, infertile and self-sanctifying piety to sustain our twitchy spirits.

I live now mainly in the House of Corpus Domini not too far from the redbrick Castle d'Este, where I've been tasked one day to write its Necrology. At least I live there most of the time, when I'm not required for a ceremonial or maternal purpose. Little Lucrezia visits me twice a year, on the Feast Days of Peter and of Paul. It remains here still so like the Subiaco of my dreams, where now little Lucrezia lives with her aunt and Roderigo, who's no longer little. Sebastian is here, missing one arrow to remind me of murder, and the ultramarine Virgin watches me from her pedestal. I think here of our beautiful Borgia Apartment and the nuns, who taught me to sew as a little girl amongst the abiding genius-painted halls, which are the only material things I miss about the Eternal City of God on His Vatican Hump. My life here nowadays is my little self-imposed exile, my thanksgiving offertory to Mother Mary for granting me my dark priesthood and the answer to my blood prayer that Sistine night. I've taken no vows, even lay vows, of this Order, though all the sweet women here welcomed me to stay and call me "Lady Sister," a not ignoble title, though only the palest specter of "Empress," "Queen of the Two Sicilies" or even "Duchess of Pesaro." Like all still-breathing myths, I've become a living ghost. I glide noiselessly through the halls like Fortunata. I pray in the chapel by myself with only an occasional, amorous glance at Sebastian's lovely bum. I sold my Borgia jewels and gave the sale's ducats to the Corpus Domini. I sold all, that is, but one; I'll wear to my grave Alphonso Bisceglie's plain gold band with its ruby pimple. I eat only coarse breads and boiled, unseasoned grains here. The wines I used to love I've returned to water. The bride of Cana in reverse.

I wear dresses I hand-sew of coarse wool. Only my gold talisman, hanging in its single loose braid down my back, is still with me of all my former Borgian treasures. I sit alone here all day and night in my bare, hard cell and scribble these words with Babylonian black ink on the best brightest Irish vellum. I listen to my charitable sisters outside and in the halls, working, teaching new little noble-bastard girls. These nuns gossip and make supernaturally unfunny jokes. Often, in secret and so no one else can see us, I take one of those girls on my lap and read this book aloud to her, pointing to each word as I say it, teaching her to read Dante's and Petrarch's Italian. I also now and then teach occasionally Greek and Latin. All these *feminae* agree with me: Roderigo's Vanita was no whore; they say she was a princess. In them—more than sufficiently—I've accomplished my girlhood oath to my mother. I'm happy—content, in any case, though lonely in the midst of all these women. Real men don't walk the halls of the Castle d'Este, and I miss men, even evil ones. I miss their bodies, the way they look at me, the way they think and their voices, thick with desire. Is that a sin? I know the Virgin would say not. Perhaps this loneliness, my new life, as Alighieri might've phrased it, in this small cell, is a good thing. I'm alone with my memories. I pray for my dead memories and they beckon me come join them. Memories of Vanita's Arabian scent, of her breast's skin, of Tuscan wine, of her carved-legged table, of my father, of Alphonso and his fields of Tivoli, of Adriatic Giovanni, fat with loveliness and truffles by a waterfall, of my young twin Lucrezia, the unknown Clytemnestra of our ambiguous age, of a pair of newborn twins, of my womanly, blessed birth-pains and my time with little Roderigo, a Gift of God beyond the Resurrection or its Shroud. And I'm even sometimes alone with my memories of Cesare, my beautiful brilliant sad brother. I bless each of these phantoms, as it passes, as if I were a Popessà. Perhaps this loneliness is the beginning of another myth. Maybe teeming solitude will scribble on my heart a new mythology of myself, of Lucrezia Borgia, the most evil woman to live on this earth, as they say, since Eve proffered Adam her apple. I've just read over what I'd planned to be my last paragraph. There's a lie in it. I had to read it twice before I could spot it. Does it stick out? No? It's the jewelry. I've kept *two* pieces, not one. The gold band with a single, ruby stone, and on the other hand a larger ring, with a hinged central sapphire. The Fishwife's ring, I call it.

Is my fable an evil one? Will Lucrezia Borgia's become the most wicked feminine myth to be told on this earth since Eve's, an evil palimpsest of a malevolent truth? Time will tell. It always does; except in Paradise. As that legendarily lusty and Hellenized Magdalen, who many say tempted God in the desert with a better offer when Satan failed, might've written of her own myth, or as Eve, that eldest mythologist, herself might write:

Πριν Σατανασ γενεσθαι, ΕΓΟ ΕΜΕΙ
Antequam Satanam fieret, EGO SUM
Before Satan was, I AM.

Exitus Clausula.

About The Author

John Faunce received a BFA in acting and an MFA in directing from Carnegie-Mellon University. Since then he has directed or produced twenty-two Broadway and Off-Broadway plays, as well as television and feature films. He lives in Los Angeles with his wife and dog. *Lucrezia Borgia* is his first novel.